GRAND CENTRAL
PUBLISHING

LARGE
PRINT

ALSO BY BENJAMIN PERCY

The Wilding
Refresh, Refresh
The Language of Elk

Red Moon

A Novel

BENJAMIN PERCY

GRAND CENTRAL
PUBLISHING

LARGE PRINT

Grand Central Publishing
Hachette Book Group
237 Park Avenue
New York, NY 10017
www.HachetteBookGroup.com

Printed in the United States of America
RRD-C

First Edition: May 2013
10 9 8 7 6 5 4 3 2 1

Published simultaneously in Great Britain by Hodder & Stoughton, May 2013.

Grand Central Publishing is a division of Hachette Book Group, Inc.
The Grand Central Publishing name and logo is a trademark of Hachette Book Group, Inc.

Library of Congress Cataloging-in-Publication Data
Percy, Benjamin.
Red moon / Benjamin Percy. — 1st ed.
p. cm.
978-1-4555-0166-3 (hc) / 978-1-4555-4535-3 (large print)
1. Werewolves—Fiction. I. Title.
PS3616.E72R39 2013
813'.6—dc23
2012016127

For Lisa, the chief
and
For my mother

Red Moon

I have realized that we all have plague, and I have lost my peace.

—ALBERT CAMUS, *THE PLAGUE*

And I lost the taste for judging right from wrong
For my flesh had turned to fur
Yeah, and my thoughts they surely were
Turned to instinct and obedience to God

—BLITZEN TRAPPER, "FURR"

Part I

CHAPTER I

HE CANNOT SLEEP. All night, even with his eyes closed, Patrick Gamble can see the red numbers of the clock as they click forward: 2:00, 3:30, 4:10, now 4:30, but he is up before the alarm can blare. He snaps on the light and pulls on the blue jeans and black T-shirt folded in a pile, ready for him, ready for this moment, the one he has been dreading for the past two months. His suitcase yawns open on the floor. He tosses his toiletry kit into it after staggering down the hall to the bathroom and rubbing his armpits with a deodorant stick and brushing his teeth, foaming his mouth full of mint toothpaste.

He stands over the suitcase, waiting, as if hoping hard enough would make his hopes come true, waiting until his raised hopes fall, waiting until he senses his father in the bedroom doorway, turning to look at him when he says, "It's time."

He will not cry. His father has taught him that, not to cry, and if he has to, he has to hide it. He zips the suitcase shut and drags it upright and stares at himself in the closet mirror—his jaw stubbled with a few days' worth of whiskers, his eyes so purple with sleeplessness they look like flowers that have wilted in on themselves—before heading down the hall to the living room, where his father is waiting for him.

The truck idles in the driveway. The air smells like pine and exhaust. Sunlight has started to creep into the night sky, but only a faint glow, a false dawn. The suitcase chews its wheels through the gravel and Patrick struggles two-handed with its weight. When his father tries to help him, Patrick says, "Don't," and heaves it up into the bed of the truck.

"Sorry," his father says, and the word hangs in the air until Patrick slams shut the tailgate. They climb into the truck and on the bench seat Patrick finds a peanut butter toast sandwich wrapped in a paper towel, but his stomach feels like a bruised fist and he can't imagine choking down more than a bite.

They follow the long gravel drive with their headlights casting twisting shadows through the tunnel of trees. They are alone on a county road, and then surrounded by traffic on I-580, heading south, toward San Francisco. Half the sky full of stars, the rest of it blurred by soot-black clouds occasionally pulsing with gold-wire lightning.

His father says he hopes the weather clears,

hopes his flight goes off without a hitch, and Patrick says, yes, he hopes so too.

"You've got Neal's number?"

"Yeah."

"In case things get weird with your mother?"

"Yeah."

"Not that I think they will, but in case they do, he's a three-hour drive away."

"I know."

The sky lightens to a plum color—and with the sun and the stars and the clouds at war in the sky, Patrick can't help but think that's how things are around here, divided, like the landscape, ocean and forest and desert and city, clouds and sun and fog, like so many worlds crushed into one.

It is another half hour before the sun crests the horizon and injures his eyes to look at. His father holds the steering wheel like it isn't going where he wants it to go unless he muscles it hard. The two of them say nothing because there is nothing to say. It has all been said. Patrick does not want to go, but that is irrelevant given the fact that he must. That goes for them both. They must.

The sky is clotted with clouds. Rain spits. Seagulls screech. The bay is walled off by fog. In the near distance the brown hills are only a hazy presence and the noise of traffic is only a vague growl as cars pour off the freeway and follow narrower roads that branch into parking ramps, rental lots, terminals. One of them, a black sedan with a silver grille, dips underground to the arrivals area at San Francisco International Airport, but it does not stop where the other cars stop, does not pull up to the curb and pop its trunk and click on its hazard lights. Instead it slides past the rest of the traffic, around the corner, to the bend in the road bordered by concrete walls, where it slows enough for the door to open and a man with a briefcase to step out and walk away without a parting word or backward glance.

He is smiling slightly when a minute later he walks beneath the sign that reads TERMINAL. He appears to be a businessman on his way to close a deal. He has the black leather briefcase with the silver snaps. The Nunn Bush wing tips shined to an opal glow. The neatly pressed charcoal suit, starched white shirt, and red tie running down his chest. His hair is severely parted to one side and dusted with gray, the gel darkening it to the color of coal. He looks like hundreds of other men in the airport this morning. His face could be anyone's face.

But if you looked closer, you might note his

pallid cheeks, his neck rashed and jeweled with scabs—where once there was a beard, razored away the night before. You might spot his white-knuckled grip on the briefcase. The redness vining the corners of his eyes after a sleepless night. And his clenched jaw, the muscles balled and jumping.

This is the busiest time of day, when the security guards, the flight attendants, his fellow travelers, notice the least, the airport a flurry of bodies, a carnival of noise. The motion detector above the entrance winks and the electronic double doors open and he enters baggage claim. Here is a gaggle of Japanese tourists wearing neon-green tracksuits. An obese man spilling out of his wheelchair. An exhausted-looking couple dragging behind them red-faced children and overstuffed backpacks. An old man in a gray Windbreaker and Velcro shoes, saying, "How did that get in here?" leaning his head back and squinting up at the metal rafters, where a crow roosts.

He cuts through them all, walking up an escalator, moving past the ticket counters to security. His eyes dart wildly about him even as his body remains tense and arrows forward. He brings his hand to his breast pocket, where his boarding pass, printed up the night before, peeks out like a neatly folded handkerchief; he fingers it, as if to reassure himself that it's actually there.

The security guard has a buzz cut and fleshy body and he barely glances up when he spotlights the man's license with a blue halogen flashlight and then initials the boarding pass before handing them back. "Okay," he says, and the man says, "Thank you."

The line is long but moves fast through the maze of black ropes. When he passes through the metal detector, he closes his eyes and holds his breath. Then the guard is waving him forward, telling him, "You're good." A moment later the X-ray machine shoots out his tray and from it he collects his shoes and briefcase and wallet and silver watch, whose face he glances at when buckling it to his wrist—his flight does not board for another forty minutes.

He has not eaten this morning, his stomach an acidic twist. But the smell of fast food, of sausage and eggs, is too much for him. His hunger rolls over inside him. He orders a breakfast sandwich and paces while he waits for it. When his number is called, when he collects the bag, he rips it open and can barely find his breath as he shoves the sandwich in his mouth and gnaws it down. Then he licks the grease off the wrapper before crumpling it up to toss in the garbage. He suckles his fingertips. He wipes his hand along his thigh, unconcerned as he smears his pants with grease, and then glances around, wondering if he has caught anyone's attention. And he has. An old woman—with a dried-apple face and dandelion-fluff hair—sits in a nearby wheelchair, watching him, her mouth open and revealing a yellowed ridgeline of teeth. "You're pretty hungry," she finally says.

He finds his gate and stands by the rain-freckled window. His reflection hangs there like a ghost, and through it he observes the plane parked at the gate. Beyond it, fuel trucks and luggage carts zoom through black puddles that splash and ripple their reflection of the world. Men wearing fluorescent orange-and-green vests over their raincoats throw luggage onto a conveyer that rises into the belly of a plane. Off in the distance, a Boeing 747 blasts down the runway like a giant bullet, steadily gaining speed, its nose lifting, the plane following, angling upward and abandoning the tarmac. And then it is gone, lost to the clouds.

He glances at his watch often. His tie is too tight. His suit is too hot. He wants to peel off his jacket but can feel his shirt sticking to his skin and knows the fabric will be spotted in places, nearly translucent along his lower back, where the sweat seems to pool. He uses his boarding pass to dab at his forehead. The ink bleeds.

The desk agent gets on the PA and lists off their flight number and destination, 373 to Portland, Oregon. Her voice is tinny and rehearsed. At this time, she says, first class is welcome to board along with premier and executive elite card carriers. He glances at his watch and checks his boarding pass for what must be the hundredth time that morning. They will depart in twenty minutes and he will board with Group 2. He wants to pace. He has to concentrate to stay footed in his place.

A few more minutes pass. He considers joining the mob of people standing next to the counter, waiting to board, but the thought of all those bodies, their heat and smell, keeps him alone by the window.

Passengers with young children and in need of extra assistance are now welcome to board. And then Group 1. And then, at last, Group 2. He hurries toward the gate but isn't sure at first where to go, who is boarding and who is waiting to board, among the confused mass of bodies and rolling suitcases. They aren't moving—they are a wall of meat—and he wants to shove them, throw something, but manages to contain himself, to steady his breathing and circle around the crowd and find the actual line of passengers shuffling toward the agent, who scans their tickets with an empty smile and a thank you, thank you, thank you.

He has not noticed up to this point the extra security detail that stands next to the jet bridge. A man and a woman, both of them big shouldered and big bellied, bulging out of their uniforms. They are studying the line. They are waiting for him, he feels certain. And soon, any second now, they will rush forward and throw him to the floor and cuff his wrists. He is only a few feet away when they pull out of line a woman in a floppy hat and floral-patterned muumuu, apologizing to her, saying they're randomly screening passengers. "For your safety," they say.

He turns his smile on the agent when she takes his ticket. "Thank you," she says, and he says, "Thank *you*." He follows the crooked line of passengers, all of them shouldering the weight of laptops and leaning to one side, as they trudge down the throat of the jet bridge. A cold, damp wind breathes through the cracks of it. He is sweat soaked and he shudders from the chill.

"Nervous flier?" A man's voice, behind him. He is short and square, with a goatee and a matching ball cap and Windbreaker bearing the black-and-orange OSU logo.

"Little bit."

The jet bridge elbows to the left, into the open door of the plane. One of the flight attendants stands in the kitchen carrel beyond the doorway. She smiles at him, her mouth heavily lipsticked. "Welcome aboard," she says, and then he is past her, into the hush of the first-class cabin, stutter-stepping down the aisle with everyone else. Those already seated turn the pages of their newspapers in rustling snaps. The storage compartments are all open, like unhinged mouths gaping at them, waiting to swallow the diaper bags and suitcases that people hoist upward before edging into their seats.

He will not need his briefcase. There is nothing in it except some pens and a day-old newspaper. So he stores it and slips into his seat, 13A. He barely has enough time to raise the window shade and glance outside before the seat next to him shakes with the weight of the body collapsing into it. "Me again," says the man with the goatee.

He responds by snapping his buckle into place and yanking on the strap to tighten it. He looks out the window—at the puddled asphalt, at the men heaving the last of the luggage onto the conveyor—hoping the man with the goatee won't say anything more.

But he does. "Where you headed?"

"Portland."

"Oh, sure. Same as the rest of us. I just wasn't sure if that's the end of the road or not."

"The end of the road." It is hard for him to make words, to engage in any sort of conversation, because it feels irrelevant and distracting, yes, but also because his mind feels elsewhere, twenty minutes ahead of the plane, already in the sky. "Yes."

"The Rose City." He stretches out the word *rose*. "From there?"

"No."

"Me either. I'm from Salem." He whistles a song that fades a moment later. He fingers through the airline magazine and SkyMall catalogue in the seat-back pocket. "I'm Troy, by the way."

Passengers continue to wobble down the aisle, while outside jets rise into and fall from the gray ceiling of the sky, vanishing one minute, appearing the next, like seaside birds hunting for food, their tails colored red and purple and blue, their brakes squawking along the runway.

The front door is latched shut. The air pressure tightens. His ears pop. The attendant gets on the intercom and welcomes them and fires off some information about the flight before settling into her singsong speech about seat belts and passenger safety. The man tunes out the cheery buzz of her voice. The air vents hiss. The engine grumbles. The plane retreats from the gate and then rolls forward, following a network of forty-five-degree turns until they have found their place on the tarmac and the pilot's voice barks from the loudspeakers, "Flight attendants, prepare for takeoff."

The raindrops on the window stream sideways into thin, shivering trails when the plane leaps forward, gaining speed. They roar along and eventually pull away from the ground, and at that first moment of flight, the man, despite the heaviness that presses him into his seat, feels ebullient, weightless. He looks down at the foggy expanse of the city. Right now, in their cars, along sidewalks, people are lifting their faces to watch his plane, he thinks. Probably they are wondering where the plane is heading, who is on board, what adventures lie in store for them—and it makes him feel dizzyingly powerful to know the answer.

Troy leans toward him until their shoulders touch. “Don’t worry so much. Flying’s a piece of cake. I do it all the time.”

The man realizes that his mouth is open, that he is breathing rapidly. He snaps his teeth together with a clack. He blinks at a shutter speed. “I’m fine.”

“Here’s the thing,” Troy says. “Almost all plane crashes happen—I read this for a fact . . . or maybe I saw it on the TV—but almost all crashes happen when the plane is taking off and when the plane is landing. Now, we’re taking off, I suppose you could say, until we’ve reached our cruising altitude. When that happens, the lady stewardess will say so, will say you can use your computer. And there will be a bong.” He makes his hand open up like a flower when he says *bong*. “Then you know you’re good. Statistically, I mean.”

For the next few minutes the man stares at the clouds curling around the plane. And then a soft-toned bell sounds from above.

"There it is!" Troy says. "We're in the clear."

The flight attendant gets on the intercom again, telling them that it's now safe to use approved portable electronic devices. They will, however, be experiencing turbulence for the next half hour or so and she asks that everyone please keep their seat belts fastened and move about the cabin only if they must.

The plane is shaking. Or maybe he is shaking. He feels a lurching sensation, as if he is being thrown out of his body. His heart hammers. His breath comes in and out in quick gasps. Troy is saying something—his mouth is moving—but the man can't hear him.

His seat belt unclicks with the noise of a switch-blade.

Patrick wishes he hadn't ordered the large Coke. But he was tired, and he doesn't drink coffee because it tastes like dirt, and the large cup cost only ten cents more than the medium—so he thought, what the hell. It's been one of those mornings. A *what the hell* morning. His father is leaving his son, is leaving his job at Anchor Steam, is leaving to fight a war, his unit activated. And Patrick is leaving his father, is leaving California, his friends, his high school, leaving behind everything that defined his life, that made him *him*. Though he feels like punching through windows, torching a building, crashing a car into a brick wall, he has to stay relatively cool. He has to say *what the hell*. Because his father asked him to. "I don't want to go. And you don't want to go. But we gotta go. And it's only for twelve months," he said. "Consider it a vacation. A chance to get to know your mom a little better." Twelve months. That's how long his father's deployment would last. Patrick has to suck it up and hang tight until then.

But now he has to pee. And he has the window seat. And there is no way he can sneak past the two women sitting next to him without making them shut their laptops, making them stand, making a big production, making everybody on the plane look up and stare at him and think, "Oh, that kid has to pee." And they will be thinking that—they will be thinking about him peeing—when he locks himself into the chemical-smelling closet of a bathroom and struggles with his zipper and tries to maintain his balance, tries not to piss all over himself while turbulence shakes the plane. Maybe he can hold it. Or maybe not—it's another two hours to Portland—and the pressure is so intense his bladder is beginning to throb. Just as he is about to touch his neighbor on the wrist, to tell her excuse me, he's sorry but he has to get up, someone two rows ahead of him, a man in a charcoal suit, rises from his seat.

His face is pale and sweating. His body seems twitchy along the edges, almost as if he were humming, vibrating. His neatly combed hair is starting to come loose in gray strands that fall across his forehead. Patrick wonders if the turbulence is getting to him, if he is going to be sick. The man staggers down the aisle, yanks open the bathroom door, and slams it shut behind him.

Patrick curses under his breath. Not only does he have to wait, but he has to wait for a puker who's going leave his chunks all over the mirror and toilet and door handle. He turns around in his seat three times in as many minutes, checking the bathroom, willing the door to open. Each time he looks there is another person standing in the aisle, all of them with their arms crossed, their faces pensive, waiting. He supposes he should join them.

He unbuckles his seat belt and opens his mouth—ready to finally excuse himself, to stand—when a ragged snarl comes from the back of the cabin. It is hard to place, with the shout of the engines, the chatter of so many voices. Patrick wonders if there is something wrong with the plane. He remembers seeing a news report about how so many planes are behind on their maintenance schedules and shouldn't be in the air at all. Maybe the turbulence has shaken loose the screws holding the tail in place.

There is a growl, a long, drawn-out guttural rumbling, and though it is hard to place, it seems more animal than machine. The cabin is now hushed except for the creaking of seats as people turn around with anxious expressions.

Then the bathroom door crashes open.

A bald man in a Rose Bowl sweatshirt is the first in line for the restroom—and so he is the first to die. The door jars him back. He would have fallen except for the narrow hallway where he stands, the wall catching him and preventing any further retreat as the thing emerges from the restroom, rushing forward like a gray wraith, a blurred mass of hair and muscle and claws. It swings an arm. The bald man's scream is cut short, his throat excised and replaced by a second red mouth that he brings his hands to, as if he could hold the blood in place. But it sprays between his fingers. As if to make up for his sudden silence, the rest of the passengers begin to scream, all of their voices coming together like a siren that rises and falls.

The thing begins to move up the aisle.

Patrick is reminded of a possum his father once trapped. They live on a hobby farm north of San Francisco, near Dogtown, a half acre of carrots and tomatoes and raspberry bushes, three goats, bee boxes, a henhouse. One night the chickens exploded into a panicked clucking, and by the time his father raced to the coop, his flashlight cutting through the dark, the whirl of feathers, he found broken eggs littering the floor and a half-dead hen in the corner missing a wing and a clump of its throat. So they set up a trap, a cage with a spring-loaded door that crashed closed. They baited it with hard-boiled eggs and old bananas. And by the next night they had their possum. It hissed and paced the length of the cage and threw itself against the bars and chewed at them with its needle teeth and reached forth a claw to rake the air. Patrick had once heard his science teacher say that animals didn't feel the same way that humans did, but Patrick was sure he was wrong. The possum felt deeply. It felt rage and hatred. It wanted to kill them for what they had done to it. And though Patrick knew he was safe, knew the cage would hold, knew his father would soon slide a pistol between the bars and fire, he kept his distance and flinched every time the possum crashed its body against the enclosure.

Of course he knows what the thing is. A lycan.

He has heard about them his whole life, has read about them in novels, history books, newspapers, watched them in movies, television shows. But he has never seen one, not in person. Transformation is forbidden.

The lycan moves so quickly it is difficult for Patrick to make sense of it—to secure an image of it—except that it looks like a man, only covered in a downy gray hair, like the hair of the possum. Teeth flash. Foam rips from a seat cushion like a strip of fat. Blood splatters, decorating the porthole windows, dripping from the ceiling. It is sometimes on all fours and sometimes balanced on its hind legs. Its back is hunched. Its face is marked by a blunt snout that flashes teeth as long and sharp as bony fingers, a skeleton's fist of a smile. And its hands—oversize and decorated with long nails—are greedily outstretched and slashing the air. A woman's face tears away like a mask. Ropes of intestine are yanked out of a belly. A neck is chewed through in a terrible kiss. A little boy is snatched up and thrown against the wall, his screams silenced.

The plane is shuddering. The pilot is yelling something over the intercom, but his voice is lost to the screams that fill the cabin. Some people are weeping. Some are praying. Some are climbing out of their seats, pushing their way up the aisle, where they bang at the cockpit door, slam their fists and feet and shoulders up against it, desperate to get in, to get away from the terror working its way toward them.

Patrick remembers watching television the other night, flipping through the channels, coming across one of those talk-show pundits. The program featured a round-cheeked man who looked more like a boy with a gray flattop. He was talking about the lycans, about the protests in D.C. and the situation in the Republic. "To hell with us all being equal," the baby-faced man was saying, staring intensely into the camera. "Nobody's saying my dog has the same rights that I do. Biology made these decisions, not me."

His father took the remote and punched the power button, and the image collapsed upon itself. "That guy makes me lose my appetite," he said and forked at his spaghetti, not eating it, stirring it up into a red mess. His face was pale and bloated from all the injections, the temporary immunizations that could help ward off infection in case he was bitten. He would be leaving in a few days—with his Bay Area unit, the 235th Engineering Company—first to the Petaluma Armory for a week of intensive briefing, then overseas to the Republic, where his primary objective was route clearance, removing and diffusing bombs from roadsides. The IEDs—and the ambushes, the firefights—had increased lately. The lycans fought with their guns and claws alike—they wanted the American forces to leave; they wanted their country back. His father's rucksack was already packed and waiting by the back door, swollen and green and reminding Patrick of an enormous gut sack pulled from a deer carcass.

The war is the reason this is happening. It is the reason he is on this plane and it is the reason the lycan is tearing the plane to pieces. Patrick curses the war and curses the lycan and curses his father, who he wishes were with him now. His father, who would ball up his fists and fight. He wouldn't piss himself, as Patrick does now, his jeans hot and soaked, the Coke finally finding its way out of him, sheeting his legs, filling his shoes.

The rear of the plane is splashed with blood that oozes from the walls in strange cave-painting designs. Bodies are strewn everywhere in various poses of death like a garden of ruined statues. Up to this point, the woman next to Patrick has not moved or said a word, frozen in her fear. Her laptop remains open, one of her hands still on its keyboard, pressed down so severely that the open document scrolls continuously, its pages filling with the letters of one long word no one will ever read. But now, as the lycan makes its way toward their row, she tries to stand and can't, held down by her seat belt. She whimpers as she fumbles with it and then abandons her seat and hesitates in the aisle, turning back for her laptop, snatching it off the tray table. At that moment the lycan lunges forward and claws away the laptop and brings it down on her head, with a wet *thunk* and a smoking spark. Pieces of plastic rain to the floor. Wires dangle like veins from around her neck, where part of the screen still hangs. The lycan pulls her close, as if to embrace her, burying its triangular face in her neck.

At that moment there is a scream that rises above all the others. An Asian man—one of the flight attendants—is hurrying up the aisle, his progress slow and stumbling due to the carnage. He has come from the rear kitchen and he has in one hand a steaming carafe of coffee and in the other a can opener with a curved silver tooth.

The lycan tosses the woman aside just as the man underhands the coffee in a sloshing brown arc. The woman's body impacts Patrick before he can see what happens, but he can hear the lycan crying out, unmistakably in pain, its voice pitched high.

He is knocked back against the wall. He does not push the woman away. He allows her to press him down between the seats, to shield him. The smell of her perfume is mixed up with the smell of her blood. It is hard to tell with the turbulence, but her body seems to tremble and he thinks she might still be alive. He hugs her close. He closes his eyes and in his own private darkness tries to imagine himself back in bed, back in California, waiting for his father to wake him up, to tell him it is time to go. He wishes that he could close his ears, too, to the screams that continue for the next thirty minutes, the longest of his life.

CHAPTER 2

AUGUST AND ALREADY it is snowing. Fat flakes brush past her window. She sits at her desk, a desk her father built from an old cherry tree, the legs carved to look like an animal's, etched with wavelike fur and clawed at their bottom. It doesn't match the rest of the room. The white four-poster bed with the stuffed animals marching across it, the matching white dresser with vines stenciled along its drawers, its top a mess of makeup and perfume bottles. The wobbly bookshelf weighed down with fantasy novels, collections of fables and fairy tales. The rank heaps of clothes, the orange throw rug, the purple walls decorated with posters for *Cats*, Wilco, *The Wizard of Oz*. The corkboard plastered with homecoming photos, a drink coaster, a smiley-face key chain, yellowed comic strips, track ribbons, an old corsage rose from some boy she couldn't care less about that now looks like a shriveled-up heart.

Claire splits open a college catalogue, one of two dozen she has stacked in a leaning pile. She has shot off hundreds of emails, it seems like, requesting information from admissions offices. This is her senior year and she is planning her escape, hunting for something other than the eternal cold, the Friday fish fries, the polka music and pine-paneled, steel-roofed taverns northern Wisconsin has to offer.

She makes notes in a yellow legal tablet about tuition, class size, acceptance rate, student population, renowned programs, touristy info about the town or city, and—of course—distance from home. Distance being one of her priorities. She doesn't care how strong the English Department is at Macalester College—if the school is within five hundred miles of home, she isn't interested.

It is not as though she comes from a broken home, an unloving family. Her mother is a bit of a scold. Her father spanked her—once, when she was little more than a toddler—for wandering out of their house, their yard, and down the street. The two of them bray constantly about politics and rarely take her on vacation to anyplace other than Wisconsin Dells. Otherwise, she is lucky, even spoiled. She knows this. But she also knows—has known since she was a child, her head buried in a book—that she craves something more, almost like a taste filling her mouth, spreading through her body, into her very marrow, the deepest part of her. Adventure. The kind that cannot be found here, in this wooded hamlet, where the pines are thick and the lakes are clear and cheese is never far from hand.

Palm trees would be nice. She imagines reading a textbook on a white sand beach running up against water as blue as the antique bottles her mother keeps lined up on the bathroom windowsill.

The lamplight burnishes the catalogues with a golden color. She flips through them once for the pictures, again for the information, the way some of her friends work their way through fashion magazines. She is a sucker for the pictures. The clock towers, the brickwork paths, the sunlit campus lawns. Celebrity speakers standing before packed auditoriums. Dark-wooded libraries aglow with light streaming through stained-glass windows. Shirtless boys in hemp necklaces tossing Frisbees. Thick-necked mud-splattered girls chasing each other on rugby fields. Circles of students sitting under elm trees with their laptops and notepads open while an oddly dressed, wild-haired professor stands over them. The sight of them warms her belly with a feeling not so different from hunger.

Some schools, she notes, advertise the percentage of lycans, the support groups, the dorms and fraternities and sororities, and others do not. Somewhere in her pile is a William Archer catalogue. Her parents are alums of the university—and though her father hasn't insisted she apply, he has brought it up several times, what a remarkable experience he had there, how they offer legacy scholarships, how safe and comfortable she would feel surrounded by her own kind. "Especially in these difficult times," he said.

She isn't interested. As it is, she hangs out with too many lycans. Her parents are always hosting meetings and potlucks—and most of the people who come are like them: obsessive, always slamming their fists into their palms, speaking in earnest, almost pleading voices about how unfairly lycans are treated, how U.S. troops remain in the Lupine Republic only to maintain control of the uranium reserves. How things *must* change. She gets it. She does. But they're always so violently leftist, and sometimes she wants to argue with them—point out how the Republic's leadership actually *supports* the U.S. role in extracting fuel and maintaining order, how only a select group of extremist lycans seem upset about the occupation—but she never feels educated enough to speak and doesn't want to rile them up further.

And she wouldn't mind talking about other things too, like, you know, her favorite episode of *Buffy the Vampire Slayer* or how Mike Romm has sewer breath or how she can see the defined bulge of Mr. Bronson's crotch when he wears his khakis in AP Calculus. Or whatever. She doesn't particularly *like* being a lycan. Her parents would hate to hear her say that, but it's true. The duality of the condition makes her feel sometimes split in two, as if she is at war with herself. Life is easier when that part of her remains dormant, neglected.

And though William Archer is located in Montana, outside Missoula, and satisfies her five-hundred-mile-radius requirement, the campus sits at the top of a bowl-like valley walled in by mountains, and—for the next four years, at least—she is done with cold. She is staring at the window as she thinks this, staring at the feathery snow dancing past it, and then her eyes focus on the nearer distance, where her reflection hangs in the glass.

She looks pale in the window and knows that the color in her face, the tan she has worked so hard on over the summer—smearing her skin with baby oil when she mows the lawn, when she water-skis at Loon Lake or sunbathes on the rocks that ring its shore—will soon drain from her skin as the clouds pile up in the sky, as she mummifies herself with hats and scarves and coats to scare away the wind that comes whistling down from Canada.

Again, the beach comes to mind, the white sand beach. She is sprawled out on a red towel that matches her painted toenails and the stripes running across her peppermint bikini. Her belly is as tan and flat as a pancake. Her nose is sugared with the freckles the sun brings out of it. She has set her textbook aside because a man—a lean, muscled, shirtless man with a black shock of hair—is walking toward her with a picnic basket full of wine and strawberries and chocolate. This is Raúl, her boyfriend. They will meet in a freshman honors seminar and will make love for the first time in a hammock strung between two palm trees. His skin will taste like salt and his smile will be as white as the meat of a coconut.

Her father shouts from downstairs, shouts at the television he has been watching most of the day, and the white sand of her dream rises in a sparkling swirl, replaced by the white snow brushing past her window.

Earlier that day, she met her friend Stacey at Starbucks, and then they walked to the park, where they drank their flavored coffees on the swings, halfheartedly kicking their legs, their sneakers nosing the gravel. The cold front was just beginning to move in, the sky a churning gray that blotted out the sun, and the swings around them began to creak alive as if inhabited by ghosts. "It's not fair," she said. "Our last days of summer—we're getting robbed."

When she came home, her nose pink and dripping from the cold, she found her mother sitting on the couch and her father pacing in front of the fireplace, the mouth of it crackling and spitting with fire. She could tell she had interrupted a conversation. The two of them stared at her, her father with his mouth open, his hand raised midgesture. The flames in the fireplace snapped and bent sideways against the wind and then licked their way upright when she closed the door. "What?" she said.

Her mother is slender and sharp edged, her graying hair cut short around a rectangular face. That morning she was wearing jeans and a red hooded sweatshirt with a UW Badger imprinted on its breast. Her legs were crossed and moving like scissors. "Something has happened," she said and looked to her husband to explain.

Claire's father sometimes appeared mismatched next to his wife, oversize and always moving, shouting, sometimes with anger but more often with enthusiasm punctuated by throaty laughter. He is a thickly built man, broad shouldered and big gutted, but with a kind face that looks like a child's, only creased around its edges like a photograph lost at the bottom of a drawer. He works independently as a carpenter—his shed built onto the back of their garage—and his fingernails are always bruised and his hair always carries wood shavings in it like dandruff.

He told her, in a gruff, halting way, about the attacks. The three planes. One had crashed outside of Denver, a fiery smear in a wheat field. The other two had landed, in Portland and Boston, the pilots locked safely in the cockpit, but with only one passenger still alive, on Flight 373, a boy, a teenager not yet identified. No one knew much else.

Her parents took her to the kitchen, where the TV was muted, the same footage cycling over and over, a faraway shot of a plane parked on a runway surrounded by emergency vehicles flashing their lights. The red banner along the bottom of the screen read that nationwide all flights had been grounded, that a lycan terrorist cell was suspected, and that the president promised a swift and severe response.

Her parents stood to either side of her, studying her, waiting for her to respond.

She understood how awful this was, but it felt so distant and unreal, like a film, someone else's nightmare, that she had difficulty processing it emotionally. She could only say, "That's terrible," like an actor trying out a line. Her father's face hardened. He had told her before—once when she said she didn't feel like visiting her grandfather in hospice—that she was empathy proof. "Typical teenager," he had said, and she had hated him for it.

She could tell he was thinking the same thing now. A blush crept up his throat like a rash.

"Why are you so upset?" she said. "I mean, I get it—it's horrible that these people died—but you're acting like you killed them or something."

Her parents shared a look full of meaning unavailable to her.

She retreated to her room for the rest of the afternoon, yelling down once, leaning over the railing, asking her mother if she was going to make dinner or what? Her mother had spoken so quietly, Claire barely caught her response: "I'm not hungry."

She could hear the television at times, and then, when it fell silent, her father's voice as he spoke on the phone, whispering harshly into the receiver.

Not long ago, he came to her room. Normally he just barged in with a "Hello, hello," but tonight he knocked and waited.

She cracked the door open and said through the crack, "What?" her hand on the knob.

He took a step forward and then back, thinking better of it, clearing his throat and asking if he might come in. He wanted to talk to her about something.

She sighed and plopped onto the bed and he wandered around as if trying to decide where to sit, before joining her, his weight depressing the mattress another few inches and making her lean toward him. He had a pensive look on his face and a white envelope pinched between his fingers that he handed to her.

"What's this?"

"I don't know what's going to happen. Maybe nothing. But if something does happen, I want you to open this."

She blew out a sigh. "Don't be so dramatic." She took the envelope and tossed it, and it twirled like a broken-winged bird onto her desk. Her father kept his eyes on it. He wouldn't look at her. She noticed a wood chip tangled in the hair above his ear and she plucked it out and he absently touched the place it had been.

"Dad," she said, and he said, "Yeah?"

She couldn't believe that anyone would care about them. They were boring. They lived in the middle of nowhere. They hadn't done anything to anyone. "You think they're going to—what?—like, put every lycan in the country in jail? This has nothing to do with us."

He opened his hands and stared at them as if the answer might lie in the rough design of his palms. "There are things you don't know."

"What's that supposed to mean?"

He smiled sadly, throwing an arm around her and

drawing her close. Her nose filled with the smells of sap and Old Spice. "I'm probably worrying for no reason. But hey, better safe than sorry."

Her mother's voice called from downstairs. "Howard? Your phone is buzzing."

"Yeah," he yelled. "Coming." He stood and the bed sprang back into its shape, the coils of the box spring creaking with relief. He walked to the desk and laid one of his square-tipped fingers on the envelope and tapped it twice. "Indulge me, okay?"

"Fine."

Now Claire shoves aside her college catalogues and purses her lips and picks up the envelope, turning it over, testing its weight with the tips of her fingers. She doesn't know if there is money in it. Or a letter. Or both. She doesn't know whether she should open it now, or if not now, then when? How will she know?

Nor does she know what's happening outside right this minute, as the small brigade of vehicles—the armored vans, the black sedans with government plates—appears at the end of her block with their headlights off. She lives in a wooded neighborhood, each house set back on a half-acre lot. There are no streetlights, no sidewalks. The vehicles purr to a stop. Their doors swing open but do not close. Any noise that might bring Claire to the window—the stomp of boots along the asphalt, the clatter of assault rifles and ammunition clips—is muffled by the steady snowfall, a white shroud thrown over the night.

She doesn't know about the Tall Man—in the black suit and black necktie, his skull as hairless as a stone—who stands next to his black Lincoln Town Car. She doesn't know that he has his hands tucked into his pockets or that the snow is melting against his scalp and dripping down his face or that he is smiling slightly.

She doesn't know that her father and mother are sitting at the kitchen table, drinking their way through a bottle of Merlot, not holding but squeezing each other's hands in reassurance as they watch CNN, the coverage of what the president called "a coordinated terror attack directed at the heart of America."

So she doesn't know that, when the front door kicks open, splintering along its hinges, her father is holding the remote in his hand, a long black remote that could be mistaken for a weapon.

She doesn't know that he stands up so suddenly his chair tips over and clatters to the floor, that he screams, "No," and holds out his hand, the hand gripping the remote, and points it at the men as they come rushing through the entryway, the dark rectangle of night, with snow fluttering around them like damp shredded paper.

She only knows—when she hears the crash, the screams, the rattle of gunfire—that she must run.

She hasn't changed often, only a handful of times. Not only because it is forbidden, because she could be jailed for it, but because she doesn't like the way it makes her feel. So grotesquely *other*. And bruised for days afterward, her body's sudden shifting like the growing pains that make children twist under their sheets and cry out at night. But her parents have occasionally insisted she do so, when they have taken her to Canada. Full-moon retreats, they call them.

She can smell the men now, deodorant and aftershave, cigarettes and gum. Gun oil. The sulfur of their weapons' discharge. She can hear their harsh breathing, their voices calling out, "Clear!" from different corners of the house. She can feel their footsteps pounding up the stairs, toward her.

Her skin itches horribly, as if bubbling over with hives, and then the hair bristles from it in a rush. Her gums recede and her teeth grind together in a mouth not yet big enough for them. Her bones stretch and bend and pop, and she yowls in pain, as if she is giving birth, one body coming out of another. She always cries. Tears of blood. This time her tears and mewling come from the pain—and also the dawning realization that everything, in an instant, has changed.

But these thoughts are fleeting. The wolf in her has no time for them. Her mind sharpens to a singular focus. Survival is what matters. There is nothing else, no love or sadness or fear or worry, only a needle stab of adrenaline that surges through her, sends her loping toward the window, toward the reflection she barely recognizes, hunched and misshapen and growing larger by the second. Then she crashes through herself, through the window.

The glass shatters, and shards of it bite at her. There is no roof to scuttle across, no lattice or gutter to climb down. There is instead the blackness of the night, the emptiness of the air she falls through, flipping and twisting as the wind shrieks in her ears and the ground rushes up to meet her. Splinters of glass, mixed up with the snow, sparkle all around her.

Two inches have already accumulated, but that isn't enough to cushion a fall from a second-story window. She lands on all fours, rolling and thudding forward, sliding across the short expanse of lawn, smearing away the snow in a ragged teardrop to reveal the green grass beneath. A tree at the edge of the lawn offers a hammer blow to her chest. Her breath is gone. Her wrist blazes as if stabbed through with a hot poker. Glass bites at her. The night seems to close upon her for a moment—and then she draws in a sucking gasp.

Her window throws a square of light broken up by triangles and hexagons of yellow and orange that spotlight her body, the spotlight blackened a moment later when the men charge into her room and pursue her exit.

She shakes away the pain and leaps to her feet and sees the man. The Tall Man in the black suit. Twenty yards away, he observes her with his head cocked curiously, and then he begins to walk—and then run, his long arms slashing the air—toward her.

She departs this place, her home, bounding off into the trees. The snow whirls around her. It is as though she is entering a cloud—with vaporous edges that thicken into a cottony tangle out of which occasionally appear windows that glow like ball lightning and tall pine forests as dark as thunderheads. Into their cover she hurries.

CHAPTER 3

MIRIAM WAKES EARLY and pulls on her jeans and a thermal and goes to the living room window. Her hair is as black and ragged as a crow's wings. Her face is as sharply angled as her body, as if honed to an edge, made to cut through things. She is in her late thirties, her age evident only in the hardness of her expression. In the half light, the tall, thick-waisted Douglas firs are swaying, bending, and creaking with the wind. The cracks around the windows and the front door emit the hollow tones that come from blowing across bottle tops.

Next to the cabin, a short clearing in the shape of a half-moon—fireweed, Indian paintbrush, moss, and stone. Her truck, an old black-and-silver Ramcharger, sits in the cinder driveway that cuts through the meadow and into the woods. It would take someone less than a minute to rush from the trees to her porch, and she keeps her eyes on the shadows between them.

Something is out there. She can feel it in the same way worms and toads can a storm, the changing air pressure making them squirm to the surface of their muddy burrows. She wouldn't be alive today if not for her heightened senses, her ability to *know*. Her eyes are narrowed and her ears seem to prick forward.

Ten minutes pass like this, and then the morning begins to catch up with her and she withdraws from the window and heads down the hall to the kitchen to brew some coffee. If something is coming, she might as well be awake for it.

She doesn't flip on the light when she enters the kitchen. The single window—looking out into the woods, much closer here, the white trunks of cottonwoods like bony teeth grinning across the glass—provides enough light. Beneath it, an L-shaped counter bends around the room, the Formica a spotted gray made to look like granite. It is interrupted by a four-burner stove and a deep-bellied sink next to which squats her coffeemaker. She grinds the beans and measures out the water, and while the pot gurgles and pops, she pulls open the silverware drawer and reaches past the knives and forks to withdraw something a little sharper still, a Glock 21, one of several weapons stashed throughout the cabin, this one a .45-caliber pistol with thirteen hollow-point rounds loaded in the magazine.

She tucks the Glock into the waistband at the small of her back. The sun is rising and the shadows are receding from the cabin, shrinking into its corners, when she splashes full her mug and returns to the living room. She stops so suddenly her coffee waves over the lip of the mug and scalds her fingers. The front door has a frosted oval of glass cut into it, and it is presently darkened by the shape of what could be a boy or could be a man, so diminutive is its shadow.

The wind is gusting. Her coffee is steaming. She sets the mug down on an end table and moves across the room, toward the door, depressing her bare feet slowly so as not to bring a creak from the wide-board flooring. She reaches for the door handle and a blue spark of electricity snaps at her when she lays a hand on it. She does not undo the lock, does not turn the handle, but lets her hand rest there and leans against it as if to buttress the door.

"Leave me alone, Puck," she says, her voice loud enough to carry through the glass.

The shadow does not respond.

"I don't want any part of it."

"We need you." She has always hated his voice, uneven and shrill, like a poorly cut flute. "Open the door."

"Go away. Get the fuck away from me."

"We need you." The wind gathers strength. She can feel it breathing around the door, a taste of snow in it maybe, with winter coming that much earlier at five thousand feet. “We want you.”

She mouths the word: *Fuck.* She thumps her forehead softly against the wall, snaps the deadbolt, and throws open the door. A cold wind envelops her. Her hair lifts from her shoulders while behind her a newspaper on the coffee table flutters its pages.

On the porch stands a small, muscular man, his feet apart, his hands at his sides. He wears a tight black T-shirt tucked into dark blue jeans. His peroxide hair—so blond, almost white—has been gelled back in a carefully messy way. This is Jonathan Puck. He is smiling at her, chewing gum. He raises his right hand in greeting, the pinky and ring finger missing from it, replaced by nubs of creamy scar tissue that she knows match the claw marks hidden beneath his clothes, along his back and chest mostly, as if he is riddled with worms. She knows because she is responsible for them.

“Come any closer, you’ll lose the rest of them.”

His hand drops. His smile trembles a little before growing wider. “I smell coffee.” His nostrils flare. “Aren’t you going to invite me in for a nice cup?”

“No.”

“I would love some coffee.” He snaps his gum. “Why don’t you let me in, dear?”

“No. I said leave me alone.”

He lets his shoulders rise and fall in a shrug. "Fair enough. I am the uninvited solicitor. We'll talk here."

"Whatever you have to say I don't want to hear."

"You've been watching the news? You have, haven't you? You know what we've done, don't you?"

As if in response, the newspaper in the living room snaps and riffles, a page of it blowing off the coffee table and onto the floor. "I know what you've done," she says.

Her covered porch opens up between two pine columns to a stone staircase that sinks into a pea-gravel path that coils into the driveway. On it—she is not surprised to see, the two of them rarely apart from each other—stands a beast of a man, Morris Magog, more than seven feet tall and seemingly half as wide. The only parts of him visible, beyond the mess of his long red hair and long red beard and long black leather duster that the wind whips around him, are his empty blue eyes and his hands, enormous and pouched. She has heard him speak on only a few occasions—once to ask Puck if he could have a bit of candy, please—his voice like shifting stone.

"You've had your time to grieve," Puck says, "and we're glad for that. We're surely glad you've had that time." Though he continues to smile, his voice has a severe edge to it. “But that time is done. Because we’ve got plans. Big plans. And you’re a part of them. And we’ve come for you now. And you’re to come with us now. And that’s the end of it.”

She knew this day was coming. She knew, when she left her husband, when she walked away from the caves, when she abandoned the Resistance, that they would allow her only so much time. These past few months she has sensed their presence, glancing often to the woods and the nighttime windows that gave back nothing but her reflection. She has discovered, on several occasions, signs of their trespass, a footprint pressed into the mud beneath her window, the lingering smell of cigarettes in the cab of her unlocked truck. They wanted her to know she was being watched.

“I won’t,” she says.

They stare at each other, Puck blowing a pink bubble that breaks with a hiss. “You really don’t have a choice, you know.” He throws a glance behind him, and—as if he has issued some silent command—Magog takes a step forward and leans his huge body toward the cabin, as if ready to break into a run. She hears a huff that could be his breath or could be the wind. “You can’t be hiding any longer. Not in times like these. Every hand on deck. That’s what your dear husband says. That’s why I’m here. To fetch you.”

She chooses this moment to reach behind her back and withdraw the Glock. Not to point it. Just to show it off.

For the first time since she opened the door, Puck stops smiling. His eyes are on the pistol when he says, “We’ll keep coming back.”

“Don’t bother.”

The light now streaming through the trees makes a series of yellow slashes across the porch. Puck wears a gold watch and it catches the sunlight and spits it on the ground like a tiny fluorescent bug. “Hey,” he says. “Look at that.” He rotates his wrist and makes the bug slide across the porch boards, where it momentarily settles on Miriam’s foot before traveling up the length of her body, zeroing in on her eye. The pupil contracts.

She lifts the Glock and stares with her good eye down the line of it. “Stop that.” She knows how fast he can move, has seen his body blur into action.

The refracted sunlight drops from her face, leaving behind its afterimage, so that for a few seconds she sees Puck surrounded by a red aura. He chews his gum slowly, considering her. “Fine. Okay. You need some time to think it over? I understand.”

Perhaps her husband sent them. Perhaps they came on their own. Puck has always wanted her, has tried to make her his—that’s why his body is gummed over with scars. Regardless of why they are here, it is based on some man's desire, not her obligation to or importance within the Resistance. "I'm done, Puck. I'm done. And if you step onto this porch again, I'll put a bullet in your mouth."

He retreats from her, his feet sliding along the porch, scraping the wood—and at the top of the steps he pauses to turn over his gum a few times with his tongue. "Not unless you're dead you're done with us."

Later, she ties on two ankle scabbards and stabs into them a matching pair of Gerber serrated combat knives. To cover them she yanks down her jeans and shoves her feet into steel-tipped cowboy boots. She straps on and tightens the shoulder holster for the Glock and pulls on a black denim jacket. She steps outside and waits on the porch for a good five minutes, listening, the wind gone now, the forest a whispery hush interrupted by the occasional bird calling, twig snapping.

She then clomps down the steps and crunches down the gravel path and circles the Ramcharger, peering in its windows and quickly under its hood, before climbing into the cab and locking the doors and keying the ignition.

Her eyes dart between the mirrors and the road

when she drives the quarter-mile driveway that leads to a pitted strip of county two-lane that snakes down the mountain before connecting up with a highway that takes her to La Pine, Oregon. Along the way her foot feathers the brake and her eyes scan back and forth across the road as if something might burst from the woods that wall her in.

At the grocery store she fills her cart with canned vegetables, dried fruit, bags of jerky, boxes of cereal, and granola bars; and at the pharmacy she collects some gauze and disinfectant, a needle and thread, an *Us Weekly*; and at the Ace hardware she buys an electric drill, an electric handsaw, a steel entry door, ten sheets of plywood, three two-by-fours, four motion-sensor lights, four Magnum flashlights, five packs of D batteries, three boxes of four-inch screws, and two empty five-gallon water bottles. On her way out of town, she swings into the service station, one final stop, where she picks up two five-gallon gas containers and fills them with unleaded.

It takes several trips to unload the truck, and she pauses to survey the woods again every time she steps outside. An open-air shed, cluttered with garbage cans, yard tools, a wheelbarrow, rusted rolls of chicken wire, stands a ways off from the driveway. She collects an extension ladder from it. The cabin is shaped like a shoebox, with its porch and entryway on the shorter face of it. She climbs the ladder to install two motion detectors beneath its gables and centers the other two along the broad sides of the cabin.

She opens the entry door and uses a hammer and flathead screwdriver to knock the pins from the hinges. She is strong enough to wobble only a little when she picks up the wooden door and lays it on the porch and excises its knob and deadbolt and hinges and then screws them into the steel door with the price still stickered to it. After thirty minutes the new door is hung, not strong enough to keep Magog out, she knows, but enough to slow him down.

Inside, she snaps her measuring tape along the windows and jots down their dimensions on a piece of paper she pockets. There are ten windows in the house, all of them the same size except for the bathroom, the kitchen, and the big bay window in the living room. She lays out each sheet of plywood in the yard and uses the measuring tape and a Magic Marker to sketch out their shape. From the shed she collects two sawhorses with lichen furring them over and sets them in the front yard and heaves the sheets up on them and sets to work cutting their edges and then, into their centers, a foot-wide slit big enough to accommodate her eyes or the muzzle of a gun.

This takes a long time because she lets the saw spin for only thirty seconds at a time, its blade spitting out sawdust like freshly fallen snow, and then she lifts her finger from the trigger, the whine of the blade receding as she surveys the woods.

There is a tall stack of firewood at the leeward side of the cabin, and she tosses the litter of plywood there before dragging the freshly cut sheets inside. Twilight has come and she claps out the remaining light by hanging the plywood blinds, bracing them with a raised knee, screwing their four corners into the window frame. Across the front door, the only door, she hammers three two-by-fours.

She fills her cupboards with the groceries. She shoves the gas containers to the back of the broom closet. She feeds batteries into the flashlights and staggers them throughout the cabin. She can't fit the water bottles in the sink so she undoes the hose from the washing machine and runs it into them, splashing them full and setting them aside.

Her dinner she doesn't taste—the chicken and pesto left over from last night—and barely remembers eating it either, surprised to scratch her fork against an empty plate.

She pads the bathtub with several blankets and a pillow, and next to it lays down a ten-inch silver dagger with a textured grip, two Glocks, six clips loaded with silver hollow-points, a shotgun with a shoulder-strap decorated with red cartridges packed tight with silver ball bearings, and finally, the photo she always keeps next to her bed, the photo of her daughter, whose face she touches before killing the light and crawling into the tub to stare at the darkness and wait for sleep.

CHAPTER 4

CHASE CAN'T GET used to it. Eight months into his first term and every time somebody nods at him and addresses him as Governor Williams, he feels like he ought to turn around, see if some blue-blood Yale grad is standing behind him. He likes to think of himself as country. He knows this is what got him elected. "He's real people," his supporters like to say.

He still wears Justin cowboy boots and Wrangler jeans, but usually with a Calvin Klein sport coat. He still speaks with a twang, but especially when he takes to the microphone at a press conference or town hall forum. But it has been a long time since he mucked out a horse stall, hefted irrigation pipe, mended a fence, fired a shot at anything except a paper target. And Salem is a long way from the ranch in Eastern Oregon, where he grew up, the three thousand acres of alfalfa, the six thousand head of cattle.

A long way indeed. Right now he sits cross-legged on the floor, holding a pair of chopsticks and clacking them together, hungrily, over a Japanese woman lying on a straw mat, her naked body decorated with a colorful array of sushi placed on tea leaves. He dines directly off her. She does not move—she barely breathes—even when he traces his chopsticks along her collarbone, to the base of her neck, where in the hollowed-out dip there rests a *gunkanzushi*—sea urchin wrapped in seaweed—that he plucks away and devours.

This is the Kazumi Teahouse, where Chase often comes for lunch, dinner, only a twenty-minute drive from the capitol building, in southeast Salem, off Lancaster Drive. Paper lanterns and tea lights softly illuminate the main dining room. Scrolls bearing Japanese characters hang from the walls, evenly spaced and separated by potted bamboo. A rectangular koi pond runs down the center of the restaurant, bright with water lilies, and to either side of the pond sit men who dine off female bodies, slowly unveiling their nakedness.

"Governor Williams?" The voice comes from behind him.

"What?" Chase turns to see the waiter—a woman in a black kimono with pink roses stitched along its edges—bowing toward him, carrying a tray on which rests the sake bomb he ordered, a ceramic bowl of Koro set next to a pint of Rogue Amber. The waiter pours the sake into the beer and hands it to Chase, who toasts the glass and takes a heavy gulp and smacks his lips and says, "Oh, is that good. That is so, so good. Thank you."

Nearby, on a spotlighted circular stage, a gray-haired Japanese woman in a dark blue kimono kneels before a koto shaped like a crouching dragon. When strummed, the thirteen woven strings stretched over ivory bridges make the air vibrate.

She watches Chase, and eventually a stare seals between them. Her eyes are black slits that swallow light and give nothing back. Maybe he sees in her face some silent disapproval, some forbidding reminder of one of his ex-wives or Augustus, his chief of staff, who tells him not to come here.

The reporters like to splash his face across the newspapers walking out of strip clubs, heckling the ref and hurling popcorn at Trail Blazers games, speedboating along the Columbia with two women half his age wearing American flag bikinis. He doesn't care.

But Augustus does. Augustus, with his buffalo head and highfalutin vocabulary, keeps imploring him—that's the word he used, *imploring*, as in *I implore you*—to think about the next election, about the ammunition he is giving his opponents. But the next election seems a long way off. And besides, he ran as an independent, and independent is who he is, and who he is got him elected, thank you very much. “I’d rather be an open door,” he told Augustus. “I don’t hide my dirty business like all the rest of these crooks. And people appreciate that. Because my dirty isn’t that dirty. What you see is what you get. Nobody’s going to catch me taking bribes or cheating on my wife.”

“You aren’t married.”

“Exactly,” he said. “Just like I was saying, independent.”

He discovered Japanese food only a few years ago, and the chopsticks are still difficult for him to handle, but with some concentration he is able to grip them steadily, to bring the *temaki* and the *gunkan* and the *norimaki* to his mouth, relishing not just the strange spongy textures and sharp spices, but the beautiful woman beneath him—her skin so pure and hairless, so different from the hands that hover over her, tanned and calloused, dark hair curling up his knuckles.

“You are a sight,” he says and mashes a roll with his teeth.

The old woman plucks the koto, and the restaurant seems to move according to the music’s slow, steady rhythm—chopsticks and teacups rising and falling—as if strings connect them all, long dangling red strings the old woman tugs.

In his pocket, his BlackBerry vibrates. He considers letting the call go. That’s the worst thing about the job, the constant questions, the pestering, everyone wanting his attention, demanding something of him, a vote, a law, a promise, a repeal, a speech. But when he pulls out the phone, the caller ID reads Augustus Remington and he knows if he doesn't answer, Augustus will simply call him back, over and over, until he answers.

He brings the phone to his ear and says, "Buffalo! Guess where I'm—"

"Be quiet. Just be quiet for a moment, please. Something has happened."

CHAPTER 5

SLEEP USED TO come like a guillotine. Patrick would crawl into bed and pull the sheets up to his neck and in less than a minute the darkness would come crashing down. It always seemed like that, like it was coming from above, suddenly descending on him.

Now when he lies awake, when the shadows creeping across the ceiling begin to coalesce and fall toward him, he will startle, snap open his eyes, shake his head. It's not that he doesn't want to sleep—he is constantly exhausted and wants more than anything to feel rested again—it's the dreams he can do without.

He is on the plane. Outside his window, clouds pearl and glimmer with lightning. He feels a hand on his wrist. He turns to the woman next to him and her mouth opens as if to tell him something. Instead a tongue falls out, a too-long tongue that rolls with her panting. Her breath smells like carrion. Her gums bleed as her teeth grow into points. Her eyes turn yellow as if lit by some sulfurous light. He looks past her, looks for help, only to discover that everyone on board is staring at him.

Even the flight attendants, the pilots in the open door of the cockpit. They all begin to wail and rip off their clothes and move toward him with their claws greedily outstretched.

If not for these dreams, he wouldn't want to wake up. He wouldn't want to throw off the covers and stumble down the hall and crunch through a bowl of cereal and scrub his armpits under the hot spray of the shower and pull on the new jeans and polo his mom bought him at the mall especially for this day, his first day at Old Mountain High.

She is already gone, his mother, off to show a house. But on the counter, beneath his keys, she has left him a note. *Good luck,* it reads. *I love you!* Her handwriting reminds him of barbed wire. He crumples up the paper and tosses it in the garbage can on his way out the door.

His black Wrangler sits in the driveway. It is his first car, a gift bought thirdhand by his mother to help with the transition. "I know this isn't easy," she said when she dropped the keys in his palm. "And I want you to be happy. I hope this helps a little." She tries. She really does. Saying "I love you," every chance she gets. Asking if he wants to talk, if not to her, then somebody else?—she knows a therapist who could help. "No, thanks," he tells her. "I'm not into that," and when she asks what he means by *that*, he says, "Talking."

The passenger-side headlight is cracked and gives off a weak, sputtery glow. Duct tape holds together sections of the soft top, which at high speeds flaps and whistles like a panicked gathering of birds. Wherever he parks he leaves behind puddles of oil and antifreeze dusted over with rust. Regardless of its disrepair, he kind of loves the Jeep.

Bits of quartz catch the sun and flash from the gravel driveway when he drives down it and turns onto the blacktop that will carry him the five miles to school. Here, along the shoulder, is where the news vans parked a month ago, the reporters huddled next to the mailbox, the cameras trained at the house like howitzers. They were waiting for him to come out, and when he didn't, they eventually left. He did only one interview—and that was enough. He didn't have anything to say. Everyone had died except for him. Not because he did anything special. But because he hid beneath a body and played dead. That wasn't something to retell, relive—that was something to forget.

The worst moment, the moment when he felt a gust of debilitating fear blow through him, was after they landed, after the plane skidded and braked along the runway and the river of blood came rushing down the aisle. They taxied a short distance and Patrick was certain that in these final moments the lycan would discover him, certain the police or military would grenade the plane, certain he wouldn't make it—he couldn't possibly make it. There had been too much death, too much to escape. In a way, he already felt like a corpse himself, unmoving, barely breathing, soaked in gore.

He couldn't see them, but he could sense them, the huddle of squad cars, fire trucks, ambulances, all with their lights flashing. Then, over the loudspeakers, came the pilot's voice: "You're going down, you fucking dog." In response the lycan made a sound like sheets of metal being torn in half.

With the woman's body draped over him, her arms wrapped around him in a limp hug and her chin resting sharply against the top of his head, Patrick could see nothing except her blood-splattered blouse and the patterned cloth of his seat cushion. He didn't dare to reposition her, not even an inch, afraid of the noise he might make.

He could hear the thing moving up and down the aisle, its feet—or paws—or whatever they were—thudding into bodies and squelching through blood, so much blood, soaked into the thin carpeting, the foam cushions, his clothes, everything around Patrick tacky and sloshing with it. When the plane at last came to a rocking halt, he could hear its claws against the plastic, fumbling with the emergency door a few rows ahead of him. There was a sudden wind, a burst of sunlight, when the lycan tore it away.

Immediately the bullets came ripping through the opening—and into its body. Patrick could hear this too. The metal impacting meat. The yowling that gurgled over with blood. The thudding collapse of its body. The gunfire continued for another few seconds. Patrick startled enough at the noise to shove away the body, slide its flopping weight away from his face. Its head thudded against his thigh while one of its hands maintained a stubborn grip on his shoulder. From where he huddled he could see white sparks, an arc of orange flame, as the bullets tore through the plane's interior, ringing off metal armrests, puncturing foam and plastic, clipping wires. The smell of smoke charred over the smell of blood.

There followed a silence long enough that he fell momentarily out of time and forgot that they had landed, that the lycan had been shot, that he was going to be all right. Then came a voice, a man's voice hopped up with fear and anger. "Is there anybody alive in here?" it said. "Is there anybody in there?"

Patrick wanted to say yes. But he couldn't. He

couldn't move either. Couldn't kick away the body now draped across his lap, his hand tangled up in her hair. Couldn't even lift an arm to signal his survival. It wasn't until later—long after the men dressed in black Kevlar and toting assault rifles crashed down the aisle and yelled, "Clear!" after the pilots escaped through the cockpit emergency hatch—that the agents climbed on board.

They were dressed in plastic goggles, elastic breathing masks, milky plastic suits, latex gloves, booties. Two of them carried clipboards and one of them a long-nosed camera. After the cameraman had taken several photos of the lycan sprawled on the floor, the carcass was zippered into a bag and dragged away. The cameraman then climbed through the puzzle of bodies, making his way to the first-class cabin, where so many had gathered and tried to escape and met their end. He was in there for some time, the bursts of his flash shimmering through the plane's interior, before he entered the main cabin again and walked row to row and snapped several photos, first of the seat number, then of the passengers in their final repose.

When he appeared at row 15, he looked at Patrick without really seeing him. It wasn't until the flash went off that Patrick flinched and the man reared back. "Holy shit," he said even as he snapped another photo, the flash blazing, melting through Patrick's eyes and his memory of the next few minutes, as he was dragged from his hiding place. "Are you hurt?" the voices said. "What happened?" "What's your name?" "Why are you alive?"

"No," he kept saying. "No," over and over again as if it were the only word he knew.

With his joints sour and aching, with his vision a white haze as if veiled by a cataract, he can only now remember feeling he had grown suddenly older, nearly dead and dragged from the grave.

Old Mountain High School is built into the side of a hill. Its walls are made of roughly hewn basalt bricks, and its roof, a red sloping steel. The parking lot is the size of a football field, and every spot seems filled as Patrick drives up and down its many rows, searching, his foot teasing the brake, depressing it frequently to make way for the students streaming toward the school, laughing and calling to each other, punching messages into their cell phones, turtling under the weight of their backpacks. The air is busy with their voices and with the country music that blasts from the rolled-down windows of jacked-up pickup trucks. The sun flashes across the hood of the Jeep, and when he blinks it away two too-tan girls—in short shorts and V-neck tops, their blond hair flattened and lustrous as though plaited from gold—appear in front of him. He stomps the brake and the Jeep shudders and creaks to a halt. The girls pause in their conversation to look at the car, and then at him, with distaste.

At the far end of the lot he finds a spot and hauls from the backseat his pack and slams shut the door. As he walks, the Jeep seems to walk with him and he realizes in a panic that it has begun to roll. He curses and tries to wrestle it to a stop with his hands and then jumps into the cab to engage the emergency brake, the only way to keep the vehicle in place.

He looks over his shoulder twice when crossing the lot, in part to make sure the Jeep hasn't rolled away or lost a tire or burst into flames, but his gaze is full of longing too as he considers climbing behind the wheel, revving the engine, driving over the mountains, then south along the coast without glancing a single time into the rearview.

Two thousand students and he knows not a single one. He brings his fingers to the bridge of his nose and pinches. Ever since he moved here he has had a vague headachy pain behind his eyes. His mother blames it on tension and altitude. He blames his bed. His mother bought it from a neighbor, a woman whose son had a job and a fiancée in Portland, so she was changing his bedroom into the guest room and upgrading from the twin to a queen-size. Every time Patrick rolls into bed, he finds it unsettling, with the impression of someone else still in the mattress, a dent where another body had been, just one more reminder that this place is not his own.

He doesn't mind the landscape. The deep-rutted glaciers glowing from the Cascades. The thickly forested foothills with their hiking trails and bear-grass meadows and white-water rivers. And then, to the east, the sprawl of the sage flats interrupted by the occasional striped canyon, the bulge of a cinder cone. Hanging above all of this a sky, that high-altitude sky, as glassy and blue as the stripe inside a marble.

But his mother is a stranger and his bed reminds him of a coffin and he wakes up in the night to pee and crashes into the wall or the bookcase because the room isn't his own. Twelve months, he thinks to himself, pushing through the glass-doored entrance, shouldering through the crowds of students. Twelve months and his father will be home, which means he will be home, and it will be as though he never climbed aboard Flight 373.

* * *

The morning passes in a blur. He forgets his locker combo. He tries to navigate the many crowded hallways and won't ask for directions and ends up slipping late into each of his classes and facing the students' hooded eyes. Teachers wearing glasses and ill-fitting slacks lick their fingers when walking up and down the desk rows, laying down syllabi, reading aloud course expectations in voices that seem already half-stunned with boredom.

He has a difficult time paying attention. He feels hopped-up, jittery. He can't seem to get enough oxygen. The lights are too bright. The chairs are too cold and rigid. He chews a hole in his cheek and drinks his blood. The clock clicks its way toward noon, and its sound reminds him of a detonator.

He remembers, in grade school, the Magic Eye books that were so popular at the time. You would stare at a patterned page until your eyes went out of focus—and then an image would rise from the page and startle you. He remembers one page in particular, a page carrying the shape of the moon—and out of its cratered grayness rose a skull. He had slammed shut the book and for some time avoided looking at the moon too closely, always closing his blinds at night for fear that it would roll past his window and grin down on him.

In this manner his day progresses, the ordinary

sharpening into the dangerous. A slammed locker is a bomb. A snapped pencil is a broken bone. A girl with her hair dyed black and her face powdered white is a corpse.

He jerks his head, hearing his name muttered everywhere, but never directly to him. “Patrick,” they say under their breath. “Patrick.” At the drinking fountain, after a splash of water, he turns to find a girl with long bangs staring at him through her hair. When he says, “What?” she half gasps, half giggles, before jogging away.

He wonders if he is hearing things, imagining things, or if anyone actually recognizes him. He hopes they don’t. His photograph, he knows, was splashed across newspapers, magazines, television reports, including the *Oregonian* and the *Old Mountain Tribune*. “Miracle Boy,” they called him. But a month has passed. And he has always thought of himself as rather nondescript—brown hair, medium height, ropily muscled, ball cap pulled low, his only distinguishing feature the red birthmark shaped like a half-moon next to his right eye.

But their eyes are on him—he is certain of it now—every face in the hallway turning to regard him, every teacher lingering on his name at roll, blinking hard when he raises his hand. He tries to shrug off the attention. Most of these students, after all, have taken classes, played sports together since they were in grade school. People notice the new guy. That's all he is to them: the new guy. They're sizing him up, trying to figure out who he is, where he'll fit.

But a group of skinheads—he thinks that's what they are, their eyes hard and their hair razored down to a bristling shadow—has him worried. He has spotted a dozen of them. Or maybe the same three or five people keep wandering past him, staring. They wear white shirts tucked into khakis, combat boots. He spots on the backs of their hands a tattoo he can't quite make sense of, some symbol that looks like a bullet.

But that isn't who knocks his hat off in the hallway. A hand cuffs the back of his head and he watches his hat flip forward, the brim of it clattering to the tile, spinning to a rest. Slowly Patrick blows out a sigh and turns around.

"Hey there, Miracle Boy." He wears cowboy boots and tight jeans with a rodeo buckle shining from the belt. He's big, nearly a head taller than Patrick, squarely built and jowly like a bulldog. "We haven't met."

Patrick shrugs off his backpack and it thuds to the floor next to his hat.

"All day long, I'm hearing about you. People

talking about Miracle Boy this, Miracle Boy that." He smiles without humor. "You're famous. I never met anybody who's famous before. You going to sign me an autograph?"

In the crowd eddying past them, people are beginning to slow and stare and whisper. Something is about to happen, they know, and whatever happens, Patrick knows, might determine how he fits into this place. "Fuck yourself," he says, his voice more like a shrug than a threat.

"That's no way to treat a fan." He mocks sadness, pooching out his lower lip. Then, in a flash, his body surges forward, his huge hand slapping the side of Patrick's head, knocking him off-balance, mussing his hair. "Miracle Boy, I'm wanting to ask you a question." He goes to slap Patrick again, this time with the opposite arm, but Patrick dances back from the swing and feels only the breeze it displaces. "Shouldn't you be dead? Why didn't you die along with everybody else?" His eyebrows rise into the shapes of crowbars. He circles Patrick and Patrick pivots to follow him. "Not a scratch on you, Miracle Boy. Hardly seems fair."

His arm shoots out again, cuffs Patrick on the side of the head, an openhanded hammerblow that makes his ear momentarily deaf, so what the boy says sounds a long way off. "Does that make you lucky or a hero or a ghost?"

People gather around them like a lasso. Some of the faces are smiling. Patrick looks to them for help, and when it doesn't come, they blur away. His mind hums like a wasp's wings. He breathes in a gulping way, as if he is choking. He has thought endlessly about what he could have done on the plane, how he might have pulled off his belt and used it to strangle the lycan, ripped the fire extinguisher from the rear cabin and bashed in its skull. Now, with his body trembling all over, it's as if all those thoughts finally find an outlet. He feels a darkness rising through him, drowning him, a wonderful, horrible feeling.

Patrick doesn't aim. He doesn't arrange his legs in a boxer's stance. He simply whips his fist into the boy's face and sends him reeling back, blood geysering from his nose and mouth. The pain catches up a moment later, a sharp volt that sizzles from his knuckles to his wrist. He shakes it off and then stares at his hand, the skin torn and raw, like a tool he doesn't recognize.

The boy hunches over and twitches, an apron of blood running down his face and chest. He keeps touching his nose and seems baffled by the red smeared across the tips of his fingers. Somebody laughs, a *haw-haw-haw* that sounds a little like a crow's cackle. At that the boy gathers himself upright and rushes Patrick with his arms out.

At the last moment Patrick leaps aside with his leg angled out to trip. He has never moved like this in his life. The boy falls heavily, his body impacting the tile with a *thud*, his face with a *thwap*. He rolls over, screaming a scream that is muffled by the hands he tents over his mouth. His eyes well with tears and stare up at Patrick with a furious sadness, like he can't figure out how this has been done to him but he will find a way to rectify it.

Principal Wetmore has a stiff broom of a mustache. He wears a baggy tan suit and a Bugs Bunny tie. His office is eerily dark, lit only by a tall lamp with a heavy shade that tints the room mustard. His bald head flashes with the light and so do his squarish glasses when he leans forward and lays his elbows on his desk. "One day in and we're already talking, huh?"

"Afraid so," Patrick says. He opens and closes his right hand, the knuckles chewed up and throbbing with what feels like an electrical current.

The walls are busy with bookcases and diplomas and a family photo taken in a JCPenney studio where the principal smiles proudly over the shoulder of his permed wife and their twin boys. On his desk sits a half-eaten bowl of peanuts with a halo of salt around it. Next to it is a nameplate that reads THE BIG CHEESE in inlaid gold lettering. The door is closed. But windows surround them, one of them looking out into the hallway, the glass-paneled trophy case. Students drift past and goggle their eyes at Patrick. He tries to imagine he is looking through a portal at the bottom of the sea and the students are strange fish with needly teeth and translucent skin.

"He started it, right?" Wetmore says. "Seth?"

At first Patrick isn't sure whether he is being sarcastic or not, so he doesn't respond except with a searching look.

"Obviously he started it. And I'm sorry for that. I'm sorry that's how you'll remember your first day here."

"Thanks."

"To be honest, to be perfectly frank, I'm glad you did what you did. Don't repeat that! But it's better that you laid him out rather than the other way around. But that's between you and me, mano a mano. You got me, amigo?"

Patrick nods and looks to the door, wishing himself on the other side of it.

"Now hopefully people will leave you alone. But I can't have fighting!" He raises his finger in the air and wags it. "I just can't."

Patrick bounces his knee, chews at the dry skin of his lower lip.

"Next time, do me a favor? Walk away?"

Patrick glances out the window. Through the crowd of students milling by, he spots two of the skinheads. They lean against the trophy case, as still as the golden runners behind them, with their arms crossed and their eyes on him. He nods at them. They give him nothing in return.

"Patrick?"

"Yes, sir. I'll try."

"Look." Wetmore steeples his hands. "You've been through a lot. Publicly. I thought about inviting you in here—did you know that? were your ears warm?—I actually thought about inviting you into my office a few weeks ago when I heard you'd enrolled. Just to say hello. I honestly wanted to tell you that I honestly didn't know how the students were going to treat you. Whether they would resent you for what you've been through or love you for it. Maybe a little of both. I just didn't know. I *do* know that it's always hard coming to a new place. Maybe not for you, but maybe so, probably so. And if so, we want you to let us know what we can do. Okay? Okay."

They stand and Patrick glances again to the window. The skinheads are gone. When he looks back, Wetmore has his hand extended for a shake. Patrick says, "Sorry," and raises his own, bloodied and trembling, in an apologetic wave.

CHAPTER 6

CLAIRE DOESN'T LIKE wide-open space. It makes her feel exposed and untethered, as if she might float off with a gust of wind. From where she stands—in the weed-choked parking lot of a Shell station in Frazee, Minnesota—she can see three different weather systems at the same time: a mushrooming collection of thunderheads that appear bruised and intermittently veined with light; an enormous cloud that reminds her of a gray jellyfish trailing its poisoned tentacles; and an anvil-shaped cumulonimbus cloud that sponges up the light of the sun. She knows its name, cumulonimbus, because her father taught her all of them, along with the different types of trees, knots, birdcalls, constellations.

She can remember lying on the driveway with her father, every light in the house extinguished, the stars sprinkled across the black reaches of the sky—this is how they spent so many summer evenings. And as the constellations wheeled past, he would test her, her eyes tracking his finger when he pointed there, and there, and there. The stars would web together into designs that seemed to glow brighter. “Carnia,” she would say, spotting the keel of a ship floating in a midnight sea. “Leo. Gemini. Hydras.”

Now she imagines her father’s upraised hand becoming translucent, the stars glowing through it, and then vanishing altogether. She pushes the thought from her head and tries to concentrate on something small and good. The endless night taught her that. If she doesn’t focus on something else, she doesn’t move, and if she doesn’t move, they will find her. She doesn’t understand why, but they want her. The men chasing up the staircase—and, waiting for her on the sidewalk, the Tall Man in the black coat. Above her—for the moment anyway; she knows better than to count on anything anymore—is a broad patch of blue sky. That is something to be grateful for.

The wind hasn’t stopped blowing since the Twin Cities, like a draft from an open door. It rises now and kicks up a tiny whirlwind of trash and grit that dies a moment later. She sinks into her Carhartt jacket—given to her by a trucker—two sizes too big and the color of the hard-packed soil and browned grass that stretches to the horizon. In one pocket rest a Snickers bar and a half-eaten bag of Cheetos, and in the other, a wad of cash and the letter from her father. She wears sneakers and jeans and a long-sleeve, blood-spotted shirt. Otherwise she has nothing—hardly even a memory of last night, so much of it a blur.

She remembers transforming, the fury and adrenaline turning over inside her like a big black dog. She remembers crashing through the glass and tumbling through the night and staggering off into the woods. She remembers the Tall Man.

In the distance, dogs bayed. Flashlights cut through the falling snow. She hoped that the wind would blow away her scent, that the snow would fill up her tracks. Her friend Stacey lived only a mile away, and Claire raced there with the intent of pounding at her window, begging for help. In her panic she almost did exactly that, stopping short, sliding in the snow and bracing herself against a tree, when she noticed, at the last minute, the black cars parked in the driveway. Every window blazed with light interrupted by moving shadows. They had come for her family too. She watched them escort Stacey and her mother out the front door and lock them in the back of a car. She watched them drag the father's body down the steps and roll it into an open trunk. And then she watched the house grow bright with fire that reached through the windows and made the snow steam.

She had run then. Run without thinking—through the night, the skeins of snow—gnashing her teeth and trying to ignore the pain in her wrist and her heart. It wasn't her plan to jump the train—she had no plan except the single-minded impulse to escape—until she heard the banshee cry of its whistle.

Tracks cleaved through the center of town, and she could see the freight cars snaking darkly through the trees. The ground tremored—even the air seemed to shake—when she burst from the woods and scampered slantingly up the gravel berm. The train was long and she could not see the engine, but she heard the faraway blast of its whistle and guessed it was nearly within city limits. The cars slowed. The wind tried to push her back. The wheels kicked up ice. The clattering roar took over every other sound in the world. She raced perilously close, reaching out with her good hand—its knuckles furred over, its fingers curled into pointed tips—and snatched hold of a short steel ladder. Her feet dragged behind her, skidding across the snow and gravel, until she hooked her other arm onto the ladder, bracing her elbow against a rung. She used her last bit of energy to haul herself up and crawl to the rear platform of a freight car, where she curled up on herself, trying to create a pocket of warmth, and only then, when she retreated into her human form, did she cry.

* * *

Deep in the night, the train lumbered into Minneapolis and came to a screeching stop at a grain elevator. She rose wearily from the freight car and wandered away in a daze, her ears aching, her body humming. She was in an industrial area. Factories. Storage centers. Big metal warehouses stained with murals of rust. Machinery hummed. Steam rose in arching columns like bridges to the moon. There was no snow here, or if there was, it had melted, but it was cold all the same and she crossed her arms against the wind and the pain nested in her wrist. She found a road with no sidewalk and walked along its grassy shoulder. She had no plan. She just wanted to feel as though she was moving, putting distance between her and whoever she felt still pursued her.

A parade of semitrailers motored by and she could feel the drivers' eyes on her. Twenty yards ahead, one of the trucks pulled over with a chirp of air brakes and clicked on its hazards. The passenger door kicked open, and when she walked by it, a man was leaning out, a thin-faced man with a gray goatee, asking if she needed a ride.

"No," she said automatically. She looked down the road as though her ride might come around the bend any minute now, then back at him. The cab of the truck, high above her, was brightly lit and seemed as big as a house. She imagined it was warm too. "I don't know."

He regarded her and chewed at his lower lip. "Look. I got a daughter about your age, and if I saw her walking around a place like this, middle of the night and all, I'd want her to get home."

When he said that, she felt at once horribly depressed and comforted. She wanted to tell him everything, to let it out in a sobbing gush. Instead she said, in a small voice that barely carried over the noise of the engine, "I can't go home."

He dropped his head in consideration and then looked at her sadly from under his eyebrows. "Then I'd want her to get herself someplace safe." He laid his hand on the door handle and pulled it inward an inch. "Your decision."

She knew she could overpower him if she had to—assuming he didn't have a gun—though she couldn't imagine her body suffering through another transformation. She decided to trust him. She needed to trust somebody right now. She took a deep, steadying breath and climbed into the cab.

It smelled like chewing tobacco and stale French fries. He gave her a long look that at first disturbed her, until he said, "You okay?" He tapped at his own forehead while looking at hers. She pulled down the visor and flipped open the mirror and gasped at her reflection. Her face was purpled, bruised from the transformation—she expected that—but not the blood, the smattering of scabs along her cheeks, the raised wormlike gash on her forehead.

"I fell," she said and spit on her thumb to wipe away what she could.

He put the truck into gear and the truck groaned forward. The CB radio was busy with jabbering conversation, and he clicked it off, its noise replaced by a country song playing quietly from the radio. He cranked up the heat and said, "Here," tossing his jacket onto her lap.

When he asked where she was headed, she said she didn't know. He shook his head but didn't say anything more as they drove on—along a series of narrow roads, through a maze of warehouses, under a graffiti-painted bridge, finally pulling onto a ramp and grinding up to speed as they filed onto the interstate, surprisingly busy for the hour. The dashboard clock read 3:03. Her wrist throbbed. She felt weighed down with exhaustion. She felt safe in the truck, surrounded by so much steel. She liked being up so high. From here, if she squinted her eyes, the lights of the city glowed like stars, the strip malls and neighborhoods like distant galaxies, and soon her eyes shuttered closed completely and she fell asleep.

He made stops all through the early morning, at grocery stores and drugstores and gas stations, leaving her in the cab with the engine idling, hauling up the rear door, yanking out the gangplank, dollying crates of milk. She examined her wrist at one point—swollen an angry red and run through with a blackened stripe—and then she blearily peered out the window and fell back into her empty dreams. Eventually the sun rose and reddened the sky and they parked behind a Mega supermarket, and when the man climbed out and slammed the door, she woke with a start and remembered the envelope.

It was wrinkled and warm from its time in her pocket. She ripped it open and found money. Two hundred dollars in twenties. And a letter. If you could call it that. A lined piece of paper dotted with pencil marks, hundreds of them, in a seemingly random design. Her father loved puzzles and games and she knew immediately this was one of them. Not out of playfulness, but because he believed someone else might come upon the note. The men in the black cars. Her skin tightened and her hair pricked. She could feel them out there—hunting her. She wondered for how long.

She studied the paper and moved her lips as

though trying to sound something out. But her mind was too gummed up with panic and exhaustion, and in the few minutes before the man returned she couldn't make sense of its cipher.

His name was Elwood, he finally told her. "Tenaya," she said, and they shook hands, which felt so silly after the hours they had already shared. She didn't know why she lied about her name—but the lie felt right and she had once read a book by a woman named Tenaya and liked it.

They stopped at a McDonald's and he bought two breakfast meals, and she chewed through her egg sandwich and hash browns so quickly that he offered her his as well. She thought that sadness was supposed to ruin an appetite, but she felt terribly hungry and wanted only to stuff herself as if to fill some gulf inside her. She tried to save her crying for when she was alone in the cab, but sometimes she couldn't hold the tears in, so she turned her face to the window. He never said anything, but at one point she noticed on the console next to her a box of tissues where none had been before.

By noon she had cried herself dry and her thoughts sharpened into questions. Why her parents? And Stacey's family? And however many other lycans? They had done nothing. They had no connection to the plane attacks. They belonged to a co-op. They drove a Prius, for God's sake. They were talkers. They hated the government—they hated the U.S. occupation of the Republic—but they had never taken any action outside of circulating petitions, holding protest signs on downtown corners. And then she remembered her father's words: "There are things you don't know."

Maybe the answer was in the letter.

When they parked at the travel plaza in Frazee, Minnesota, Elwood left his hand on the gearshift and said, "End of the road." He lifted his eyebrows expectantly. "Unless you want to head back to Twin Cities?"

She did not.

"Didn't think so."

She had been using his jacket as a blanket, and when she tried to hand it back, he shook his head, told her to keep it. "Somebody looking for you?" he asked, and when she did not respond he blew out a sigh and said, "You be careful. And you stay off the interstate if you don't want to get found."

It isn't until he drives away—the gray exhaust rising from the truck's bullhorn pipes—that she realizes she forgot to thank him. She lifts a hand as the truck departs, growing smaller in the distance, and she hopes he sees the gesture in his mirror.

Then she turns around in a circle and feels lost and utterly alone, realizing she has no one to trust, nowhere to go.

The gas station is part of a larger travel plaza. There is a Subway attached to it and a video-game parlor she can see flashing through the windows. The parking lot is busy with cars and trucks, people pumping gas, cracking open sodas, sipping from steaming mugs of coffee. An SUV beeps its horn and the driver irritably lifts his hand off the wheel and she realizes she is in the way, standing in the middle of the lot, in the middle of all this traffic.

She starts toward the store, her wrist pulsing with every step, and when she pushes through the door, a bell chimes. One thing at a time, her mother always said. She tries to wrap her head around a plan. She needs a bathroom, a map, some ibuprofen and food. She can manage that at least. The rest can wait.

Behind the register stands a heavy woman with black roots showing through her bleached-blond hair. She stares a beat too long and Claire feels a surge of panic, wondering if her face has appeared on television, if the woman recognizes her. It seems impossible, but so does everything that has happened to her.

Once in the bathroom, she feels encouraged by

her reflection in the mirror. She looks like hell. Her hair—which has always been a problem, a wavy blond tangle she conditions and straightens every morning—is snarled up in every direction. Her face looks like a piece of old, darkened fruit. And then there is the gash across her forehead, a second mouth. Who wouldn't stare?

The daisy-patterned linoleum, peeling up at the corners, is littered with cigarette butts and toilet paper confetti. It is a four-stall bathroom, and as women walk in and out, their voices chattering, their eyes lingering on her, she tries to pay them no mind, draping her jacket over the paper-towel dispenser, tearing off a long sheet, dampening it, frothing it up with soap. She cleans up as best she can.

The travel mart has bins of five-dollar DVDs, open-air coolers full of cheese and sausage, racks of T-shirts with eagles and wolves silk-screened across them, display cases full of lacquered log clocks, and several grocery aisles crowded mostly with chips, pretzels, cookies, and candy. She selects an off-brand backpack from a rack, unzips its mouth, braces its strap in the crook of her elbow, and begins to stock up. A Rand McNally road atlas, ibuprofen, tampons, a blister pack of pens, a notebook with a cartoon football on its cover, two wolf T-shirts, duct tape, a bag of jerky, a box of granola bars, a bottle of Coke. And a newspaper, its headlines concerning the terrorist attacks.

She tries to smile at the woman behind the register—tries not to wince when she jars her wrist with the backpack, lifting it onto the counter—and when she has finished paying, nearly a third of her money spent, she says thank you in a voice that needs a glass of water.

She heads toward town, the cluster of buildings and trees a half mile down the road, the only variation in a landscape otherwise sprawling with corn and soybeans. This is the kind of country, her father used to say, where you could watch your dog run away for three days. Used to say. Because he wouldn't say again. He wouldn't say anything ever again. Neither would her mother. The dead didn't speak. She knows she will never see them again.

The day is warming up and she is thankful when she steps into the shade thrown by the knuckly oak trees lining this main street, the older Victorian and Colonial homes set back on browning lawns. The occasional car whooshes by, but otherwise, it seems like a quiet place, where nothing horrible could ever happen. The houses are soon replaced by small businesses. Next to a steepled church sits a small park with paths running through it and a play structure in its center. The trees are big here, some of their gnarled branches as wide as a man's middle. She circles them, collecting several smaller branches knocked down by the wind. Two girls in bright floral dresses play on the swings while their mother watches. At a nearby picnic table, an older woman, dressed in black rags, rocks back and forth, the town crazy. Claire finds a bench and scares off a squirrel before taking a seat. Out of her bag she pulls the ibuprofen. She pinches the bottle between her thighs and clumsily pulls off the cap, then punches through the foil and washes down three pills with a gulp of Coke.

Next she withdraws a wolf T-shirt and duct tape. She takes off her jacket and slides back her shirt-sleeve to the elbow. Over her arm she pulls the T-shirt, a child's small, running her thumb through a sleeve and her fingers through the neck, flopping the shirt over several times, wrapping the material tight around her arm.

She then lays the sticks across her forearm, two of them pressed tightly together, hoping to make a splint. But when she reaches for the duct tape, her arm wobbles and the sticks fall out of place. And when she tries the duct tape, using her fingers, and then her teeth, to unpeel a long strip of tape, she only ends up tearing and twisting it. "Damn it," she says and almost hurls the tape away to strike a squirrel or robin. It's heavy in her hand, as though made of metal, and she bets it could do some damage. That might make her feel better.

Instead she looks around for help. The mother and her children are already gone, the girls skipping down a distant sidewalk, which leaves the old woman sitting ten yards away, staring off into nothing, rocking back and forth as though lost in the rhythm of a prayer.

"Excuse me," Claire says. The woman makes no response, so she yells this time, "Excuse me!"

The woman goes still and glances in Claire's direction. She could be fifty or could be seventy—it is hard to tell. Her hair is dishwater gray and cut choppily around her ears, her skin deeply wrinkled from too much sun. Claire says, "I need some help. Can you help me?"

The woman nods and mutters something under her breath, then rises with some difficulty and totters like a vulture over to where Claire sits. An unwashed smell comes off her. Her eyes appear filmed completely over with cataracts. And her smile, if that's what it is, has holes in it from her missing teeth. "Need help," she says, her voice like a rusty hinge. "I can help. What help do you need? Tell me. Tell me."

"What's your name?"

The woman says her name is Strawhacker, Ms.

Strawhacker, and Claire addresses her as such and explains what to do, how to slowly spin the duct tape around the splint, beginning at her elbow, moving forward to her wrist, finally knotting it between her thumb and forefinger.

"Why not a doctor?" The woman, Strawhacker, touches Claire's knee. "A doctor is what you need, dear. A good cast. Not sticks and tape."

"That's not an option," she says in a dead voice that quiets the woman, makes her peer around and lick her lips and finally say all right, all right. How she can see, Claire doesn't know, the cataracts like puddles of old milk. Her knuckles are swollen, but she moves nimbly enough, uncurling the tape, around and around Claire's arm, making a mummy of her. "Like this?" the woman says, speaking to herself. "Yes. Yes. Good." Claire tells her to do it again, and then again, three times over, until her arm feels properly armored.

When they are finished, Claire pulls her sleeve down, so that the only visible part of the makeshift cast is a silvery mitten with a bit of white padding peeking out from beneath.

"There now," Strawhacker says. "Not bad."

Claire thanks her and expects Strawhacker to leave, to return to her picnic table and resume her rocking trance, but she does not. She remains seated on the bench, staring at Claire with her milky eyes, smiling softly. Then she reaches out a hand and lays it on hers, a hand as dry as paper. At first Claire thinks she means to shake, to wish her well. Instead she says, "Your fortune?"

"Excuse me?"

"I can tell it. I tell fortunes. With cards, tea leaves, palms. Would you like that? For me to read your fortune? Something to pass the time."

"I guess."

"Yes, because everyone likes to hear their fortune. Everyone does." She begins to run a fingernail along Claire's palm, tracking the lines. "But once your future is spoken, you cannot stop it from happening."

Then no, Claire decides, wrenching away her hand and tucking it into her armpit as though scalded. She'd rather not. Thank you.

It's easier not to think about the future—it's easier to think of her palm as blank. The future is an ambush. The future is pain and absence. She has decided she can only bear to look a mile down the road, to think in terms of minutes instead of years. What am I going to eat, where am I going to sleep, how am I going to escape the rain? That's the only future she's interested in right now.

The woman leans closer, her hair a nest around her shriveled face. "Will you at least tell me your sign, then?"

"Aries."

Her face bunches up in a smile and she pats Claire on the thigh and stands wobbling upright. "That's good," she says. "This will be a good month for Aries. Your planet is in a good place."

Then it strikes Claire, the answer. She prays fiercely that she is right. The lines on her palm like the lines in the sky. The lines of a constellation. She hurries the letter out of her jacket pocket and unfolds it, smooths out its wrinkles with her palm. Her mind is like a spider weaving together the dots on the page with gossamer threads, uniting them as constellations. Yes. She doesn't know why she didn't recognize them before. Probably because she was out of her head with pain and fear and grief and exhaustion, but also because the constellations appear so out of context on lined paper, black instead of bright, small instead of far-flung in the night.

She rips a pen out of its packaging and begins to connect the dots, sketch out their designs. Grus. Octans, Taurus. What they mean, she doesn't know. But at least a trapdoor has opened in the sky and she was lucky enough to fall through it.

In her excitement, Claire has forgotten about the old woman, who hobbles closer and gestures with her crooked hand. "What are you drawing, dear?"

"My future," Claire says.

CHAPTER 7

WALT PULLS ASIDE the curtain and cups his hands around his eyes and leans into the dark window. Something has spooked the cattle. His hearing isn't what it used to be, he'll admit, which means they must be making quite the ruckus if he can make out their mewling and bawling over the television. His breath fogs the window and he swipes a hand through it, smearing his vision of the night. He cannot see anything, not from here, but beyond the barn and the corrals, dust rises like smoke through the blue cone of light thrown by the sodium-vapor lamp. He imagines he can feel a tremor in the air, hooves thudding in the pasture.

There. Three sharp barks. Followed by yammering. Coyotes. This sort of thing happens often enough—the coyotes seeming to outnumber people in Central Oregon—that he isn't concerned so much as he is annoyed. Beyond the barn stands a whitewashed coop fenced in by chicken wire that runs three feet into the ground to keep the coyotes from digging their way in after prowling near for a sniff. He imagines coyotes, like gray phantoms, circling the enclosure, and the chickens clucking in a panic, nervously fluttering their wings, filling the coop with a cloud of thrown feathers.

He could take a rifle out on the porch, fire three rounds into the sky. Or stamp down the steps and into the night to pursue any that linger near the coop, the barn. But he has had a long day—leading cattle down the chute, punching them with a vaccination gun—and up until a moment ago he was half-asleep in his La-Z-Boy, sipping a tumbler of bourbon, watching Fox News.

The last thing he wants to do is pull on his boots, zip up his jacket, head into the cold that made his nose run and his hands numb all day. He hired on a gang of Mexicans to help. To usher the cattle from the holding pen to the chute, to tighten the sidebars, to thrust the vaccine into the cows' rumps—Scourguard 3KC to boost immunity before calving, Ivomec Plus for liver flukes, intestinal worms. The men's faces were reddened from the weather when they waved their arms and clapped their hands and zapped the cows with electric prods—the cows snorting and trotting away from them, kicking up clods of dirt, stacking up at the far end of the lot.

That's all there is anymore for help—Mexicans. Used to be, he kept a hired man who lived onsite in a trailer. Then, ten years ago, when he hit sixty, when he decided to run for city council, he sold four hundred acres and as many head of cattle. His driveway is still flanked by pine columns with the Bar J brand chiseled into them, but as a hobby he keeps only a small herd on his twenty acres. When he needs help—with shots, with calving, with bucking alfalfa—he advertises in the classifieds, and the only ones who call have those drawn-out vowels, those sentences like songs he has trouble deciphering. “I don’t understand. Slower this time,” he often hears himself saying.

The window has fogged over again. He lets the curtain swing shut. He flips on a tableside lamp, and then another, not liking how dark the living room suddenly feels, the pine paneling soaking up the light. He falls back into his recliner and pulls over his lap a stars-and-stripes blanket. He sips at his bourbon until the ice cubes rattle against his teeth and his face feels flushed. On television he half tunes in to the familiar footage of the planes and then the goddamn president giving another goddamn speech instead of *doing* something.

Walt knows what he’d do. Right after the attacks, he brought to the city council an emergency proposal that would make public every registered lycan. Put it in the papers, he’d said. Put it on the Internet. Put it on their IDs, for God’s sake. That was the real no-brainer, something that had been discussed for years without success, a slot on the driver's license, right next to blue eyes and brown hair: lycan.

We need to know who we're up against, he'd said. It was a bluff, completely illegal. He knew the needle-dick mayor would try to shame him. But he felt he needed to say what everybody else was too chickenshit to admit: humans and animals don't mix and it was time to build some fences between the two, go back to the old ways. The *Oregonian* ran a condemning piece about Walt alongside the worst photo in world history, him with his mouth open, a gaping black hole to match his shadowy pocketed eyes.

There comes a high-pitched bawling from outside. The noise a cow makes when dehorned or branded, when their black muzzles lift to the sky and their eyes bulge and roll back in their heads. Walt feels seized by it and goes utterly still as though waiting for the pain that caused the sound to arrive.

Then it dies out. Walt utters a long string of curses and with some effort kicks down the leg rest and stands up, nearly tripping in the tangle of his blanket. He kicks it away and scrambles for the remote on the end table. He punches the power button. The image of the newscast falls into darkness. He can see himself reflected on the screen, standing and holding out the remote like a drawn pistol. His eyes are crinkled and buried in the folds of his face. His nose is like the head of a hammer. His hair is buzzed down to a silver brush. He might be old, but he can still do some damage. You bet.

He drops the remote on the chair and heads to the kitchen. He could never find anybody worth marrying—that's what he said whenever asked what's kept him single all these years—but his home has no piles of rank laundry, no empty beer bottles lined up on the counter or stacks of dirty dishes moldering in the sink. The world is too messy; he wants his life clean. A place for everything and everything in its place: that was another thing he said.

So he knows exactly where to find what he's looking for, in this case a handgun. He keeps weapons throughout the house—a .22, three revolvers, even his father's World War II bayonet—the nearest handgun hidden behind the cereal in the cupboard, a loaded S&W .357. He thumbs off the safety and snaps the lock on the door and swings it open. The noise comes rushing out of the night to greet him. Coyotes babbling. Hens squawking. Horses and cattle shrieking.

In his surprise he brings the handgun to his ear. He hesitates a moment, one foot out the door, the other anchoring him to the kitchen. Then he casts off his surprise and joins the din by screaming, not a curse, but a garbled cry of anger. He stomps down the steps and along the path that leads to the barn, the ground biting his bare feet. In his hurry he has forgotten his boots and jacket. His breath clouds from his mouth—he is panting—but otherwise he feels oblivious to the cold. Warm even, with two tumblers of bourbon sloshing inside him.

The moon hangs in the sky like a skull. In its pale light he circles the barn. Its panels shake, as if the building is stirring to life, from where the horses kick in their stalls. The noise—a zoo of noise—is such that he cannot think, can concentrate only on dragging his feet forward, maintaining his grip on the revolver. The air smells like alfalfa and musk and something sharper: copper.

Next to the holding pen, a forty-by-forty-foot square encased by a split-rail fence, the sodium-vapor lamp hangs in the sky like a second moon. He lifts the bar to the gate and pushes his way into the holding pen and stumbles across the uneven, hoof-pocked ground. Earlier today he left behind a red heifer with a pale face who is too old to calf and who will be trucked off tomorrow to slaughter. No longer. Now, against the far edge of the pen, she lies on her side, her broad back to him. The ground is soft and steaming with her blood. His bare feet squelch through the mud to examine her. Two hundred and fifty pounds of packaged beef—gone.

Walt has always been sensitive to high-pitched sounds. The coyotes are howling, their howls merging into one distressing note that trembles the air and sends Walt reeling. He drops to one knee to observe the heifer's torso rent open, her slatted ribs like long teeth grinning at him from a bloody mouth. He remembers one afternoon when—after he lifted her tail and pushed his gloved hand into her, after he reached around the hot emptiness and determined she wasn't carrying again, after he released her—she kicked the sidebars hard enough to dent the metal. No matter how old she was, she still had fight in her. A pack of coyotes couldn't have done this.

To steady himself he rests a hand on her sledgehammer-shaped head. The fading warmth of it makes him realize for the first time the cold. Maybe it is this that makes the revolver shake in his hand when he aims it into the darkness. His breath puffs out of him in white scarves. And he realizes that the night has gone quiet except for the lamp buzzing overhead.

He does not hear the whispering tread of footsteps moving through cheatgrass or the groaning complaint of wood as something large clambers up the side of the corral, but he notices the shift in the light, and when he finally turns, the last thing he will see is the creature balanced on the fence post, like a gargoyle, its shape occulting the moon behind it.

CHAPTER 8

SOMETIMES PATRICK PLAYS this game when he is bored. He will doodle a shape. Say, a hand. And then he will transform it, see what else might come out of it, whether a turkey or the starburst of a gunshot window. Now, in third-period English, in the margins of his notebook, he draws a circle. The circle becomes the moon—pocked with shadowy craters. The moon becomes a face with wild eyes, a nose and mouth. Then he fills the mouth with fangs and draws black squiggles through the eyes.

An aisle runs down the middle of the room with three tables to either side of it. He hides in the back right corner. Next to him sits a girl—he noticed her earlier when she sat down, smelling of raspberries—and he realizes that she is now leaning toward him, peering at his notebook. He slides his hand over the drawing, which makes it especially obvious how empty the page is, void of any notes except for the title of the play, *Othello*, also scrawled on the chalkboard in looping script.

The teacher, Mrs. O'Neil, has squinty eyes, an embarrassed smile, and a gray helmet of hair. With her hands clasped, she paces back and forth before the chalkboard, and whatever she says—something about betrayal and "the Other"—everyone scribbles into their notebooks. She makes her fingers into quotation marks whenever she says "the Other."

He tries to pay attention, but then he glances at the girl and loses the lecture once more. Her hair is cut short, ending at her ears in curling points that frame her face like a pair of red wings. She doesn't move her head, but her eyes dart sideways and catch him. She gives him a small smile that doesn't go away, even as her attention returns to the front of the room.

Mrs. O'Neil is droning on about the film they'll watch next week, the one directed by and starring Kenneth Branagh, who plays the moor as a lycan. "Won't that be interesting?" she says. Someone's phone goes off—and just as suddenly goes silent. Mrs. O'Neil smiles in a way that makes many more wrinkles appear like fissures on her face. Everyone, she says, please turn to act two, scene one.

It is then, when the room fills with the flutter and slash of turned pages, that the girl draws her chair toward Patrick with a screech. He smells again her raspberry shampoo—the smell of red, the color of her hair—and breathes deeply of it, his breath catching when her hand finds his thigh beneath the table.

The weight of it is tremendous. He does not move. All of his blood seems to rush to the center of his body. He cannot look at her and he cannot look at the teacher, so he looks to the classroom's east-facing windows, ablaze with light.

Her fingers are moving. A gentle clawing, prying, as though trying to find the softest spot on him to pierce. His mouth is full of saliva and he swallows it in a gulp. The chalk screeches when Mrs. O'Neil writes, in block capital letters, the word *LUST* on the board.

The windows. Patrick tries to concentrate on the windows. They glow orange, as though made of fire, as though the sun has pinpointed the room to burn through a magnifying glass. It is hot in here, terribly hot. And her hand, so dexterous, is unbuttoning his jeans, unzipping his fly, grabbing hold of him—he has never felt so hard, as if his skin might split, when she gives him first an appreciative squeeze and then a caress that takes in the length of him.

The students around them hurry their pens across their notebooks and Mrs. O'Neil scratches her chalk across the board and her shadow capers along the wall, like a dancing crow, and the dust motes twirl in the sunbeams cutting through the window and the girl moves her hand faster now, and faster yet, her eyes fixed straight ahead, her arm appearing still, all of the movement in her fingers, her wrist—and Patrick can feel the building pressure, can feel himself losing control, can feel the heat of the sun inside of him, the wonderful heat, and the sudden pressure that gives way to a loosening, a surge.

He coughs into his fist when he finishes. He can't not make noise.

While he sits there—his posture slumped, his breath whistling fiercely through his nose—she wipes her palm on his jeans, retrieves her pen, and begins to take notes. He watches her hand, its glossy fingernails, its faint green veins, for maybe five minutes, and then the bell rings and she rises from the table without a word or parting glance and leaves him.

Patrick takes his packed lunch to the gym, to the mirror-walled room with the rubber floor, located off the basketball courts. His father kept a bench and some dumbbells in their garage, and in the afternoons, they would lift together, not saying a lot except to shout encouragement on those final wobbly reps, simply taking pleasure in each other's company. That used to be their routine anyway.

His father, in the months leading up to his deployment, spent more and more time alone in his home-brew lab, more and more time on the phone with his friend Neal, an old college pal, now a researcher based out of the University of Oregon. They were working on something—that's all his father would say—a biochem problem. Making beer better, Patrick assumed.

In the mirrors of the high school gym, Patrick sees himself reflected endlessly and imagines one of those far-off figures as his father when he works out—chins, benches, dips, rows, military presses, curls—as much as he can fit into thirty minutes, taking breaks between sets to snap bites from his apple.

He never asks anyone if it's all right. And when he first senses a figure in the room—when he pumps away at the bench and hears the cludding footsteps, catches movement at the bottom of his eye, he guesses he's in for a lecture. *You can't be in here without a spotter,* the teacher, hands on hips, will tell him. Or, *You're never going to fit in if you isolate yourself like this.*

Patrick racks the weight and rolls into a seated position and sees, not a teacher, but a boy. He is tall and plump, baby faced, which makes it difficult to tell how old he is, fifteen, nineteen. His head is shaved-down brown bristle. He wears a white T-shirt tucked into khakis, combat boots. On the back of his hand, the bullet-shaped tattoo.

The boy stares, his eyes wide and damp and gray, but says nothing. A moment ago Patrick was thinking about the girl—about what compelled her to reach out for him, about how nothing like that has ever happened to him and whether it even happened, whether he imagined it, and what he should say the next time he sees her—and now this, all those good anxious thoughts interrupted by some skinhead who won't blink.

Patrick doesn't know what to expect, another fight maybe? But fights like an audience. Fights feed off the energy of a crowd. And they are alone except for their hundreds of reflections. Then what? Patrick grows tired of the staring contest, stands and slides on another twenty pounds of plates, and says, "You guys have some sort of problem with me?"

"We don't have a problem with you, Patrick." The boy's voice has the surprising clarity and resonance of a radio announcer's. An adult's voice.

"Then what?"

His name is Max, he says, and he has some friends he wants Patrick to meet. "Let me ask you something," Max says and shoves his hands in his pockets as though sleeving a weapon, offering a truce. "What are you doing this Friday?"

Nothing. He has nothing going on, but he doesn't want to say as much. This might be a gesture or might be some kind of trap, him walking through a door to greet a roomful of guys swinging lead pipes and baseball bats. "Friday," Patrick says. Friday there is no school for the full-moon Sabbath. A law that has been around so long no one knows its origin: nobody is to work, nobody is to go anywhere except in the case of an emergency. He says as much.

"You're not a lycan," Max says, "so what's the problem?"

"No problem."

Talking to girls has never come easily to him. Sometimes, at the mall, the bowling alley, a restaurant, he'll dream up a bad line—"I've seen you around, right?" or "If I hear this song again, I might rip my ears off"—good enough to make them look his way, get them talking, but after that, he's worthless, smiling, nodding his head, letting his eyes drop to his shoes. So usually he doesn't bother.

She makes it easy on him, surprising him that afternoon, appearing out of the river of students flowing down the hall, her shoulder brushing up against his. "Did you hear a single thing Mrs. O'Neil was talking about today?" she says.

At first he has no words. He can only think of her hand, the heat and pressure of it. "Not really."

"That's what I thought."

He tries to control his bewildered smile. He tries to come up with something more to say, but he is too busy studying her, her yellow V-neck and dark jeans slung so low he can see the blade of her hip-bone.

"Did you even read the play?" she says.

"No." He closes his eyes. That helps. "I want to. I just haven't been able to concentrate."

"Because of what you've been through." Not a question.

"Yeah."

He waits for her to give him a sympathetic nod, to touch him on the shoulder, to ask him a million questions about what it was like to hear all of those people dying around him while he hid under a body like a blanket. She doesn't. He figures this is a good sign. "So you know me?"

"Everybody knows you, even if they pretend not to."

Lockers slam. Voices call around them. Bodies mash them closer together. Every other hand with a cell phone in it. Patrick isn't even sure where he's going—he's just walking.

She says something, but he doesn't hear her. "Sorry?"

She leans in to his ear so that he can feel her breath. “You’re a celebrity.” She overenunciates the word, making it sound like many words.

He almost says, “I wish that wasn’t the case,” but doesn’t want to sound like a whiner. Instead he says, “You know me, but I don’t know you.”

She says her name and holds out a hand, the same hand, for a shake.

“Malerie?” he says.

“Malerie.”

“Malerie.”

“Yeah.”

He repeats the name three times, making it into a song.

“Is something wrong?”

“It’s just that I’ve never met anybody with that name, Malerie.”

They talk for another minute—about what, he isn’t sure—school probably, the town maybe. His mouth is moving and words are coming out of it. Then the bell rings.

He has never liked saying good-bye. On the phone, after someone says, “All right, I guess I got to—,” he throws out a question to keep the conversation going. And in person, after raising a hand to wave so long, he can never depart more than a few paces without looking back. It always surprises him how easily other people hurry away, their faces already different, walled off and occupied with the next place they will go, the next person they will meet.

But she is different. When he walks five steps, he pivots on his heel—not to stare at her ass, just to watch her, he likes watching her—and at that same moment, as though she can sense him, she slows her pace and turns and smiles but casts down her eyes as though he has caught her doing something forbidden.

"It's French, you know," she yells to him. "My name. It means bad luck!"

CHAPTER 9

CLAIRE FELT SO CLEVER when she realized the note revealed a string of constellations. And she feels so stupid now, two weeks later, with no better understanding of what they mean, what her father was trying to tell her. She knows they can't be directions—a map written in the night sky—for if she were to follow them, she would go nowhere, turning this way and that, wheeling along with the stars. She tries spitting out the names in a hurry—"Grus, Octans, Taurus, Orion"—thinking their sound might hold a secret. She brings the paper directly before her eyes and pulls it slowly away, as if a picture might reveal itself. She considers the mythology of each constellation, overanalyzing them like lines of some sonnet assigned to her in English. She scribbles out page after page of theories in her notebook—the one with the cartoon football on the cover—until her fingers ache from gripping the pen.

It's enough to make her want to tear the note in half, and in half again, letting the wind carry the pieces away like the snow that fell the night this all began. And then, with her hands and her mind empty, she will crawl under some porch and curl up in a ball and close her eyes—which feel as poisoned as her wrist from staring endlessly at the note—and wait to die. That would be easier.

The landscape here is flat, parceled up into brown and yellow squares edged by barbed wire, so that Claire feels she is crossing a giant board game. The shape of the wind is visible in the fields of trembling wheat and soybeans that stretch to the horizon. Trees appear only when clustered around houses as a windbreak. The distance between towns grows greater. Yellow-bellied marmots poke their heads out of their burrows and chirp at her, as if to say, *Where do you think you're going?* and *Why bother?*

She has felt, these past few years especially, like the center of something. Her shoes mattered. Her jeans and jackets. Her grades. Her friends. Her text messages. Her opinions about movies and music and television shows. Her love and hate for certain boys. All of that is gone now. Especially in these northern plains, where the wind never stops blowing and the sky seems bigger than the ground beneath her feet, she feels smaller and more insignificant than ever before. A tiny harmless thing that could be swallowed up and no one would notice.

She asks for a ride outside a grocery store from

a gray-haired, one-eyed woman pushing a shopping cart full of frozen dinners. She asks if she can sleep on the covered porch of a squat white house where four children race around the front yard, capturing grasshoppers to toss into a fat-bodied spider's web. She asks for directions at the edge of a field where two men wearing seed caps and heavy leather gloves toss hay bales into the back of a pickup. But mostly she keeps to herself, afraid that someone will squint at her and say, *You're that girl I heard about on the news?*

Though she knows that's unlikely. She has been reading the newspapers, stopping at convenience stores to scan the headlines. "Terror in the Skies," "Lycan Terror Plot," "The Terror Among Us," they read. Photos of the wreckage outside Denver, the blackened metal, the scar charred into a wheat field. Photos of the planes in Portland and Boston, parked on the taxiway, the red and blue lights of dozens of emergency vehicles reflected on the fuselage. Photos of body bags organized in a long black row along the tarmac. Photos of mourners piled up against the hurricane fence, clutching it and each other, their faces crumpled like damp tissues. Photos of the boy—"the Miracle Boy"—his expression grainy, a blanket shrouding his shoulders, escorted by police. Photos of the dead, a special insert in *USA Today* memorializing them, their names, ages, hometowns, occupations, hobbies, surviving family. Three 737s—553 corpses.

Nothing about her.

American flags snap from every porch. Stars-and-stripes magnets decorate every bumper. And this morning, outside a McDonald's, a man with a bucket and a sudsy scrub brush works over the brick exterior where someone has spray-painted *Eye for an eye, lycans should die*.

The kind of rhetoric she's read about in books, seen in movies, heard about from her parents, but never experienced firsthand. She debates whether she should go in, the building seeming poisoned, but the smell is too good, the fryer grease making her mouth damp, and the day is so cold, chasing her into the warm, brightly lit space. She buys a large coffee—two creams, two sugars—and a Big Mac, large fries. She has never had a better meal in all her life.

She pulls from her backpack the *Bismarck Tribune*, found in a garbage can outside. Its paper retains the cold and carries it to her fingertips. She finds on the front page an article that makes her lean forward. "Retribution," it reads, accompanied by a shot of the president standing before a black bouquet of microphones, talking about the "swift, severe, and immediate response taking place at this very moment." He could not go into details, for fear of tipping off those they pursued, but the American public should rest easy knowing that several arrests had already been made and scores more would occur over the next few weeks. "This is not a time to panic," he was quoted as saying. "This is not a time to lash out at our lycan neighbors, who live peacefully among us and who are registered and monitored and, with the help of strictly prescribed medication, have forgone their ability to transform. Remember that to be a lycan is not to be an extremist, and I would encourage patience among the public while the government practices its due diligence in pursuing those responsible for this terrible, unforgivable catastrophe." This was followed by a small quote from a lycan-rights group claiming widespread harassment and persecution in the days following the attacks.

That was it. Nothing about a house stormed, semiautomatics barking, her parents killed. The men in the black cars and the black body armor were at Stacey's house too, which means they were probably at other houses, maybe all across the country. She imagines a hundred doors kicked down, the noise like a hundred bones broken, and she imagines the Tall Man stepping through them all. Why wasn't this news?

* * *

She doesn't know where to go, so she goes nowhere, holing up for ten days in an abandoned motel on the outskirts of Fargo. The Seahorse Inn, it's called, the paint a faded and peeling aquamarine. The parking lot is riven with weed-filled cracks. The windows are blinded by sheets of plywood. There are twelve rooms, all of them locked, but when she walks around back, she finds an open window, the plywood crowbarred off and tossed into the tall grass. She calls out, "Hello," and hears no answer. She peers in the window for a long time, the threadbare curtain moving with the wind licking her cheek, until her eyes adjust to the dim light, and then she crawls in, stepping onto a cinder block, slinging her good arm over the sill. Her feet rattle against the many crushed beer cans that litter the floor. Keystone Light. She guesses some teenagers broke in and used the place to party. The wallpaper is patterned with sailboats and starfish. There are light squares on it where paintings used to hang. A hole punched through the drywall. A chair tipped over. The mattress stripped bare and stained with what she hopes is spilled beer. She knows sleep won't come easily in a place like this, but it ranks better than the nights she has so far spent beneath porches and in barns, truck beds, old campers.

She can smell the mess in the bathroom before she steps into the dark cave, barely able to make out the dried fecal matter muddying the toilet. Someone has destroyed the mirror, and the thousands of shards glimmer faintly from the floor. She closes the door and wanders around the room again and shrugs off her backpack and decides to call this home for a little while at least.

She smells like herself. That's what her father used to say after a long day of work, lifting his arm, sniffing: "I smell like myself." She has washed daily in rivers, in rest-stop and convenience store bathrooms, but her clothes feel as oily as a second skin. And her wrist. The wrappings stink like congealed grease at the bottom of a pan after frying bacon. She continues to wrap more and more tape around it, sealing the tatters, creating a fat silver mitten. She has swallowed her way through a bottle of ibuprofen, and though the pain has ebbed, she gets a fresh jolt now and then when she bangs her arm against something.

She has learned to do everything with one hand—eating, tying her shoes, unbuttoning her pants—her other hand uselessly tucked into her coat pocket. She tries to concentrate on the letter, to break its code, but after all this time without success, her mind wanders easily. She finds herself zoned out and staring at the wall, thinking about how much she misses her phone, how she once made a birdhouse from a dried and hollowed gourd, how one September a cold front blew through northern Wisconsin and dropped the temperature into the single digits, and when she and her parents drove to Loon Lake and clambered out on the ice and augered holes and arranged their tip-ups, the ice was so clear they could see the walleye and smallmouth and sunfish whirling beneath their boots.

She knows the cold is coming. Severe cold that will blacken fingers and make teeth chatter so violently they shatter. The weathermen love to talk about Fargo, a place where you can hurl a glass of water into the air and watch it vanish, leave out a banana overnight and use it to hammer a nail into a plank of wood.

She can't stay here long. Every day she climbs out the window of the Seahorse Inn and wanders the town—and every day the grass grows browner, the tree branches grow barer, until they appear skinned, their leaves clattering along the streets. She has bought a black knit cap from Walmart to fight the deepening chill. Her mind circles around the letter as her body circles stores and neighborhoods, and more than once her steps slow, nearly stop, as if a hard wind is trying to blow her back the way she came.

But what if she does go home? What waits for her there? She imagines walking through her darkened house, fingering the bullet holes in the walls, stepping around the puddles of blood dried into the linoleum. She imagines opening closets full of clothes no one will ever wear, bringing her parents' pillows to her face to smell them, finding their hairs curled up in a brush.

Or not. Maybe they aren't dead. Maybe they were only injured. Maybe the semiautomatics were shot in warning, into the ceiling, chunks of drywall snowing around them. Maybe, if she found a pay phone and dialed 911 and gave herself up, maybe then she would see them, as soon as tomorrow. They would clutch each other in a holding area, tiles white and lit with fluorescent bulbs, the three of them laughing and crying with relief at the mix-up—because they hadn't done anything. She hadn't done anything. Right?

Or she could visit her nana. In the Sleepy Hollow Assisted Living Center. The Tall Man wouldn't have bothered her, with one side of her face appearing melted, her words a mushy slur. And though the two of them had never gotten along, she was family—there was comfort in that—and maybe Nana knew something. Claire imagines the curl of a beckoning finger as the old woman leaned forward in her wheelchair to whisper a secret.

Or maybe she should go south, like the geese she sees cutting across the sky in the shape of spearheads, where she could walk barefoot on the beach and waitress at a restaurant with tiki torches flaming in the beer garden. Or maybe she should consult her horoscope, flip a coin, sit in the back pew of a church and pray. She can't make up her mind, can't trust herself, her mind like the sky, muddled up into a soupy gray cloud from which competing thoughts rain.

It takes her a long time to drop the quarter in the pay phone and dial her landline, but it takes only one ring for an automated voice to tell her this number is no longer in service. She hangs up, stares at the phone, then sinks another quarter into the slot and dials her father's cell. After two rings, someone answers but says nothing. She can hear the person's breath.

"Hello?" she says. "Mom? Dad?"

The breathing continues. Then comes the staticky pop of saliva as a mouth opens into a smile. The voice that speaks to her—a crisp baritone—isn't one she recognizes, though it recognizes her. "Where are you, Claire?" it says.

The Tall Man. Who else could it be except him?

"Tell me where you are," he says.

She slams down the phone with such force that it rings like a hammer striking an anvil.

Her nose burns and drips, her feet ache, and her fingers feel numb at the tips when she returns to the Seahorse Inn. She doesn't understand what he wants from her. She doesn't know whether he can find her now, whether the pay phone came up on the cell as unlisted, whether he can trace its origin. She doesn't know whether she should leave immediately, but she knows she must leave.

When she drops through the window, she freezes in a half crouch. From somewhere in the room comes a rustling. And then silence. Her eyes adjust and distinguish in the gray light the black shapes of the desk, the chair, the bed. The beer cans are long gone, hurled into the woods. Her first instinct is to retreat, but she is too tired to leap again from a window into the black square of the night. And if she did, what then? Where would she run to this time?

She steps slowly forward, flat-footed, trying to distribute her weight, hoping the floor won't creak beneath her. It takes her a minute to make her way around the bed, where the shadows pool, black and impenetrable.

She keeps a flashlight—a plastic two-dollar cheapie the size of a pen—in her pocket. She withdraws it now to click on and scare away the shadows. Nothing.

Then she hears it—a series of scrapes and clicks—the sound a skeleton might make if animated. The bathroom. Its door is open. Maybe from the wind, which funnels constantly into the room, fluttering the curtains, or maybe not.

As a child, maybe five or six or seven, she was once so afraid of the dark, so certain a pale-faced creature with long, bony fingers hid in her closet, that she wet herself rather than use the bathroom. She feels something similar—a bladder-bursting pressure—when she looks at the open bathroom door and imagines the possibilities that might lie concealed in the wedge of darkness. The Tall Man in his black suit. A mossy-toothed drifter with jigsaw tattoos covering his face. The ghosts of her parents, their arms encircling her like a cold mist.

Her voice is rusty when she says, “Come out of there.”

As if in response the wind dies out, and in the silence that follows she can hear a faint clicking. She has no gun, only the ability to let the wolf turn over inside her, which feels impossible to someone in her condition, half-alive with grief and exhaustion.

A *scritching* now—she hears it—followed by the rustle of what could be cloth.

Enough. She hurries forward and raises her flashlight. The weak yellow light seeps into the bathroom but fails to penetrate a shadow darker than the rest. Its eyes flash red. A crow, she realizes, as it lets out a screech and leaps from its perch on the toilet. Its wings beat the air and its claws rake at her and she swings her arm and her flashlight goes whirling off and for a moment she is uncertain which way is up or down, left or right, with the crow screeching and flapping its wings and crashing off the walls, finally escaping through the open window.

She is huddled on the floor. She laughs and the laugh cracks into a sob.

She and her father used to count crows. For the times they spotted the birds roosting in a tree, wheeling in and out of low-hanging clouds, he taught her an old Irish rhyme. One for sorrow, two for joy, three for a girl, four for a boy, five for silver, six for gold, seven for a story that's never been told. "Seven. That's the one I want," he used to say, squinting up at the sky. "I want that story."

Anything but one. If they spotted a single crow, they would look around hurriedly, seeking another—as she does now, finding nothing but shadows all around her.

* * *

She packs what little she has and hikes her way out of town. A drop of rain strikes her cheek, and then another, and another still, and through the thickening downpour, she hurries to the nearest building, a Tesoro gas station, to wait out what she hopes is a passing storm.

She spins the card rack and chooses one at random. Its cover is cartooned with a baby in a sagging soiled diaper, a scab-kneed toddler picking her nose, a teenage boy clutching a sandwich and wearing sunglasses, a raggedy dog and spectacled grandparents, and, in the middle of them all, a bald middle-aged man in a white undershirt that can't contain his potbelly. Inside, MOM—an acronym for Mother of Multiples—and a message from the sender, presumably a husband: *Thanks for taking such good care of us*.

Claire reads her way through all the cards, imagining whom she might send them to, and then wanders to the magazine rack and flips through a copy of *People*. Here is a shot of a starlet rising out of the ocean with her bikini dragged off her by a wave, a black censor bar covering her breasts. *Oops* is the caption. Claire wants to be interested—wants to read the articles as she would gobble candy—but part of her knows that her days of gossiping about celebrity nonsense are over.

Rain lashes the window. Out of the windswept

murkiness comes a police cruiser, turning off the highway, into the parking lot, the tires splashing through puddles and throwing up fans of water.

Claire blindly sets the magazine on the rack and doesn't pick it up when it flutters to the tile floor. Surely, she thinks, this is a sign, when a moment later the door chimes as the trooper pushes through it. He has the beginnings of both a mustache and a gut. His gun is holstered in his belt. He swings his arm wide around it, and in his hand dangles an oversize plastic mug with a bendable straw. He splashes it full of Cherry Pepsi and caps it and heads to the counter, whistling, the whistle cut short when Claire steps out from behind the greeting-card rack and says, "Excuse me?"

His feet drag to a stop. "What?" His mike squawks. His hand goes to it and he drops the volume as tinny voices chatter back and forth between blasts of static.

Then Claire tells him everything. But only in her head. In fact she only looks up at him, a man with handcuffs clipped to his belt, knowing that he could drop her, force a knee to her back, clip her wrists, pepper-spray her face in less than a minute. She finds it so strange that this is the situation she is in when about a month ago, around this same time of the day, she was sitting down to lunch with her parents—grilled ham and cheese, that was what they ate, along with small bowls of tomato soup—while NPR played from the faux-antique radio on the kitchen counter. The most ordinary thing in the world made suddenly extraordinary by the fact that she would never experience it again.

"What?" The trooper lifts the mug to his mouth and the straw becomes as dark as a vein when he sucks from it. "What do you want?"

She feels so naked under his gaze, under the fluorescent lights that hide nothing and make everyone appear as though they are dying. She imagines what she must look like to him: oversize coat, ratty hair, greasy skin, a faded bruise with an angry red gash running across her forehead. A runaway. That's what he'll think. And then he'll make the connection—he'll realize she is *the girl*—the one from the notice that could very well be circulating through every police station in the Upper Midwest.

She takes a step back and the rack rattles behind her and for a moment she can't help but think of that card, the stupid one with the cartooned family on it. In her mind it flips open as her mouth opens and she says, "My friend says you can go seven miles over the speed limit and not get pulled over." With every word she expects her voice to shake, but it doesn't. "That you guys have, like, a seven-mile-per-hour cushion you give people. Is that true?"

"Don't speed," he says.

"Okay. I won't. But do you?"

"I don't speed."

Inside the card. *MOM. Mother of Multiples. M-O-M.* An acronym. She is a few seconds behind the conversation when she says, "But do you pull people over if they're only seven miles over?"

He sips again from his soda and then sets it in front of the register for the clerk to ring up. "Everybody is different. Maybe it will be your day to get pulled over and maybe it won't. Maybe I'm feeling nice or maybe I'm feeling mean." He digs in his pocket and rattles out some change. Behind him a wall of cigarettes and lighters and energy pills. "The next time you think about doing something foolish, think of me mean."

"I will," she says, but he is already out the door and she has already forgotten him. Her backpack drops to the floor and she digs through it for a pen and paper. Her eyes are blinking rapid-fire and her jaw is clamped so tightly it clicks. Her mind cycles through the constellations. "Grus. Octans," she says. "Taurus. Orion. Mensa. Indus. Reticulum." She continues to speak to the empty store, her voice solemn, as if performing some ancient rite. "Indus. Aries. Musca."

CHAPTER 10

MIRIAM IS TIRED of waiting. For two weeks she has remained in the cabin, pacing the hardwood floors, waiting for the power to flicker out, the water to gurgle to a stop in the faucet. Her neck aches from sleeping in the bathtub. Her teeth ache from grinding. Her eyes ache from peering constantly out the slots sawed into the plywood sheets hammered to the windows.

Sometimes she thinks she hears laughter in the forest. Sometimes the motion detectors go off and bring a ghostly pallor to the night. One morning she woke to a *thunk* against the front door and thought dreamily to herself, it's the paper, only to later discover a rabbit bleeding out on the welcome mat. Otherwise, two weeks of nothing.

She has never gone this long without transforming. She doesn't trust that part of herself these days, like an alcoholic eyeing a whiskey bottle, knowing the promise of one sip will lead to a gurgling swallow and the night will end with broken dishes, bruised flesh, sirens. She will either tear apart the cabin or claw her way outside.

She tries to keep herself occupied. She jumps

rope until her legs ache. She does push-ups and crunches on the oval rug in the middle of the living room. She plays chess, spinning the board with every turn, pretending herself the enemy. She reads her way through the paperbacks on the bookcase, among them a Dover edition of *Dr. Jekyll and Mr. Hyde*. The bottom shelf is crowded with children's stories and on more than one occasion she opens them as if to make sure their words and drawings haven't vanished. Her eyes flit to her husband's book—a self-published manifesto the size of a brick called *The Revolution*—its cover bearing the image of a man casting a wolf's shadow, but this is a book she won't read, no matter how bored she gets.

She crunches her way through a bag of tortilla chips and then licks her finger to pilfer the crumbs and salt. She eats peanuts, Oreos, Nutri-Grain bars. She cracks six eggs and grates cheese and chops peppers and stirs up a steaming omelet. She always has a coffee in hand, the mug clacking against her teeth. She is so hungry.

Tonight is especially bad. The moon is nearly full, and it pulls at her blood. Her mouth drowns in saliva. Her muscles feel like tightly coiled springs that no amount of stretching can loosen. She gnashes her teeth and breathes as though back from a run. Every noise draws her to the window, gun in hand. Every shadow makes her eyes narrow. She walks from room to room, a clockwise rotation of the windows of the house, peering out into the clearing walled by woods.

She keeps the cabin dark so as not to ruin her night vision, and the slots in the windows glow like slanted blue eyes. In the living room she drops to the floor and hurries out a set of twenty-five push-ups. After the last rep she pauses with her chest and cheek against the rug. She does not breathe. Something has changed. She can sense it like an open door, a shift in sound and pressure.

She rises slowly from the floor and approaches the front window and releases the safety. The slot is the size of a ruler and she must press her eyes against the wood to get any sort of view. Splinters chafe her nose and forehead. A good minute passes before she sees, at the edge of the woods, a shadow come alive and separate itself from the rest, moving into the clearing, seeming very much a part of the forest, with its antlers forking upward like a cluster of branches and the band of white beneath its muzzle as bright as the moon rising over the tree line. A buck.

She closes her eyes, and when they snap open the rest of the world has fallen away, except for the deer, as if spotlighted. It lowers its head now to taste some grass, and she too opens her mouth and runs her tongue along her teeth. Through her body she feels a rush of blood that finds its focus in her chest, a throbbing pressure. She imagines her rib cage as a cell that cannot contain much longer the black fingers gripping it, shaking it.

If she does not hurry, the deer will step into the range of the motion detector and the explosion of light will startle it away. The door is braced by three two-by-fours. She sets down the gun and picks up the drill and hesitates, knowing the deer will hear the sound. She rattles around in a junk drawer for a screwdriver instead. She hardly notices the cramps in her hand when she twists out the eight screws the length of her finger.

The voice that scolds her, that begs restraint, that tells her to stay put, is a mere whimper, easily ignored. She sheds her clothes like a skin no longer needed. When she pulls open the door, ripping off the two-by-fours, and takes in her first shuddering breath of fresh air in two weeks—when she steps across the threshold, from the shadowy pocket of the cabin to the moonlit expanse of the night—she is already changing, the process as simple and liquid for her as diving into a pond.

The deer raises its head to study her. Its eyes black. Its ears twitching. It lifts one of its hooves, ready to move—and then, when she starts off the porch at a dead sprint, it twists away from her, bounding toward the cover of the trees. The motion detector flashes—instant daylight—and throws her shadow before her, a long black seam she pursues.

The wind shushes her ears, trembles her hair, making her feel as though she rides its currents, weaving past trees and cutting through bushes and curling over logs, the deer always within sight. It is faster than her but compromised by its size. Its body thuds off tree trunks; its antlers clack against low-hanging branches, finally tangling in one, dragging the deer to a stop.

It shakes its head furiously, trying to tear away from the tree. Wood cracks but does not give. Needles rain down. The weight of her body knocks the deer free, the two of them a mess of flailing limbs, and then it is too late, her claws dragging across its throat. Its bones are pearly. Its blood is warm and steams like a ghost released. For a long time she is lost to hunger.

Then her muscles tighten, knot up. For the first time she feels the air's chill. She is aware of herself as a wolf and a woman, the woman only faintly realized, like a burr in a sock, an abrasion that makes her lift her head from the carcass and recognize the danger of the night.

A cloud spills over the moon and momentarily dims the forest. She feels a pang of dread and rises from her crouch. Her sense of smell is compromised by the blood that sleeves her arms, masks her face, clots the hair that has risen from her skin. A scudding sound makes her flip around. The moon breaks from the clouds and splashes its light across what at first appears to be a boulder furred over with moss.

Its eyes sparkle like bits of quartz and its teeth glimmer when it rises into the massive figure of Morris Magog. She can see his breath trailing upward and imagines it as hot as the breath of an oven.

She does not whimper. She is not paralyzed by the terrible sight of him. A gust of wind is the only prompting she needs. She runs on all fours, letting the wolf lead her. Branches claw at her. The deer's blood dries against her in a tacky patina. The thrill of the earlier chase is gone, replaced by a cold, emotionless need to escape. Fear can come later.

She never glances over her shoulder, but she can hear his passage close behind—wood snapping, a deep-throated growling that sounds like shifting stone—and she can picture him clearly enough, appearing more bear than wolf, a surging mass of hair and muscle with a mouth of darkest black.

There it is. The woods open into a clearing with a driveway snaking through it. The shed. The Ramcharger. The squat shape of the cabin. She feels more vulnerable in the open space and wonders for the first time if Magog is alone. An explosion of light blinds her. The motion detector. Through the yellow haze she finds the steps and clambers up them—the open door waits for her, a rectangular black slash that she dives through. She does not allow herself the time to look, to see how close he is behind her, but slams the deadbolt home and backs away from the door, certain it will explode inward at any moment.

Already she is retreating into her human form, and as always she feels small and bewildered and achy, like someone rising from a dreamscape to find herself gripped by a hangover. Without looking, she crabs her hand across the coffee table and finds the Glock.

She knows she should retrieve the shotgun, the machete, the extra clips of ammo. But right now her body only wants to curl up in the corner, the wood of the wall digging into her naked back. She hears the porch boards rasp. And then, a moment later, a faint scratching at the door, a nail teased across its exterior. The knob turns slowly—catches against the lock—then rattles back into place.

A minute passes. The motion detector clicks off. The harsh white light is replaced by a watery blue glow seeping through the window slots. One of them goes suddenly dark. She breathes through her nose with a high-pitched whistle. She wills her body to recede into the wall, to appear as another piece of furniture in the room. She aims the Glock. Her finger tightens on the trigger. A half pound of pressure is all it takes.

The darkness retreats and the space glows blue again—and then, a moment later, white, the motion detector activated.

She does not feel relieved. She feels like she has a noose around her neck and it is only a matter of time before the trapdoor gives out beneath her. She waits for one of the longest silences of her life, barely breathing in an effort to listen more closely. Then the cabin shakes as something lights upon the roof. She does not cry out but brings a hand to her mouth and bites down on it.

The pitched ceiling is made of tongue-and-groove fitted pine planks. When the footsteps come, slow and thudding, fifty years of dust rains down. She blinks away the grit in her eyes and squeezes the pistol so tightly that the grip bites her palm. She concentrates on the impact of each footstep, the complaint of the wood, until she feels she could sketch a circle on the ceiling that targets Magog.

He is fucking with her. She is done being fucked with. She raises the Glock and fires.

She squeezes off five rounds, and the spent hulls

litter her lap and burn her but she hardly notices. The cabin quakes as though struck by a car. She has hit her mark. The fallen body rolls, thundering its way down the roof. There comes a brief silence punctuated by a heavy *whump*.

CHAPTER 11

CHASE REMEMBERS the first time he talked to Augustus. Seventh grade, Obsidian Junior High, after gym class, he walks into the locker room. Showers sizzle. Steam fills the air. Boys are scrubbing their armpits with soap or toweling off in front of their open lockers. He spins his combo and pauses before yanking the lock—because of the voices he hears, jeering, laughing like jackals.

Three boys—still in their shorts and tank tops—stand outside a toilet stall and kick at the door hard enough to dent the thin sheet metal. "Come on," they say. "Come out and show us your pussy." Another kick and the door jars open.

Chase recognizes the kid inside. They're in the same section of math, and the other day, in line at the cafeteria, a girl wearing bell-bottoms and her hair pulled back in a ponytail turned to the kid, who had accidentally rubbed up against her, and said, "Don't touch me. You haven't even gone through puberty yet."

He wears small glasses on a head too big for his body. His hair is the wispy blond of cornsilk. His arms and legs are stumpy, his torso round. All of this giving him the appearance of an enormous baby.

The same can't be said of Chase, who feels so much younger than his body. A few years ago his bones began to ache and he developed a vicious hunger, gobbling up six eggs for breakfast, a whole pizza for dinner, sucking down five gallons of milk every week. He studied himself often in the mirror, as his limbs stretched to match his oversize feet, his hands, what his mother called puppy paws. He started rubbing himself off in fifth grade, shaving in sixth grade with his father's razor and Barbasol. He is taller than most of his teachers and plays forward on the varsity basketball team.

He's not a good guy—he knows that has nothing to do with what happens next. He hates the Methodist church his parents drag him to every Sunday and smokes cigarettes under the football bleachers and sneaks cheat sheets into exams and every chance he gets tries to slide his hand up a girl's skirt. But most of his trespasses have to do with pleasure, seeking it out, the buzz of a beer, the way a blow job makes his whole body feel like a tingly nerve ending.

He's not a bad guy either—he has a certain sense of righteousness motivated now by these three punks, with their braces and pimply backs, getting off on ganging up on somebody weaker than them.

From what Chase gathers, as he moves toward them, the kid has been camping out in the toilet stall after gym, skipping his shower, changing where no one can observe him. A pile of clothes remains in the stall as he is dragged across the wet tile floor, half-dressed in a button-up short-sleeve and white briefs that match the paleness of his skin. He struggles but does not cry out when the boys reach for his underwear and try to yank it off him.

Chase comes up behind them. Without pause he kicks one of the boys square in the ass and sends him keeling into the wall—striking it with a wet thud, crumpling into a mewling ball. Chase cracks together the skulls of the other two boys and then shoves them headfirst into the nearby urinals. He holds them there for a good five seconds, mashing their mouths into the deodorant pucks. Then he slams the flush bars and leaves them sputtering.

The kid has gathered up his clothes. His face is impassive, and his glasses have fogged over, hiding his eyes. Neither of them says anything. Not until the next day, after algebra, when the kid introduces himself as Augustus and asks what he can do for Chase.

"You don't owe me nothing."

The rest of the class is filing out of the room, glancing at the strange pair, Augustus standing with his arms crossed and Chase sitting with his legs sprawled out, their height about equal. "I disagree," the kid says. "And maybe you will as well when you hear my proposal." The precision of the kid's words, the confident purse of his mouth—the white short-sleeve shirt, like something an accountant would wear in the summer. Chase might as well be having a conversation with an alien. He has no idea how to respond and finds he doesn't have to, because the kid is filling the silence, explaining how, if protected, Augustus will do any homework assignments Chase finds tiresome.

"I'm not stupid. And I'm not looking for help." Chase is less angered than amused. "My grades are fine."

"You have obligations I do not: sports and socializing. Homework gets in the way of these, yes? If you feel like completing your assignments on your own, great. But if on occasion you have an away game or a hot, sexy date—then you will hand the work off to me and I will happily oblige."

"And for this I kick anybody's ass who messes with you?"

A curt nod. "Tit for tat."

Chase stands. He towers over the kid, could smash him into his backpack if he wanted. "We don't have to hang out or anything, do we?"

"Not unless you want to."

"I don't."

A contract they have more or less honored for the past thirty years.

Chase has never called Augustus by his name. It was a mouthful, and obnoxious, the name of some old poet who liked to write about the pansies growing in his garden. The kid. That's what Chase called him—until they enrolled at the University of Oregon, when the kid took Chase aside during orientation and said he would rather not be called *that* anymore.

"Why not?"

"It implies a lack of strength."

"Then what the hell am I supposed to call you?"

"My name."

"Out of the question."

He settled on Buffalo. For the enormous head, too big for any hat, that seems to grow directly out of his sloped shoulders. Chase nicknames everyone he meets. His administrative assistant, Moneypenny. His legal counsel, No Fun. The head of his security detail, Shrek, for his bald head, his jutting forehead, his barrel of a torso balanced on tiny legs. Even the people he doesn't know, he finds a way to name them—a bartender is *honey* or *sugar*, a valet or groundskeeper is *buddy* or *friend*.

It's his way of making people come a little closer, look him in the eye and smile.

Sweetheart is what he calls the woman working the front desk at the Kazumi Day Spa. He recognizes her from the teahouse. The wrinkled face and square body and silvery hair pulled back into a bun stabbed through with chopsticks. A potted bamboo sits in the corner. A scroll bearing a string of Japanese characters hangs behind her. She doesn't smile at him but lifts her arm, gesturing to a dark hallway, and says, with a heavy accent, "Last door on the left."

The spa is in southwest Salem—not too far from the teahouse—a nondescript windowless brick building tucked between a pawnshop and a moneylender, the street busy with rusted-out cars missing their mufflers.

In a back room, the recessed lighting gives off a dim orange glow. Music trembles—piped in through the overhead speakers—something acoustic, what Chase recognizes as the same instrument played at the teahouse, the koto, the plucked strings making him think of spiders' legs dancing across a web. In the center of the room waits the massage table and against the wall squats a glass-doored, marbled-topped bureau, full of white downy towels, bottles of oil and lotion. On top of it, a plug-in fountain, water gurgling over colored stones.

Buffalo used to tell him not to come here. For a long time, his principal duty, as chief of staff, seemed to be telling Chase what not to do. Do not bad-mouth Weyerhaeuser. Do not make fun of the Trail Blazers. Do not curse during live press conferences. Do not get intoxicated at black-tie fund-raisers. Do not punch Ron Wyden. Do not tell the *Oregonian* that you think Nancy Pelosi is one smoking-hot old lady.

The attacks changed everything. "You realize," Buffalo said, more than a month ago, when the planes came down, "that this is the best thing that could have possibly happened?" At the time they were at Mahonia Hall, the governor's mansion, a place Chase never liked much. The pretention of it—Tudor-style, ballroom, wine cellar, surrounded by thorny rose gardens. Not to mention that ten thousand square feet can feel pretty lonely in the middle of the night, when the dreams come to him. Sometimes he wakes up gasping—believing he is still in the Republic, where he served two tours—his nose choked with the smell of cooking flesh, his eyes imagining clawed hands scrabbling out from beneath the bed like a pair of gray spiders. He has more than once brought the security guard a beer to split on the front steps at three a.m.

The afternoon of the attacks, he and Buffalo were sitting in wingback oxblood leather chairs, watching the flat-screen, flipping back and forth between CNN and Fox News. Same footage, different talking heads. Outside Denver, the wreckage smoldered in a wheat field. At PDX and Logan International, the planes were parked on the tarmac like giant white coffins.

A reporter interviewed a woman wearing a Looney Tunes sweatshirt and purple leggings. The tape at the bottom of the screen identified her as a family member of one of the passengers. "It's the most horrible thing in the world," she said, roughing away her tears with the remains of a tissue. "And it's happening right here."

The footage cut to Jeremy Saber, the leader of the Resistance movement, which claimed responsibility for the attacks. In a video he posted online, he sat at a desk in a collared shirt with the sleeves rolled up. His hair was a mess of curls—his face square and shadowed with whiskers—and his arms were sheathed with tattoos. He looked more like a barista or hip college instructor than the spokesperson for an extremist group. "Some will say we do not value human life. We value it very much. That is why we have taken it away. We do it with remorseful intention. You are paying attention now. That is what we need for you to do. Pay attention. Our demands have not been met." He went on to list enforced medication and blood testing, limited employment opportunities, the U.S. occupation of the Republic, and the proposed construction of a public lycan database as chief among his complaints. "If the government does not respond to these very reasonable requests, we will be forced to be unreasonable again. The terror will continue."

Buffalo stood then and tucked his hands in the pockets of his sport coat and walked over to the window, the gray light coming through the water-spotted glass reminding Chase of his Marine Corps woodland-pattern cammies.

"One way of looking at it is this," Buffalo said. "As a tragedy." He turned to Chase and removed a hand from his pocket and pointed it like a gun. "Here is another. It is a game changer. It is timely. It is advantageous. You are the only politician in the country who has fought in the Republic. We need to remind people of that." He has a way of talking, carefully enunciating each word as if it were a tiny gem delivered between his teeth.

He worked as a lawyer for ten years before joining a management consulting firm that told businesses what machines to buy, which people to fire and locations to close. He developed strategic marketing platforms to boost or reinvent a corporation, making a WorldCom into an MCI, he liked to say. He was the one who approached Chase about running for governor. And now, for the first time—Chase can see it in his trembling mouth—Buffalo seems to believe in the possibility of reelection. "We need to get you behind a microphone by this evening, ideally with that plane in the background."

"We'll bang out a speech on the drive up?"

He considers this a moment. "No. Speak from the heart. Just make sure your heart is more furious than mournful." On the television, another shot of the flaming wreckage. Buffalo's glasses catch the shimmering orange light and the lenses glow like twin suns. "People are ready for fury."

Fury is what Chase gave them, two hours later, outside the open hangar that now housed the plane, rain wetting his face, a crowd of reporters gathered around him. "What do I think?" he said to them. "I think it's time to tighten the leash, roll up a newspaper, say *bad dog*."

Since then he has spoken to every major news network, every magazine and newspaper, made a villain and a hero. He has earned, for the first time, his own nicknames. Dog Soldier is one. The Game Warden another. He sees his face when he logs on to AOL, when he opens *Newsweek* to read the editorial comics, when he flips the channels on the flat-screen with a cold Coors resting against his crotch. He supports a continued occupation of the

Republic and a greater reliance on nuclear energy and quotes polls that indicate that the Republic by and large feels the same, its citizens dependent on the jobs and infrastructure and security the U.S. supplies. He supports the public registry—a watchdog list, he calls it. He supports vaccine research, segregation, suspended rights. "Extremism in the face of extremism," he calls it.

All this talking exhausts him. He keeps a handful of lozenges in his pocket and finds an antidote to all the noise on the treadmill—pounding out five miles every evening, sweating through his clothes—and in sex. Sometimes he seduces women—the blond reporter at KOIN 6, the redheaded waitress at the Book of Kells Irish pub—and sometimes he pays for them.

Today he pays. At the day spa, in the back room, a digital thermostat on the wall reveals the temperature to be seventy-five degrees, warm enough to make him eager to kick off his boots, peel off his clothes, pile them in a heap in the corner. Jeans and a denim shirt. Corduroy jacket. Belt with a Buck knife holstered to it. Silver six-inch blade, a birthday present from his father when he turned sixteen. He carried it in the Republic and doesn't go anywhere without it now. He retired as a colonel, and across his naked shoulder, like a bruise, he carries the faded ink of the anchor-and-eagle tattoo.

He palms a condom from his pocket. A white towel hangs from a hook. He ties it around his middle. The light is such that his shadow hardly seems to exist, oozing faintly across the floor and then the massage table. He climbs up and settles his face into the cushioned groove.

He hears the knob rattle, the door click closed, the footsteps whisper across the carpet. Her name is Choko. They visit for an hour every few weeks. Sometimes he lets her dampen his back with oil, rub the poison out of his muscles—and sometimes he does not. Sometimes he asks her to flip him over. Sometimes she takes him in her mouth or her hand. And sometimes she climbs onto the table with him.

"Hey, you," he says and raises his head to peer at the woman standing a few feet away. She wears a red kimono with a black dragon stitched into it. Hair down to her elbows. She smiles. The fountain gurgles. He lets his head drop into the groove again. "Give me a little rub, will you? I'm knotted up. Then we can get busy."

He feels a hungry anticipation. The blood pools in his center. His erection presses uncomfortably against the table. He hears her clothes drop. He hears her breathing heavily, almost panting.

"Hey, what kind of a party's going on without me?" He is smiling when he rises on his elbow.

The pressure of the table has made his vision muddy. At first he believes this is why her nude form seems to shift, to bulge and bend, like a reflection seen on the body of a passing car. And then he blinks hard and observes between blinks the contorted posture, the lengthening teeth, the black hair bristling like quills from her skin. He feels a hole in his stomach like he used to get when small-arms fire popped in the near distance, when tracer rounds streaked through the night like blood-red comets.

Her voice is guttural when she says, "I have a message from the Resistance."

Before he can slide off the table, she has his leg—snatching it up—her claws and then her teeth sinking into his calf. He kicks at her and she falls with a mouth full of blood. His blood. He doesn't take the time to examine the wound, to recognize what this means, infection.

The towel slips off him when he falls off the table. His first impulse is to stupidly grab for it, cover himself—and then, equally stupid, to race for the door, call for help. But he realizes midshout that this was a planned attack and plans are rarely made alone.

She growls. It is a bestial sound. He can feel it. Feel it in his bones like when bass pours from a too-loud stereo. He has never been more vulnerable, naked and unarmed, bleeding. He doesn't feel any pain, not yet. Only the warmth of blood running along his leg, its tackiness underfoot when he stumbles back, looking for a weapon, something to swing.

The bureau jars against his spine, preventing any further retreat. The mist from the fountain licks his back. He yanks its cord from the outlet and scoops it up and hurls it at the lycan. Its stones are like a brightly colored hail rattling the floor. The bowl arcs toward her, and she puts out her arms to catch it and it thuds against her chest and the water dampens her hair and makes it appear a rippling shadow.

She is on one side of the massage table—the padding torn through in yellow slashes—and he is on the other. He needs to get to the pile of clothes, the knife nested in it, on the opposite side of the room. He can smell her. He would recognize that smell anywhere, the smell of a lycan. Like an unwashed crotch. Supposedly set off by their hyperstimulated pituitary gland.

Her posture is hunched and her breasts dangle pendulously and her arms rake the air and her face is nearly impossible to decipher beneath all that hair. She makes a noise that sounds like a guttural string of words. His skin goes tight. She begins to climb over the table, toward him, one arm and then the other. He tries to run and nearly topples, his feet sliding across the stones.

He is to the clothes when she leaps and knocks him to the floor. For a moment they might be lovers, a tangle of limbs, breathing heavily. She is faster than him, but he is stronger. He loops an arm around her throat and drags them back against the wall. Her body bucks against his but he holds her in place. She wears his arm like a necklace. He is choking her and she claws at him, tearing away ribbons of skin from his forearm, his thighs, his ribs, wherever she can reach, while he sets his jaw against the pain and uses his free arm to seek out the knife, yanking his belt from the pile of clothes, fumbling with the leather casing.

Finally he withdraws it and unfolds the blade. In its silvery flash he catches a glimpse of his eyes, wide with fright. Then he draws the knife toward them in an arc. The woman—no, the lycan, the *thing*—tries to block the blade, swatting and tearing at him, but her strength is fading and after a few wild swings he sneaks the knife to her chest, where it catches against a rib—and grinds its way inside her.

What would have been a growl, against the pressure of his chokehold, escapes as a plaintive mewl. He stabs her again and again, so many times—*knife*, *knife*, *knife*—far more than necessary, her body limp in his lap. She doesn't reassume her human form. Not like in the fairy tales. She dies a beast and a beast she remains.

He feels faint. The room seems so cold and her body so warm. He could fall asleep with her draped over him like this. But he doesn't. He shoves her aside and stands with great difficulty and fights the gray wings beating at the edge of his vision. He tries not to look at his ruined arm when he retrieves the towel from the floor and makes a tourniquet of it. Roses of blood bloom immediately through the cotton.

There are no windows. There is only one way out. And only one way in. It takes him a while, but he drags the bureau against the door. He remembers how severely the old woman stared at him, and he knows Choko did not act alone. He needs help. His hand is trembling and slick with blood, but somehow he manages to retrieve the handheld from his jacket pocket and call Buffalo, telling him what happened, telling him to hurry.

CHAPTER 12

PATRICK SPENDS several days planning his escape—figuring out which stairs creak, spritzing the door hinges with WD-40, backing his Jeep into his parking spot and testing how easily it rolls in neutral—and then his mother tells him she's going out of town. The National Association of Realtors. They're having a conference in Portland this weekend.

He is so thrilled he doesn't sigh or roll his eyes when she asks him to join her this afternoon to freshen up a house. "It will be fun," she says. He is lying on the couch, reading the newspaper, some article about the ongoing investigation into the death of a local rancher and city council member. The ground around the corpse was a mess of coyote tracks, but the game warden claims it was highly unusual and even beyond reason to believe coyotes capable of such behavior.

The couch is leather. So is the matching armchair next to it. The living room looks like something out of a Pottery Barn catalogue. Wool carpet. Wrought-iron lamps. Dark-wooded end tables. His mother does all right.

She finishes clipping on an earring and then roughs her hair with a pick. A silver stripe flares at her left temple and curls all the way to the base of her neck, through hair that is otherwise thick and black. She hides her age well, the wrinkles fanning from her eyes caked with a layer of foundation. "So you'll come?" she says.

"I guess."

Her cheeks dimple when she smiles. Like his. These past few weeks, he's spent a lot of time studying her, trying to figure out how they match up. He's a lot like his father—that's what people say—same hawkish nose and high forehead, same square-tipped fingers and huge hands dangling from thin wrists like shovel heads. But he belongs to them both.

She pokes him with the pick on her way out of the living room—gives his cheek a little bite with it—and he swats it away with a "Quit."

She's trying—he'll give her that—trying to make him feel welcome. And he tries to reciprocate, to make himself available, answering her incessant questions, sitting at the kitchen table to do his homework, joining her when she watches the stupid television show about the horny doctors.

He's not looking for drama. His life needs the volume turned down, not up. He knows a lot of crybabies in his situation would probably lock themselves in their rooms and eventually throw a damp-eyed fit about how Mommy abandoned them. Whenever he feels tense and ready to shatter a dish against the wall, he remembers his father, who demanded he not feel sorry for himself.

Still, there are little things that bother him. The way she uses her hands when she speaks, pointing and pinching and swinging and flapping. The way she's always losing lids—the milk, the mustard, the oatmeal—everything in the house uncapped. The way she programs the thermostat. All of August she kept the air-conditioning at seventy-four—and now that the weather has turned cold she keeps the heat at sixty-seven. "Jesus," he says. "Wouldn't it make sense to negotiate between the seasons, keep it at seventy year-round?"

And she's a bit of a freak when it comes to messes. She'll pull a shirt right off him if it's wrinkled. She'll scoop up a dish the moment he drops it on the counter and rinse it off to set in the dishwasher. And he could tell, when she put down the money on the used Jeep, how disgusted she was by it. "Are you sure?" she said, too many times, pointing out the other cars in the lot, all of them sedans, only going along with his insistence on the run-down Wrangler because she would do anything right then to make him happy.

She drives a white Camry so clean the sky

streams across its hood like water. The interior still smells new, despite the car being a few years old, so different from his father's pickup, with the dust coughing from the vents and the French fries moldering under the seats. Before they left, she grabbed a vented carrier from the garage and set it in the backseat. Inside sits a calico cat that paws and bites at the caged door and hisses when Patrick turns around. "What's with the cat?" he says, and his mother says, "It's for a friend. They were giving them away at the gas station."

They drive through Old Mountain, a place that has transformed from mill town to luxury outpost for Californians looking for a second home or a place to retire. His mother tells him they came for the skiing, the fly-fishing and mountain biking and horseback riding. "Fifteen years ago, when I first moved here," she says, "fifteen thousand people. Now? Two hundred fifty thousand in the metro." Making it one of the fastest-growing communities in the country and creating fault-line abrasion between the old and the new.

The mill is long gone, the industrial district replaced by condos, organic coffeehouses, boutique clothing stores, a brickwork river walk. There are few intersections, everything a roundabout that makes Patrick feel dizzy and lost.

She points out the section of town where the lycans used to live—before the Struggle, when lycan segregation was mandatory in housing, schools, bathrooms, restaurants—a collection of quaint one-story bungalows that now, his mother says, cost three hundred thousand a pop.

The road inclines as they drive up the side of a butte—into a neighborhood that is a carbon copy of his mother's. These faux-rustic developments are all over town, as far as Patrick can tell, many with golf courses spilling greenly through them. They have names like Elk Ridge and Bear Hollow, and every house seems to come with a river-rock chimney and rough-hewn pine pillars flanking the front porch.

The sky is a pale and depthless blue. A gusty September breeze sends leaves skittering across lawns, and one of them catches on Patrick's shoe—a round leaf, as gold as a coin, as though money indeed grows on trees here—when he steps out of the car next to the Century 21 sign staked in the front yard.

From the car trunk, his mother retrieves a broom, a Dirt Devil, and a paper bag full of cleaning supplies. They roll down the windows for the cat.

The family moved out last week. She vacuums the footprints from the carpet, massages away the divots from where tables and couches stood. She Windexes the fingerprints smeared across the storm door and arranges scented candles throughout the house to light before the showing. She clips flowers from the garden and fits them in a short vase on the kitchen island. He yanks the cheatgrass flaming up between the four cement squares of the driveway. He sweeps the stone entryway, the tile bathrooms, the oil-spotted garage. He lifts a window and clambers across the roof and cleans out the pine needles clogging the gutters.

When they finish, an hour later, he asks if she does this for every house and she says she does, more or less. He asks if it really makes that big of a difference, a candle sputtering in the bathroom, and she says absolutely. "Because appearances matter." She snaps her seat belt into place and readjusts the mirror and feathers her hair with her fingers. "That's the world we live in."

☽

From the day Chase took the oath of office, he refused police escorts. They cost taxpayers too much, thirty-eight million in California the previous year. Besides, he claimed, he could protect himself. For the past month, ever since Chase began to regularly appear on the lecture and talk-show circuit, Augustus forced a compromise and hired a private security detail from Lazer Ltd., mostly thick-necked, thin-waisted ex-military. Chase calls them babysitters and refuses their protection except during speaking engagements. Augustus tries to get him to reconsider, telling him the worst can happen when you least expect it.

The worst has happened. Four men, all wearing tracksuits, pick up Augustus in a black Chevy Suburban and drive at a perilous speed to the Kazumi Day Spa, honking their way through red lights, screeching their way around corners. It's an unlisted address, but Augustus knows the way and directs them from the backseat—telling them to hurry, goddammit, *hurry*—even as he leans into a turn and braces an arm against the window to keep his balance.

They find the front door locked and use a metal battering ram to splinter it from its hinges. One man remains posted at the entrance while the others, their Glocks unholstered, charge inside. They give the all clear and Augustus walks into the dim entryway. The lights are off, the hallways and rooms empty—except for one barricaded door. They shove at it and a crack of orange light appears and only then does Augustus tell them, "*Stop.*"

The men step away and wait for him to tell them what to do. "Stay here," he says and shoulders past them and puts all of his weight against the door until the bureau slides away and allows him entrance.

He hurries the door closed before the men can spot Chase, curled up on the floor—dizzy and naked and shivering from blood loss, but alive.

There is blood smeared across the wall and soaked into the carpet that squelches underfoot. "I'm here," Augustus says, not daring to touch his friend, not knowing how long the disease can live once exposed to the air.

He toes the slumped body of the transformed lycan. Her hair, tacky with blood, has the look of seaweed plastered across the beach at low tide. "Bitch," he says, "you really fucked things up." The governor attacked in a whorehouse. Half-dead and likely infected. His political career finished. Augustus brings back his foot and considers kicking her face but doesn't, not wanting to dirty his shoe.

Instead he covers her body with towels so that the others won't see her. Red splotches soak through immediately. He pulls a terry-cloth robe off a hook and tucks it around Chase. No one can know about this or everything will be ruined. There is only one choice. He opens the door and tells the men to get a makeshift stretcher for Chase, and then, once they get him to the car, "Burn the place. Burn it to the ground."

Patrick's mother needs to make a stop on the way home. Just for a minute. To drop something off. "The cat," she says. "I hope that's all right."

They drive past several car dealerships, where dozens of American flags snap in the breeze, and past the dump, where crows and seagulls darken the sky, and here, his mother says, pointing to an abandoned whitewashed cinder-block building, is the old school where the lycan children went. Its windows are thorned with broken glass, its front door yawns open, and a pine tree twists through its roof.

Another mile and they turn off into Juniper Creek, a wooded neighborhood on the outskirts of town, every driveway curling away from the road into an acre lot. Browned pine needles rain down on the windshield. Patrick can see the house, twenty yards ahead, a ranch home with a lava-rock exterior that makes it appear as though it is rising out of the ground.

Then his attention is lost to movement all around them. Out of the bushes, from behind trees and under the front porch, come dogs. More than a dozen of them. They kick up dust when they tear toward the car. Among the assorted mutts, Patrick spots a German shepherd, a Rottweiler, and a wiener dog. They bark furiously, surrounding the car, pacing it as it crawls up the driveway.

His mother does not seem to notice them, humming along with the radio. She shifts into park, kills the engine, and swings open her door before Patrick can tell her, “No!”

The barking ceases, replaced by whimpers and soft cries for attention. His mother speaks to them in baby talk and ruffles their ears and pats their backs.

“Who lives here?” Patrick says.

“A friend.”

She doesn’t invite him to join her, doesn’t ask for his help with the carrier she removes from the backseat. “Back in a flash,” she says when she starts toward the house, not bothering to nudge a hip against the driver’s-side door and close it. Some of the dogs follow her, darting in front of her, begging for her attention, all tongues and tails—excited by the scent of the cat—and others remain with the car, including the Rottweiler, who observes Patrick from the open door, panting, licking its chops.

A minute passes before Patrick says, “Good dog?” and the Rottweiler considers this encouragement enough to leap onto the front seat, its face inches from his. All Patrick can focus on is its mouth. Its breath smells like old hamburger. Its gums are a spotted black, its teeth the size of his thumbs.

He does not breathe when he raises his hand, so slowly, to pet the dog. It sniffs his hand once, gives him a lick, then nudges—with its cold, damp nose—his hand upward for a scratch behind the ears.

It isn't long before Patrick stands outside the car with his arm cocked and a stick in his hand. The dogs surround him, their eyes on the stick. "Ready?" he says, and they yap and their paws drum the ground. He hurls the stick and it flies end over end into the woods and the dogs go ripping away, their paws kicking the ground hard enough that Patrick can feel the tremor in his chest like a furious heartbeat. A moment later the German shepherd appears, smiling around the stick, the rest of the pack trailing behind.

Patrick throws the stick, now damp with slobber and dented with tooth marks, a good twenty times. The dachshund grows tired and stays behind after the last toss, and Patrick picks the dog up and cradles it in his arms. He can't believe he felt afraid, a few minutes ago, when they first drove up. The dachshund licks him, a tongue worming from a snout run through with white hairs. Harmless. But when Patrick peels back the skin, he exposes the jagged line of teeth hidden inside this tiny old dog.

At that moment the front door swings open and his mother starts down the porch midconversation. "Which will be good, I think," she says. "So I'll see you soon."

A man stands in the doorway, watching them.

He wears a dress shirt tucked into khakis. He is tall and eerily lean and bald except for a silver horseshoe of hair. He gives an almost imperceptible nod, a slight dip of his chin, which Patrick does not return.

☽

Chase shivers in and out of consciousness. His skin is as pale as the bone peeking out of his shredded arm. Every heartbeat brings an electric surge of pain. He is lying on a blue tarp, he realizes. A blue tarp in a white room. Not a hospital; they can't risk a hospital. His head rolls to the side and the tarp pops beneath him and he recognizes the couch against the wall, the tacky white leather couch, as Buffalo's. His living room.

Buffalo. Chase can hear him, dimly. It's a comforting sound. Like when, as a child, on long car trips, he would intermittently wake to the murmur of his parents talking in the front seat. He strains his neck to observe his friend pacing back and forth with his handheld pressed against his ear. His voice is panicked, hurried. Chase wants to tell him to take it easy, but then the darkness of sleep once again overtakes him.

CHAPTER 13

THE GRAY-EYED BOY named Max lives in old town. A neighborhood of Old Mountain untouched by all the new development, every house on his street a one-story shoebox with a concrete-slab porch and a mature maple tree planted left of the cracked driveway. Three cars and a truck are parked out front, all Chevys. The streetlamps buzz and telephone lines crisscross the moonlit sky. Before Patrick can knock, the door cracks and in the crack hangs the craggy face of a man—Max's father, Patrick guesses—who waves him in, says the boys are downstairs.

The basement is pine paneled and smells vaguely of mothballs. Mounted on the wall, three trophy bucks, a lacquered rainbow trout, and a shelf busy with beer steins and age-tarnished softball trophies. A gun cabinet stacked with rifles and shotguns. Minor Threat plays from a laptop set on top of an ancient minifridge. When Patrick thumps down the stairs, a dozen faces turn toward him, some nodding along with the music, some still and expressionless. Everyone wears their head shaved, so at first it's difficult to distinguish between them, and then one steps forward and comes into focus: Max. “We’re glad you came,” he says.

Patrick notices for the first time the tracheotomy scar, like a bright red worm nesting in the cup of his neck. The air is dry and the carpet shag, so that a spark snaps between them when they bring their hands together to shake, a jolt that makes Patrick blink fast and stutter out his thanks. One by one, the boys in the room introduce themselves—this one chinless, this one rashed over with acne, this one freakishly muscled, the tendons jumping from his neck like piano wires—and their socks sizzle across the carpet and their hands emit tiny blue balls of light.

They don’t linger but return to whatever previously occupied them, darts, foosball, something on the laptop. A wood-paneled TV set squats in the corner, the image of a soldier frozen on the screen, his teeth gritted. A video-game console nests in a black tangle of wires. Two of the boys punch their controllers and the screen comes to life. Patrick recognizes *Call of Duty: Lycan Wars*, a shooter game set in the Lupine Republic, your level-by-level mission to kill as many lycan insurgents as possible while collecting stores of energy and weapons—a silver chainsaw, a Gatling gun that rattles out ammo with a sound like a shuffled deck of cards.

A few times a month, Max says, they make an effort to get together. Nothing formal. Just a chance to hang. Feel connected. Patrick doesn't know what to say—doesn't know if he should ask what exactly connects them, makes them a group—so he simply says, cool. Their talk turns to school, how Patrick is liking it, how Max believes one teacher is worthless and another is smart but clouded by his liberal agenda. His eye contact is unrelenting. He taps his middle finger into his opposing palm to punctuate his sentences.

"You want a drink, by the way?" Max says, and Patrick says sure and wonders for a second if that means a beer before noticing that everyone in the room is sucking on a pop, Coke, Squirt, Dr Pepper. The minifridge is stocked full and Patrick cracks a Coke and Max snaps his fingers and says, "Before I forget." His voice rises to address the room. "Guys. Heads up. Listen up." The volume of the music lowers, the video game pauses, heads swivel in their direction. "Next Wednesday, four o'clock, don't forget, we're stopping by Desert Flower, the old folks' home on O.B. Riley. Groundskeeping first. Then card games. And, Dan, you're going to play the piano at dinner."

Everyone nods and then the foosball table rattles and shudders and the video game and conversations start back up. Max raises his eyebrows and lowers his voice and says to Patrick, "Not what you expected, right?"

He's not sure what he expected. Yelling maybe. A swastika flag. "You guys straight edge or something?"

"Not exactly."

"Then what?"

"We call ourselves the Americans."

They talk about immigration. They talk about guns. They talk about the viability of Chase Williams as a presidential candidate. And when they talk, Max seems to end every sentence with "right?"—in a prodding, corrective way—as if to make sure they share the same beliefs.

They talk about the attacks, and when Patrick says he doesn't understand why *now*, why all of a sudden the seeming escalation in the size and strength of the Resistance, Max appears insulted. "It isn't all of a sudden. This has been going on for years. This has been going on since our parents were our age, since the Struggle."

He holds out a finger for the failed Times Square bombing, for the anthrax scare, for the mail bombs, for the mall shooting, for the subway gassing. "All of those were relative failures. A few headlines, a few dead bodies, and then everybody moves on to the next earthquake or tsunami news tragedy. This is just the first time the mutts have actually been able to pull something off, something big. And you, my friend, found yourself in the middle of it and somehow walked away alive. Which is pretty amazing. You're part of history. You're a walking emblem of their failure, our hope." Max's voice seems to grow louder with every sentence, and his head bobs on his shoulders like a balloon on a ribbon.

Patrick hates it when people talk about him as if he were an idea. That's why he stopped meeting with reporters. He tries to change the subject, asking Max if he thinks the average lycan is dangerous, if it's fair to lump them all together as part of the Resistance. "I can't say I know that many lycans, but it seems like they're living pretty normal lives. They don't have much to complain about. They seem pretty happy, pretty safe."

Max shakes his head with disappointment. He puts his arms on Patrick's shoulders. "Listen to me. They are a public health risk and a biological abomination. Don't ever forget that, okay?"

"Okay."

Max releases him and Patrick drains the last of his soda and shakes it to indicate he is going to get another. Max follows him to the minifridge and says, "Now I want you to tell me about your father."

He cracks the can, slurps the foam. "What do you want to know?"

"Everything."

Patrick doesn't know what to say. His father wears Levi's, motorcycle boots, white T-shirts ripped from clear plastic packs. His fingernails always carry bruises and crescents of dirt. Every few weeks he cuts his own hair in the mirror with a pair of clippers, shearing it down to a high-and-tight. In college, he was a biochem major, a gifted slacker. That's where he met Neal—at UC Davis—where they went by the nicknames Kirk and Spock. Keith drove motorcycles and carried a knife on his belt and found himself bored in the lab, excited more by big ideas than by carrying them out—while Neal wore khakis, sandals with socks, the detail-oriented workman who went on to make a name for himself as a researcher in animal diseases.

Whereas his father eventually put his bad grades and chemistry genius to work at Anchor Steam Brewing. He drives a Dodge Ram and an Indian motorcycle. He has a diamond-shaped scar on his forehead from when he struck an open cabinet during a Christmas party. He fell to the linoleum with a shocked look on his face and blood welling from between his fingers, one of the most terrifying moments of Patrick's life, when for the first time he saw his father hurt and embarrassed by the group of people hovering over him.

About halfway through college—he took six years to graduate—he ran out of money and signed on with the National Guard to pay his tuition, and today he serves as a staff sergeant with the California National Guard currently stationed at Combat Outpost Tuonela in the eastern Republic. He supervises a platoon of men, twenty-five soldiers of the seven thousand deployed from California. Years ago, he served a tour—back when Patrick's grandparents were still alive—but that was before the conflict escalated, before the marches and rock-slinging riots protesting U.S. occupation, before newspaper headlines were inked in the blood of soldiers killed in IED blasts, tooth-and-claw street battles.

His father jokes, by Skype, by email and instant message, that he didn't have any gray hair before his unit was activated, but now it's coming in strong. He writes that he feels like an old man among all these kids, most of them not much older than Patrick. He writes about his conflicted feelings, how he wishes he were home but how he knows they're doing good. "It's only a few rotten eggs over here. They get all the news. The rest of the citizens, and that's the majority by a long shot, are happy we're here. Remember that just because you're lycan doesn't mean you're a monster. Really remember that."

He writes that he hears small-arms fire on patrol and lycans baying outside the compound at night. He writes that a bomb exploded near the Humvee in which he was riding. The truck flipped twice, when it banked a hard right and rolled down an embankment, but somehow they got away with nothing but a few cuts and ringing ears. "Made my heart jump. Too many close calls for kids I'm responsible for. Stay safe, buddy. Love ya."

For this he has gone on leave as an assistant brewmaster at Anchor, where he spends much of his days in white coveralls, moving among the big-bellied copper vats, the clouds of yeasty steam, checking and double-checking on fermentation, hosing down tanks, dollying barrels, jotting down temperatures and yeast-cell concentrations in a notebook, giving the occasional tour for gangs of tourists wearing fanny packs and white sneakers. His hair smells of malt. He often talks about whole grains and oaken casks and in everyday conversation uses words like *hydrometer*, *glycol*, *sparge paddle*.

There is so much to tell about his father, but before Patrick can piece together more than a few sentences, the door at the top of the landing creaks open and footsteps boom down the stairs and his voice dies away when he sees who it is—the red-headed girl, Malerie.

He feels, then, a hole open up in his stomach through which all his blood seems to drain.

She does not look at Patrick, not at first, but walks directly to Max and snakes an arm around his neck and kisses him loudly on the cheek. His face pinches and reddens. He shrugs off her arm and glances around, as though embarrassed by her affection. An electric guitar shrieks, the only sound in the room, until Max says to Patrick, "This is my girlfriend, Malerie."

It is only then that she looks at him—with a blank expression—and says, "Nice to meet you." She raises her hand in a half wave, her fingernails as red as a stop sign.

CHAPTER 14

CLAIRE IS HERE. It hardly seems possible, after all this time, but the sign at the side of the road reads LA PINE, POPULATION 5,799. Its letters glow with the silvery light thrown by the full moon.

She is here because of her father's note, because an acronym on a stupid greeting card finally helped her read what he had written. She studied the constellations he sketched and jotted down the first letter of each. From this she built the words, *Go to Miriam Ten Twenty Battle Creek Rd La Pine Oregon.*

No wisdom beyond that. No clue as to why, out of all the people in the world, he chose his sister, a woman who is more a blank-faced mystery than an aunt, who ten years ago was excised from the family for reasons not entirely clear, who might not even be at the address listed, and even if she is, might not want anything to do with Claire.

She headed west, constantly studying her creased map, realizing sadly one afternoon that she had achieved her dream, making it more than five hundred miles from home. She caught rides with a lesbian couple driving a minivan with three pugs barking and snorting in the backseat, with a rancher with hay in his hair and heavy gloves and a tin of chewing tobacco on his dashboard. She slept on porches, in barns and sheds and campers, under pine boughs. She woke up one morning to hail and another to what sounded like hail but turned out to be a group of children clacking sticks together, pretending them into swords. "You're dead, lycan monster," one of them cried, slashing at his friend's belly.

When she couldn't bum a ride, she walked. Sometimes during the day and sometimes at night, the night so monstrously dark in the Plains, its star-sprinkled blackness broken by the occasional red halo of light emitted by towns with names like Snakebite, Elkhorn. Always the wind blew, flapping her pants, ruffling the oily strands of hair that hang from beneath her wool cap.

In a pole barn she found a workbench with a pegboard hanging from the wall behind it. Wrenches and screwdrivers and hammers and pliers surrounded two Craftsman toolboxes, one red, one black, with their lids thrown open. A set of socket wrenches. A ratchet. She picked up a few of the hammers, tested their weight, decided on a ball-peen with a rubber grip, and slid it into her backpack—and then her eyes paused on a pair of heavy-duty wire cutters.

She flexed the fingers of her left hand. The tendons felt tight, the muscles tender and unfamiliar, but otherwise fine. She spent the next few minutes clumsily snipping through her homemade cast, and when it finally fell away, the skin beneath was as damp and pale as something drawn from a shell.

She blows into her hand now, trying to warm it, her breath puffing between her fingers in short-lived clouds. The moon glows and casts a sickly light. Claire tries not to look at it. She hates it. She knows how ridiculous it is to hate a spinning ball of rock, but she does, she hates it, as someone can hate a flag tacked to a wall or a corporate logo emblazoned on a smokestack. It reminds her, like a grinning skull, of what she is.

She has never taken Volpexx, has never had to, her doctor a sympathizer, a family friend who falsely reports their monthly blood tests. But she saw the drug's effects in her friend Stacey, who sometimes seemed deadened, especially when the moon fattened, when the dosage was most potent. Her words slurred. Her posture hunched. Her skin appeared yellow except for the purplish half-moons beneath her eyes. She fell asleep in class, forgot her homework.

Even unmedicated, Claire feels no desire to transform. And that's what it's about, desire. Letting go, they call it. Letting go, allowing the animal to take over, like an unleashed id. Most can control the change, as you might anger or desire—choosing not to swing a fist, cop a feel—but when stressed or exhausted, when pushed too hard, overwhelmed by the weight of the world, not everyone can hold back, the animal rising unbidden, invading the body and mind. The moon makes it worse. The lunar effect, they call it, for the spike in robberies, suicides, murders, births, car accidents, transformations.

The road is walled by pine trees. Her footsteps, following the white line that edges the asphalt, are the only sound. At the edge of town she passes a Burger King, its sign glowing, its windows dark. In observance of the full-moon Sabbath, restaurants close; only vital services remain open. Hotels, hospitals, police. Gas stations. The red star of a Texaco blazes up ahead, and a few minutes later, when she walks past the pumps, the fluorescent lights buzz above her like sick cicadas.

The store is empty save for the man behind the counter. Thirties. Hollow eyed. Mossy goatee hanging as low as the crucifix flashing around his neck. She asks if he knows where to find Battle Creek Road. He says he's never heard of it. She asks if he has a smart phone she could borrow and he says if he could afford a smart phone he wouldn't be working the late shift at the Texaco.

Outside, a semi idles at the diesel island. She can barely make out the shape of the driver, a shadow darker than the rest inside the cab, but she knows he is watching her. She can feel it. Her skin tightens. The red tip of a cigarette glows in the cab and the semi seems to expel its smoke in the exhaust rising from the bullhorn pipes. The steel trailer behind the cab is pocked with air vents. Sheep on their way to slaughter. She can hear their panicked bleating, can see here and there a bulging eye, a damp black snout.

Another quarter mile and a sidewalk and streetlamps appear. She hurries between their cones of light. Three cars are parked at the AmericInn and she guesses the purple Datsun belongs to the night clerk, a woman with dream-catcher earrings and a coal-black dye job that doesn't match her wrinkled face. Claire tries to keep her voice calm, even when the woman looks around as if for another customer and asks if Claire plans to get a room or what, then sighs heavily when the answer is no. But Claire doesn't move and the woman at last gives in and taps the address into Google Maps and says, "Battle Creek?"

"Yes."

"Not Battle River?"

"The note says Battle Creek."

"Got nothing for Battle Creek, but I got Battle

River. Ten-twenty Battle River." Her throat is corroded, her breath smelling like the ghosts of a thousand dead cigarettes. "South of town a ways. Then west. You got a ways to go. Five miles at least." She clicks the mouse and the printer hums and spits out a piece of paper bearing a map in gray scale. "Hope you find what you're looking for."

She follows Highway 97 south of town. Streetlights vanish. Houses appear less and less frequently, islands of light set back in the woods. Now and then the trees break and she can make out the white glowing jawline of the Cascade Mountains. Every time she passes a road, many of them gravel, she consults the sheet of paper with her flashlight, as if the map might have shifted when she wasn't looking.

Her feet can't move fast enough, not out of excitement but from worry. Her father made a mistake. Maybe the street is wrong—or maybe the town is wrong—or maybe they're both wrong. Maybe it's all wrong, even the house number. He was hurried and nervous, after all, penning a note he knew might be his last. She can't help but curse him. Just as she can't help but push forward.

Her mind is so busy, she does not notice the semi until it is nearly upon her. Its headlights brighten the night to the color of an old bruise. It blasts past her, and in the air it displaces, she smells the sheep in the trailer, the shit-soaked heat of them. Another hundred yards and its taillights flash red. The semi rolls to a stop, braking with the sound of a big animal clearing its throat.

She slows her pace. She remembers the truck driver in Minneapolis, how worried she was and how kind he turned out to be. Her hand fumbles with the zipper of his coat, now hers, and draws it snug to her neck. She glances behind her—at the empty stretch of road, like a long black snake banded with black and yellow stripes—and tries to remember the last time she saw a car.

She removes the hammer from her backpack and holds it against her leg. The distance closes between her and the semi, and soon she can hear hooves tocking against steel, can hear a waterfall of piss splash through the grating and onto the asphalt. She walks the length of the trailer, and, now ten yards ahead, the passenger door yawns open and emits the faint orange glow of a furnace. She stops and says, at a yell she hopes will carry over the noise of the engine, "I didn't have my thumb out."

No response. The engine idles. She can feel it inside her, a trembling. She doesn't know whether to run away or run toward the open door and beg a ride. She knows five miles should feel like nothing after two thousand, but the night is cold and she is tired and her aunt—is that possible?—might be waiting for her. She can't picture a face—it's been too long—but she imagines a straight-backed woman in a kitchen, pulling mugs from the cupboard, setting a kettle on the burner and looking toward the front door expectantly, anticipating her knock.

Her grip on the hammer tightens. Her feet make chewed-ice sounds along the shoulder when she creeps forward. She half expects to recognize the driver, the man from Minneapolis here to rescue her once more, a kindly smile on his face, his hand outstretched. But of course it is not him.

He is wearing a clown mask. That's the first thing that goes through her head when she steps into view: he is wearing a clown mask, why on earth is he wearing a clown mask? He perches on the passenger seat, backlit by the overhead light. The mask's eyes are black hollows, the hair a wild red color that matches the too-big lips stretching around a too-big grin.

The sheep bleat and the engine hums and he says, "Come here. Come here right now." He speaks in the tone of a man commenting on the price of gas—quietly terse—and this is what scares her most, his calmness. Before she can spin away, he launches himself off the seat, onto her.

They crash to the ground. Her backpack digs painfully into her spine. He lays an arm across her chest, pinning her. She must be dreaming. Isn't that what people always think when faced with the impossible? And what could be more impossible than this: her parents are dead—her house is riddled with bullets—and now, after traveling halfway across the country, she will be raped by a stranger in a clown mask who crushes her with his weight, the shape of him blotting out the stars above, erasing the constellations that brought her this far.

But in dreams you wake up when the worst happens. In dreams you cannot feel as she does now: the cold of the cinder at the small of her back, the heat of his sour breath on her face, the scrabble of his bony fingers working their way under her shirt. The sheep whine and stamp their hooves.

She should transform. She knows this. And for one moment she thinks she might—when an electric tremor runs through her, when her body tightens like a fist—and then she swings the hammer and it glances off the man's shoulder. "You'll pay for that," he says and strikes her temple with his fist. She hears a sound like a pool ball dropped on a wooden floor. Now she is adrift, swimming between two worlds, and loses her will to do anything but close her eyes and try to find some dark closet in her mind to hide in, latch the door.

☽

Patrick needs to drive, windows down, the night air cold, as sharp as a slap in clearing his head. He leaves behind Old Mountain and the glow of its outlying neighborhoods, preferring the company of darkness, not knowing where he is going, only wanting to get away. Moving is what matters. And being alone in the only space that really feels like his, this shitty Jeep.

The roads are empty. For a good minute he drops his foot to the floor and the engine screams and the speedometer trembles around eighty—and then he eases up, knowing the Jeep will rattle apart if driven too hard.

It's close to midnight, but he doesn't feel the least bit tired, hopped-up as he is now on adrenaline, thinking about Malerie leaning in to kiss Max and then addressing Patrick like a stranger, holding up her hand—the same hand she grabbed him with, now unfamiliar. He was scared of the Americans before she walked in the door—and now they have cause to hurt him if Max ever learns what happened.

"What kind of game are you playing?" he says.

Only the wind replies, whistling through the cracks in the nylon shell. He has his arm out the window, flattening his palm and cutting through the cool air that drags against it so that his hand looks like a pale fish struggling against a dark current.

Some movement catches his eye, and he glances past his hand and nearly jumps at what he sees. At first he mistakes them for wolves, the dozen or so coyotes that pour out of the forest and move as a pack along the shoulder of the highway. He slows, and for a while the coyotes keep pace with him, a rippling wave of gray. Then he accelerates and watches them fall away in the rearview mirror, their eyes reflecting the taillights, glowing red.

Later, he will wonder if they were summoned by the smell of sheep, and if he was driven wild by the full moon, but now, when he rounds a bend and comes upon the parked semi and the two figures struggling in the anemic wash of its headlights, his mind is empty, his body seemingly separate and acting on its own impulse when he stomps the brake and jumps out of the Jeep and races toward them—a man struggling to hold down a woman.

"Hey," Patrick yells, and at the last second the man lifts his head and reveals the powder-white face and red toothy grin of a clown. By then it is too late for Patrick to reel back—he is already arrowing through the air. Someone cries out, maybe Patrick, when their bodies impact painfully. Then they are rolling down the shoulder, into the ditch's weedy bottom, where they come to a rest with Patrick on top, the man below him. He snatches the mask and rips it off with a damp, sucking sound.

Beneath it is a flushed pink face, as hairless as an eraser. A man. No matter what kind of monster he first appeared, he is just a man. And a man can bleed. Patrick lashes out, striking him once, twice, mashing his lips against his teeth—and then realizes, too late, why the man is not holding up his arms in defense. He is reaching for something, a rock as big as a fist that comes whistling toward Patrick, a blow to the side of the head that he hears more than feels, his vision momentarily black.

He is on the ground—he knows that—choking on the dust thrown up by their struggle. His vision wobbles into focus in time for him to see the man scramble into the truck and drag the door closed behind him. There is a hiss and a chirp as the brakes release.

Patrick shakes off the pain and struggles to his feet, but the ground seems to be shifting beneath him. He claws up a rock and hurls it after the semi—not even close, twenty feet wide, thwacking the blacktop. Before he can find another, the engine is bellowing and the trailer is shuddering off the shoulder, onto the highway, the red taillights like the eyes of some retreating beast. He watches until it vanishes around a bend, the muggy smell of sheep the only proof it was ever there.

He touches his fingers to his forehead—blood and a loose flap of skin—hopefully nothing serious. At his feet he finds the mask. The red hair frizzes around its head; the red lips stretch around its grin. Where its eyes should be there is only blackness, the kind of black encountered at the bottom of a well too deep to draw a bucket from. He kicks it away in disgust.

The girl remains on the ground. He looks at her and she looks at him and the air feels at once static and loaded, as if there is some kind of undersound his ear can't quite decipher. Like after a bell rings. That's how it is between them. There is something celestial about her, her skin a pale color, but a paleness of the softest gray-white imaginable, as if she had been soaking for years in a bath of moonlight.

"I have a hammer," she says and holds it up for proof.

"You don't need to worry about me."

"I didn't think so. But I want you to know, I have a hammer."

He almost asks if she is okay and then stops himself. Of course she isn't okay. Is she hurt? That's what he wants to know.

"I'll be okay," she says. Her clothes are intact. She isn't bleeding. That might not be the case, Patrick guesses, if he had arrived even a minute later. A minute later and the man might have carried her into the cab of his truck like a spider scuttling to his burrow.

He holds out his hand and she takes it and he hauls her up and for a moment they are too close. "Do you have somewhere to go?" he says.

She takes a step back. "Yes."

"Can I take you there?"

"Yes." She hurries out her answers. No matter what he asked, she would likely say the same, yes. When she follows him to the Jeep, she does so slowly, as if trying to remember how to walk.

Her hand goes for the door handle and misses it. He opens it for her, and when she crawls inside, he asks if she wants to call the police. He didn't catch the license plate, he says, but if they call now, the man won't be able to get far. It is only then, with her teeth bared, that she says, "*No.*" He darts aside when she reaches out and slams shut her door. "No police."

He climbs in the driver's side and grinds the engine to a start. The radio blares—some pop song that comes across as mockingly sweet—and he hurries to snap it off. He checks his reflection in the rearview. His hair hides the wound. The skin is swollen and pouchy, the blood already tacky. His eyes seem all right, no dilation. He'll live.

It's only then that she says, "Thank you," so quietly he almost misses it.

"Forget about it." His fingers close numbly around the steering wheel and he sees his knuckles are torn up. "Where to?"

She hands him a crinkled piece of paper and he studies it a moment. "I don't even know where we are, so this doesn't mean much." He pulls out his handheld and plugs in the address, and a map appears with a red pin tacked in the center of it and a route from their current location. He holds it out to her and the glowing screen chases the shadows from a face that seems at odds with her clothes. She's his age, maybe a little older, and pretty, not the type he'd peg for a runaway or drifter or whatever it is that brings a person to the side of the road in the middle of the night clutching a hammer. "Not far."

They drive. The crowns of the trees are silvered with moonlight and their bottoms skirted with an impenetrable blackness. He steals glances at her often—whatever her name is, he is afraid to ask. Her eyes spill tears, but she doesn't appear to be crying, not in the standard sense. She is so still, sitting ramrod straight, hugging the backpack in her lap. She hasn't even blinked.

What is the proper response in a situation like this? Should he offer a comforting touch or reassuring word? Curse the man for his wretchedness? Crack a joke to ease the tension?

"Hey," he finally says, touching her wrist. He can't find the words—words never come readily to him—but he hopes touching her tells her okay, everything is going to be okay.

☽

She is tired of this nightmare. And now it is almost over. The boy drives her to Battle River, glancing back and forth between his phone and the road, slowing to peer at the mailboxes staked at the end of every driveway. Moonlight falls through the trees in blue patches that tremble at their edges when the breeze blows. He almost misses the driveway, no mailbox, the reflective numbers 1020 nailed to a tree. "There," he says and cranks the wheel hard. Gravel ticks and pops as they shoot down a tunnel of trees several hundred yards long that opens into a clearing.

The headlights illuminate a modest cabin, and parked next to it, a black Ramcharger. They roll to a stop. When a bright white light explodes from the cabin, Claire feels a flare in her chest, believing it to be a porch lamp, someone welcoming them.

Then she realizes what it is, a motion detector, and feels instead like an intruder.

"This isn't your house," the boy says.

"No."

"But you know who lives here?"

"Yes," she says, and then, "No."

The heater wheezes. She unclips her seat belt.

"Do you want me to come with you?" the boy says and she says no and he says, "I'll wait and make sure somebody answers."

"Don't worry. Somebody's home." And indeed, she feels something, as though she has come upon a place where deer slept in the woods, the flattened grass still warm. Someone is here, if not in the cabin, then nearby.

She swings open her door and shoulders her backpack. She needs the boy to leave, to forget about her. She supposes she shouldn't have shared the address with him—not knowing what kind of trouble her aunt might be in—just as she shouldn't have approached the open door of the semi. She needs to be more careful. She has lost her trust in the world. There are too many monsters. "You can go now."

"Just knock and—"

"*Go.*" The word comes out more forcefully than she intended, and the boy's face tightens with concern. It occurs to her that he is kind and handsome, that this sort of thing used to matter to her. "Thank you," she says. "But I'm fine."

He stares at her another moment, then nods, but instead of driving off he retrieves a notebook from the backseat and a pen from his pocket. He scrawls his name and phone number on a piece of paper he rips out and hands to her. "Just in case."

She scrunches it into her pocket, and when his hand rises to the gearshift she closes the door on him. The Jeep swings around and putters down the driveway, soon lost from sight except as a ghostly sphere of light floating through the trees.

Her mind feels unnervingly heightened. It is the moon, she suspects, the moon and the attack and the chance that she has finally made it, that she will soon be safe. She shivers not from the cold but from nerves. Anyone else, she supposes, would be in shock right now. She is beyond shock.

A gravel path is the only thing that separates her from the cabin. The longer she looks at it, the longer it seems to grow, taunting her, daring her forward. She squints into the harsh light of the motion detector mounted at the peak of the roof. If the porch beneath it was brightly lit, then maybe she would feel a greater sense of urgency, but the windows are dark, meaning no one is home or someone is sleeping, maybe her aunt or maybe not, and if not, then what? She will have no one; she will be nowhere. She has no defense against these thoughts that flit through her mind like ragged-winged moths.

She tries to command her feet to move—to get it over with already—and at first her body falters, not listening to her. She leans forward and that does it, the weight pulling her onward, one step and then another. Her shadow rolls alongside her, a small black ball, maybe all that remains of the old Claire shackled to her. She crunches down the path and climbs the front porch and knocks at the front door. And waits. She hears no footsteps inside and no crickets in the forest, only the hush of a breeze that carries the smell of snow down from the mountains.

Again she raps her knuckles against the door, more insistent this time, until her knuckles feel like they might split. Someone is here—someone has to be here. She feels it. "Hello," she says.

From behind her comes a voice: "I'm right here, Claire."

CHAPTER 15

AUGUSTUS NURSES CHASE through the next few weeks. The living room becomes a makeshift hospital. An air mattress replaces the bloodstained tarp. He smears disinfectant and changes bandages. He draws a warm bath and seasons it with alcohol and tincture of iodine. He buys OxyContin off one of his neighbors, a doctor and campaign donor, and dopes away the pain with 160 mg doses. He serves Chase Gatorade to get his electrolytes up, brings him platters of eggs and toast when he has an appetite. All the while Augustus wears a mask, goggles, and latex gloves. Every day he disposes of the black plastic garbage bag that grows big bellied with soiled bandages and washcloths and latex gloves he peels off as carefully as if they were a diseased condom.

He tells the staff, the reporters, that Chase is at a strategy retreat. When they ask if the rumors are true, if he has taken ill, Augustus laughs and says, "He's, as always, the picture of health."

When Chase sleeps—and he sleeps often, sometimes sixteen hours a day—Augustus sits at the kitchen table with his laptop open, a pen and yellow legal tablet arranged next to it. He plugs into Google different word combinations involving lycans, lobos, prions. He knows he ought to know more, but as with AIDS, the disease feels so *other* that he has learned only to fear it in the abstract. Here are some of the things he discovers:

The earliest documentation of a lycan can be found in the cave systems of Revsvika, on the island of Moskenesøy, Lofoten. You must worm through a tunnel only a few feet wide until you come to an open cavern full of shamanistic pictographs, one of them a man with the head of a wolf. His hands—with long claws in place of fingers—are held above his head as if in benediction. And at his feet lies the carcass of what appears to be a sheep. Carbon dating estimates the drawing as seventh century.

The latest U.S. census lists persons infected with lobos at 5.2 percent.

Lobos is not a bacteria and it is not a virus, despite its commonly being referred to as such. It is a *prion*—a word derived from *protein* and *infection* and assigned to infectious agents that are made not of nucleic acids but instead of misfolded protein. Prions come in multiple strains, like viruses, capable of producing different symptoms in different hosts. Mad cow disease is another common example, chronic wasting disease another. All known prion diseases affect the brain and neural tissue, creating vacuoles in the nerve fibers that eventually lesion and degenerate into spongiform encephalopathy. The pathogen is untreatable but the degenerative process is slow enough that humans typically do not live long enough for the pathogen to prove fatal.

In an article by Amant J. Dewan, professor of history at Harvard University, Augustus learns that widespread infection began in Scandinavia, where, in the Faroe Islands, the brains of wolves were ritually eaten on the night of the winter solstice. It is believed—through the cross-checking of dozens of runic Old Norse documents—that lobos first broke out in the early seventh century among the wolf population, as chronicled in their loss of balance, shaking, and physical wasting. An apparent incessant itching overcame the animals and caused them to scratch their hindquarters on anything available, even after their fur and skin were scraped away. The villagers had always believed they consumed the strength and cunning of the wolf—but at this time, they feasted instead on highly infectious prions that mutated in their human host.

Everyone responds to the pathogen differently. For some, the incubation period is several weeks. For others, ten years or more. The adrenal gland stimulates the lobos prions. The parts of the brain most affected: the amygdala, which controls anger, and the hypothalamus, which controls hunger. Like a virus, its aim is to reproduce. It does so when the host lashes out. Because the gums bleed during transformation, the prions propagate themselves through a bite, often directed to the back of the neck, seeking out the closest route to neural tissue.

Sweat cannot carry the disease; a cough or a sneeze cannot carry the disease. You cannot get lobos from shaking hands or sharing a soda. You cannot get lobos from a scratch. Like AIDS, it can pass from parent to child and must be blood-borne or sexually transmitted to successfully find a new host. Whether the host is in a latent or heightened (commonly known as "transformed") state does not matter: the disease is in the host's blood and that blood remains contagious.

The word *lobos* comes from *wolf*, as does *lobotomy*, an operation that puts one out of one's mind—and isn't that the very essence of the infection?

Most people with the disease live healthy, happy lives. Volpexx, lycan groups claim, is merely a safeguard. Lycan attacks are in fact as uncommon as shark attacks—but in both cases, media attention makes them seem more prevalent than they are. The average lycan, one website says, would no more attack a human than the average hunter would turn a gun on a friend.

The Lupine Republic was established in 1948 after nearly two thousand years of dispersal and more than fifty years of attempts to create a lycan homeland. It is located between Finland and Russia, a northern territory largely uninhabited at the time and now populated by several million lycans and U.S. personnel. The country has prospered, with the discovery of uranium reserves, but the past fifteen years especially have been rife with conflict as a result of terror attacks by extremist forces protesting U.S. occupation and advocating state autonomy. They are in the minority, with 80 percent of lycans supporting uranium extraction and U.S. involvement for the economic stability and physical security.

Augustus creates a favorites folder for several dozen webpages—and then pauses for a long time, with his pen in his hand and the glow of his laptop swimming across his glasses, when he discovers there are five prion research centers in the country, one of them based at the University of Oregon.

☽

The showerhead is caked white with mineral deposits. From it comes sulfur-smelling water, but

Claire steps into it happily. For too long she has not bathed except to splash herself with water and soap in gas station restrooms. A whorl of dirt forms around the drain and doesn't go away. Nothing has ever felt so good. She showers until the hot water fades and she begins to shiver. When she pulls aside the curtain, the air eddies with fog as though a cloud has descended upon the room.

She has conditioned her hair three times and even then cannot get the knots out of it. After she towels off, she opens the vanity and finds a pair of styling scissors. She swipes a hand across the mirror and almost immediately the clear patch gives way to fog. She turns on the fan and the fog spins slowly away. For some time she regards her reflection in the mirror. A swollen black bruise veins out of her temple.

She grips the scissors. She holds out a length of hair. She snips, once, and then again. It gets easier with every cut. She tosses big damp clumps in the toilet. She stops when her hair is jaw length and the person in the mirror looks like a stranger.

She steps from the bathroom wrapped in a towel. Miriam appears in the doorway of her bedroom and blinks hard at the sight of her. "Hardly recognize you."

"That's the idea, I guess."

Miriam waves Claire into the room. Her bed, a

queen with a wrought-iron frame, takes up most of the space. A lamp and a handgun rest on the nightstand. A pine bureau squats beneath one of the two windows, both of them boarded over. Miriam says, "You a size four?"

"Used to be."

"We're about the same." Miriam motions to the bureau and closet. "Try on whatever."

Weekends, back in Wisconsin, Claire used to sleep ten-, twelve-hour stretches. Around noon her father would knock gently on her door and say, "Claire? That's enough, don't you think?" But it never seemed to be—she could never get her fill—a yawn stretching her face as she stumbled down the hall for a cup of coffee, a bowl of Apple Jacks.

Her first few days at the cabin, tired as she is, she cannot fall asleep, and once she does, she cannot stay asleep, so that her days and nights are hazily threaded with dreaming and waking, her eyes shuttering closed when flipping through a novel and then snapping open again at the dinner table with a cold plate of spaghetti before her and her aunt studying her. She is hiking along the shoulder of the road, staring at a dark bank of clouds that might carry rain. She is standing in a gas station restroom, letting the dryer blast her hands just to get warm. She is struggling against the weight of a man in a clown mask, and when she rips it away, a red skull grins back at her. The whole world seems a threat; the whole world wears a mask.

As much as she wants to, she can't allow herself to relax, can't feel safe, the weapons arranged throughout the cabin and the plywood planks shielding the windows making her feel as if she has stumbled into an uncertain fortress.

When Claire asks Miriam why—why the stronghold defenses?—she says, "Because there are people hunting me."

"The same people who came for my parents?"

"Different people. But just as dangerous."

☽

The dinette runs up against the living room and Augustus sits at the table, spooning into a bowl of cottage cheese, while Chase weakly attempts to exercise. For the past few weeks he has done nothing but sleep and stumble back and forth to the bathroom. He needs to get the blood flowing again, he says, or he might rot away into a husk.

"You understand the way this works, I assume?" Augustus says.

Chase is wearing a pair of gray sweatpants and

nothing else except for the bandages that patch his arm and torso. He dips up and down, his face red and wet with sweat. "You get bit by a rabid dog, you get rabies—isn't that the gist of it?"

"Not exactly. Saliva isn't enough—thank God—or every sneeze on a subway would infect a dozen people." The spoon clicks against the bowl and then his teeth. "We're fortunate that lobos is more like HIV, a blood-borne contagion. A bite doesn't guarantee infection, but it's quite possible. A lycan's gums bleed after they transform, and it's a great way for the prion to propagate itself."

"I'm fucked."

"If by that you mean, 'Am I infected?' Yes, I think we can assume as much. But if by that you mean, 'Am I finished as a politician?' Not necessarily. Three people know what happened in that room. One of them is dead."

Chase dips down and tries to hold his position but wobbles and loses his balance. "You think we can hide this?"

"It will require lifestyle changes." Augustus shoves another spoon of cottage cheese into his mouth and speaks through his chewing, his voice thick and mucousy. "I'm going to look into getting you a prescription for medicinal marijuana. And it looks like I can get Volpexx delivered from Canada—maybe we can try that in low doses. But right now you need to stay calm, stay in control, stay human. That means no more women. No more binges. No more temper tantrums."

Chase gives up on the squats and walks to the window and stares out into the day. Clouds hang like a dark, low ceiling. A maple sapling, stripped of its leaves, shakes against the wind. "That's not really my style, is it?"

"No," Augustus says. "No, it is not."

☽

Miriam is handsome more than pretty. Claire can see her father in her. The muscular jaw and squared shoulders. Eyes as blue as an acetylene torch. But while her father always had a smile flashing beneath his beard, Miriam seems incapable of humor, her expression stony, her mouth a lipless black slit. She never stops moving and wears a black tank top that shows off arms roped with muscle.

The idea of family has, up to this point, evaded Claire. When she complained about visiting her nana at the nursing home, or about attending a barbecue with her cousins, her mother would always say, "They're family," as if that explained everything. Now Claire finally understands it, the importance of blood. That someone like Miriam, who is otherwise a stranger, would take her in without question.

Their conversations, rushed and interrogative, are broken up by long silences. They sit on opposite ends of the couch. Claire has her legs tucked under her and her aunt leans forward with her forearms on her knees. At first Miriam has only questions—"And then what happened?" is one of her favorites—about the home invasion, her father's note, the seemingly endless passage from Wisconsin. Claire expects more of a reaction when she describes the gunfire erupting downstairs, but Miriam only lowers her head and says, in a muted voice, that she knew, from the moment she spotted Claire on her doorstep, that her brother must be dead.

Then her voice is sharp once more. "Who was that boy? The one in the Jeep."

"He was nobody." Claire explains what happened—everything about the night, including the truck driver, whom up to this point she has kept secret. She braces herself, expecting Miriam to pull her into a hug and tell her how sorry she is. Instead her aunt rises from the couch and disappears from the living room. Claire can hear her aunt down the hall, in the kitchen, a cupboard closing, glasses rattling. A moment later she appears with two tumblers of whiskey. Without a word she hands one to

Claire. They raise the glasses in a grim toast and drain them. Claire coughs into her fist. Her chest blazes as though she has swallowed a coal.

Miriam sets down her glass on the coffee table with a click. "That was stupid, you know, bringing that boy here. Really stupid."

"I know."

"He knows your face. He knows where we live."

"I know," Claire says and drops her gaze to the floor, but really, despite the strong poison of what Miriam has to say, all Claire can concentrate on is a single word, *we*. Where *we* live. It makes her want to cry out with relief.

☾

Claire tries to keep busy. She sweeps the floor. She turns the toilet paper around so that it pulls forward. She alphabetizes the books. She washes the dishes, letting the towel linger on a plate before setting it on the rack to dry. She opens up the fridge and stares into its cold white hum. Small tasks, everyday rituals, bring her comfort after living in a free fall.

She finds flies in the sinks. Flies on the windowsills. Flies on bedcovers, flies even beneath her sheets, buzzing. The cabin hasn't been opened in a long time and the air has a stale, rank quality.

She has longed for a roof over her head, but she finds herself so used to the open sky that the boarded-up windows make her feel trapped.

She tells her aunt as much. At that moment Miriam is peering out one of the window slits, and when she glances at Claire a band of light divides her face. “You want to chop wood?”

“Anything. So long as it’s outside.”

Miriam returns her gaze to the window and uses her teeth to shred dry skin off her lower lip. “I suppose it’s safe. So long as we’re armed. And you stay close.”

“You think somebody might be out there?”

“I don’t know. I don’t think so. Not right now. But somebody came for me a few weeks ago.”

“What happened to him?”

Miriam makes her hand into the shape of a gun and points it at Claire. “Bang.”

Chase appears in the statehouse rotunda in dress uniform—peaked cap, midnight-blue jacket with red trim and a standing collar. Behind him, when he tromps down the marble stairs, follow members of the Oregon National Guard. He approaches the podium, its front adorned with the Oregon seal, and pauses there as the soldiers perform a traditional march. Their swords slash the air and their boots thud the stone floor and make the air tremble. They come to a stop beneath a massive American flag suspended between two pillars.

Chase snaps off a salute and removes his hat to set on the podium. "Thank you," he says, first to the guardsmen and then to the reporters who sit in folding chairs twenty rows deep. Their cameras flash and create a strobe-like effect that blinds him. For three weeks he has not made a public appearance. After appearing everywhere, he was suddenly nowhere, and the media took note. His official statement claimed he was hunkering down for a restful strategy session, but many believed he had fallen ill. The press conference is Buffalo's idea: a show of strength and a bold declaration that will distract from the gossip of his sudden absence.

Despite his rigid posture, despite his small smile, Chase does not feel well. He doesn't feel like himself—maybe that's a better way to put it. He is a man divided, host to a pathogen that can overtake him at any moment. Sometimes his heart races and his breath comes in hurried pants. His muscles ache. His toothbrush pulls away from his mouth bloody. He rakes a hand through his hair and finds it wet with sweat. He can smell himself, his armpits and crotch damp musky pockets. His consciousness sometimes feels as though it has short-circuited, whirling with lights, through which dart, alternately, the silhouette of a man, and then a wolf.

Buffalo warned him about this. It will take time to get used to his condition, physically, emotionally, an alien pregnancy capable of tearing through his belly, strangling him with its umbilical cord. *Symbiotic* is the word Buffalo used. Cursed is how Chase thinks of it. Volpexx will make things easier. Volpexx—Buffalo promised, once they get their hands on a shipment of it—will be the equivalent of a choke chain.

Good thing. The infection has a tumorous effect on the adrenal glands, causing them to double in size. The section of the brain known as the amygdala—which controls emotion—is part of the limbic system and communicates with the hypothalamus, where hormones take effect. Rage or fear or excitement results in a hormonal cue results in an adrenal flood. The effect on the body, during transformation, is equivalent to a towering dose of PCP.

The reporters lower their cameras and the white haze of his vision solidifies. "I stand here a proud, humble Oregon boy." He pauses and cocks his head, at first wondering what he hears, realizing it is their pens scratching across paper, like the noise of hundreds of insects chewing something fibrous. All of his senses have amplified these past few days especially. He can feel the tags on his shirts and the stitching in his socks. Nothing tastes right—even tap water carries strange flavors of fluoride and metal. He can smell a dead squirrel rotting beneath a bush three blocks away.

Beyond the crowd of reporters stands Buffalo, who makes a get-on-with-it motion with his hand. Chase clears his throat. "My family has lived in this state for three generations. My great-grandfather laid roads in Eastern Oregon. My grandfather designed the lumber mill that was for so many years the industrial heart of Old Mountain. My father ran a six-thousand-head cattle ranch. My roots go deep." He almost never speaks from scripted material, but Buffalo says that has to change, that he can no longer leave anything to chance and risk a flash of fear or anger.

Somewhere in the distance he hears a siren. A police cruiser, he feels certain, though really he has no idea how to tell the difference between the wail of one compared to that of an ambulance or fire truck. Regardless, someone is in trouble.

"Some of you might remember there was a time when the billboards at our state's border read WELCOME TO OREGON. NOW GO HOME." Many in the audience smile. "It was a joke, but not really. Oregon is a treasure. And we did not want it spoiled by outsiders. Which is exactly what has happened.

We've become a haven—especially those liberal enclaves of Eugene and Portland—for lycans. We have compromised our borders and our safety. One thing I know as a rancher, you've got to build good fences.

"I am introducing legislation that I hope will be approved by year's end." He pauses when the cameras flash again and the reporters whisper among each other, the sound like a gathering wind. "Initiatives include stricter testing, criminal penalties, and lifetime supervision as well as a public registry containing names, photographs, and addresses, accessible online. We will also reconstitute the Lycan Advisory Board—dissolved in the 1970s—and I have asked Chief of Staff Augustus Remington to serve as chair."

For the moment no one speaks—no one looks up—all of them bent over their notebooks and laptops, writing furiously. A cell phone rings and goes unanswered. He spots the red eye of a video camera blinking at him. He stares into it. "There should be absolutely no mercy shown to any lycan offenders in our state, and our legislation serves to impose the strictest standards of supervision to ensure that we are protected. Our old way of worrying about who might be offended must be radically altered to account for keeping people safe. New policies will require open minds, a willingness to do things differently, more strictly. The expense to some will be to the benefit of many. This state can benchmark the nation's policies. And to those who think my goals are too high, too extreme, I say, you ain't seen nothing yet."

He ends the speech by facing the flag, placing a hand over his heart, and offering a somber rendition of "America the Beautiful."

He doesn't field questions, but they ask them anyway. When he escapes up the stairs, he can hear every one of their voices calling after him. But as Buffalo predicted, not one of them wants to know about job growth or corporate income taxes or commercial property taxes or whether it's true he's taken ill.

The chopping block is a scarred, ancient stump. Next to it sits a pile of freshly chainsawed logs that smell of pine resin. They heft the logs, one by one, onto the stump to split twice over. Then they carry the armful of sticks to the woodpile stacked the length of the cabin.

This was her favorite fall chore. Her father would buy a permit and the two of them would drive along Forest Service roads and buzz down a few tagged trees and shave away the branches and load the logs into the bed of the truck to take home and spend the next few weeks splitting.

She thinks of him now, the pain in her heart matching the pain in her wrist, which she tries to ignore when she hefts the splitting maul. The two women sweat, despite the day's chill. They take off their sweatshirts, and their forearms rash over from carrying the wood. Miriam keeps her eyes on the forest and occasionally touches the Glock holstered at her belt for reassurance.

The ax's wooden handle is polished to a hard gloss from the hands that have constantly gripped it. Claire swings it in an arc and it catches, with a sound like a cough, in the log, which hasn't been properly seasoned, its wood hard to split, as white and wet as an apple's core. Some of the logs are so tight grained they must use a sledgehammer and a wedge. Her arms ache pleasantly.

They work in a comfortable silence that Miriam finally breaks. "How much do you know about your parents?"

Claire has been waiting for this moment, has been waiting for what she doesn't know how to ask. Her swing falters and the ax blade catches in the log and she wobbles it back and forth and then kicks the log to release it. "My mother likes to quilt. She doesn't wear makeup. She cans beets and pickles and tomatoes. She reads a book a week, usually something historical or political. Her favorite color is yellow." She realizes she is talking in the present tense and doesn't bother correcting herself. "My father—"

Miriam steals the ax from Claire and lifts it over her head. "You're saying you don't know anything."

"They're the most boring people in the world. What's there to know?"

Miriam steps forward and drops the ax and the wood splinters and the blade buries itself in the anchor log. "You have no fucking idea."

☽

The sky is closing down and dark is coming. It's that time when the day isn't really gone but isn't really here. Augustus escorts Chase to his home in Keizer, a white neocolonial with black shutters. He does not entertain visitors, so the walls are as white and bare now as they were the day he moved in, the rooms mostly empty except for an IKEA table and chairs in the dinette, a couch set before a widescreen television in the living room, a mattress and box spring in the master suite upstairs. The office is the only room that matters to him, and it is busy with file cabinets, crowded bookshelves, and two desks arranged in the shape of an L.

The basement remains unfinished, the ceiling bare studs, the walls cinder block, the floor a sloping concrete with a central drain. Three naked lightbulbs offer meager light. Augustus stuffed the recessed windows with insulation and covered them with plywood to muffle the sound and prevent anyone from peering inside. He hired a security firm to install a steel cage, its panels built out of heavy-duty six-gauge wire welded at every wire contact point. The swinging door is hinged with flanged head bolts and fitted with an industrial padlock made with a case-hardened alloy steel shackle.

A garden hose runs from the industrial sink into a coil on the floor. Later, he will use it to spray away the shit and piss and blood, the foaming tide of it swirling down the central floor drain.

Chase pauses before the cage and says, “I hate this,” and Augustus says, “I know,” and puts a hand on his shoulder to show his support and encourage him forward. “Take off your clothes,” Augustus says. “You don’t want to ruin them like the last time.”

It is not that he grows larger. It is that he soils himself in excitement, claws himself in agitation. Chase peels off his uniform and tosses it into a ball outside the cage. Thin scars crosshatch his shoulders and chest where the claw marks healed over.

His left forearm is a lumpy mass of reddish scar tissue.

The door clicks shut and the padlock snaps into place and Augustus settles into the aluminum folding chair and adjusts his glasses and rests his hands on his knees like a theater patron who waits for the lights to dim, the curtains to part.

Every night, he transforms. Augustus demands it. To get it out of his system and exhaust his body. To normalize it, control it. Transformation does not come easily, he has told Augustus, every bone seeming to break, his skin crawling with angry wasps. He cries out and falls to the floor. His body contorts itself as if run through with electricity. From what Augustus has read, this will get easier over time, like a nerve deadened by repeated blows.

"This never would have happened," Augustus says under his breath, "if you had just listened to me."

As if in response, Chase hurls himself against the bars of the cage. He would have made a fine berserker, Augustus thinks, those Norse lycans who so long ago worked themselves into a frenzy, transforming before battle and fighting in a savage trance.

This would take time, months maybe, but Augustus, as a boy, owned several dogs, and with discipline and patience they all learned to fetch his slippers and shit outside. He has no doubt the same will be true of Chase. “Isn’t that right, old friend?”

Chase circles his enclosure. His arms lash at nothing but air. His teeth snap together as though chattering out some code. He presses his face, wild-eyed and misshapen and split by a fanged grin, against the cage.

There is a fridge in the corner, and Buffalo withdraws from it a package of raw hamburger. He tears off the plastic and crushes his fingers into the bloody mess. He molds tiny red balls and tosses them into the cage and, with a peculiar little smile, watches Chase devour them, one after another.

CHAPTER 16

A FROG LIES on a black dissection tray, the flaps of its belly pinned open to reveal guts like damp jewels. Patrick prods it with a scalpel and scissors and makes notes on his lab report. He breathes through his mouth and can vaguely taste the smell of formaldehyde. His right hand, gripping the scissors, still hurts. It has been a week since the full moon—since he saved the girl from the side of the road—and when he woke the next morning, he wasn't sure if she was real or the shades of a dream that settled into the bruises ruining his knuckles.

Across the room, the teacher—Mr. Niday, a goateed man with sweat stains constantly darkening his armpits—comments on a three-legged frog, how common mutations are due to pesticides and parasites and how frog populations are declining precipitously and how something needs to be done and—

Patrick's attention turns to his pocket as it buzzes twice. He checks to make sure Mr. Niday is still occupied with the three-legged frog and pulls out his handheld. A text from Malerie reads, "Skip lunch. Meet @ ur Jeep."

He is so distracted that, when a few minutes later Mr. Niday appears behind him and asks how he is doing, Patrick says fine even as he slices through the heart he didn't know was there.

He has been avoiding her. But now—God knows why; sometimes he can't help himself—he is driving around Old Mountain with her. The day is bright and washed of its color. She has the radio up and the windows down. She sings the Stones around a lit cigarette—"Well, you've got your diamonds and you've got your pretty clothes"—the lyrics carried by clouds of smoke.

He turns off the radio and she keeps singing another moment without it. In the silence that settles between them, he licks his lips, not sure what to say. "I don't understand what's going on."

"We skipped school and now we're driving around."

"You and Max. You're together."

The tip of her cigarette burns as bright as a cherry. "He's all right."

"If he finds out there's something between us..."

"Scared?"

Something in the engine block whines. His

odometer flips over to 145,000. “I don’t like trouble. I’ve had too much trouble.”

The road angles and the sun flashes through the window and settles on her hair to create a blazing red halo. “I’m hungry.” She snaps on the radio again and says over the music, “Where are you taking me?”

He shakes his head, not knowing whether to smile or kick her out the door. A few miles later, he pulls in to Hamburger Patties, where they order shakes and burgers, a basket of waffle fries, splats of mustard and ketchup in tiny paper cups.

“You believe in Max?” he says. “The Americans and all that?”

“And all that.” She shrugs and finishes off a bite of hamburger. “It’s something to do, people to be with.” She darts her tongue out and tastes her milk shake, her tongue lingering in it before curling upward, like a beckoning finger, back into her mouth.

“Jesus,” he says. “You are pushing all kinds of buttons.”

She wants to drive around. Someplace remote. He knows better but can’t stop himself. When she touches him on the shoulder or the hand, it’s like a jolt from a live wire. “I think I know a place,” he says.

He glances at his handheld to study a map of the town he hasn't yet memorized. The app boots up and displays his last entry, Battle River Drive. He hesitates—too long; he can feel her eyes on him—before thumbing *save* and then views a map of Old Mountain and orients himself.

They trail a garbage truck on its way to the dump. A damp sheet of newspaper flutters out of it and splats onto his windshield, flattening there, the Sunday comics. Malerie screams with delight. The sun soaks through the paper and colors their bodies with squares of light. Patrick kicks on the wipers and the newspaper is gone and they are driving past the dump and hanging a left onto a chained-off driveway that leads to the abandoned lycan school. He takes the Jeep off road, to avoid the chained entry, and then chunks back onto the driveway, which opens into a weed-choked parking lot. Broken asphalt mutters beneath the tires.

Malerie smears ChapStick across her lips and pops them. "You know Max is straight edge, right?"

Patrick negotiates the Jeep through an old basketball court, the chain nets like rusted chandeliers, and then they are behind the school, out of view from the road. "He said kind of."

"Yeah, kind of." She snorts more than says this.

"No drugs, no smoke, no booze." He parks the Jeep and kills the ignition. "He doesn't even let me do this." She unbuckles her seat belt. His eyes dart to meet hers just as she drops her head to his lap.

There is a car coming toward him when he hits his blinker and gets ready to turn back onto the road—a Camry, as white as a polished bone. Behind the wheel he spots his mother. She has her cell phone pressed to her ear and doesn't see him, he's sure of it, distracted by her conversation.

He hesitates a moment before ignoring his blinker, heading in the opposite direction, pulling onto the road behind her, following as she heads out of town.

"What are you doing?" Malerie says.

"I want to check on something."

His dashboard clock reads 88:88. Malerie hits it with the heel of her hand, then goes digging in her purse, withdrawing a hot pink Motorola Razr to check the time. "I need to get to work soon." Three afternoons a week, she doles out pills at Walgreens as a pharmacy tech, and he agreed to drop her off.

"This will only take a minute."

He keeps a hundred yards between her car and his. Another mile and his mother pulls off into the Juniper Creek development, as he guessed she would. He taps the brake and slows nearly to a stop.

"What?" Malerie says.

"Nothing."

CHAPTER 17

MIRIAM CALLS HER WEAK. Her voice is not cruel so much as it is cold and precise. "You haven't been sleeping enough. You haven't been eating and exercising properly. You look scared of your own shadow." If Claire is going to live with her—no, if Claire is going to *live*—she needs to toughen up.

They begin the day with muscle building. They do wide-arm and narrow-grip push-ups on the living room floor. They do dips balanced between the coffee table and couch. Crunches and cherry pickers and leg lifts and lunges and planks. They hurl a medicine ball back and forth as if blasting it from a cannon. Miriam holds up her hands and Claire punches them, one-two, one-two, fast jabs, knuckles smacking palms.

They make a grocery run and fill the cart. They drink protein shakes. They cook a half pound of bacon and scramble eggs in the grease coating the cast-iron pan. They eat beans, thick slices of cheese, summer sausage. Apples. Within five days Claire begins to fill out. She can't see her ribs and she can feel the muscle and fat cording around her bones.

And all this while, usually when they're eating or stretching between workouts, Miriam tells Claire about her parents.

They were part of a radical-line movement, what Miriam calls an underground conscience. This began in the sixties, when they enrolled at William Archer University and lycan political resistance was at its height.

The information is readily available. A quick Google search of their names would have revealed a long string of articles, but it has never occurred to Claire to look. It has never occurred to her that her parents were anything other than NPR-listening armchair philosophers. They talked often about the Struggle, which peaked a few decades ago, but now she sees they were directly part of it—leading May Day demonstrations, joining labor unions, organizing boycotts—their aim to end segregation in schools, segregation in the workplace, segregation in restaurants and bathrooms and pools and hotels and retail stores, and the continued U.S. occupation of the Lupine Republic.

They marched. They hurled rocks and eggs at police. They wrote letters to congressmen and shook signs from street corners. They staged full-moon frenzies in which they would transform en masse in a park or town square. They were arrested and posted bail and were arrested again. The Fourteenth Amendment passed with some concessions but not enough. Lycans could not work in education or medicine or law enforcement, could not serve in the military except in a designated frontline unit nicknamed the Dog Soldiers. Mandatory prescriptions and monthly blood tests remained in effect.

Miriam says, "My brother's principal stance, which I'm sure you've heard ten thousand times before, is that lycans are their own category of person. It is not a disease. It is an identity and way of life." She explains that it was difficult to talk about this scientifically until the discovery of prions in the early eighties. The way the pathogen inhabits the body results in a symbiotic organism that is fundamentally part man and part wolf. "He was arguing for a new categorization of race, which most people aren't willing to consider."

Then, Miriam says, then came the Days of Rage.

Neither Patrick nor his father is much of a talker, and ever since his unit was activated, on the two occasions they have Skyped, fidgety silence has defined their conversations. When they do speak, because of the slow connection, their words garble together so that they constantly say, "What? What was that?" On the computer, his father's face appears pixilated and run through with lines of static. His mouth does not align with his words when he says, "Makes me sick thinking about what happened to you on that plane."

Email is better. They come every day, or every other, usually something small, like "What did u do today?" or "Love ya, bud." His father tells him he should go for a drive, should go visit Neal, and Patrick wants to say he has enough strangers in his life, but he doesn't. His father complains about the snow that won't quit, the wind that blackens skin, the MREs that taste like glue. The temperature dropped below zero the other night and a pipe burst on base and the water pressure coughed out for two days. Occasionally he writes about the war, telling Patrick about the rocket blast that woke him or how his platoon fought their way through an ambush as they humped five miles over steep, rugged terrain, sometimes thigh-deep in snow, only one man injured after getting blown off his feet by a land mine. Telling Patrick, too, that not everyone there is opposed to their presence. That most, in fact, seem pretty happy to see them patrolling the streets, guarding the mines. They work with local police. They meet with villagers, shake hands, share coffee and some godforsaken dish called lutefisk made from stockfish soaked in lye.

Today Patrick's handheld buzzes and he glances at the screen to find an email from his father, keithgamble1@gmail.com. The message reads, "Mountains. Forests. Lakes. This would be a beautiful place if not for all the fuckers who want to kill me."

Patrick nudges Max with his elbow, says take a look at this. They're raking leaves and planting bulbs—tulips, irises, daffodils—outside the local women's shelter. Max pulls off his dirt-smeared gloves and takes the phone and smiles and asks Patrick if he knows how lucky he is, having a father like that. "First thing I do when I hit eighteen," Max says and flips his trowel in the air and catches it, a flash of sunlight on the metal. "I'm heading to that recruitment station, signing on to fight. I assume you feel the same?"

In truth Patrick has been off and on researching colleges but can't help but feel a twinge for Max's approval. "Sure," he says. "I've been thinking about it."

Claire has learned not to ask too many questions at once or Miriam will grow short or cagey or stop talking altogether. She has learned, in small doses, over the past few weeks, that since the 1960s her parents have been on a government watch list, that they have been jailed more times than Miriam can recall, that they eventually lost faith in violence as a strategy for anything but trouble and began, in the eighties, to put their energy into pacifism buttressed by action, organizing nonviolent campaigns that called attention to social injustice. "And then they gave up altogether."

"What happened?"

"They had you."

Miriam says she can smell snow. "Any day now." They are outside the cabin, in the scrub meadow that surrounds it, the sky as gray as concrete, the weeds browned and snapping underfoot. Miriam unrolls a Pendleton blanket and reveals a Glock, a .357, and a shotgun. Claire sets clips and bricks of ammo next to them.

Miriam gives her a quick lesson on the Glock 17. Austrian-made semiautomatic pistol. Self-loading. Polymer frame. Checkered grip. Used by virtually every law enforcement agency. Outperforms any other handgun on the market for ease, accuracy, and durability. Seventeen-round double-stack magazines.

Miriam shows Claire how to feed the magazine, how to disengage the safety, how to aim down the line of the barrel, the ramped front sight, the notched rear sight. "It's got good bark, good bite, so be ready. You're going to have to correct the muzzle rise after every shot."

Claire asks what she should aim for and Miriam points to the edge of the meadow, a pine tree, maybe ten years old, as tall as two men and as wide around as a leg.

The pistol jumps in her hand like something alive when she squeezes off round after round. The gunshots slap through the trees and thunder in her ears so forcibly her hearing feels bruised. Brass casings spit like peanut shells. The smell of sulfur sharpens the air. Most of her shots miss the tree, but a few make it dance, knock pulpy white wads from the trunk.

When she ejects the magazine and slams another into place, she thinks of her parents and the Days of Rage, the three days of demonstrations that took place at this same time of year, October 1969. "The Power Is in the Street" was the heading of the chapter Miriam showed her, apologetically calling the book leftist propaganda. The pages detailed how—during the late sixties and early seventies, at the height of the Struggle, as it came to be known—many lycans came to believe in direct action and violence as political strategy. Anti-government graffiti appeared on buildings, statues were defaced, and leaflets were distributed at high schools and on college campuses. In Chicago, a bomb ripped apart a statue commemorating a policeman who died in the Haymarket Affair. In Milwaukee, a bomb exploded outside city hall and a passenger train was derailed by a slab of concrete set on the tracks; and in Lincoln, several mail trucks and police cars were set on fire. Thousands attended the demonstration in Chicago, where protesters turned over cars and smashed windows in homes and businesses and were beaten and firehosed and teargassed and dragged away by fascist police and National Guard members in full riot gear.

And there was the black-and-white photo of her father, standing before the Chicago federal courthouse, fully transformed, his arms outstretched and his head thrown back in lamentation, standing on a stage before hundreds of people pumping their fists in the air. In his claw of a hand he clutched a burning American flag.

It was beyond surreal, the equivalent of an adult looking up to see Santa and his reindeer track their way across a winter sky; terrifying, almost comical if not for the severe expression on Miriam's face when Claire dropped the book to her lap and said, "This is hard to process." The book was called *The Revolution* and its cover bore the image of a man casting a wolf's shadow. She flipped it over to study the photo on its back cover. A curly-haired man glowered back at her. "Who wrote this anyway?"

"Jeremy Saber. My husband," Miriam said before departing the room and leaving Claire with a mouthful of unanswered questions.

And now Miriam is correcting her stance, educating her in the design and temperament of each weapon, the .357 Smith & Wesson, the Browning pump-action. Another hour and her arm is trembling and her ears are throbbing. She levers the final smoking cartridge and when she lowers the shotgun, the pine tree seems to mimic her, groaning and splintering and slowly bowing until it rests on its side.

"Wow," Claire says. "I am such a badass now."

"Not really."

"Look at that tree! I destroyed it."

"A tree doesn't move. A tree doesn't fight back."

Claire rolls her eyes.

Miriam studies her a moment, hardening her gaze; then—before Claire can register what is happening—her aunt crouches, snaps up a Glock, rolls forward, and blasts three pinecones off the branches of three different trees. Then she brings the pistol to her mouth and sucks the smoke rising from the muzzle and blows it in Claire's face.

Claire stands in stunned silence, then gives a hard swallow. "How do you do that?"

"Do what?"

"React like that? Like you see something coming before anybody else can?"

"How many times have you changed?"

"Maybe ten." Exactly nine.

"In your life?" Miriam shows her teeth when she says this.

"I don't like how it feels."

"*Claire.*" She says the word like a curse. Her mouth quivers as though too full of words ready to come spilling out. But she doesn't say anything more. She marches into the cabin and closes herself away in her room. Thirty minutes later, her door jars open and she grabs Claire by the forearm with enough force to leave a bruise and says, "You are going to learn."

Patrick can't get her out of his head, the girl from the other night. The girl he saved. He saved her. It feels good to think about her that way. After the whole world wanted to call him a hero—for doing nothing, for hiding while everyone on board the plane was ripped to pieces—he cherishes the possibility that he might be capable of something truly good, that the words written about him in articles and spoken to him by reporters might be genuine even if misplaced.

Every time the thought or sight of Malerie makes him feel wrong, his mind circles back to the girl for whom he did something unequivocally right. And every time his phone buzzes, he expects it to be her, her voice hesitant but warm. "I wanted to thank you again," she would say, and he would ask her if she wanted to meet up and she would say yes and he would buy her coffee and they would sit by the sun-soaked window and when their feet touched beneath the table by accident they would smile and make eyes at each other through the steam rising from each of their cups brought simultaneously to their mouths for a taste.

He is thinking about her now—even as Malerie stands before him in Max's basement.

She says it was easy. No trouble at all.

She went to work like always—through the glass-doored entry, between the cash registers, past the photo department, to the office door that opened into a room lit with harsh fluorescent light. She punched her three-digit code into the clock and tossed her purse in her locker and changed into the shapeless dark blue scrubs she hates to wear. Lands' End. The seams irritate her skin and the sizing is all jacked up so they don't fit right. Anyway.

She has three primary functions as a pharmacy tech—*functions*, that's her boss's language. She fills or she works the drop-off or pickup window.

Filling is boring. She hates filling. She rips the patient leaflets off the printer, checks the promised times to make sure they're in order, and fills, fills, fills, the pills clattering like hail into their containers, the containers then slipped into plastic totes, the totes dropped on a conveyor belt where the pharmacists can grab them and verify the product.

Max tells her to get on with it, they don't have all night.

Tonight is Halloween and in the basement everyone is dressed in too-big cammies bought from the army surplus—all except for Malerie, who wears a devil costume, plastic horns and a red Lycra bodysuit from which a barbed tail dangles. She stands before them, her posture bent at the hip. In her hand, a small piece of lined notebook paper with handwriting crisscrossing it. Patrick sits crushed on the couch between Max and a hulking guy named Cash who smells like beef jerky.

Malerie rolls her eyes at Max and continues her story. All this week she's been filling, which she hates, because you don't get to talk to anyone. She likes old people and old people like her. They're sweet. That's why she was happy to get bumped to the drop-off window. So she could talk to people—

and do the job Max asked her to do. The job that, by the way, could easily get her ass fired. Not that she wasn't willing to stick her neck out. "Anything for Max," she says, her eyes on Patrick.

At the window, she takes in prescriptions as people drop them off or when the fax whirs out an order. She scans the Rx into the computer and then types the info and sends it to the pharmacists for review. So she normally enters her initials and an alphanumeric password, which is kind of a problem, since she'll be tagged to anything she does, but luckily, one of the pharmacists hadn't logged out, so it was doubtful anyone would look twice at the record. She opened up the work queue and searched Volpexx and it listed everyone who'd picked up their prescription in the past ten days. All their information is included in their profile: name, address, phone number. She could have print-screened anything she found, but that was too risky because the printer sits by the pharmacists. She keeps a little notebook in her pocket. Everybody does. For passwords and common overrides needed for various insurances. So nobody thought anything of her scribbling away. "And here I am. Here it is," she says and holds out the sheet of paper to Max, at first teasing it away when he reaches for it, then handing it over when he stares hard at her and says, "This isn't a joke, Malerie."

He tells her she can go and she lingers a moment in defiance before turning so quickly her tail whips around her leg. She tromps up the stairs and everyone watches her go except for Max, who scans the names for a long thirty seconds and then raises his eyes to study the group. “Let’s do this.”

They wear camo jackets and pants tucked into black combat boots. They pull white pillowcases over their heads with eyeholes and crooked mouths scissored into them. They shove their hands into black leather gloves. “Keep them on, no matter if you get hot,” Max says. “No fingerprints.” And then they pile into three cars and caravan to the first name on the list, a Mr. James Duncan, at 312 Terrabonne Road.

Trick-or-treating took place earlier in the day, before nightfall, so no children crowd the sidewalks, the side roads mostly empty. Pumpkins glow on porches, the candle flames within them sputtering in the breeze and making their triangle eyes and toothy grins tremble with shadows.

“You’re with us, right?” Max says to Patrick, and Patrick says, “I’m with you.”

They park blocks away from their target. Their boots drum out an angry song on the sidewalk. The night is cold and their breath blooms gray. On

Terrabonne, with baseball bats, they smash out the windows of the car parked in the driveway. On Macintosh and on Ridgeway, they spray-paint a pentagram on a garage door, the hood of a car. On Thirteenth Street, they toss an M-80 with a spitting fuse into a mailbox and run like hell and turn around in time to see the white-orange carnation of flame—the thunder of the explosion knocking them back a step and making them holler with pleasure.

In the Malibu Village trailer court, they navigate the maze of single-wides, the chicken coops, the rusted-out cars up on blocks with mullein flowers spiking through their engine blocks, and find the trailer, a gray vinyl dead whale of a thing. There is a bare-branched tree in the front yard decorated with fishing lures and empty cans of Budweiser and they soak it with lighter fluid and spark a Zippo and it lights like a blue torch.

At the B&B auto detailer, they scale the chain-link fence and move across the asphalt lot lit by high-intensity arc lights. They stare into the security cameras, not worried, hidden by their hoods, when they spray-paint *LYCAN* across the office windows in dribbling black capital letters.

All this time Patrick tries to think of the plane—the lycan exploding from the bathroom, the blood sluicing down the aisle, the bodies stacked and splayed all around him—and he admits to feeling good. Hurting back those who hurt him is a good thing. His heart beats madly, as if it were a poisonous toad trying to leap out of his chest.

When they roar through a high-end development—most of the windows dark at this hour, but a few living rooms still swimming with the blue light of televisions—he is the one who hurls a brick through a window and rains the living room with glittering shards of glass.

They run. And when they do, he might hear a voice calling angrily behind him—"I'm going to kill you, you sons o' bitches!"—as if this were *his* fault, as if he *wanted* this to happen, his life's goal to see his parents split up, his father shipped off to war, a plane full of passengers slaughtered, and when he finally takes the opportunity to lash out and abandon all the vinegary pain stewing inside him, somebody has the gall to threaten him? Part of him wants to rush back with a baseball bat—and the other part of him wants to yell over his shoulder, sorry, he thought things would turn out differently.

CHAPTER 18

IN THE FOOTHILLS of the Cascades, near the base of the North Sister, the forest opens into a red rocky clearing where the air smells sulfuric and steam rises in columns as if from secret chimneys. These are the Blood Bath Hot Springs, pockets of grainy water stained red from the iron in the ground. Around the springs lie tangles of clothes, heaps of beach towels. The rocks are warm to the touch and free of snow. And people, old men and women mostly, are bobbing in the red water up to their chins.

Many believe the water has a medicinal effect. That is why Alice is here with her husband, Craig, who is suffering from a head cold. He is naked now, his coat and collared short-sleeve shirt and pale blue jeans and white tennis shoes stacked on the rocks next to him. His hair is flecked with gray. He wears owlishly round-framed bifocals. And though he is thin, his cheeks are a bit jowly, making his mouth appear downturned, sour. He has a fondness for whistling Christmas carols year-round. You might peg him as the most normal man in the world, but Alice knows better. His breath smells of the tonic water he drinks all day. He has one testicle and a small, thin, uncircumcised penis. She once watched him kill a puppy—that she had brought home from the shelter and that messed on the rug—by stomping on it. He meets people on the Internet and forces her to have sex with them while he watches. He says it's good for her.

Just as he said it would be good for them to visit the hot springs, to soak in them nude, along with the rest of this strange mix of hippies and tourist Europeans floating in the pools around them. She can't tell if his eyes are open or closed, his glasses fogged over, when he sighs deeply and says, "That's better. That's the ticket."

His contentedness will not last long, she knows. Soon he will go back to his sharp-voiced bullying, reminding her how fat she is, how dumb, how boring. She tries to enjoy the moment and leans her head back against the stone lip of the spring and takes in the view. The North Sister rises like a fang. The air is blurry with snow, none of it touching down on the springs, erased by the updraft of heat, and it is as if an invisible dome surrounds them.

Her face drips with sweat. Her heart thuds slowly in her chest. Her skin feels scorched by the heat of the water that she lowered herself into with a hiss. She can see, rising up the nearby hillside, a glacier-fed creek running through a glen fringed with browned ferns that give way to thickly clustered noble firs. Her eyes pause on a log or a boulder—it is hard to tell with snow fuzzing the air—maybe two hundred yards away. She's drowsy from the heat, and her eyelids slip closed—and then snap open as the thing in the glen, whatever it is, a deer or a bear, rises and bounds off into the woods.

"Craig," she says, standing up so quickly she makes a wave that crashes against his face. "Craig, I saw something."

He licks his lips, tasting what splashed across his mouth. His glasses are spotted with water. He takes them off and streaks a thumb across their lenses and sets them on top of his pile of clothes. "You got water on me."

"Up there. Like a wild animal. It was—"

"Shut up. Just shut up. Shut your mouth. Okay? I'm so sick of you. Your voice. It's like a bird being strangled. *God.*"

She realizes her nakedness and sinks into the scalding spring.

She expects him to say something more, but his eyes are closed. It is a relief, not having his gaze on her. In the corner of their bedroom, he arranged a chair, a wooden chair they bought from the Saturday market, rough-hewn and whorled, and this is where he sits when he watches her on their bed. A stranger tearing open a foil packet or smearing oil across her back. Craig never masturbates. He only sits there, so still, his chin in his hand, watching, his eyes swimming behind his glasses.

She surveys the woods, and then this humped and jumbled acre of red rock, wondering if anybody else saw what she saw. An animal. Central Oregon is known for its outdoor recreation, but she can count on one hand the number of hikes she's taken. All of her time is spent at her job, as an office manager for Grayson Insurance Company, or at home, making a hamburger hot dish or folding Craig's underwear into white triangles. The closest she gets to wildlife is the occasional dead deer smeared across the side of the road.

She hears muted conversation, laughter that sounds a long way off. Then a splashing. From one of the springs crawls an old man. Saggy skin, egg-white belly. "My bones," he says and sighs contentedly and stands there a moment, stretching, the water dripping and the steam rising off his skin. When he reaches for his towel, she spots the first lycan.

Though she doesn't immediately recognize it as such. It is standing at the edge of the clearing, seen through churning steam, so still that it appears a part of the forest. A troll, she thinks, a troll like something out of the fairy-tale books she used to read as a child, something that lives in the woods, under bridges.

The old man has a towel over his head like a shroud. He does not see the lycan when it scrabbles across the rocks on all fours and then rises behind him and reaches a claw and pulls away his throat. The old man staggers. The towel remains over his head as a red beard of blood curls down his chest. His arms are outstretched as if to welcome someone into an embrace. But there is no one there to meet him. He falls into the spring from which he rose a minute ago—and the effect is that of a trapdoor. He vanishes from sight. A splash is followed by screams that sound, from a distance, a little like laughter.

Alice joins the noise, crying out. The woods come alive—three, four, five lycans exploding from the trees—clambering across the rocks to enclose the bathers. Water sloshes as people turn in panicked circles or clamber from the springs, running naked across the rocks, the rocks shredding their feet and making them stumble and fall.

She startles at a noise behind her, a clatter of displaced rocks, and spins around to see a lycan approaching them, a small one, the hair on its head the white-yellow of lightning. "Craig," she says, and then again and again, in a rapid-fire string.

Her husband opens one eye to observe her. "Didn't I tell you to shut up?" The eye closes.

She has never seen a lycan before, not outside of a magazine or television program, and what bothers her most are the teeth, too big for their mouths, arranged in bleeding grins. One look and you recognize evil. Unlike her husband—who might as well wear a mask—his ugliness hidden from the rest of the world. She wishes all danger was as obvious as this—a black cape, a third eye, a bleeding grin.

And she can't help but smile back when the lycan moves forward another two steps, its grin seeming to widen as it balances at the opposite edge of the pool, as though considering a soak. Then its arms shoot down and latch hold of her husband and drag him out of the water by his head. He barely has a chance to respond, and then it is too late: the lycan has burrowed its snout into his neck as though to seek out the darkness inside him that is selfsame with its appearance.

She can't help but think, when she turns to run, that she would like to stay. For once she would like to be the one to watch.

CHAPTER 19

SNOW DUSTS THE CLEARING. Their footsteps track a dark stream through it. A minute ago, Miriam led Claire from the cabin, telling her nothing except to strip, and then motioning with her hand to follow. The sun glows through the clouds like a hazy specter but offers no warmth, and when they stand there, Miriam seeming to stare into her, Claire begins to shiver, naked except for her underwear.

Finally Miriam says, "Enough bullshit. It's time."

"I don't know."

"Think of the Tall Man. Think of what he did to your parents."

Claire's throat tightens. "Don't."

Her voice is low and slow, almost a chant. "Think of the bullets cutting through their flesh. Think of them trying to cry out. Think of the footsteps pursuing you. Think about after. After you left. The breath of those men rasping through your house, filling it up. Think of their hands ripping open drawers, digging through them."

"Stop." She feels something deep inside her—

maybe fear or fury—springing open like a black umbrella. Tears make icy trails down her cheeks.

"Go back to that night."

The clouds hang low, a dark ceiling that seems to press downward as if it might collapse under the weight of the sun. Her body no longer shivers—it tremors. She can hear the scuff of her feet shifting beneath her.

"Go back to that night. Instead of running, I want you to fight. I want you to kill those men."

The new Claire likes this idea very much. She knows that if one of those men—in their black body armor—were before her now, she would, without hesitation, claw the skin from his face, revealing a red skull with bulging eyeballs and a tongue that trembles when it screams. She imagines the warm blood gushing when she brings her mouth to his soft white belly, hollowing him out.

And then, as if a key has toothed its way past the rusted tumblers and sprung a stubborn lock, she gives in. She begins to transform.

"Good," Miriam says, but her voice sounds far away.

It is different this time. She doesn't resist the feeling, doesn't push back. She summons it and lets it grip her completely. Her heartbeat spikes with the rush of adrenaline. Her skin goes warm and prickles with hair. Her bones make noises not unlike a series of wet gasps. When her gums recede, she tastes the coppery blood flooding her mouth. For the briefest moment the sun breaks through the clouds and her shadow appears suddenly before her, tethered to her feet and shifting like a tree in a hard wind.

She has more energy sizzling through her than her body can contain. And a door seems to have swung open in her mind to allow everything in at once. A vole scurries through the underbrush. An owl breaks a bone with its beak. Sagebrush rattles against the breeze. She hears and smells and sees it all. It is as if, up to this point, her brain was muffled, everything experienced through a filter of wet wool. And now so many senses emerge from the blur. She has changed—she has opened up and tuned in to some dead transmission that has suddenly buzzed to life inside her and allowed in all the richness of the world.

It is then that she hears the car engine.

In the near distance, maybe a quarter mile away, a faint rumble. When the vehicle turns down their driveway, the gravel rattling its undercarriage, she jerks around and tears off in the direction of it—driven by some animal impulse that responds to trespass. It is the Tall Man, she is certain. Miriam wanted her to fight. Miriam wanted her to kill. And now Miriam is going to get her wish.

Claire doesn't hear, or doesn't care to hear, her aunt yelling "No!" behind her.

Patrick drives the road that winds out of La Pine and toward the Cascades, feeling sweet abandon, the best kind of risk. He saved her. He keeps going back to that. He saved her, and when you save somebody that means your life and hers are irrevocably linked. The feeling inside him must be similar to what a parent feels, a fawning sense of creation, ownership.

He brakes, signals, steers down the rutted driveway, bumping along the washboard, following the lines of the ponderosa pines. Fifty yards in, a deer bounds in front of him, so fast his foot hasn't even reached the brake before it is gone, diving into the woods, its raised tail a white flash. He skids to a stop just as two more follow, slower, trotting, their heads low, their hooves tocking the gravel. He laughs with relief.

The laugh is cut short when he catches a glimpse of movement out his driver's-side window and the Jeep lurches. He assumes he isn't so lucky after all—another deer has come vaulting out of the woods and struck him.

Then the nylon shell rips open. The fog of his

breath is sucked away by the breeze rushing freely into the Jeep. He looks up and there she is. He knows her instantly, despite her changed appearance, like someone recognized through a Halloween mask. The bloodshot eyes and bleeding mouth. A lycan.

He feels a jolt of fear, as if run through with electricity, when she reaches for him, snatches his shoulder. He barely feels her claws pierce his skin, too overwhelmed by the sight of her, as if he has somehow fallen back in time, back into his hiding place on the plane, only this time the lycan has found him. This time he will be as dead as everyone else.

He cannot breathe. He cannot move. She can do with him what she will. Her arm pulls back, he assumes for a slash, but no, she is retreating from him, dropping from the Jeep, stumbling away, breathing heavily and observing him with eyes that glow with recognition. She is crying. He isn't sure why, maybe as a side effect of transforming, but she is crying and her tears are red and trailing down her face.

She turns away from him and launches herself into the woods and vanishes from sight.

He takes the first sucking breath he might have taken in a minute. His head buzzes with blood and his hand is over his heart and his foot is jammed against the brake so hard his leg is cramping up.

Before he can decide whether to knock the gearshift into park or reverse, the door swings open. He is staring into the muzzle of a pistol. His eyes have trouble focusing on the woman beyond it, her face as narrow as a blade. "Kill the ignition and get on the ground," she says.

Earlier that day, he stood in his room, his closet door hanging ajar. In his hand was the T-shirt. The one he was wearing that day on the plane. A continent of blood dried across it. They cut it off him and tossed it in a plastic biohazard bag that he later swiped on impulse and hid away. He doesn't know why. Maybe the same thing that compels people to keep a lost tooth in an envelope or an appendix in a glass jar. It seemed important. He held the shirt up, stiff and rust colored, like a second skin he had outgrown. It smelled like metal and sharpened his breathing and made him feel stabbed through with shame. He balled it up, bits of blood flaking off it, and shoved it into the back corner of his closet and covered it with a magazine.

Now he has another shirt to add to the collection, its fabric ripped and spotted red along his left shoulder. A smear of dirt runs along the belly from when the woman shoved him and he stumbled and fell and caught himself with an outstretched hand.

"Why did you come back? What are you doing here?" she says and kicks him in the hip. "Speak."

Pricks of pain bother his shoulder when he pushes himself into a seated position. The woman is standing over him with the pistol an inch from his eye, and then closer still, so that his vision waters and he can smell the gun oil. His voice comes out strangled when he says he wanted to check on her, that's all, to see if she was all right.

She cocks her head, searching his face. "Bad choice." She motions with the gun, tells him to get up, walk ahead of her. With the Jeep ticking behind them, they start off in the direction of the cabin. He puts his hands in his pockets and she says, no, keep them out and keep walking. A cold wind blows and a gray dust devil rises from the gravel and twists its way toward him and batters him with its grit.

The cabin, smaller than he remembers it, raised foundation, railed-in porch. The woman tells him to open the door and he does and a slab of light falls across the floor, punched through with his shadow, and then the woman's, when she comes up behind him and nudges him forward, the pistol biting his spine.

The girl is waiting for him. The girl, no longer

transformed. Lights off, curled up on the couch, her posture hunched over, as though she has a hook inside her. She wears a gray hooded sweatshirt and black sweatpants. Her sandy hair is chopped short now, and though he doesn't like that look on everybody, he likes it on her. Her nose and cheeks are dusted with freckles that get lost in the fresh bruises darkening her face—the effect of transforming. She sucks at her mouth and runs a tongue along her teeth. A dime of blood has dried beneath her lips and she knuckles it away.

"It hurts," she says to the woman.

"Get used to it."

The air smells stale. Dust and grease and body odor. The woman snaps on a lamp and splashes the room with light, and it is then that he notices the boarded-up windows, making the small room seem even smaller, a couch, a chair, a coffee table, a bureau, and barely space for their three bodies. The woman closes the door behind them, twists the deadbolt into place. The high ceiling with exposed rafters is the only thing that fights the claustrophobia.

The girl looks at him for the first time since he entered the cabin, her eyes red puddles. "Why did you come back?"

"I wanted to see you."

A small smile dies as soon as it forms. "You shouldn't have."

The woman, still behind him, says, "I told you you were stupid to bring him here."

"Too late for that."

He feels the gun at his ear. It seems to give off its own noise, an undersound, like a struck tuning fork. "But not too late to put a bullet in his head."

Some silent message seems to pass between the girl and the woman. They leave him in the living room—the woman first patting him down, telling him he cannot run fast enough to escape her, so don't bother—and retreat to the back of the cabin, thunking closed a door behind them.

He can hear their voices snapping back and forth, but not what they say. His initial fear has faded, replaced by a sickening confusion. She is a lycan. She scratched him, but he thinks—he hopes—the disease spreads only through blood, through sex.

She is what his father fights. She is what Max rails against. She is what brought down three planes and their passengers. The face of the plague, the creature made monstrous in so many novels and films and cop dramas and comic books—

But now she's just a girl with choppy hair, wearing a sweatshirt and sweatpants, who walks past him, opens the door, and says, "Come on." When he doesn't follow, she stops there, hand on the knob, framed in a rectangle of daylight, and looks back at him. "Come on already."

They walk from the cabin and into the dark breadth of trees. The ground is dusted with snow. She doesn't look back at him—she just assumes he will follow—and he does. He glances over his shoulder, just before the cabin disappears from sight, and sees the woman standing on the porch, watching them go.

"You're not going to kill me, are you?" He isn't sure whether this is a joke. No one knows he is here and he can't help but imagine his body buried somewhere deep in the woods, a little rock for a marker.

CHAPTER 20

THE TALL MAN climbs out of his Lincoln Town Car, his beltline nearly parallel with the roof of the car. He wears a long-sleeve button-down wrinkled from the long drive. His jacket is folded neatly over the passenger seat, and he pulls it out now and meticulously brushes the lint off it before sliding one arm and then the other into its sleeves. His head is hairless, not because he shaves his head clean every morning, but because he has been burned terribly. His skin has the wrinkly gloss of chewed bubblegum. It isn't clear where his lips begin and end. His dark eyes appear lidless. His nose is small and upturned and from a distance appears like no nose at all, slitted like a skull.

Three police cruisers, a Forest Service Bronco, and a forensics van are parked nearby, in a parking lot corralled by a split-rail fence. A sign hangs from a post—a varnished block of wood with the letters carved out of it—Blood Bath Hot Springs. A rime of snow coats the letters.

The half-mile trail takes him no time to walk, his long legs scissoring quickly, his black wing tips dusted red when the pines open up into a rocky clearing busy with police. Tendrils of steam come off the springs as if something beneath their surface is alive and breathing. The smell of sulfur, like eggs on their way to going bad, is such that more than a few men have their shirts tented over their noses.

They don't have enough tape to cordon off the crime scene. So there is a strip of black and yellow hanging across the trailhead. Most would duck under it, but the Tall Man steps over. A goateed man in a black North Face fleece approaches him with a question on his face he doesn't have to ask. The Tall Man already has his identification out, and the goateed man nods at it and says, "Never seen you before."

"You wouldn't have." His voice is baritone, every word he speaks cleanly enunciated.

The policeman is studying the Tall Man, arrested by the sight of him. He eventually says his name is Don and identifies himself as a sheriff's deputy. He pulls out a pack of Juicy Fruit and pops a piece in his mouth and jaws at it. "You come from the office in Portland or Salem?"

"Neither."

The deputy chews the gum another moment. "All right. Be a mysterious asshole. Let me know what you need to know."

The bodies are several days' dead. They would

have been perfectly preserved except for the heat of the springs. As is, their skin is blackened and occasionally split red from swelling, like a hot dog left too long on the grill. The severed head of an old man, his mouth gaping open, peers at the Tall Man from the top of a spiked boulder. Here is a body of a woman splayed like an X, her belly hollowed out, a brown-and-yellow tangle of intestines piled nearby.

Policemen in blue Windbreakers snap photos. The flashes explode. The ground is uneven with red blistery rocks that their boots thud against often and that send them stumbling forward. Except for the Tall Man, who walks slowly and cleanly around the springs, stepping over bodies, balancing on the rocks, sometimes turning in a circle to look thoughtfully off into the woods.

He spots something in the red puddle of spring water. A naked body, boiled and egg white, floating belly-up. Don stands nearby, talking into a handheld, and when he ends the conversation, he looks at the Tall Man looking at the body. "Lycans."

"I am aware."

"What are you thinking?"

"I am thinking about how, when I was in college, I thought I was going to be a volcanologist. Isn't that a funny thing to want to be? There is something about them, volcanoes, that has always appealed to me. I have stood at the smoking rim of Saint Helens and flown a helicopter over Kilauea and stared down into its terrible orange eye. In the end, I didn't have the head for chemistry and physics, but I took enough classes and read enough books to know that eruption is about force and time." He visors his eyes with his hand and looks at the cloud-shrouded mountains above them. "Did you know that the Three Sisters, even though they are quiescent, have magmatic activity beneath them? Did you know that their elevation changes, sometimes by several inches, every year? They will erupt again, and this very place we are presently standing in will be a bright-red sea. It is only a matter of time."

The head of the body is sunken, barely visible in the red murkiness, but when the Tall Man dips his foot into the spring, as if testing the water, to toe the body, it bobs upward and the face gapes back at him, looking like a pencil drawing smeared over by wet fingers.

"Force and time."

CHAPTER 21

NEAL DESAI'S DAUGHTER is having one of her dark days. That's what his wife tells him over the phone, asking him to come home early if he can. His daughter needs him. "Yes," he says. "Of course." But then his lab work distracts him and the next time he glances at the clock it is seven thirty. There are no windows here. Hours often pass without him lifting his head from a microscope or computer. Another missed meal. Another night coming home to an upset wife, her face hidden behind a novel or focused on the TV turned up too loud.

He works in the Pacific Northwest Regional Biocontainment Laboratory in the Infectious Disease Research Center. They are part of the University of Oregon, but located outside Eugene, a collection of mostly windowless concrete buildings surrounded by electrified barbed wire and patrolled by armed security guards. From a distance his workplace could easily be mistaken for a prison.

His title is professor, but aside from a few lectures a year, he does not teach, his primary duty research. The center houses five barns and ten acres of pasture, and today he is supervising his graduate students and postdocs as they inoculate calves. They are sedated with xylazine, a midline incision is made in the skull and a hole drilled through the calvarium, and then the inoculum is injected into the midbrain via a disposable needle. The incision is closed with a single suture, and the surgical instruments, including the drill bits, are disposed of in a hazmat bag. You can't be too careful when you're deliberately infecting an animal with prions.

This is his specialty, prions, and as interested as he is in mad cow and chronic wasting disease, most of his research over the past ten years has concerned lobos.

His daughter, Sridavi, is a lost girl. That's how he thinks of her—though really she is not so much a girl anymore at twenty-two. Her eyes swim with drugs. Her skin always has a sheen of sweat to it. Her bones press against her skin so harshly he fears they might cut through. The black smears beneath her eyes darken her otherwise yellowish complexion. Looking at her makes him feel scraped out by something sharp, a wound that no suture can help heal.

Ten years ago, he heard a crash in her room followed by a banshee scream. Her door was locked and she did not respond when he knocked or called her name, so he splintered the hinges with his weight. He has always been a big man, though not as big then as he is now, drinking gallons of sugary coffee, regularly peeling open candy bars for the rush that keeps him going all these long hours.

He barged into his daughter's room and found the bookcase overturned and a pair of pants poking beneath it so that at first he thought her crushed. A growl rose from the corner. He spotted her then, at the head of her bed, curled up in a ball nearly curtained by her long black hair. His relief was short-lived. When he called out her name again, her hair parted and a demon's face emerged from it, the eyes and mouth pocketed with blood.

He knew immediately what had befallen her even though he did not want to believe it. He should have retreated from the room, drawn closed the broken door, but he ran to her instead, stumbling over the mess of books, saying, no, no, no, as if to chase the demon out of her.

She sprang off her bed and he held out his arms to greet her. The impact knocked them both to the floor, where she clawed at him, parting the buttons of his shirt, flaying the skin from his chest, as if to tear the heart from him.

Though Neal outweighed his daughter by more than a hundred pounds, he could barely hold her down, her body rigid and humming with power, as if he were wrestling a sprung diving board. His wife stood in the doorway with her hand over her mouth, and he told her to hurry, damn it, call 911.

And while he waited for the sirens to wail, for the police to tromp down the hallway with a tranquilizer syringe, while his daughter bucked against him and he strangled away her snapping jaw, his chest hurt in a way that had nothing to do with the shredded skin and blood pouring from it.

He strips off his booties and hazmat suit and tosses them in a bagged bin. He punches his personal code into the keypad and the light flashes green and the door unlocks with the *shunk* of the automatic deadbolt and he enters a white-tiled room and strips off his shoes and socks and underwear and undershirt and tosses them in another bin before standing under a blistering shower and scrubbing off and toweling dry and then heading into the locker room, where he spins his combo and yanks the lock and pulls out his gym bag and dresses in jeans and a long-sleeve collared Izod, a birthday present from his wife, not that he has any time or desire to golf anymore. His jacket he drapes over his arm.

He signs out with the night secretary, a woman

named Beatrice, whose pink scalp glows through her thinning red hair. She buzzes him out of the lab and into a short gray hallway, undecorated except for a plastic ficus tree, its leaves leavened with dust. At the end of the hallway, a metal detector and X-ray machine. He says hello to the security guard, one of several posted at every building, then empties his pockets and tosses his bag on the conveyer and picks it up on the other side and says so long. He gets buzzed through another door and heads not into a reception area—they rarely see visitors here—but directly into the chill of the night.

He knows the Willamette Valley is temperate compared to the other side of the state, where he hears a snowstorm is dropping several inches tonight, but even after thirty years of living here, he can't get used to the temperature dropping below fifty. The air is misting, a hesitant rain. He zips his jacket so quickly that the metal bites his neck, what his wife teasingly calls his second chin. He checks his fingers for blood when he walks a winding concrete path that takes him to the gate.

He can hear the electricity humming in the fence when he approaches. The guard here sits behind a sliding Plexiglas window that he opens to hand Neal a clipboard and pen. He smacks Nicorette and makes small talk about the Trail Blazers sucking it up again as Neal signs out. On his desk, a mess of log sheets and several television screens that offer fish-eye views of the center. The gate buzzes open and the two men wish each other good night.

He pulls out his keys and shakes them away from the remote clicker and punches the autostart on his Honda Accord to get the heater and butt warmer going. In the lot ahead of him, a scattering of cars and SUVs lit by lamps, the asphalt running up against a gully tangled with blackberry vines, plastic bags caught up in them like spider eggs.

The space behind his eyes throbs with the exhaustion of the day and the anticipation of what awaits him at home, his daughter likely glassy-eyed and catatonic and soiling herself from some combination of snorting too much Volpexx and smoking too much of the medical marijuana she's prescribed. The last thing he wants to do is talk to someone—the gauntlet of security was bad enough—so he loudly sighs when he hears his name, "Dr. Desai?"

He turns and sees that the voice comes from the SUV next to his, a silver Chevy Equinox, its window down and dome light on, the soft yellow glow illuminating a round face that appears almost childish except for the wrinkles framing his mouth and the gray hairs collaring an otherwise bald head. "I'm sorry to bother you at this late hour."

He holds out a hand that is small and damp when Neal hesitantly shakes it. "But I have a business proposition for you."

At the McMenamins brewpub, along the Willamette River, they sit by the rain-dotted window. A bridge reaches over the water and the lights staggered across it diamond the ripples beneath. Neal turns down the craft beer on special tonight, a nut brown, and orders tea instead.

The man—Augustus—folds his hands on the table, one on top of the other, as if they were napkins. "Are you Muslim?"

He is not. He is nothing. "I am exhausted."

The waiter brings an ale for Augustus and a tray for Neal on which rests a small ceramic pot and an assortment of tea bags arranged like a fan. The waiter has a forked goatee and wears a hemp bracelet. He pulls a pen and pad from his apron and says, "And will we be ordering anything to eat this evening?"

Neal says no at the same time that Augustus says maybe. "Maybe," Augustus says again, and the waiter says he'll be back to check on them in a minute.

Neal selects a black tea and drops it in the cup and pours steaming water over it.

"Long day," Augustus says.

"Yes." He lets the tea steep another moment and then raises the cup for a drink.

"And a long night ahead?"

Neal says nothing, the teacup hanging before his lips, the steam warming his chin and making the image of the man before him warp. Augustus smiles, his teeth as small and white as corn kernels, and says, "Your poor daughter."

The tea is hot in his hand. "What do you know of my daughter? Has she done something?" The steam trembles with his words.

"No." Augustus laughs, a sharp little bark. "She hasn't done a thing." He sips from his beer and uses his napkin to dab the foam mustache from his upper lip. "Excuse me for prying. But she was bitten? Was that how she became infected?"

"No," Neal responds automatically, though he isn't sure why he is talking about this very private matter with a stranger. "She was exposed in another way." He doesn't elaborate. The disease had been sexually transmitted. Fifteen years old and sexually active and not using protection. The thought still makes him close his eyes with shame. He wishes she had been bitten instead—then maybe he wouldn't blame her for what happened, her recklessness the cause of their life's ruin.

"I'm sorry."

The tea is bitter. He sets it down with a rattle and tears two sugar packs into it. "You'll forgive me. I don't follow politics. What is it that you do again?"

"Like I said, I'm chief of staff to the governor."

"Yes, but what do you *do*?"

"I suppose I do what I have always done. I am a consultant. The presumption of my job is that management or boards or whoever—a politician, say—might not be...capable in all situations." The lamplight makes his glasses glow. "I am the external competency."

"I see." He takes another drink of his tea, better now, and then stands to pull on his jacket and says sorry, he really ought to be going. He needs to get home to his family. If Augustus insists, the secretary can make an appointment during regular business hours and—

Augustus talks over the top of him. "Since your center is, as I see it, severely underfunded—even more so lately, with the budget cuts. And since I can be of service in this matter—if I feel so inclined. And since your daughter suffers from the very ailment we are both interested in curing, I don't think you have any choice but to sit down and listen." He drinks again from his beer, an ale as dark as the night. "Sit down, please."

Neal does, slowly dropping back into his chair, his jacket still on.

The waiter appears again. "Have we made up our minds, gentlemen?"

"No, we have not," Augustus says. "Not yet." And the waiter wanders away again.

Neal listens to what Augustus has to say. Halfway through he realizes his tea has gone cold. And a few minutes after that he quiets his cell phone when it rings, not bothering to glance at the caller ID, knowing it is his wife wondering where he is. Except for occasionally nodding his head and smiling sadly, he hardly moves until Augustus stops talking, and then the two of them sit in silence for a long time, Neal avoiding eye contact, staring into his teacup as if there might be some message encoded in its leaves.

Augustus sips loudly from his glass. "Gosh, this beer is good."

Neal does not like this man very much, but he can't help but like what he has to say. He looks out the window. Dripping beards of moss hang from the trees. The river twists off into the distance. He sees their reflections hanging in the glass and studies the profile of the man studying him. It's easier to look at him this way, avoiding his fixed gaze.

"Sometimes," Neal says, "I think it would be easier if she had died."

"Easier on her? Or easier on you?"

"Yes."

CHAPTER 22

THE TEMPERATURE SHARPENS and the wind picks up and the sun cuts a shorter arc across the sky. Patrick has not answered the phone, though Malerie has called him more than a dozen times in the past few days. Three voice mails, the first cheery babble, the second a long sigh, the third asking him what the hell was going on. "Patrick? Seriously. You better call back." Here her voice grew cruel. "Or maybe it's time Max finds out about us."

He doesn't know what he'll do after the long weekend, the Sabbath on Monday, when she seeks him out at school—tell her the truth? That he had fun? More than fun—the swell of her breasts, the vacuum of her mouth, the thrill of sneaking around—but he's just not feeling it anymore? Screwing around with her is no way to repay the kindness Max has shown him?

He is sitting upright in bed, a pillow braced behind his back, with the laptop warming his thighs. Outside, the sky is a dying purple. The lamp in his room is dim and at odds with the bright glow the screen makes. His eyes ache. He feels mildly nauseous, mixed up inside.

He browses the news sites. First the nationals, hunting for updates about the Lupine Republic. He knows there will be casualties, and there are, but every one of them brings him a sick kind of relief, because he knows some must die—that there is a quota to fill—and one man dying means his father goes on living. He reads an editorial titled "Extremist Groups Do *Not* Define Lycans," all about how a small percentage of radicals are defining the larger population of peaceable lycans in the U.S. and in the Republic. He reads about a raid in Florida, a terrorist cell that had been building a fertilizer bomb. He reads about the lycan no-fly, now more than three months old and facing legal opposition from the ACLU. He reads about how the security threat level has dropped from red to orange but airports and train stations will maintain increased security and random passenger checks.

Then Patrick hits up the local papers, the *Oregonian*, the *Old Mountain Tribune*, to read up on the governor, whom everyone seems to have a loudmouthed opinion on. Here is an article about Chase Williams advocating nuclear energy and endorsing a power plant along the Columbia, and here is an editorial that claims the governor's plans will only tighten the collar on the uranium-rich Lupine Republic.

He spots a headline that reads "Blood Bath at Blood Bath." Yesterday, a naked woman—identified as Alice Slade—was discovered along the shoulder of the Santiam Pass, naked and hypothermic and babbling about wolves in the woods. After hospitalization and questioning, it was discovered that an alleged lycan attack took place at the remote Blood Bath Hot Springs north of Sisters. She is believed to be the wife of local insurance agent Craig Slade, whose corpse was found at the springs, along with eleven others, some of them mangled beyond recognition.

He clicks on an ad for a new phone plan. He clicks on an ad for Victoria's Secret. Click, click, click. He opens ESPN and checks the scores on the Saturday football games. He tries to instant-message a few pals from back home—to catch up; he's been neglectful—but everyone is away from their computers. He watches a video for the Marines in which a young soldier slays a dragon with a sword. He downloads a few college applications—UCLA, UC Davis, UC Irvine—to fill out later, the deadlines a few months away.

Then he stares out the window, watching the stars brighten in the sky. The wind rises and makes the glass shudder. Snow is expected tonight, the first winter storm. When he turns back to his computer, he opens Google and plugs in Blood Bath Hot Springs and finds it on the map and sees it is no more than an hour's drive from here. He thinks of the girl, Claire. In truth he has thought of little else lately. She is always flitting at the edge of his mind like a moth with a sinister pattern on its wings.

She finally told him her name in the woods. He didn't initially respond, not knowing what to say. Nice to meet you? Though they had already met, and the circumstances then and now were hardly nice.

"And you're Patrick," she said, still not looking at him, tromping ahead. "Don't worry, Patrick. I'm not going to kill you. Though I think my aunt might have if we didn't get away from her."

When he drove out there, he had planned their conversation, readying every smooth response. But now everything had changed. She was not who he thought she was. And when he reached for that store of memories now, his hand passed through it, all the words evaporated. She was a lycan. And not just a lycan but unmedicated. An illegal, a resister. Max calls them a plague. The governor calls them the biggest threat to this country, a threat he is working brutally to remedy. Even as Patrick was aware of this, he could not catalogue his feelings, nor could he reconcile the political rhetoric with the sight of the pretty girl walking before and then slowing next to him.

"Thank you again," she said. "Maybe that's why you're back. Because I didn't thank you."

"That's not why I'm back."

"Well, thank you." She leaned suddenly toward him and he stiffened and threw up his hands, thinking she would bite him—her mouth open, only inches from his face—and he noticed then the blackness of his fingertips, stained from the spray paint that soaked through his gloves the other night. He dropped his hands and said, "Sorry."

She did not seem offended, studying him another moment before she said, "Ever kissed a lycan before?" She seemed as surprised by the question as he.

"No," he said.

Her lips lingered for a beat on his cheek. "Now you have."

Then she began to talk, her words coming fast, as if they'd been dammed up. She said she moved here from Wisconsin. Or maybe *moved* was the wrong word. She came here from Wisconsin. And how, growing up, for the longest time, that was all she wanted, to get out, away from the snow and boredom, off on her own for the first time. But now she wishes she hadn't gotten her wish after all.

She went quiet then and he supposed he ought to say something. "Isn't that how it always works? In the stories about genies, people end up screwing themselves up with all their wishing."

She nodded. "It's better not to wish."

They stood there, in the middle of the woods, under a sky simmering with clouds, half looking at each other. He kicked at a buried rock that coughed out of the frozen ground. It sparkled with quartz. His father knew everything there was to know about rocks, minerals, and the two of them used to go hounding on the weekends, the bed of the truck full of shovels and picks. On their front porch he kept a geode the size of a child's skull, carved open to reveal a violet crystal core. Sometimes they would visit old hardrock mines in California, and when they moved through the tunnels framed with old timbers, his father would tell him about silver. It is designated by the chemical symbol Ag, for *argentum*, Latin for *shining*. It has the highest electrical and thermal conductivity of any metal. The father of medicine, Hippocrates, believed that it had medical abilities, the power to heal, to fight infection and disease, and it was used widely in medicines and ointments during the world wars—and now most famously in Volpexx. When his father held a flashlight to a vein of silver, it shimmered like an underground river.

When Patrick thinks about all the years those minerals were rolled and grinded and baked by the earth, the precious veins hidden away by a hard ugly shell, until one day along comes somebody with a pile of dynamite to ravage a mountainside and reveal its glimmering guts—he thinks maybe that was what the girl, Claire, had done. Cracked him wide open.

He is not sure why he wakes up. But when his dreams blur away he discovers he is sitting upright in bed. Still fully clothed. His laptop in sleep mode beside him. The light of a streetlamp pours through the venetian blinds and decorates the wall with shadowed bars.

And then he hears it. A quiet padding and scratching in the hallway. His door is closed, but beyond it, he is certain he can distinguish the sound of something trying not to make a sound. He swings his legs out of his bed. He cringes when the box spring creaks. He creeps forward, depressing his weight slowly. He brings his ear close to the door and tries to open it up to accept every sound in the world. In the distance a train rattles along to some midnight destination. A long, lonely whistle cries out—the noise hushed by the snow but still loud enough to eat up anything he might have heard in the hallway. He waits for it to pass—the seconds dragging on—and then it is gone, a fading grumble.

The loaded silence of the house takes over. And there it is again, the sound. *Click-click-click*. Like someone teasing chalk across a chalkboard. Close. Right outside. The knob does not move, but the door clatters softly in its frame, barely displaced, the way it would if a window opened or someone braced a hand against it.

He keeps a baseball bat beneath his bed. He can't understand why he didn't grab it on his way across the room. He feels naked and small. He raises his trembling hand and lays it flat against the wood, not pushing back, not yet, but ready if the door bursts inward. Two inches of wood, not even, the door hollow core. On the other side of it, he imagines a shadow figure mirroring his own, its arm also outstretched, its mouth tusked with teeth.

His mind flips through a Rolodex of possibilities. It could be Claire's hard-faced aunt, convinced he would expose them. Could be Malerie, her eyes raccooned by mascara, gone all *Fatal Attraction* on him with a butcher knife in her hand. Could be some lycan, connected to the cell that took down the planes, come to finish him off. Or it could be nothing. It could be he is imagining things.

He waits for a long time, so long he fades in and out of sleep, so long he can't be sure he ever heard anything, before his free hand rises to the knob and depresses the spring lock. The noise is a startlingly loud *snap*, the tumblers falling into place like the hammer of a gun.

Whatever is on the other side of his door lurches back. He hears, moving across the landing and then dropping quickly down the stairs, what must be claws *click-click-click-clicking* their way to the entryway, where the hardwood turns to tile, the noise changing its timbre then, louder, more echoey.

His phone is on the night table—and he grabs it and nearly powers it on to call the cops. He could call them and he could stay here, stay safe—the door locked, his back against the wall. He shoves the handheld in his pocket instead. No more hiding. Not with his mother downstairs. He retrieves the baseball bat and strangles his hands around the grip and swings open the door and steps into the dark throat of the hallway.

CHAPTER 23

OVER THE CASCADES rolls a bruise-black cloud bank. From it, snow falls. Big flakes. It clings to Claire's hair, her clothes, fills an outstretched palm when she steps outside, early this morning, for a walk.

Miriam is sleeping off a hangover. Sometimes her aunt seems like an alien, cold and unfamiliar with human emotion, but every now and then, she'll do something that surprises Claire. Pour some tea and say, in a Cockney accent, "You want a little sugar with that, guvnah?" Or snort out a laugh when paging through a novel. Or go silent and drink whiskey and lock herself away in her room. From behind the door Claire will discern a high, keening sound and the occasional sniff that sounds like a tissue tugged from a box.

This is what happened last night, when Claire finally asked whether she had a cousin. "The children's books," she said. "I keep looking at them on the bookshelf."

They were sitting at the kitchen table and Miriam was sawing her knife through her round steak. Blood pooled around it. "Had."

"What?"

"Had a cousin." She brought her fork to her mouth and then changed her mind and set down her silverware. "You had a cousin. I had a daughter."

Claire didn't need to ask what happened. Miriam told her, in a flood of words, as if Claire had taken a knife to a seam in her throat that had been holding all this back. Her name was Meg. She was seven, nearly eight. Curly brown hair like her father. Smart as hell. Could name all the capitals and recite the alphabet backward. Her father was building fertilizer bombs. He planned to enter six floats in Fourth of July parades across the state, detonating them at once, ripping apart all the clowns shooting water guns and ladies tossing their batons and children racing for candy. "Instead he ripped his own child apart. We don't know what happened, not exactly. We know the bomb went off. That's what we know, and I suppose that's all there is to know. This was in an open-air shed with a tin roof. She was snooping or playing one moment, dead the next. I remember running and looking into the sky and thinking it was full of bats. But it was tin, smoking pieces of tin, twisting their way to the ground." She is not crying. She has dried herself out with all her crying. She grips the knife on her plate with such strength that her knuckles go white.

"Your parents were right. They were right to step away when they had you. I realized that too late."

Miriam has told Claire, over and over, not to leave the cabin without her, not to let her guard down for a second. But Claire is tired of the paranoia. She has been here more than a month, and during this time, despite Miriam's constantly fingering a weapon, peering out the window, nothing has happened, no shadow has slipped from the forest to their doorstep. Especially in weather like this, the air a blinding whirl of flakes, what danger could possibly present itself?

She needs to escape, antidote the day's drag of hours. Her wrist aches in the cold. She wears boots that shush through the snow. A hooded sweatshirt beneath the old Carhartt jacket that her aunt wanted to burn but Claire wanted to keep for sentimental reasons. "It's like a graduation tassel or something." Paper crackles against her hand and she withdraws from the pocket a torn slip with Patrick's name and phone number scrawled across it. She smiles and feels a snowflake catch against her lip and melt.

He was muscular and taller than her by a few inches and had bright green eyes that would alternately stare hard at her and then turn shyly away.

His hair was a dark brown and cut short, and she could tell it would have a little curl to it if he grew it out. The other day, when he came for her, she could smell him—she could smell everything, the residual effects of transforming—and he smelled good, even when a little sweaty, like black dirt. She liked how still he was, only moving when he had to. And the way he talked, slow and careful with his words, making sure each one mattered.

It was a relief to talk to someone her age, to anyone besides Miriam.

And so she drank up everything he told her. She asked where he was from and he said California and she said to tell her about it and he did, talking about his father's hobby farm. How he spent his childhood collecting eggs from beneath hens and ducking under barbed-wire fences and firing slingshots at jackrabbits and cutting the tails off lizards to keep in a glass jar and swiping grasshoppers from the air to toss in a spider's web. He told her about Big Sur. He told her about driving Highway 1 on the back of his father's Indian motorcycle. He told her about the fog breathing off the ocean. The clang of buoys and the barking conversation of sea lions. He told her about San Francisco, fishing off the wharfs, jumping onto the back of a moving trolley.

"Sounds like you miss it."

“Yeah.” He did, but less so than before. He said he had been through so much, and when he looks back, that life seemed to belong to someone else.

“I know the feeling,” she said, the feeling that she wasn’t the only one holding back, who could have said more. She felt a tug then. Like those stories her father used to tell around the fireplace, the ones about ghosts that grabbed you around the neck when you were sleeping, by your ankle when you were swimming, and never let go. He had her.

Now her boots whisper through the calf-deep snow. The windward sides of the ponderosas are clotted with white, making the exposed bark startlingly red. Branches slant downward, weighed and frosted with snow. She walks among the white, huddled shapes of the underbrush—and then runs a few steps, just for the thrill of it.

Yesterday, with the temperature plummeting, she heard, way off in the woods, what she at first mistook for gunfire. Echoing *cracks*. “Don’t worry,” Miriam said. “It’s just the trees.” Freezing and splitting in half. One explodes next to her now, an old pine that breaches, its two halves ripping away from each other with a splintery rasp. She cries out in terror and then covers her mouth with her hand, muffling the laugh that follows.

She pauses next to a mound of snow, what must be a boulder frosted over. The wind rises and she sees the shape of it in the scarves of snow that blow all around her. The chatter of her thoughts quiets and she realizes the only sound is the wind and the only color, white. The mound trembles. She notices a red strain of moss—what looks so much like hair but can't be—curling out of all that white.

She turns around in a circle. Something is wrong. She senses it in the air, like the echo of a scream, some disturbance she can't quite hear. The snowbank pulses again, as though breathing—and then explodes upward, making a small blizzard. She cannot seem to move, and a vast stretch of time—enough time for her to feel her breath leaving her, her eyes widening in terror—seems to unfold before a massive set of arms encircles her.

Patrick is at the kitchen table, his head full of fog. He spent most of the night with his back against the locked door of his bedroom, a baseball bat resting across his lap. A few minutes ago he woke and tromped downstairs when he heard the pipes clanking, the downstairs shower spitting on.

Now he spoons into his cereal and sips a Mountain Dew and turns to watch his mother clatter down the hall in her high heels. She wears a black pantsuit with a cream collar that matches the pearls strung around her neck. "You look good," he says, and she curtsies and then winces.

"What's the matter?"

She rubs her knee. "Just my joints. Getting old, I guess."

He tells her he thought he heard something last night. He does not tell her that he searched the house with his baseball bat cocked and ready to swing, that he found her room empty and the back door open, breathing in and out slightly, snowflakes fluttering into the house to perish on the floor.

He unlocked his phone then, ready to punch 911, when he saw her old text message and remembered that she hadn't come home that evening, that she was staying over with a friend who was "having some trouble," and that she would see Patrick the next morning. In his dream-addled state, he had forgotten.

She ceases her rubbing, her body frozen for the space of a breath. Then she is on her way to the kitchen, where she opens a drawer, rattling with silverware, and closes it without pulling anything out. "Well, like they say in the movies, it was probably only the wind."

"They're always wrong in the movies."

She gives him a rigid smile and pulls a carton of orange juice from the fridge and a glass out of the cupboard and fills it and drinks it in a gulping way. "Something has come up. Not going to be here tonight."

Again. She is gone so often these days, at least two nights a week. He thinks about the thin man stepping out of his house, nodding at him. He thinks about spotting his mother's car heading toward his home in the middle of a workday. "What's come up?"

"A convention."

"Another one? But it's the Sabbath."

"Uh-huh." Her eyes are on her hands, not him, picking at a hangnail. "Busy, busy, busy."

He notices then the black bruise along her cheek that not even her makeup can hide. "Who gave you that?" He brushes a knuckle along his cheek and she raises a hand to touch the purplish swelling.

"Nothing. Nobody. I was doing a showing the other day and walked into an open door. Stupid of me. Really embarrassing."

A twenty-inch TV sits on the kitchen counter. She picks up the remote and punches the power. The volume kicks on before the image. "What's the worst part?" That's the voice coming out of the darkness—the voice of Anderson Cooper, it turns out, reporting live from the Lupine Republic, wearing a down jacket and holding out a microphone to a soldier. His ears are bright red and his face appears windburned. Beyond them, the snow-covered landscape matches the sight seen out their kitchen window.

"Worst part?" The soldier wears winter cammies patterned with white and black and gray blotches. His face could be anyone's, obscured by goggles and a helmet. "Carrying your buddies on a litter to the birds. To the medevac. That's the worst."

Cooper gives a brief history lesson, talking about the Republic as a melting pot of cultures, all of them united by their infection. "The world's biggest leper colony," Chase Williams, the governor of Oregon, recently called it. Virtually everyone, besides the U.S. personnel stationed there, is infected. Some have lived there for several generations, but families who want a homeland they can't find elsewhere immigrate every day.

The segment then cuts to Tuonela, the largest uranium mine in the Lupine Republic and a major U.S. supplier. Cooper dons a hazmat suit, readying for a tour of the facilities, while his voice-over describes the codependency of the U.S. and the Republic—and how a small militia of extremist lycans continues to threaten that relationship.

His mother hits the remote again and the TV goes dark. She mutters something about nothing but bad news anymore and then says, "Your father is fine, you know. If anybody can take care of himself... Your father is fine."

Patrick almost says, *What about my mother?*

She pulls her jacket out of the hallway closet and digs around in the pockets until she jangles out her keys. "So long," she calls over her shoulder when she closes the door to the garage behind her.

He doesn't respond. He's still looking at the black rectangle of the TV. He pulls out his handheld. He hasn't heard from his father in three days; the last email Patrick didn't understand. "Breakthrough!" it read and nothing more. Whether he meant success in a military campaign or something else, Patrick doesn't know, and the reply he sent—"???"—remains unanswered.

He shoots his father another email: "You okay? Tell me about this breakthrough thing." He hesitates, his thumbs hovering over the keypad, before writing, "Nothing new here," when of course the very opposite is true, but his father has so much already to worry about, like staying alive.

By the time Miriam discovers the cabin empty, the snow has stopped. Her stomach is sour and her brain sluggish, but she manages a few clear thoughts. The child has merely disobeyed her. That is what teenagers do. She is testing boundaries. When Miriam peers out the front door, squinting against the brightness of the snow, only a single set of tracks runs from the porch into the woods, and Claire is tethered to the end of it. That's what Miriam tells herself as she throws on a jacket and steps into her Sorels and snatches a Glock off the bureau and hurries outside, pausing briefly to puke between her boots, before running a sleeve across her mouth and continuing on.

The air has that special hushed quality, as if the world is holding its breath, waiting. The only sound is the snow creaking underfoot and thumping off branches and hissing across the ground in serpenty wisps. The tracks are gray with shadow and half-filled and Miriam wonders what she would have done if there were no tracks, if the snow kept falling and erased them completely. She puts the thought out of her mind. Best not to think about the worst that can happen.

But the worst has happened, she soon realizes, when she comes to that place in the trees where the tracks vanish into a messy crater of exploded snow. She stands still for a long time, breathing through her nose, and then she circles the crater, a muddle of prints, another set heading off deep into the woods. Claire's tracks were the same size as her own—following them felt as if she were following herself. But these tracks, when Miriam sets her boot inside them, are twice the size of hers, swallowing hers up.

Magog is alive. After she fired through the roof, after she heard him fall heavily to the ground, she checked outside and found no body but enough blood to make death a possibility.

Now he has come for Claire. And though they are long gone, she can feel them—their smell and taste like a memory imprinted in the air. She kneels down and scoops a handful of snow brightened by a spot of blood and crushes it in her hand until it becomes a red ball of ice.

She sees something nearby, caught in a bush, white and flapping like a bird's wing. A piece of paper. It makes a rasping noise when she pulls it out—and reads, in blocky handwriting, the boy's name, Patrick.

CHAPTER 24

THE MOON IS FAT and aglow and seemingly balanced on the chimney of the house Patrick stands before. A few minutes ago, he parked his Jeep on the snowy shoulder of the road. Though he duct-taped the hole Claire tore in his roof, the cold still finds its way in, and he is shivering from the drive when he walks the unplowed tire-rutted driveway. The wind is at his back. He hopes the dogs will remember his scent.

They do. A few preliminary barks give way to mewling and whining and huffing, and he tells them *shh* and kneels down to face their slobbering tongues, flopping their ears and making their legs kick with his rough scratching. As he suspected, his mother's car is parked nearby, glowing as white as the snowbound woods around him.

When he circles the house and crunches through the drifts and peers in the windows, the dogs trail him, nudging at his hand with their cold noses. In every room he expects to find his mother cowering on the floor with her hand held over a swollen eye, a bleeding mouth. She divorced his father more than fifteen years ago—she can see who she pleases; he understands that—but if this man is hurting her, then Patrick plans to hurt him back.

But the house is seemingly empty. He is surprised by what he sees, every room clean and sparely decorated with the kind of modern hard-edged bright-colored furniture on television shows that take place in fancy apartments in LA or New York. Not what he expected from a guy who owns twenty dogs and lives in an outlying neighborhood whose defining landmark is the city dump.

Then he hears a scream. Muffled as if filtered through a pillow. He pounds up the front porch and tries the door, the knob loose. He pushes inside. Vanilla candles burn on the kitchen counter. Soft jazz mumbles and hoots from the stereo. He hurries through the house, checking every room twice, not sure whether he should call out for his mother—and then he hears it again, almost a squeal, from behind a door in the kitchen.

He yanks it open and the floor falls away, a wooden staircase with rubber grips leading into the dimly lit basement. There is a terrible tang to the air—like the worst the zoo has to offer—that he barely registers when dropping down a few steps and leaning over the railing to take in the view.

His guts go cold, as if he has just gulped down an icy glass of water.

At first he isn't sure what he's looking at, the

splatter of bones and blood, and then he spots the tufts of white fur and realizes it must be a goat. Perhaps. It's difficult to tell. Hunched over it, with the posture of buzzards, are two naked figures. They are feeding. He remembers the cat his mother brought here the other day and wonders if it met a similar fate.

He cries out for his mother—and then, too late, brings a hand to his mouth. They both swing toward him at once. The white stripe of hair gives her away, though her face is otherwise unrecognizable, deformed and bloodied. The man is covered with a thick down of hair, everywhere but his head, which remains ridiculously bald. His mother rises and moves toward him, and her feet smear the concrete with tacky prints the color of molasses. Her mouth is moving—she is either gnashing the air or trying to speak—but he doesn't wait to find out.

Claire is not sure how much time has passed. A day, maybe two. She has messed herself. She has not eaten or had anything to drink. She has slept some, but even when awake, she might as well be sleeping, the world dark and unavailable to her. Her hands are cuffed to her opposite ankles, making an X of steel chain that rattles when she moves and makes it impossible to pull the burlap sack off her head. She finally does so by rubbing her head against the stone wall and licking the sack upward with her tongue. When it peels away, she sees that she is at the end of a shadowy corridor. The floor is black sand. Along each wall hangs a strand of LED lights that give off a blue glow and lend to the air an underwater quality.

She can see that the ribbed lava tube reaches for twenty yards before elbowing to the left. She guesses she is deep underground—the air is still and musty, smelling of mud and sulfur—in one chamber of many that network the ground.

She has called out for help a few times before with no response. But this time, after fifteen minutes, someone comes. She hears first his whistle. A low-noted song that comes from a long way off and that she does not recognize until the distance closes. "All around the mulberry bush, the monkey chased the weasel." The slowness of the song is maddening. It reverberates with an eerie echo, sounding like many more than one whistler coming toward her. "The monkey thought 'twas all in good fun." And with that he steps into view, his body slowly bending around the corner when he whistles the final notes. "Pop goes the weasel."

His hair is the color of electricity. That's the first thing she notices. The way it glows weirdly in the light thrown by the strand of LEDs. And then his size, as small and muscular as a gymnast. He wears black boots and black jeans and a black leather jacket. Now in the room with her, he has his hands in his pockets and kicks his way through the sand, kicking a small wave onto her when he comes to a stop a few feet away.

"Hello, little missus," he says, his voice high and vaguely accented, maybe British.

"Little," she says. "Look who's talking."

He smiles without humor. "Got a mouth on you, do you? Just like your bitch of an aunt." He takes his right hand out of his pocket. It is a small hand, made even smaller by his missing two fingers, the ring and pinky, the place where they ought to be mucked over with scar tissue. But it grows bigger a moment later when it curls into a fist and comes speeding toward her, filling her vision.

She hears a muffled thud and realizes it is her head impacting the cave wall.

When she comes to, her nose is throbbing and swollen, crusted with blood. She cannot breathe through it. She is on the floor, her head pillowed by the sand that crumbles off her cheek when she raises her head to observe the three men standing nearby.

There is the man who hit her—who seems more sprite than man, someone out of a fairy tale—someone you'd come across on a dark forest path who would try to trick you or knife you. And there, next to him, the man who stole her away. The giant. As unreasonably wide as he is tall, his head nearly touching the cave's ceiling. Long red hair, long red beard obscuring what little face she could see, two small eyes that seemed to look nowhere and everywhere. A black leather duster flaps loosely around him like a set of baggy bat wings. Hands that could palm and crush a basketball. She knows their strength from when they clamped hold of her, dragged a bag over her head, tossed her over his shoulder, where she spent the better part of a day jostling through the woods.

The third man she recognizes but at first cannot place. He has a broad face with a pile of brown curls surrounding it. His cheeks are dirtied with week-old whiskers. He wears jeans and a flannel shirt with the sleeves rolled up, his arms tattooed with running wolves whose bodies melt into each other in a surging wave of hair and paws and fangs. He is pacing, raking a hand through his hair. "You're out of control."

Peroxide Hair has his arms crossed. His voice is high and reedy when he says, "Some say the same of you."

Then the man with the sleeve tats says something Claire doesn't understand, something about a hot springs, about the foolishness and impulsiveness of his actions, about how he has put everyone at risk. Then his eyes fall on her. "Don't touch her."

"Not even for a squeeze? A peek at her little cunnie?"

And now she places the man with the tattoos, the brooding photo on the back of the book, *The Revolution*. Jeremy. Miriam's husband. Her uncle. His eyes are wide with barely controlled rage. "Don't touch her, Puck."

"Supposing I do?"

"I'll touch you back." He cocks his arm and the wolves inked there seem to crouch, readying to leap.

The giant—so still until now, seeming a part of the cave, a stalagmite mounded over thousands of years of dripping from some poisonous source—comes alive and steps between Puck and Jeremy—her uncle? can she really think of him like that?—who appears suddenly so small.

☽

In that moment, halfway down the basement steps and ready to bolt back up them, Patrick did not know that sixteen years ago, a homeless man crashed onto the trail and tackled and bit his mother as she was hiking John Muir Woods—a man who turned out to be an unmedicated lycan—the sort of encounter that these days happened so rarely, like a grizzly attack, but when it did happen ended up highlighted in the news and played into everyone's worst fears and set off two days' worth of television interviews and newspaper editorials about stricter regulation and enforcement.

Nor did Patrick know that his parents divorced because of it, that her infection became more divisive to their marriage than politics or religion, that Volpexx spiraled her into a gray-skinned, sour-stomach depression, that she once swept Patrick's cereal bowl off the table and hurled his milk glass against the wall because he wouldn't stop whining, that she eventually decided life would be easier and safer for him if she just went away. But she was better now. Still infected, of course, but better mentally, able to manage her urges and transform only in contained circumstances, so that she knew it was safe for Patrick. She wouldn't have ever let him come otherwise.

He did not know, either, that the man she has been seeing for the past two years is a physician, that he was infected with lobos when treating a patient who, in a fevered delirium, bit him, that his mother met him in an Internet chat room for lycan singles, that they have fallen in love and that he freed her from Volpexx by falsely reporting her blood tests.

That comes later.

After Patrick races from the house in Juniper Creek and kicks through the snowy woods and leaps into his Jeep and slams the gas and drives for hours, directionless, not going anywhere, just moving, hurrying away from what he has discovered, checking the rearview constantly as if worried what might race out of the shadows behind him, until his heart stops pounding and his balled-up muscles loosen and his eyes shutter with exhaustion and he pulls into a truck stop where sleep finally drags a black bag over his head.

After he wakes with his face against the steering wheel, after he drives home, the inside of his windshield glazed with the frost of his breath, he finds his mother waiting for him on the living room couch. She wears a sweatshirt and jeans and her face is weirdly absent of makeup, puffy and unfamiliar, splotchy with bruises.

It is a struggle to keep from shaking. "You don't look good," he finally says.

"That's how I always look." Without the makeup, she meant. Without the mask. "You don't look so good yourself." She tries to smile and he tries to smile back.

"I didn't sleep much."

"I don't imagine you did." Her face seems to crease and pale. She pats the cushion next to her and tells him to come, come sit, she'll explain everything.

He skips school. It would be impossible to concentrate. It would be impossible to look anyone in the eye. It would be impossible to make his way through the swarm of bodies, to suffer through droning lectures and math quizzes and a lunchtime conversation with Max when he has lost, in the space of a few hours, all sense of who he is.

He spends the morning with his mother and the afternoon alone. He goes for a drive, and the rumble of the engine makes his entire body shake and a bitter taste fills his mouth like week-old coffee. The sun sets so early these days. In Old Mountain, in the deepening gloom, he passes a construction site for yet another new development. Trucks with generators and hydraulic lifts spotlight the frames of half-built homes and cast skeletal shadows. Everyone is working overtime, chasing the final days of November.

In the middle of town rises a cinder cone called Lava Butte. At the last minute, he yanks the wheel and heads up the road that curls around and around to the summit, because what the hell, when you needed perspective, you were supposed to go up high, right? The road hasn't been plowed and his wheels slip and scud over the ice pack.

He parks and sits on the hood of the Jeep and watches the sun die and the moon rise and the stars blink to life. Below him the city glimmers like a pond reflecting the sky above, making this butte an island looking over the drowned.

His mother, when he asked what it felt like to transform, gave him a smile with a troubling quiver. It feels good, she said. Not the first few times. The first few times you wake up with a suck of air, naked and blue lipped and curled up in a ball and covered in bruises and scratches and blinking confusedly in the morning sun. You feel hungover, unsure of what's happened, of where you've been, what you've done. And then—snap—a memory from the night before.

But later, when you've gained control, later it feels like being a child again, which is the only time you're ever truly alive, unrestrained, driven by hunger.

Below him, in the near distance, he can see the construction site, glowing blue like an underwater city. He can hear the distant rumble of tractors and payloaders, the whine of circular saws and clatter of hammers and shouts of foremen and beep of back-up alarms. Yet another subdivision. The town looks less like itself every day. The town Max grew up in—that his father grew up in, and his grandfather before them both—is a new kind of creature that has condos in place of mills, roundabouts instead of intersections, white and Mexican and Asian and black and lycan. Everything is getting eaten up and spit out differently. Patrick sees for the first time how small Max is, how impossible his resistance to change.

Patrick isn't much for reading, let alone the plays his English teacher is always shoving down their throats, but the last guy they read, whatever his name was, was all right. No annoying symbolism and pointed pushy message, just a bunch of smartasses saying things that made his head spin, like: "It's the best possible time to be alive, when almost everything you thought you knew is wrong." A line he streaked a highlighter through.

His phone buzzes and he rushes to check it, hoping for a message from his father, whom he still hasn't heard from. No luck. It's Max.

His thumb hesitates over the phone. The wind is cold and blustery, as high up as he is, and for a moment he wonders if he'll go spinning away, as light as a leaf. He opens the message. "Hunting season," it reads. "Be ready at dawn. Will pick you up."

CHAPTER 25

NEAL'S DAUGHTER HAS sunk unkindly into middle age. She looks as old as if not older than his wife. Her face, at one time more a fleshy moon, has grown sharply defined. She is beginning to go gray, the gray standing out so brightly against hair that is otherwise the glossy black of a gun barrel. He notices this most on weekends, the only time he is home to see her rise from bed, usually in the early afternoon, dragging herself to the kitchen to make coffee. Her eyes are dark craters. Her back hunched. Moving like a thing half-alive.

Every now and then he will come down hard on her, usually at his wife's behest. "We are supporting you," he will tell her, "and you need to support us. You need to contribute to the household." She will cry and through her tears tell him how hard it is, how terrible she feels. He will comb his fingers through her hair and say, "There, there," and she will dab her eyes and wipe her nose with a shirtsleeve and promise to do better. And she will.

He is always working, his wife is always working, and while they are gone Sridavi will make their beds, vacuum the carpets, scrub the coffee grounds and red wine blotches from the counters—and then, after a week or two, her room, and the rest of the house, will slip into the disrepair that is her standard. The coffee table has ghostly rings on it, like raindrops in a mud puddle. Unfolded laundry remains piled in the hamper. Crumbs spot the carpet. Mildew crawls along the corners of the shower. When doing yard work, she will leave the lawn half-mowed, a pile of branches trimmed but not bundled, everything unfinished, as she goes inside to get a drink of water and then forgets.

Sometimes, when he is on the phone with his friend Keith, when they are talking about prions, about the possibility of an inoculation, Neal will grow weary and distracted and interrupt the conversation to ask about Keith's boy. "Is he the same? Is he like Sridavi? Lazy and unmanageable, sneaking away at night and sleeping all hours of the day?" But Keith always says, no, no, his boy's a pretty good shit. And Neal is happy for him, he is, but another part of him wishes the boy were a problem. Then he could write off his daughter's affliction as a product of her age instead of this disease. Something she might grow out of.

Sometimes, when he comes home from the lab, he has no energy to do anything but watch television with a plate of cold food in his lap. Usually he flips to the History or Discovery Channel and watches shows about evil dictators, Sasquatch and Loch Ness, the predictions of Nostradamus, what the world will look like after the people are wiped out by a disease that eats its way through the population or an asteroid that comes flaming out of the sky. He particularly loves the shows about haunted castles, houses, caves, catacombs.

He remembers one episode about a suburban home in Pennsylvania. A family moved in, and soon after, strange things began to happen. The lights would flicker and dim. The windows would open and close. A glass of water would drag across the table and shatter on the floor. One night, when the parents were reading in the living room, the couch turned over and the windows blasted open and from them came a wailing, like the noise of banshees. And another time, in the bathroom, the father noticed the paint bubbling and when he pressed his finger to it, it popped and bled. Soon after that, they brought in a psychic, a large black woman in a purple muumuu named Madam Serena, thinking she might identify a demon or an Indian burial ground.

Instead she claimed the haunting came from the daughter, a teenager, black haired, black fingernailed, dosed up on medication for her depression. She was possessed by a darkness that had in turn possessed their home. “She is devouring you,” Madam Serena said.

When Neal sits in the living room illuminated by the flickering light of the television, when he sees the vomit-splattered toilet bowl and hears the moans coming from his daughter’s room and faces the stiff, cold silence of his wife in bed, he, too, feels as though his daughter is slowly devouring him, devouring them all.

He isn’t sure what to blame, the drugs or the disease. Sometimes the drugs seem like the disease. He remembers a story his amah told him when he was a boy. He would help her in the kitchen, standing on a chair so that he could reach the counter—blending spices, mashing peas and potatoes, sculpting samosas—and she would tell him fairy tales about tigers and rupees, asses and elephants, magic fiddles, broken pots, the boy with the moon on his forehead and a star on his chin.

One of these stories was about a village that hired a snake to kill a troublesome jackal that ate babies and stole treasure and kept everyone awake at night with its cackling. The snake spread its jaws wide and ate the jackal whole, and for many minutes its wriggling form could be seen surging its way down the snake’s throat and distending its belly, where it at last went still. The snake then curled up and slept in the village square and digested the jackal and around it the villagers danced for many days in celebration, and eventually their stomping feet and jangly music woke the snake, which turned to them to satisfy its renewed hunger. In this way one beast replaced another. That is how he feels about his daughter.

Lycans used to take a high dosage of quaaludes—labeled Wolfsbane. Then, in the eighties, Volpexx hit the market, a chemical cocktail of antipsychotics and benzodiazepines / sedative-hypnotics. Over the years the formula has undergone many changes, but in its current form, the pills—taken twice daily, as round and white as miniature moons—are a stiff blend of 20 mg haloperidol and 4 mg lorazepam laced with silver. The drug is mandatory and available free to all registered lycans. There is no limit on the number of refills—there is only the demand that a patient test positive during the monthly blood test or face imprisonment. All one needs is an excuse—a bottle of pills misplaced—and a new prescription is filled.

Most people would not want to take more pills. Most people find the drug imprisoning, deadening, a denial of self. But his daughter is not most people. She takes Volpexx with Robitussin and NyQuil. She takes it with weed, with Red Bull, with Sudafed and Benadryl. She pops it and snorts it. Sometimes her skin seems so thin, as transparent as cellophane, that he can see her pulse in her veins from across the room. And sometimes she cries for no reason at all, cries for hours on end, her tears like dark rivers.

Neal does not mention this—not even when Augustus asks about his daughter—at the Deerstalker Golf Club outside of Eugene. "She's good," he says, and Augustus says, "Good. That's good." The day is damp and gray, the grass still heavy with last night's rain, soaking their shoes and slowing their balls and giving the men a good excuse for their frequent slices and mulligans. Chase wears jeans and a Windbreaker, Neal and Augustus slacks and sweaters. They drive a golf cart along the slick asphalt path—the tires spitting, the clubs rattling when they round a corner—and behind them follows another cart carrying a two-man security detail.

At the eighth hole, a par five that doglegs left, Augustus and Chase both end up blasting away with their fat-headed drivers and hooking into the woods. Neal opts instead for a five iron, takes a few practice swings, and then gently thwacks his ball in a long, curving arc that comes to a rolling stop right where the fairway elbows.

Chase whistles appreciatively. "A real golfer."

"Used to be."

"What's your handicap?"

"My handicap is golf." He pats his stomach. "And ice cream."

A quiet joke. In response Chase laughs a little too loudly. This is, Neal suspects, because of the Volpexx. More than an hour ago, when they met in the parking lot, Neal removed from his trunk a carton packed with one hundred bottles, each rattling with one hundred pills. He ordered them shipped to his campus office, instead of the lab, charging them to his discretionary fund.

Immediately Chase pulled a jackknife from his pocket and slashed open the box and popped open a canister and punched through the foil. "When I was growing up," Chase said, "my cousin started getting these headaches. They'd come and go at first. Then it didn't matter how much aspirin he took. They took him in after the nosebleeds started. Brain cancer. Inoperable. Thirteen years old. Tumor the size of a starfish. In the end, he started saying and doing the most terrible things. Nobody wanted to be around him because nobody recognized him."

He used his sleeve to dry off the rain-spotted spoiler of a car. On it he crushed three pills with the cap of the bottle until they were a mess of white powder. He pulled out his wallet and cut the powder into two lines with a credit card. "That's how I feel these days. With this *thing* inside me. I want you to kill it, Doc."

Then he rolled a dollar into a straw and brought it to one nostril while plugging the other. He staggered back with his eyes watering, furiously rubbing his nose. Then he sneezed into his elbow and gave them a dopey grin and slapped both his knees and said, "Phew. That's a dose of death right there."

Now Neal joins the two men in the woods. They wade through the damp cover of oak leaves, the leaves slurping and squelching underfoot. They turn their faces downward and hunt for the balls they know they will not find. And while they move among the thick-waisted trees, ten feet apart, Augustus talks about the plan. It is a good plan, he thinks. They will start by making a call to Senators Wyden and Merkley.

Chase kicks over a pile of leaves and says, "I've punched Wyden. Twice."

"He'll forgive you. Because this is what we're going to promise our dear senators: major campaign donations from Nike, Intel, Lithia, Harry and David, and Alliance Energy. Alliance Energy being the key. One of our major talking points over the next few months being nuclear energy.

In turn, the Senate earmarks a lump sum from the federal budget for the Center for Lobos Studies, which will remain affiliated with the Infectious Disease Research Center and which our man, the distinguished Dr. Desai, will direct. And hopefully we will have a vaccine in place within the next two years. That's completely possible. You've said that's possible."

Neal peers out of the woods and eyes the fairway and judges the angle of their drive and guesses again the placement of the balls. He does not look at Augustus when he says, "Creating the vaccine is not a problem. Implementing it is. The ACLU has blocked vaccine research the past twenty years."

"These are special times. America is under attack."

When Neal was a boy—in Los Angeles, his father first generation and a professor of psychiatric studies—he would spend his weekends hunting for golf balls. Trolling the woods, raking the sand traps, wading the ponds. The courses would pay him a nickel a ball. The groundskeepers thought he was Mexican and called him José. He said he was Indian and they asked about his headdress and tomahawk and he said, "Not that kind of Indian. *Indian* Indian." He carried a backpack with him and by the end of the day it would be full of Titleists and Dunlops. He would bring his goggles and wear his swim trunks and dive down into the gray-green murkiness of the course's ponds and lakes, holding his breath until his lungs ached, until his vision went spotty, clawing golf balls from the muddy bottom like pearls.

Now he approaches a rhododendron and peaks under it and spies the dimpled white ball and feels that old excitement that comes whenever he discovers what no one else can. He holds his breath as he bends over his gut and palms the ball. "So it's as simple as that?"

"There's nothing simple about it. But it will work." Augustus removes his glasses and untucks a flap of his shirt to clean the lenses and inspects Neal as if he might need some polishing as well. "We're going to make certain you get the support you deserve."

"Are you?"

"We are." Two angry red lines run from his ears to his eyes, the skin pinched by the stems of his glasses. "Because once you develop the vaccine, you will be both the governor's benefactor and beneficiary."

Chase has given up his search. At the edge of the woods, he leans against a tree with a glassy-eyed look and smokes a cigarette. Neal approaches him and holds up the ball and says, “Found what you were looking for,” and Chase draws on his cigarette and blinks confusedly through the smoke and then reaches out his hands, palms up, as though he hopes Neal will join him in prayer.

CHAPTER 26

TIME PASSES. How much, Claire doesn't know, whether minutes or hours or days, with no light except the glow of the LED strand, no company outside of the black stone and black sand, so that she is nearly unconscious, somewhere between sleeping and waking, the cold making her body and mind numb, and even when she tries to collect her thoughts they flutter away like the bats roosting among the cracks. In the corner sits a bucket and a roll of toilet paper. Her feet remain handcuffed, but her arms are free. "I don't want to make you miserable," her uncle said when he snapped them into place. "But I need to know I can trust you before I take these off." She feels no emotion, no panic or anger or fear, just blankness, when she stares at a block of basalt, at the porous holes and knuckly bumps of its black surface like a landscape of its own, like a hidden world within this world, no different from the community that exists in these lava tubes.

She isn't sure how many lycans there are, maybe dozens, maybe more, but she understands from the electricity flowing through the tunnels and the conversations overheard and the many men who have brought her food—on a tray, no less, with a plate and a glass and silverware and a napkin, venison sausage and a beet vinaigrette salad, rice and rosemary chicken, food that could not have been cooked without a working kitchen—that this is more than a camp; it is a kind of undertown.

She wakes to Puck standing over her. "You shouldn't be here," she says.

"Why not?"

"Because my uncle told you not to bother me."

"Some uncle. Handcuffs on your ankles. Nothing but a pot to piss in."

"I never said I liked him."

He has been smiling all along, but now the smile grows wider. He holds up his disfigured hand, the one missing its pinky and ring finger, a gummy nub of tissue. The remaining fingers carry thick yellow nails. "Compliments of your aunt. Do you want to know how it happened?" He does not wait for her response. "The slut always walks around in next to nothing. Little tank tops and such. Wanting everyone looking at her, wishing for a peek, hoping for a squeeze. So that's what she gets. I come up behind her one day when she's working in the kitchen, cutting some vegetables, and I give her a nice rub. Hands on her shoulders. Real friendly. Not in the least inappropriate. Just wanting to ease some tension. She's a tense person, your aunt. And what does she do to repay my kindness? Flips around without warning, swings the knife, cuts me to the bone. I'm not one to take my punishment sitting down. We got into a bit of a row."

She notices his crotch bulging with an erection. His eyes go someplace far away before focusing in on her once again. "I could take those cuffs off, you know? It wouldn't be much trouble at all." He takes a step toward her and the cave seems suddenly very small.

All the men carry walkie-talkies on their belts, and his sizzles to life then. A voice calling for him. He unclips it and says, "What?" as if the word were a curse.

There is a shipping problem. A delay. The nitro. They need his help. "Will be right there," he says and then bites down on the antenna and stares at her.

"I'm going to tell Jeremy about this," she says, just to say something, to stop the penetrating silence of his stare.

His teeth unclip from the antenna. "Child." His hair is so white it might be aflame. "You seem to think he's in charge. He would like that. He would very much like that. But he's not, not at all. Despite the fact that he's always rubbing it in my face what a big shit he is."

"If he's not in charge, then who is?"

His expression goes slack and his eyes seem to pulse, to widen. "Balor."

The .30-06 was a birthday gift when Patrick turned fourteen. It was his father's, a Mossberg. Walnut forearm, checkered stock, bluish metal, worn leather strap. Holding it, breathing in the smell of gun oil, brings him back to California. Rising well before dawn, his father opening his door, gently saying up and at 'em, a breakfast of eggs and bacon waiting at the table. Blaze-orange jackets and hats. A thermos of coffee set between them on the bench seat of the truck. The empty highway, the gravel side roads, the thick black forest into which they hiked when the horizon began to brighten pinkly with dawn.

He shipped the rifle, along with a few boxes of books and clothes, back in August. That was one of the things his father stressed, how good the hunting was up in Oregon, as though Patrick were headed off on vacation.

Now the rifle is in the bed of a Chevy Silverado and he is crushed into the club cab. There are five of them in the truck, all wearing a blend of camo and denim and blaze orange. Max drives. When they picked Patrick up, he asked where they were going and Max said, "On a wolf hunt." He says he has a feeling about the hot springs. It's too random of a place to attack otherwise. Why not a mall or a park or a church service? He figures some lycans came across the bathers by accident, saw an opportunity. They're in, they're out, just as the snow starts falling to cover their tracks, and a few days later, when the bodies are discovered, they're holed up, nowhere to be found.

Before Patrick can respond, Max snaps on the radio. Nobody talks, not that they could, the speakers blasting some punk band called Slovak, the electric guitar sounding like knives on knives, the words garbled into screaming that makes Patrick's ears feel as though they might bleed. At one point he asks if they can turn it down a little.

"Max?" he says. "Max?"

Nothing. The other Americans stare straight ahead as if so intent on the music blasting from the stereo they do not recognize his voice. Not for the first time, he wonders what he is doing in their company.

They follow paved roads that branch off into cinder and dirt slippery with snow. They drive past houses and single-wides that give way to timber broken up by five-acre clear-cuts. They pass logging trucks, the trees in their beds whittled down to pencils. The Forest Service road they follow angles steeply upward, deeply rutted and choked with weeds, the trees growing closer, the braches occasionally reaching out like icy claws to screech on the windshield until finally they come to a place where a landslide washes out the road and they park beside the tide of boulders and frozen mud.

"Here we are," Max says and kills the ignition.

A few years ago, at her friend Stacey's, Claire was sunbathing in the backyard when a shadow fell across her—she felt the cool of it like a wet towel—and she opened her eyes to find Stacey's younger brother hovering over them with an air rifle in one hand and a rabbit in the other. He had killed it in the woods near the house. He flopped its body at the girls and they said gross and threatened to rip out his hair and paint his toenails if he kept bothering them. And then something came over Claire—she wasn't sure what—and she stole the air rifle from his hands. There was a robin singing in a nearby tree and she stalked toward it, wearing her purple bikini, rifle at her shoulder. She fired. There was a snap sound. The robin dropped from the tree and lay still. Stacey's brother whooped, but she was quiet when she crouched by the bird and scooped it up. It weighed nothing. Its eyes were glassy—its beak swelling with a bubble of blood. She had never felt so horrible in her life and swore she would never kill anything again—that is, until later that afternoon, when she ate a steak her father had grilled. But still, she felt horrible and preferred not to think about killing as a part of life.

Yet here she is, trying to decide how best to kill Puck—or whoever comes along first; she isn't picky—and all the different ways she might escape. She needs to stay sharp. She needs to be ready, as Miriam taught her.

So she does as Miriam taught her and transforms. Lets the wolf turn over inside her, at first to test her strength, to see if she can snap the chain, and then to pass the time. She isn't sure how much noise she makes—she isn't sure how she gets from one side of the cave to the other—she isn't sure how her clothes tear or a gash appears in her forehead. Whenever she settles down—when her heartbeat slows and her breathing calms and her body resumes its original form—her memory of the past few minutes is like a cloudy dream.

Her ankles bleed from yanking at the cuffs. But the pain doesn't bother her. If there is anything the past few months have taught her, it is that the familiarity of pain makes it easier to manage, her body like one big nerve deadened by affliction.

Her senses grow heightened. She notices the whisper of a bat's wing, the faraway char of meat cooking, the small shifts in the air as the cave breathes. She knows someone is coming—like an image glimpsed in a lamplit window or a conversation overheard in the buzz of a bar—she knows this long before she hears the footsteps in the sand. Soon he will turn the corner. Soon he will be within reach. If it is Puck, and if he comes close enough, she will go for his neck and his eyes. She will kill him.

It takes Patrick time to make sense of what he sees. The circumference of strewn carcass—the hair and the blood and the bone—reaches fifteen feet across. And then he recognizes the head of a doe, still attached to the spine, a little ways off. A beetle lumbers out of its mouth and creeps along its snout to sample the black pool of its eye.

He is alone. Ten minutes ago, he and the others split up, stalking different sections of the woods. It wasn't long before their footsteps fell away. Now the wind rises and a drift of ice-polished leaves twirls up into a small cyclone before falling apart with a rattle. There are piles of snow here and there, but much of it has melted and frozen again. He isn't sure whether he should call out or not, tell the others to come see. But what would a dead deer prove? A cougar could have done this as well as a lycan.

His phone buzzes and he pulls it out, surprised he gets service this far from town. The message, from Malerie, reads, "I was protecting you. But I guess you don't need my protection."

He has no idea what to make of this and considers ignoring her altogether but feels enough concern to fire off a question mark in response. Before he can think any further, he hears a thrashing, faint and far ahead, something pressing through the undergrowth. He clicks off the safety of his rifle and starts forward, taking care not to step on a stick or crunch through an ice puddle or kick through a bush. After a minute the sound dies away and he pauses, cocking his head until he hears it again, tracking it. In this stop-and-go manner he proceeds for a good five minutes.

He tries to steady his breathing. It could be one of the Americans after all. It could be anyone, anything. He can feel his heartbeat in his fingertips. He imagines the trees parting like a curtain to reveal the lycan from the plane, crouched on a stump like a gargoyle, with a grin full of far too many teeth. Patrick wonders what chance he will stand this time, with no body to drape over him, nowhere to hide. He of course wishes he could run as fast as his legs will carry him, until the forest is a brown blur, back to the truck. But every time he feels rooted in place, ready to turn and flee, he thinks of his father, who would not run.

The sound, he realizes, has not moved. It comes from roughly the same place—now thirty paces ahead, where the ground angles downward into a coulee. He hears the faint trickle of water, and—interrupting it—a splash.

He reaches the lip of the coulee, where the land drops and the trees angle upward like arms crooked at the elbow. He sees, at the bottom of it, through a willow cluster, in the spring-fed stream, the mule deer. Two big bucks facing off.

He lifts the rifle and glasses them with his scope. He tries to count their points and cannot, their crowns tangled together in combat. The larger of the two weeps blood from where a tine punctured its eye. A red trail oozes from its ear—and several more from its neck—where it has been speared. The animals are silent except for the occasional snort, the splash of a hoof when they redistribute their weight, whip their heads around. The water, as dark as blackberry wine, rushes along beneath them, but mostly they are still, seeming to rest against each other. Patrick then realizes their antlers are locked, so tightly entwined they cannot release.

His finger slides off the guard and caresses the trigger as he imagines the racks mounted in his bedroom. He can see them so clearly, it is as though they are already there, anchored above his bed and casting their shadows like forking branches on the wall when he walks in and flips on the light.

He fires. The larger deer collapses. The creek runs over its body like a boulder and makes a foaming collar around its raised neck. Their crowns remain locked and the smaller of the bucks stands frozen in place with its head bowed toward the river as if for an endless drink.

His handheld buzzes. The deer isn't going anywhere, so he checks the message before reloading. Malerie again. "I know about your mother," she writes, "and now Max does 2."

He nearly drops the phone, forgetting all about the woods and the deer and everything else, all his attention crushed down to a single sentence that makes his chest seem to collapse so that he can barely draw a breath, when his mind makes a swift series of calculations—Malerie, Walgreens, the list of names—and still he doesn't really understand what this means until he looks up and sees

Max standing on the other side of the coulee, rifle in hand, looking at him.

☽

Claire pretends to sleep. She hears the footsteps grow near, hears breathing. She imagines Puck standing there, his hair fluorescent, watching her, maybe toying with his belt or zipper. Her blood goes hot, that catch-flame feeling that precedes transformation. She opens her eyes slightly, just enough to spy through her lashes, and discerns a shadow far larger than she expected. She flinches—sure that the giant is leaning over her, the black flaps of his leather duster opening, spreading as wide as buzzards' wings—ready to cry out.

But it is only her uncle. He holds up his hands as if she were the threat. "Hey, hey," he says. "It's all right." His face is broad and kind, haloed by thick brown curls, and though she wants to hate him, it's hard to feel anything but relief when he digs in his pocket and removes a key and nods at her cuffs. "I thought I'd show you around. As long as you promise not to try anything stupid?" At first she doesn't respond and his hand closes around the key and hides it from view. Only then does she nod, and he says, "Good."

Her feet, once free, still feel bound, every step she takes somehow wrong. Her leg muscles are at first heavy and unresponsive, and she touches her toes and does a few lunges and jumps up and down before telling Jeremy she is ready.

In the sand their footsteps make sounds like paper shredding. She follows him through the tunnel, which forks and then forks again. She makes an effort to remember the way—in case she should ever get the opportunity to escape—left, left, for starters.

"This is home," he says, this network of lava tubes, an underground village protected by vast rocky armor. In some places the walls glimmer and trickle, slick with moisture, and in other places they go chalky with calcite and lichen. She follows him up a kind of stairway, flattopped rocks stationed in the black sand, and the tunnel opens up into a vast chamber, as big as a ballroom. She cannot make out the ceiling—the LED lights cast an uncertain glow beyond which hangs the deepest darkness—but from it hang roots, like tentacles, hundreds of them dangling all around them. Jeremy takes hold of one and swings a few feet and trippingly looks back at her with a grin. "Try it."

She will not.

"You're upset at me?" he says.

"What do you think?"

"I'm sorry we've had to meet this way."

She asks whose fault that is. She says he's her uncle, but until a month ago, she didn't even know he existed. She doesn't know anything about him.

"That's not my fault. That's your parents'. They didn't want anything to do with us, not the other way around."

"I don't know anything about you," she says again, and he says, "What do you want to know?"

"Nothing," she says, and then, "Where do you get your power? Electricity, I mean."

"That's what you want to know? Where we get our power?"

It is. So he explains how the dams on the Columbia River produce electricity that gets outsourced to California. Many high-voltage and secondary lines are strung across the Cascades, and no, to answer her question, it's not possible to tap into a twenty-five-thousand-volt structure to run computers or small appliances. Power is stepped down as it goes to homes through multiple levels of transformers that lower the voltage. Less than a half mile away from where they stand, there is a PacifiCorp maintenance shed with a residential transformer in it that brings the voltage down to 120. "That's our keg to tap."

Claire asks what if PacifiCorp detects a power drain, what if they get caught?

"That won't happen," he says. "Because we work for PacifiCorp. Just as we work for UPS and the Port Authority and Nosler and Union Pacific and American Airlines." He lists off names and holds out a finger for each one until he runs out of fingers. He smiles when he says, "We're everywhere."

They move through the roots, brushing them aside, some of them as thickly clustered as hair. They approach a brightly lit chamber. Voices mutter from it, voices that go silent when they enter, ducking their heads through the low entryway. The room, twenty yards in circumference, is shaped like a dome. The floor is a mess of black and white cords that vine from tables crowded with desktop and laptop computers, printers, a scanner, a blinking green modem and wireless transmitter. A map of the country hangs on the wall right next to a map of Oregon, with different colored pins quilling them both. White Christmas lights are strung overhead in an impression of a starlit sky.

Ten men, seated at computer terminals or standing around a table littered with paper, are staring at them. At Claire. Some of them are as pale and swollen as grubs, and some of them are leathery and appear clownish in their mismatched clothing, a too-large Gap shirt and pants sewn out of doeskin and stitched with sinew.

"The latest?" Jeremy says.

One of the pale men, dressed in a Darth Vader sweatshirt and blue jeans, says, "Problem solved." His eyes flicker to her and back to Jeremy. "Freight from Canada is delayed but on its way. We've got a truck on standby at the intermodal rail yard. He'll meet us at the farm in Sandy. We won't have long to get ready."

"Then we better get moving."

She filters out the rest of the conversation—because nearby, peeking from beneath a pile of paper, she has spotted a pair of scissors. She tries to be casual when she rests her flattened hand on the table. She thinks about lurching forward, grabbing the scissors, swinging them into Jeremy's temple. Then she spots a web hanging between two computers, a spider balanced in the center of it like the pupil of an eye watching her. So she swings the scissors, and then what? And then what would she do? They would have her on the floor within seconds. She creeps her hand around the blade and secrets it up her sleeve. She can be patient.

Another minute and Jeremy leads Claire from the room—down a corridor lined with yellowed newspaper clippings that flap and whisper with their passing. She glances at the headlines. "Terror in the Air," they read. "Hundreds Dead." "Nation of Fear." "Lycan Uprising." She slows when she spots the front page of *USA Today*. "Miracle Boy" is the headline, and below it she spots a familiar face. The boy, Patrick.

She nearly cries out to him, like a friend spotted in an unfamiliar city. He is surrounded by police who usher him toward an ambulance. He is staring directly at the camera, staring directly at her. A spot of mold darkens one of his eyes.

"What are you planning?" Claire says.

Jeremy keeps walking, not looking back at her when he says, "You'll know soon enough. Along with everyone else."

"Is something wrong?" Patrick says. He doesn't know what else to say. He has to say something—has to break the long silence that hangs between them, Max on one side of the coulee, him on the other.

No response outside of an unblinking stare. Maybe his words were lost, carried away by the rushing water, the wind whining through the trees. Maybe he is jumping to conclusions. Maybe Max doesn't know what Malerie said he knows.

"Is something wrong?" Max finally says. "Is lying wrong? Is betrayal wrong? Is fucking somebody else's girlfriend wrong?"

Patrick has never heard him swear before, so the word seems as sharp as a sword. "We never did that."

"You did enough!" Max screams this, his voice filling up the forest, drawing from it other figures, the Americans. They step from behind trees, their eyes hooded, their boots dragging through the pine needles. "Half-breed."

"I'm not a lycan." He realizes this will make no difference to them, realizes they have already made up their minds to hate him, but he can't stop himself, as if to affirm his identity. "She was bitten after I was born."

"That still makes you a son of a bitch." Max points his rifle at him.

He raises his own in defense. They have brought him here to hurt him. Deep in the woods. A place where no one will hear him scream. A place where he will never be found. He isn't sure what they are capable of—but he is about to learn.

Max keeps his eyes on Patrick but speaks to the others. "He hasn't reloaded. Get to him before he does."

They leap off the ledge and kick their way down the hill and splash through the stream and scramble up the other side, moving steadily toward him, and all the while Patrick stands there, as frozen as the deer in the river, too tired to run, too tired to do anything but ratchet the breech and eject the cylinder, not bothering to reload. "I'm sorry about Malerie," he says.

"Too late for sorry."

The boys close the distance quickly, clambering over the lip of the coulee, racing in his direction with their arms out. He can't fight them—there are too many and their punishment will be that much more severe if he puts up a struggle—so he tosses the rifle aside and crouches down in a ball and they are on top of him. He is ready for the pain. Their fists and their boots thudding against his spine and ribs, his ass, the back of his head. First the impact, then the bruised heat that follows, until his entire body feels inflamed, every throb like an ember glowing orange beneath his skin.

Somehow, through the tangle of bodies, he makes out Max on top of him. His belly is soft and damp, like a pillow soaked with water. His voice pants in his ear. "We could kill you, you know. Say it was an accident. No one would know. Maybe I'd even speak at your funeral, run a hand along your coffin, which would be closed of course, since your skull would be split open like a cantaloupe."

Somebody punches him in the ear, a hand as hard as a sledgehammer. A steady rain of black spots falls along the edges of his vision, and he ends up on his back—staring through the animal bodies looming over him—staring at the sky beyond them, where jets rumble and their contrails criss-cross the pale blue like badly cast fishing lines across the surface of a lake.

He wishes them safe travels.

Jeremy shows her a room with a groined ceiling. Three moldy couches are arranged around an old wood-paneled television with a VCR and DVD player stacked on top of it. And then they walk past a sleeping chamber full of cots and a supply room busy with bags and boxes and crates, some arranged on shelves, some heaped and scattered on the floor. The tang of gun oil hangs in the air.

The kitchen is a space similar to the computer lab. Six mismatched lamps are staggered through the chamber to give off enough light to cook by. A skinned headless deer hangs from a rope, turning slowly, the rope creaking and knotted through its hind hock. The scent of blood comes off it and she resists the peculiar desire to slide a finger along the haunch and lick it.

Next to the deer sits a dented gas stove with a dirty propane tank hosed up behind it. And then a woodstove piped out through a crack in the wall, some other channel that sucks away the smoke.

Several folding tables are pushed against the walls, their tops cluttered with cutting boards and knife blocks and cutlery jars packed with spatulas and wooden spoons like vases full of flowers. An old yellow fridge hums in the corner, surrounded by stand-alone cabinets, many of them without doors, their insides jammed with pans, pots, glasses, plates, spices.

Claire notices a trickling sound and goes to it, a spring dribbling from a hole in the wall and pooling in a rock basin the size of a bathtub. Jeremy kneels down and unhooks a ladle with a screened filter and dips it into the spring. He drinks from it and dips it again and asks, "You thirsty?"

She is more than thirsty, her lips cracked and peeling, and she nods and brings her mouth greedily to the ladle, the same place his mouth had been. She fills it four times before she nods to him and their tour resumes.

"Who's Balor?" she says.

"Where did you hear that name?"

She shrugs. "Who is he?"

"Tell me about your aunt."

"Your wife."

"Yes."

"Why do you want me?"

"Because I want her. She'll come for you. Can you tell me about her?"

"I'm guessing she's a whole lot of pissed off and worried sick right now."

"I'm counting on that," he says. "I'm hoping we'll be seeing her soon."

She can feel a breeze now, as they move up an incline, the floor a jumble of boulders. They hold out their arms for balance and leap from rock to rock, moving upward, the air steadily growing brighter.

"She hasn't mentioned anything about the police?"

"Why would she?"

"Going to them, talking to them? She hasn't mentioned that?"

"She just wants to be alone. You should leave her alone. Why do you want her anyway?"

"I need her. A wife should be with her husband." He blinks rapidly, and then his voice grows louder and hurried as if to overwhelm what he has already said. "And she's an important part of what we're doing here. She's an important part of the revolution."

"Don't you think that's a little dramatic?"

"We're the revolution." He slips on a slick rock and catches himself with his hands and scrambles to right himself. "We're the leather-fringe revolutionaries fighting against the blood-coat British. We're the blacks boycotting the buses in Montgomery. We're the fist-pumping protesters who took over Tahir Square. This is grassroots democracy."

Claire realizes the illogic of what he's saying—a true democracy would leave Miriam alone if she voted to separate herself from the group—just as she realizes the brokenhearted can create any sort of justification, can make sense out of no sense. His daughter died. His wife abandoned him. He wants to fill up the emptiness he feels. Claire can relate.

But she is also a teenager, so she views everything through a cynical lens, and she finds it annoying that he is costuming his desire to regain his wife with political zealotry. He sounds like an actor reciting lines he hasn't quite mastered. She can't hold back the sarcasm. "Did you say democrazy?"

He frowns and stops climbing and stares until her eyes drop. "Are you making a joke?" he says and she senses for the first time how he could be dangerous to her if pushed too far.

"You kill people."

He takes a step toward her, stepping across a black gap of air, onto her boulder, less than a foot between them, but she doesn't back down. She can feel his breath on her when he says, "People die. That's what they do."

"Like your daughter."

He hits her openhanded. She doesn't see it coming—the slap hard—a sting followed by a swelling flush. She imagines, on her cheek, the white shape of a hand blooming bright red.

His eyes, at first black slits, soften. He hangs his head and turns away and continues to climb upward. "Come on," he says, and, after a moment, she follows, her hand holding the place his had been.

The air brightens. The incline flattens and they come to a door made of cross-stitched nylon rope—messy with browned vines—that parts like a curtain. This is one of four entrances, he says, and the netting provides camouflage and blocks the worst of the wind but also keeps the cave system breathing. "Essential, considering the smell the raggedy lot of us gives off." His voice full of humor, as if what happened a moment before did not.

Outside the sun is red and the trees are black. Dawn. She has lost all sense of time underground. She tries to take in as much of her surroundings as she can. A tangle of manzanita, stacks of lichen-encrusted rocks, a valley shoulder busy with scree. They are high up, near a lava cone frosted with snow, the Cascades rising jaggedly behind them. She imagines, at night, she would be able to distinguish—in the distance—some town, the faraway grid of streetlights. But now, squinting against the rising sun, she can distinguish nothing but hundreds of miles of woods that eventually give way to a wash of desert.

"Where are we?"

He looks at her with eyes the same color as the winter sky above them. "Your new home."

Max picks up Patrick's rifle and tests its weight in his hands as if it were a baseball bat. Then he swings into a tree, once, twice, three times, the bark chipping away, revealing the pulpy yellow wood beneath—and the rifle shatters, the stock splinters.

Patrick does not so much as lift his head in protest, his cheek to the forest floor, one of his eyes swollen to a slit. His mouth is full of blood and his tongue feels like an eel twisting around in it. Everything hurts, his entire body a pulsing wound. A headache tightens like a hot belt around his skull.

Max kicks at the remains of the rifle and shakes off the pain in his hands, and then, after one final withering glance at Patrick, he heads back the way they came with the other boys trailing him. One of them asks, "What about the deer?" and Max says, "Let it rot."

Patrick lays there a long time, feeling sorry for himself, caught up equally in the pain and humiliation of the moment. The woods seem suddenly leached of color, a nearby pine gray and gaunt and pocked with woodpecker burrows.

They have abandoned him here. A ten-mile hike from the nearest asphalt road, and from there, forty miles or more to Old Mountain. But he is alive. He rolls onto his side, bringing his knees to his chest, and imagines the bruises darkening his skin. He breathes through the pain in his ribs and listens to the trickle of the stream and the far cry of an owl.

Then he hears what he at first mistakes for the blood-pounding pulse in his ears—footsteps. Moving toward him. The Americans returning to finish him off. He lifts his head and blinks away the blood that films his vision and still he cannot make sense of what he sees. Walking along the edge of the coulee, a woman in full-body camouflage, Miriam.

"You're not dead anyway." She holds out a hand. "Come on. Get up."

CHAPTER 27

SOMETHING IS HAPPENING. When Jeremy escorts her back to her cell—she isn't sure what else to call it, the dark sandy recess she is consigned to—men rush through the underground passages, many of them speaking into walkie-talkies, one of them carrying a tangle of cords and video equipment, another huffing along with an oil-stained cardboard box that rattles in his arms. Jeremy says things to them—like "Go time" and "Let's do this"—and in their passing he pats them on the back or grips their shoulders.

Then, when the two of them descend the staircase, the corridor curls around a corner and she sees him, Puck. Unlike the others, he is not moving. He is leaning against the wall, hands in his pockets, with no other task except to wait for them. "I was told I won't be joining you in the field," he says, his voice as high-pitched as a bat's screech. "I was told I would be staying behind."

That stops Jeremy, who—head down, lost in his thoughts—hadn't yet noticed Puck. "Your work is here."

"You're punishing me? For the hot springs? Because I didn't ask for your *approval*?" This last word said with more than a little venom.

Jeremy looks at Claire, looks at Puck, and says, "We'll talk about this later." He starts down the staircase again, and Claire reluctantly follows, crossing her arms, walking directly behind Jeremy as if he were a blind. She feels electricity in the air, the crackling possibility of violence.

The corridor is thin and Puck does not move to accommodate them, so that Jeremy and then Claire have to brush against him, and when she does, she feels as she might when brushing up against a lightning-scarred tree, the char rubbing off on her, staining her with its shadow. She tries to keep her head down but can't help glancing his way, and when she does, he slides his tongue between his teeth and bites down.

☽

Patrick isn't sure what it is, maybe the sight of the knives on the counter or the pistol holstered around her shoulder, but he can't help asking, "You're not bad, are you?" The most childish question in the world, he knows.

"No," Miriam says. "Are you?"

He can't tell for sure, since her back is to him, but he thinks he detects a smile in her voice. He is in her cabin once again, feeling no less like a prisoner than last time, but something has changed, her attitude toward him softer. He sits at a round wooden kitchen table and she stands at the sink, wearing camo pants and a black tank top that reveals black wings tattooed across her shoulders, their color the color of her hair.

Next to the table sits an openmouthed trash bag full of driver's licenses. A dozen of them, like a strewn deck of cards, are spread across the table, all bearing photos of young women who look an awful lot like Claire.

Miriam fills a bowl with hot soapy water and carries it steaming to the table. She sweeps away the licenses and arranges a chair opposite him and dips a washcloth into the bowl and wrings it out with a splash. "Hold still," she says and begins to clean him. The washcloth is as rough as a cat's tongue. He closes his eyes and tries not to wince at the pressure against his swollen, cracked skin. All the while she hums, something barely audible, a lullaby. Before long the water in the bowl is flat and pink. She pats him dry with a hand towel and then unpeels several Band-Aids to hold together the places his skin split.

He has his arm wrapped tightly around his chest, hugging his ribs. "Better take off your shirt," she says, and he tries, but it hurts too much to lift his arms over his head. She helps him peel away the shirt to reveal a torso colored with angry red welts, a purplish black bruise along his rib cage.

He can see in her fingernails the telltale thickness of a lycan. He remembers Max talking about that, about the different ways you could detect infection, and fingernails were one of them, as thick as teeth, as thick as bone. His mother's are not so noticeable since she keeps them painted and filed. He can feel her nails on his skin now when she runs a hand along his ribs. "Maybe broken," she says, "maybe not. Either way, you'll live." She retrieves a bottle of ibuprofen from the bathroom and rattles out four pills, which he swallows with a tall glass of water.

Then she asks if he is ready to listen and he says he supposes so. She begins to talk. "Some of this you might already know. Some of this you will not." The light shifts and the shadows darken, when she tells him at length about the Resistance, about their ideology and activity over the past few decades, about her abandonment of them, about their harassment and the eventual kidnapping, the place in the snow where Claire's tracks ended, taken over by an abominably larger set she recognized.

"The bad guys," he says.

"Definitely the bad guys," she says.

"Did they leave you a note?"

"They didn't need to leave me a note. I know where to find them and their message was clear. Come back to us. Or else."

She tells him she was scouting the woods near their hideout when she heard the gunshot, when she found him enclosed in a knot of bodies. She tells him she plans to return there. She tells him that they will be expecting her and that there are many of them, but despite this, despite their force, she will get Claire back. And she tells him, finally, that he is going to help her.

"How soon are we going to do this?"

"We are going to do this now."

He feels afraid, very much so, but that is not why he hesitates. He hesitates because he has not said anything about the plane attacks and wonders if he should, wonders if she was somehow involved despite her disavowal. And he hesitates, too, because the beating has left him weak and addled. He worries he'll be useless. When he squeezes his hands into fists, they tremble like tools capable of breaking down when he needs them most.

Miriam is leaning toward him, her arms resting on her thighs. Her face is so pointed it is like its own kind of weapon. "You care about her?"

He is surprised by how automatic his response is. "Yes."

"I suppose you wouldn't have come back for her, right? You wouldn't have gone for your little walk in the woods if you didn't feel something for her, right?"

Her voice and expression are so stony he can't tell whether she is messing with him or not. "Right."

"I want you to know that she's not safe. The longer we wait, the more likely it is that something will happen to her."

He tries to harden his face when he says, "Okay," but really he feels small enough to put in his own pocket. The whole world seems suddenly against him, and he doubts, when he thinks of the Americans in town, or the lycans in the mountains, that he is up to the fight. His headache, at least, is fading to a hum, the ibuprofen numbing him.

Her hand drops to the table and caresses the pistol. "You know how to use one of these?"

"A little." Never pistols, only revolvers and rifles really, hunting deer or blasting pop bottles at the rock quarry.

She thumbs the safety off, then on. Ejects the magazine and slams it back home. "Seventeen rounds, double-stack magazines. Keep track. Finger on the guard unless you're ready to kill. Otherwise, bam, bam."

She rises and returns with two Magnum flashlights, two penlights, four folding knives with Teflon grips, a sheathed machete, a twelve-gauge pump shotgun, stacking them on the table. She goes to the cupboard next to the stove as if to withdraw a pot but instead grabs a half dozen clips of ammo. Then she creaks open the hall closet and pulls from the shelves several holsters, each with a backing plate of saddle leather, worn tucked inside the waistband.

She tells him to stand up and he does, still shirtless. Without asking for help, she grabs his belt and loosens it by two notches to accommodate the holsters, one on either hip, the pistol butts facing forward for a cross-arm draw.

She stares at him for a long while and sighs, as if finally recognizing him for the kid he feels like. "Let me put on some coffee," she says. "Sharpen us up."

Outside, the paling sky has the look of a watercolor. She hand-grinds beans and fills a kettle with water to set on the stove while he experiments with the pistols, unlimbering them from their holsters, holding them out before him, like the gunslingers in the movies; only his arms waver no matter how hard he tries to keep them steady. It's more than the pain in his ribs—like a knife wound—it's the weakness he feels.

He thinks of Claire, huddled somewhere in the

dark, and imagines her face turning toward him with relief. That numbs his pain more than the drugs breaking down inside him. He saved her once; he will save her again.

The stove *tick-tick-ticks* as the burner fails to catch. The smell of natural gas sours the air.

Patrick says, "So they've taken her because of you?"

The stove continues to tick like a bomb, and she curses under her breath and opens a drawer and knocks open a box of matches. "Yes."

"Why do they want you back so badly?"

She strikes a match and drops it on the burner and a blue flare the size of a child *foomps* to life and knocks them back a step—and then the flame settles. "Because I'm married to one of them."

When Jeremy tells her to please sit down, when he cuffs her wrists, when he tells her he enjoyed their little walk and asks whether she needs anything, she almost tells him about Puck, almost.

Then she realizes this is her chance. Something has been set into motion, something Puck is not a part of, something that will draw from the mountain many men, including Jeremy, who might otherwise bar her escape.

"No." She fiddles with the cuffs and casts down her eyes in case they might reveal her excitement. "I'm good. Thank you."

She knows it is only a matter of time before Puck comes for her. From only a few conversations, she has gleaned that he desires her, yes—but for reasons even more complicated he will punish her as if punishing Jeremy.

Her ankles he leaves free. The scissors remain hidden up her sleeve, the blades of them cold against her forearm. She feels her pulse throbbing against the metal, counting down the seconds, the minutes, the hours, until the tunnel system goes quiet, vacated—and then, as expected, she hears the approaching footsteps, kicking through sand like a gathering whisper.

It isn't clear where her cell begins—there is no definitive space designated as hers, no bars to peer through and knock a tin cup against. The lava tube simply ends—as if, eons ago, some large worm burrowed through the earth until it expired here, its flesh crumbling to sand, its shape remembered in the rocky husk of the tunnel. But if there were an entrance, a line within which she felt jailed, it is where Puck stands now, ten yards away, the bend in the corridor.

Neither of them says anything at first. They both know why he is there.

She can see his jaw working up and down, chewing gum, wetly mashing it with his teeth, snapping it. "It's snowing, you know," he finally says.

"That's nice." She isn't sure what to make of this, him talking about the weather. The weather is what you talk about when there is nothing else to talk about. "I like snow." Nothing could be further from the truth, but she tries to make her voice as sincere and pleasant as possible. She wants his guard down.

He pauses his chewing to say, "Really?" With that, he comes forward, one slow step, then another, the look on his face leading her to believe he is as surprised by what she says as by her seeming friendliness. "Most don't."

"This time of year, I do. Christmastime."

"But then it gets to be too long."

"I guess."

His voice lowers. "Around here the winters can be very, very long." The whites of his eyes glow, but his pupils appear as black as burrows. She feels as if she is falling into them. He has closed the distance between them by half. She is sitting on a rock the size of a buffalo skull, the closest thing she has to a seat, hunched over as if exhausted, but really, she is approximating a crouch, ready to spring forward. She tries to be casual, pretending to scratch an itch, when she pulls the scissors halfway from her sleeve, the blades now tucked sharply against her palm.

He pops his gum again, the sharp report making her flinch, reminding her of the time a boy at school came up behind her and snapped her bra. "Your bitch of an aunt isn't going to do anything stupid, is she? Isn't going to tuck tail to the police, spill her guts, tattle?"

"She wouldn't do that."

"Everyone has their breaking point." He crouches and reaches out an arm to touch her ankle. "Pretty."

She shivers. He's still too far away, faster than her, stronger, and she can't risk lunging that distance, giving him time to respond. She tries not to be bothered by his touch, but that's like trying to hold still when a spider dashes across your face. A shiver runs through her and she pulls away her feet. "Stop."

"Stop?" He works the gum from one side of his mouth to the other. She can smell it now, something fruity. "You think I'm going to stop? You think any of this is going to stop? We're just getting started. And if you think I'm going to use common words—like 'You better obey me' and 'You ought to treat me with respect' and 'You better shut your mouth'—you're mistaken. Because we don't believe in words here. We believe in doing. I'm going to *do* things to you. That's how you really get people to listen. You do things to them, and when those things are horrible, they listen very carefully. I want you to listen very carefully. You might think you're being imprisoned in this far dark corner, but you're in fact being protected. Forget about Jeremy. I am your protector. I am protecting you. All I need to do is snap my fingers and you'll be cast out to the wolves. The wolves like to bite and they like to sodomize. You'll feel like you've been turned inside out, like you've been fucked by a dozen swords. Maybe after they're done with you, they'll keep you around for another round or two, or maybe they'll be bored and bothered by your whimpering, and if that's the case, maybe we'll have a bonfire, a big one. We'll throw you in it and your skin will melt off and we'll all laugh and howl and dance around the flames and afterward gnaw on your blackened bones. How does that sound, Claire?"

He is reaching for her now. He is reaching for her, and if he touches her again, she imagines breaking apart into so many blackbirds that would screech and scratch and peck and finally flap in a dark cloud out of this place and take to the sky. He is reaching for her with his scarred hand, the hand Miriam disfigured with a knife, and now he touches her cheek, softly. Caressing her. She closes her eyes and takes a deep, trembling breath, laced with the flavor of his strawberry-sweet gum, and realizes, by breathing in the smell of him, he is already inside her. His fingers suddenly dig into her cheek and chin, and she snaps open her eyes to see his face transformed, his teeth fanged, his eyes as red rimmed as a smoldering coal. "Everyone has their breaking point."

It is then that she swings the scissors upward—into him.

☽

The cratered cheek of the moon hangs low in the sky, soon to be overtaken by a dark bank of clouds. In the Ramcharger, Miriam drives, Patrick sits shotgun, weapons piled and rattling behind them. The road hums under their tires and a light snow falls through the yellow glow of the high beams.

She pulls off the highway into a gas station with old-time pumps and a cedar-shingle mercantile. She does not stop but drives around back, where she says her husband keeps ten vans and cars and trucks parked. This morning, three were missing. Now it is early evening, and she counts seven of them gone, the empty squares of blacktop dusted white.

"What does that mean?" Patrick says.

"That means they're up to something."

He asks if they would have taken Claire with them, and Miriam is silent for the time it takes her to spin the wheel and loop the Ramcharger around and head back toward the highway. "Doubt it. She'd be in their way."

They drive another five minutes before hanging a hard left onto a road that branches several times and narrows, hemmed in by pines.

His mind is sharp with caffeine and adrenaline when they park at a power shed made of corrugated metal and surrounded by a hurricane fence and a metal sign that reads PACIFICORP. The trees here have been razed to make way for the twelve-line high-voltage high-wire utility poles that march off into the distance. Patrick can hear the electricity humming, as if the forest were alive with locusts, when he steps out of the Ram and they unload their backpacks and hoist their weapons. A lamp glows above the entry door.

Miriam tells him to wait here. He asks where she is going but she does not respond. She leaves her backpack with him but shoulders her shotgun, the black nylon strap cutting between her breasts. As quick as a cat, she scales the hurricane fence and drops to the other side and walks the perimeter of the power shed until she finds what she is looking for, a hole drilled through the metal siding, a power line the size of a garden hose snaking through it. She pulls down her shotgun, takes aim, and unloads both shells. Fire spits from the twin barrels. A thunderclap fills the night.

Patrick curses and ducks down behind the Ram and unholsters a pistol and looks around as if expecting shadowy figures to come pouring out of the woods. But the night is still and quiet except for the uninterrupted hum of the electricity overhead and the violent spitting of the severed cord.

He hears Miriam drop over the fence, her boots squeaking toward him, and when she appears next around the corner of the Ram, he says, "Now they know we're coming."

"They can't see shit. That's what they know."

He follows her into the woods, hushed as if listening in on their every move, and it isn't more than ten minutes before they come to the mouth of the cave system. Patrick does not recognize it as such until Miriam draws aside the ice-clotted drapery that covers the entry.

She disappears into it. For a moment he is alone, trying not to think too deeply about the necropolis he is about to enter, the risk and impossibility of the situation. He pauses, as if drawing a breath before diving underwater, and then clicks on his Mag light and plunges into darkness.

CHAPTER 28

CLAIRE HAD HOPED to hit his throat with the scissors. But Puck was faster than she expected and lurched back in time to save his life but not to dodge her completely. She plunged the scissors into the fleshy spot beneath his chin, knifing upward, into his mouth, the blades coming to a rest in his soft palate. He cries out, but the cry is muffled by a mouth stapled shut.

Wide-eyed, he stumbles back, a fistful of hair tearing away in her grip. He trembles his hands to the scissors and drags them slowly from his jaw. Blood gushes down his neck and patters the sand. He hurls aside the scissors and they clatter against the wall and he opens his mouth to test it and in doing so reveals teeth sharpening with his rage and fear.

And then, in a blink, the lights go out.

When Patrick first steps inside and out of the wind, he is surprised by the temperature difference, the cave significantly warmer. His father would sometimes take him spelunking, at Lava Beds National Monument, and he remembers strapping on a hard hat and running his hand along stalagmites and burrowing through crawl spaces and hearing some bit of wisdom from long ago, that caves and caverns year-round maintained a constant temperature, somewhere in the fifties.

The air smells sweetly fungal, some mixture of mold and guano and the sulfuric oxidation that stains the walls orange in places and yellow in others. The constant hissing of the wind and the dripping of water make it difficult to hear Miriam when she says, "Follow me closely." They have their Mag lights in one hand, their pistols in the other. The lava tube pitches downward and he sweeps his light across the cave floor and walls, black except for the occasional crust of lichen or sulfite, a white vein of quartz that catches the light and sparkles. The stalactites dangling from the ceiling remind him of nothing so much as teeth.

He has a knife in one pocket, clips of ammo in another. His belt creaks and his backpack clinks and his breath quivers out clouds. The noise seems impossibly loud. He trips several times over debris and knobs of basalt, always catching his balance, and Miriam looks back at him in irritation. He whispers sorry and feels fear and the fear feels something like wasps under his skin, a thrumming of wings, a prickle of legs and stingers.

One moment she is watching Puck. The next moment, darkness. She wonders, at first, if she is dead. If he has somehow already closed the distance between them and ripped her heart from her chest. If a rock has come loose from the ceiling and clubbed her skull. Or if her body has finally decided enough is enough and simply given up.

Then she hears his long, agonized wail, an animal in pain, and realizes that she is not dead, not yet. But death is close. Death has never been more of a possibility—buried as she is in a sulfuric dark beneath hundreds of thousands of pounds of rock. This will be her grave if she does not act quickly.

She recalls her last image of the chamber and wonders if she has moved since, if she is still facing the open tunnel. She steps sideways, her hand outstretched, until her fingers jam against rock. She scrabbles her hands along the wall and then shoots them out before her, as if sweeping the air free of cobwebs. She raises her knees high with every step, trying to avoid any debris on the floor, not worrying about her hurried stomping, knowing Puck cannot hear her over his own noise, as he alternately whimpers and bawls.

She is moving along the tunnel now. Her eyes are wide open but her fingers are her way of seeing, nosing through the dark like many moles that feel her way forward. The wailing behind her grows softer and then silent, and it is the silence that worries her. She tries to be as quiet as she can, but every other step she kicks a rock or sends something crumbling from the wall.

She remembers the way—left and then left again—noticing the shifts in air, the cold drafts when the tunnel forks. She nearly trips over the first step of the staircase. She clumsily climbs, wishing she knew how many steps awaited her, expecting any minute for something to come rushing out of the dark to seize and caress her. Another minute and her foot falls flat where she expects another step. The walls open up into a chamber. Her breathing and her footsteps sound softer here. She knows it would be wiser to follow the wall, to travel the chamber's circumference, but she cannot recall if there were other corridors that intersected here and she cannot risk wandering off into some channel that takes her deeper underground. She knows the computer room lies directly ahead. She decides to trust her eyeless sense of direction and starts forward. She smells the earthiness of the roots dangling from the ceiling, the roots that startle a scream out of her when they seem suddenly to swarm her, licking her face like dry tongues.

The cave is as black as bile. As black as ink. The black of a place sealed by stone and buried deep beneath the earth—a place no one should ever go. Penetrating, infectious, a black that soaks into her and drowns her lungs and leadens her muscles and makes her want to shrink into a ball and wait for the worst to happen because the worst seems an inevitability when lost in the dark with something fanged in pursuit.

She stops to listen. There is movement in the darkness. A rustling. Then footsteps. The noise, the soft padding over rocks, the shooshing through sand, grows louder, closer. The darkness invites the worst of her imagination, and instead of Puck creeping toward her, she imagines the man in the clown mask, his eyes black pools, his lips the red of fresh meat. When he found her, when he sniffed her out, his mouth would open as large as this chamber before swallowing her.

She feels the wolf welling inside her, willing her to let go, but so far she resists. She does not trust her wild mindlessness once transformed and worries she might end up, panicked as she is by the dark, clawing at the walls until her fingers peel away to bone.

She keeps *trying* to see. As if, by force of will, she will develop extrasensory sight. The strain makes her eyeballs ache as if full of too much blood. She hears Puck bark out a laugh, but it's difficult to place him, whether five or fifteen or fifty yards away, the noise echoing off the curved walls and toothy ceiling of this chamber and carrying through the many rooms and pits and corridors that reach into the darkness all around her.

Then she screams when right next to her she hears a voice damp and bubbling with blood: "I can smell you, pretty."

By his best guess they have been underground an hour. They have heard things—sand whispering, bats fluttering, rocks coming loose from the ceiling with a click and then slamming the cave floor with an echoing boom. At one point, something with red eyes scuttled through their flashlights' beams, never to be seen again.

He taps Miriam on the shoulder and she flinches at his touch. He asks how much farther and she says, "How much farther to what?" her annoyance obvious even at a whisper.

“To where they’re keeping Claire.”

“I have no idea. She could be in one of twenty different places.”

His flashlight sweeps the kitchen into sight. He is surprised, not for the first time, with their civility. He doesn’t know what he expected—straw and animal skins for bedding, a fire pit with gnawed bones stacked around it—but certainly not this. Glasses and knives and pots wink back at him. The fridge is messy with magnetic poetry. A can of Diet Coke is tipped over on a counter with a small brown puddle around its mouth. The smell of chili hangs in the air.

Miriam opens and closes the fridge, her hand lingering on the handle, as if she is remembering something.

He hears the trickle of water and seeks out the source among the cabinets. Here the cave wall sparkles with water. A ladle flashes silver. A stream of water seeps from the wall into a pool big enough for him to dive into with a splash.

It is here that he first sees her. Reflected in the moisture of the wall. A warped rippling figure darting from a nearby tunnel and coming rapidly toward him. He swings the flashlight and his pistol at once, almost firing and then nearly crying out when he recognizes her, Claire.

She is running toward him, toward the flashlight,

as though traveling down a tunnel of light, the white eye of the beam shrinking to home in on her chest. He feels such excitement he does not notice her expression, gray with fear and spotted with blood, until she is upon him. He catches her and she struggles against him a moment. He says her name and recognition dawns on her face and she says, "Run." She is pushing him, dragging him away.

He is about to question her when a half-glimpsed shape knocks him to the cave floor. His ribs scream with agony. He nearly blacks out. His Mag light skitters away and the shadows reel and make the kitchen swarm with black wraiths. He can smell blood, maybe his own. A figure crouches nearby, encased in shadow, unseen except for the faint glow of what must be hair, almost phosphorescent. It is breathing heavily, and every breath has enough damp throatiness to sound almost like a word.

Patrick is on his back and crabbing backward on his hands and legs when the figure blurs toward him. Gunfire shouts. Amplified painfully by their enclosure, the sound echoes around him, clapping off the walls and making one shot into a fusillade. Patrick is so stunned he can't register who has been shot, if anyone, until a flashlight arrests the figure—a man, Patrick can now see, a lycan with a narrow face and a body barely bigger than a child's. He is crumpling sideways, clawing at the air with one hand and clutching his belly with the other.

Miriam has both arms outstretched, casting the beam of her Mag light and firing her pistol into its glowing funnel. She fires again, and again, and every gunshot brings with it a blast of daylight that dies as soon as it appears. She marches forward, and the circle thrown by the Mag light grows smaller until it pinpoints the lycan. She fires again. The lycan's eyes roll back in his head and his body shakes as if possessed by a spirit he is trying to resist.

CHAPTER 29

THE CEREMONY IS to take place at nightfall, only minutes away, the sun cutting the sky with one last blade of light before sinking from sight. The windows of Fox Tower and the surrounding mall and office buildings glow yellow. Pioneer Courthouse Square—known affectionately as the living room—is a tiered and bricked crater in the heart of downtown Portland. A full city block decorated with fountains, now dry, and potted plants, now empty, and edged with pillars and trees through which, like a tangled spiderweb, hang garlands and strings of lights. The light-rail rolls by, its bell mixed up with the bell rung by the Salvation Army volunteer stationed at the corner.

On this cold November night, thousands of people have gathered. Breath plumes from their mouths. They stamp their feet to stay warm. They wear fleece and wool caps and red-and-green holiday sweaters. Daughters in Santa hats roost on their fathers' shoulders. Boys sip from paper cups of hot cocoa and ask, dozens of times, how long it will be until the lights come on, and their parents say, soon, soon. All eyes are on the dark-limbed seventy-five-foot Douglas fir erected in the center of the square.

A fat, white-bearded man in a Santa suit walks through the crowd, ho-ho-hoing and patting heads and handing out tiny candy canes wrapped in clear plastic and crouching down to gaze kindly at shy children who hide behind their parents' legs.

The sky is clear, but when the wind rises, it appears to snow, ice crystals blowing off the buildings and trees, making the darkened air sparkle.

Reporters from KGW and KATU and KOIN, wearing red scarves and black peacoats, stand before video cameras on tripods. They say that any minute now, the governor will appear for the annual Christmas tree lighting, any minute now—and *wait*—they bring a hand to their earpieces and listen and look over their shoulders and say, here he is now.

He wears a cowboy hat, a sport coat, and jeans. His teeth are bared in a smile. His cheeks are reddened from the cold. He works his way down a set of stairs, flanked by a seven-man security detail. He shakes hands, claps shoulders. There is applause, but under the applause, some muttering, a few boos.

Another minute and he is at the bottom of the amphitheater, standing before a microphoned podium with a rounded top, its dark wood polished to a glow, making it appear like an upright coffin.

"It's that time, friends," he says, his voice becoming many voices that boom from speakers stationed throughout the square. "The most wonderful time of the year." He takes in the sight of the tree, a black silhouette against a purple sky, and his eyes crinkle with seeming wonder when he talks of Christmas, the season of peace and giving, of goodness.

He makes no mention of lycans or of a presidential run or of any of the other sound bites he is so well-known for these days. Instead he talks about candy canes and sugarplums and the magic of the season and the gift of kindness. He talks about Christmas growing up on the cattle ranch. He quotes Charles Dickens. For a few minutes everyone feels good—everyone looks at him with kind crinkly eyed smiles—as if they each carried inside them invisible candles that he has lit so that the square seems illumined before he even flips the switch, as he does now, and everyone gasps with delight and applauds as the tree explodes with colored lights that chase the shadows from every face and make every wide-open eye glimmer like a star.

The choir from Oregon Episcopal, a group of teenagers dressed in red and black, gathers before the tree and sings, "Chestnuts roasting by an open fire, Jack Frost nipping at your nose," their voices as clear and bright as the pillar of light that rises behind them. Children sway and smile and husbands kiss their wives on the cheek and they hug arms around each other.

All this time a white windowless van circles the block. A decal along the body reads DEDMEN PARTY AND CATERING SHOPPE, a cluster of colored balloons rising above the black capital letters. The reflection of the Christmas tree streams across the black windows. The fifth time it circles the square, its engine shouts and it gathers speed and lurches sideways, off the street, into the square. Its tires thud over the curb.

The first few people don't even have time to scream, hammered by the grille, lost beneath the tires, their bodies cleaved. And then, all at once, as if everyone is connected by an invisible string, the crowd comes alive with a collective shout. Bodies shake, surge one way, then the other.

The choir is still singing when the van drops into the amphitheater. Their voices call out beautifully—soon lost against the harsh metallic bang when the undercarriage first slams the brick. The noise that follows is like the crash and crunch and shriek of the heaviest toolbox in the world hurled down a stone stairwell. Yellow sparks, like those of a failed Zippo, spit from the wheel wells.

The van is nearly to the tree when, in an orange flash, it is gone. A great boom sounds. Blackened strips of metal fling through the air, the shell of the van peeled away by its explosive core, the flames fingering their way outward, seizing and igniting so many bodies, flinging fistfuls of nails and screws and stainless-steel balls that blister brick and concrete and tear through flesh like buckshot through a road sign.

The brightness of the explosion—which for a few seconds chases away all the darkness and brings a hellish daylight to the square—has been replaced by a charred and smoking crater. Bodies lie in heaps, some of them moving, some not, their skin blackened and marred by many strange openings like diseased mouths.

A woman sits on a bench; the top of her skull is gone. The grayish nub of her brain peeks out. Threads of blood run down her face and dampen her jacket. She seems unaware of her injury, staring into the glow of her smart phone as if deciding whether or not she ought to call someone.

A man staggers by nearly naked, the clothes shredded off him, what remains hanging in blackened and bloody tatters like old bandages. His genitals are missing and blood streams down the insides of his legs. Another man walks by with no nose, another with no teeth, another with no lower jaw, his tongue dangling from a ragged toothy cavity.

"Help," says a woman in a Rudolph sweater. "Can somebody help me?" But even if someone could, she wouldn't be able to hear them. Her eardrums have ruptured and made her red sweater even redder along the shoulders. Rudolph's red nose—powered by a battery pack—blinks a distress signal.

Santa's body lies sprawled out in the shape of an X. His head is missing.

Chase sits in the center of the square. He cannot hear anything except the ringing in his ears. Only *ringing* is the wrong word. This is more like screaming, the screaming of a thousand cicadas. Around him he sees all these victims, bloodied and charred, some of them crawling and some staggering and some motionless. He sees them through the roiling smoke, sees them lit with flame, and his concussed brain believes he is at war again.

A man rushes toward him, a man in a smoking sport coat. He carries a pistol. Chase vaguely recognizes him. His mouth is moving but all Chase can hear is the sound of screaming insects. Another man joins him. And then another. More and more come out of the smoke, crowding around him, opening and closing their mouths, but the only noise is this terrible insect rasp that seems to emanate from them. He would love to run away, but his limbs feel loose in their sockets. He would love to close his eyes and pretend they didn't exist, but they reach out and touch him all over, trying to move him, to wrestle him up, and as they press upon him, he lashes out and screams something garbled.

He sees, through the smoke, in the deepening black of the sky, a crescent moon. He feels a heat rising inside him. For the past twenty-four hours, at Buffalo's orders, he has not taken Volpexx. He needed to be *present* for the ceremony. So long as he stayed calm, everything would be fine, Buffalo assured him. They talked about breathing—peach in, green out—good in, poisons out. They talked about what to do in case of hecklers. They talked about enjoying the moment.

Chase can feel his heartbeat crashing in his chest, can taste the blood in his mouth, can feel the wolf turning over inside him. He is breathing out of his mouth and he is rolling onto his knees and arching his back when he feels a sharp stabbing pain in his left buttock.

He flips over with a shriek and finds Buffalo leaning over him, drawing him into a suffocating hug. He says *sh-sh-sh*. In his hand is a tranquilizer the size of a fountain pen. He has stabbed it into Chase and already he feels its effects, a dopey calmness overtaking him, numbing any fear or desire.

Buffalo. Chase studies his old friend. His enormous forehead is bleeding and Chase wants to ask if he's okay but can't manage the words. One eye of his glasses is sooted over, but the other is clear and in it Chase can see his reflection. Though the air is cold, sweat has sprung from his skin and he takes on a paler color so that there seems to be something about him already embalmed.

Two of the news cameras are still rolling. They will close in on the governor, and then swing suddenly away. There are a series of pops, like the gunshots of a .22, that draw their attention skyward, finally settling into wobbly focus on the tree, which has caught fire. It begins with a yellow edging along some of the branches. Then, as the fire eats its way quickly through the needles, the swish and snap of flame grow louder, overtaking the screams and car alarms and sirens in the distance.

The Christmas lights—big red and green and blue lights the size of bell peppers—explode, two pops, then six pops, then fourteen in rapid-fire—filling the air with tiny clouds of glass powder, sparkling and seemingly motionless.

In less than a minute the flames have overtaken the entire tree, now a towering cone of fire that breathes heat that sends the survivors scurrying from the square and melts the glasses and wristwatches and rubber-soled boots of the corpses left behind. A black cord of smoke coils upward, beyond the reaches of any skyscraper, to bring a tremendous black cloud to an otherwise clear sky.

CHAPTER 30

PATRICK PARKS HIS JEEP and sits with his hands on the wheel and the engine idling for a long time. The strip mall in front of him houses a Shopko, Supercuts, Pizza Hut, Old Mountain Liquor, and the Armed Forces Recruitment Center. This is December, six days since he turned eighteen and nearly a month since the three of them emerged from the caves, filthy and bloody and bleary-eyed, but alive. They drove down the mountain together, silent in the cab of the Ramcharger. Claire sat in the middle of the bench seat, her head resting on his shoulder. He remembers how he felt then, trembling with relief and excitement, so utterly alive.

Night had given way to day during their time underground. The rumble of the engine and the tick of cinders in the wheel wells and snow falling off a tree branch in a crystalline scarf and the sun flaring in the blue dome of the sky with little puffs of clouds hanging under it and the weight and warmth of Claire's head on his shoulder came together to give him an overwhelming sense of peace and relief. The worst was over and new things were coming. A knot inside him seemed to loosen, unravel.

Until they pulled up to his house and discovered the sedan with military plates in the driveway. He did not say anything. He did not think anything. A dark instinct sent him leaping out of the Ram and storming toward the house. He pushed open the front door and stood in its dark rectangle and called out for his mother even as he saw her on the love seat with the two men seated on the couch opposite her, the CNO and chaplain in military dress with their hats in their hands and their biceps darkened by black bands.

His mother stood at the sight of him. "What's happened?" they said at the same time. She was referring to his black lump of an eye, and he was referring to what really mattered, the reason her tears washed away her makeup. When she didn't respond, he looked away from her, looked to the street, where through the glare of the Ramcharger's windshield he saw the faint image of Claire looking back at him.

Just as he is looking now at the windowed door of the recruitment center, glazed with a cataract of ice, so that in a few minutes' time someone outside could barely see a figure—whether a boy or a man, it would be too hard to tell—approach the reception desk and shake the hand of the officer sitting behind it.

CHAPTER 31

THE TALL MAN STANDS at the base of a mountain lost to the clouds. A long stream of footprints runs from the woods to the open mouth of the cave, the trail hard-packed from the weight of so many men. The ice-stiffened drapery has been torn away and tossed aside. Three agents in watch caps and Kevlar vests are stationed in this clearing, three more at the power station down the hill. The rest of his team, two dozen of them, stormed the lava tubes more than an hour ago and have maintained radio contact. "Clear," they tell him. "There's a lot of blood, but nobody here. Over."

He holds the walkie-talkie to his mouth, close enough to lick it. "Nobody," he says, not a question.

A burst of static and then, "They've gone and vanished on us."

"No one vanishes. They've just blown off somewhere else." His voice is soft and meditative, not meant for the walkie-talkie, which is already at his belt. "We'll find them," he says to himself. Something catches his eye and he crouches to pluck it from the stamped and polished snow at his feet. A twist of hair, bleached an unnatural shade of white. He kneads it between his fingers. Bits of skin dangle from the roots. He brings it to his nose for a sniff and then tucks it into his breast pocket and pats it. “And when we do, they’ll be dead.”

Part II

CHAPTER 32

HER NAME—rather, the name she goes by these days, Hope Robinson—is written in bold black capital letters on the manila envelope, a rumpled nine-by-twelve, folded in half to fit into her campus mailbox. There is no return address. The same as last time, the postmark comes from Seattle. The same as last time, quotation marks surround her name.

She knows people often punctuate incorrectly. "Employees must wash their hands," a notice will read in a restroom, as if quoting someone, maybe the germ-phobic manager. But quotation marks around a name? That's different, too strange to be anything but purposeful.

Last time, she opened her mailbox to find a standard business-size envelope, and when she ripped it open she found and unfolded a lined piece of paper that read *Boo!* Nothing more.

Now this. Claire holds the envelope with the tips of her fingers. When she flips it over, to see if anything is written on its back, she hears something solid slide around inside with a rasping noise.

She stands before the bank of mailboxes, a few

thousand of them altogether, each numbered and decorated with a tiny window and brass knobs tarnished from so many years of fingers twirling combinations. Normally the mailroom is busy with jostling bodies and student organization booths requesting signatures and volunteers, but at this time of night, the space is dim and empty. She can hear voices and music filtering from another part of the student union, beyond the marble arches and down a hallway, where the Stomping Grounds coffee shop remains open until midnight.

She thinks about tearing open the envelope but feels too exposed. She tucks it into her backpack, along with her laptop, a spiral notebook. Her cowboy boots—slick black ones, Stetsons, a treat Miriam bought her before the move to Montana—clomp against the tile floors. The bulletin boards that line the walls are busy with flyers advertising bands, sketch comedy shows, student council candidates, lycan support groups. They flutter when she passes them on her way to the glass entry. She jars against the first door, already locked, and then hurries out the other.

The night is cool and bugs orbit the lampposts and make their pools of light appear like crazed water. She zips her fleece snugly around her. In front of the union sits a fountain with four wolves arranged around it, their mouths bubbling out arcs of water that splash into a greenly lit pool. The union is aglow with spotlights. She learned during orientation that it has been here as long as the university, since 1875, and appears on the homepage of the website and on the cover of the catalogue, all columns and Palladian windows and triangular pediments, its classical style so different from the rest of campus, the Nixon-era architecture, square, featureless, riot-proof buildings with cinder-block walls and windows that won't open.

She follows the concrete path through the central quad to her dormitory. She keeps her hand closed around the knife in her pocket and her eyes on the bushes and pine trees clustered here and there, black shadows oozing around them. A blue-light security phone glows in the near distance, one of dozens positioned throughout campus. All she has to do is slam the red call button and one of the many guards patrolling campus will rush to her aid. They carry nets and Tasers and tranquilizers and pistols. This is supposed to make her feel better, but she does not. Dead dogs show up on campus every week. She has seen pentagrams spray-painted across the sides of buildings, choke chains hung from trees like tinsel. It has always been like this, she hears, but since the plane attacks and the courthouse square bombing, with anti-lycan sentiment at its peak, the campus is more than ever in the crosshairs. The other night Fox News ran a segment that questioned whether it was a training camp for terrorists.

Funny, given the reasons she enrolled. "You'll be safer there." That's what Miriam told her. Safe with a new name. Safe with a new life. Safe among her own kind. Miriam owed that to her brother. She knew a network of lycans and sympathizers who helped open a bank account for Claire with a credit union and secure the required documents, the transcripts, the driver's license and birth certificate and lycan registration. "Not good enough to get you on a plane, but good enough to get you into William Archer." She helped dye her hair chestnut brown. She bought her the black-frame glasses from Urban Outfitters. For the next few years, Claire—no, Hope—needed to lie low and stay safe and abandon herself to her studies. "Forget the boy," Miriam said. She rarely referred to him by his name, Patrick. To her he was "the boy." And the boy betrayed them. The boy enlisted after his father disappeared in the Republic. Claire wanted to hate him for it, as Miriam did, but could not muster the energy.

Miriam would be in touch. She had business to attend to, and when Claire asked if that business had anything to do with Jeremy's capture following the Pioneer Square bombing, Miriam said nothing—and has said nothing since August, the last time they saw each other at the Amtrak station in Portland, where Miriam gave her a stiff hug and said so long.

"Not too long, I hope," Claire said.

This is October. Soon the cold will come and the bugs and leaves and grass will wither and brown and go white with the cover of snow. The campus is located near Missoula, in a bowl-shaped valley that butts up against the Rockies. Its location, combined with the architecture, makes the campus appear like a military compound.

A half-moon glows. The sky is a spackling of stars and a plane winks through them and makes her think of far-off places, Patrick. Damn him. Every now and then they email. Every now and then she would google his name and battalion, check for casualties, but only when she couldn't help it. Her breath fills the air before her with ghostly steam that she then passes through. Her dorm is one of five, arranged like a pentagon with a bench-lined atrium at its center.

Her glasses fog over as she enters the building. Rather than wipe them off, she perches them on her head. The lenses are clear glass—she can see fine—but she knows that she ought to be more careful, knows that if she gets in the habit of absentmindedness, she will end up in trouble one of these days. She climbs the stairs and glances both ways down the empty hallway before keying open her door. She finds the light on but the room empty. Andrea is off somewhere, likely upstairs drinking with friends, despite this being a weeknight. Claire feels a mixture of relief and emptiness, the emptiness gnawing her out so that by the time she closes the door and shrugs off her backpack she feels like a chitinous husk that might crumble against the slightest pressure.

A stripe of moonlight runs across the wall. She squints into it when she collapses her blinds to keep the night at bay.

The wall next to Claire's bed is blank except for tack holes and the gummy spots where tape once held posters in place. The books on her shelves are alphabetized. Her clothes are folded in drawers, the socks balled and arranged in colored stripes of white, brown, gray and black. She didn't used to be this way. But after everything that has happened to her, she has decided if life is going to be messy, she needs everything else in perfect order. She knows it is only a stupid gesture toward stability and she doesn't care: it makes her feel better.

For this same reason she can hardly abide her roommate, Andrea. There is a clear line that runs down the middle of the room, the floor on the other side barely visible beneath chip bags, lace bras and sweatpants and T-shirts, crushed cans of Diet Cherry Pepsi. Andrea has never made her bed, not in the two months they've lived together, the duvet always peeled back like a sneering mouth. The wall above it is a collage of magazine clippings from *US Weekly* and photos of friends on beaches or around campfires or at house parties, always with lips pursed, cheeks sucked in, always with arms draped around shoulders and beer bottles raised to the camera. It is this wall, more than anything, that makes Claire feel alone.

She is absent of pictures. Absent of history. Whenever she thinks about her parents and starts to feel sorry for herself, she tries to make the choice not to feel that way any longer.

She digs through her backpack and shreds open the envelope. The inside is a shadowy mouth that at first appears empty. She drops her hand in and her fingers close around something hard, a DVD that flashes when she pulls it into the light.

She slides the DVD into the slit on the side of the television. The screen goes dark. There is a click and a whir as the disc begins to spin. She has no idea what to expect, her mind as empty as the envelope she tosses to the messy floor. She crosses her arms and steps back and nearly trips over a tangle of clothes.

The screen brightens. She is looking at a building. The outside of what appears to be a motel, though she sees no sign. The camera shakes, a handheld. She hears no noise outside of the wind whistling against the mike. She can see very little besides the motel and its crumbly parking lot. Then she recognizes, with an intake of breath, the front end of a silver-and-black Ramcharger. It is parked before the last room at the edge of the brown one-story building. She can barely make out, above the roof, the green blur of trees. Then the camera zooms in on a door. From it hangs a silver number seven. The recording continues for a long time—what turns out to be five minutes but feels much longer—before the door jars open and Miriam steps out. Her hair is longer, pulled back in a ponytail, and she wears sunglasses, but Claire recognizes her stiff posture and locked jaw. She swivels her head, scanning the parking lot, before locking the door and climbing into the Ramcharger and barreling away. The camera lingers on the empty parking space another thirty seconds and then the recording ends.

CHAPTER 33

THERE ARE PLENTY of ways to stay awake, the corporal told Patrick. He could drink coffee and crunch caffeine pills. He could concentrate on his muscles, hardening them one at a time, maintaining the flex for thirty seconds. He could recite the Marine's Hymn in his head: "From the halls of Montezuma, to the shores of Tripoli; we fight our country's battles in the air, on land, and sea." He could recall his orders as a sentry—memorized from the handbook—to take charge of this post and all government property in view, to report immediately to the corporal of the guard every unusual or suspicious occurrence noted, to halt and detain all persons on or near the post whose presence or actions are subject to suspicion. He could go on, but as tired as he feels, he is in no danger of falling asleep when on sentry duty with Trevor.

Trevor is a nineteen-year-old private, a wiry redhead from Tuscaloosa, Alabama, whose talking never ceases and whose pale skin is darkened by freckles and whose jaw is always humped with dip that flavors his breath wintergreen. He talks about being a kicker for Tuscaloosa High and how nobody respected a kicker but they ought to respect a kicker because a kicker was quite regularly the difference between a win and a loss. He talks about Archibald's, the best barbecue in the world as far as he's concerned, though you couldn't find it in the white pages and you couldn't find so much as a sign out front, because it was a house, just a house, with all sorts of people waiting in line, people driving a twenty-year-old Buick and people driving a brand-spanking-new Lexus, all waiting in line for a pile of Wonder Bread and those ribs that would give your mouth an orgasm. He talks about the mile-wide tornado that went ripping through Tuscaloosa not so long ago and how he used to joke about the city having a church on every corner, but by God those churches stepped up and provided all the food and shelter anybody without a roof or a hot meal needed and how he was working at the convenience store when the tornado hit and the whole place collapsed around him and he hid under the register and managed to crawl out of the rubble on his own and spent the rest of the day digging other people out of their destroyed homes and apartments. That was something else.

Patrick half tunes in to the endless stream of words. The night has his attention. The night that grows longer and longer, darkness outlasting daylight by many hours. The night that spills beyond this guard tower that rises thirty feet in the air like a gargoyle looming over the base entrance. Their post is unlit, but along the perimeter, floodlights cast a harsh glow that makes the snow sparkle and the barbs of Constantine wire gleam.

Their M4s rest on a concrete shelf stacked with sandbags. The rifles are held in place by carbine bipods with a forty-five-degree swivel. Between them sit three bricks of ammo, a two-way radio, and a bag of frozen sunflower seeds. Patrick sometimes squints into the darkness and sometimes glasses it with his binoculars. The base is located on a hillside barren of trees and undergrowth, of everything but snow, a white expanse that drifts off for a square mile before running into the piney woods that channel cut through the two ridges walling this valley, fifty miles long, seven miles wide.

Beyond the brightness of the floods, the valley is dark except for the half-moon peeking over a ridgeline and the faint glimmer of lamplit windows in the town of Hiisi and the hellish radiance of the Tuonela uranium mine. From here, several miles away, it appears encased in a globe of light. It operates day and night, a city of giant metal sheds. Red lights blink and black clouds cough from its smokestacks. He doesn't want to ruin his night vision, but if he glassed the mine, he would be able to make out the railcars and tankers, the freight elevators and conveyer belts. And if the wind was right, he could hear the dump trucks beeping and grumbling, the big booms of dropped loads and the screech of metal against rock, the faraway thunder of dynamite. A train departs the mine, rattling up to speed, and releases a mournful whistle that gets mixed up with the wolves crying in the distance.

The mine is the reason the base is here. The mine—and others like it, nearly a dozen of them strung throughout the Republic, all owned and operated by Alliance Energy—are the reason, some say, the U.S. is here at all. Some call it a war. Some call it a conflict, and some an occupation. Some call it a mistake and some call it necessary. Some call it endless. It is what it is—as it has been since 1948, when the Republic was established as a paramilitary lycan-majority state, and all the labels and opinions in the world mean nothing, Patrick knows, because nothing will change. The Republic needs the U.S. and the U.S. needs the Republic. They can no longer exist without each other, like an inoperable tumor that has fingered its way through a brain.

The population is estimated at 5,507,300, all infected, a number that does not account for the 64,000 U.S. personnel stationed there, these twenty thousand square miles bordering Finland

and Russia and the White and Barents Seas, a place no one wanted. During the short-lived summers it is pocked with lakes and strung with silvery rivers and bearded with forests of pine and spruce that during the long winters are invisible beneath the snow and ice and the shroud of many sunless days. It is a place of bracingly low temperatures and winds that can blacken skin within seconds of exposure. A wintry ruined mantle of a country with a hot, poisonous core.

A space heater glows orange in the corner, giving off some but not enough heat. The thermostat on the wall reads fifteen degrees and the wind probably shaves it down to five. They aren't far from an inlet, and when he first arrived, when the weather was warm and the wind was right, he could smell algae and mudflats, hear seagulls screeching overhead. Whenever the snow seems too much, when his lip splits and his nose bleeds on guard duty, when he has to knuckle the icicle off the showerhead before stepping under it, he reminds himself that in a few months, when it gets warmer, things will get better; everything won't seem so forbidding. He imagines standing on a pebble-strewn beach and watching the wind whip the water into white crowns and wading out into the slow breakers and breathing in the salt air and knifing forward into the water.

Now he wears a watch cap under his helmet and a wool sweater under his winter fatigues. Every now and then he flexes his knees and stamps his boots to shake the blood back into them. A stack of creased porno magazines sits in the corner. Some of the men use the women inside them to warm up.

Every time he thinks of himself with a woman he thinks of Claire. She hated him for enlisting. Called him a hypocrite. Said he disgusted her. He tried to explain, tried to tell her about his father, but nothing he said could leaven her temper. There was only the unavoidable truth that he was going. It was a betrayal—to her, to his mother. She would not respond to his emails for months, until one day she did.

Sometimes the two of them fire back and forth dozens of messages a day—and sometimes there are long silences between them, punctuated by some point of disagreement, often the differences between the infected and the uninfected. She would not let the argument drop. Just when he thought it was over, she would come back with another email about that guy who killed the old folks and stole their social security checks or that experiment where people happily electrocuted others or the child prostitution rings in Thailand. "But psychotic disorders are not contagious," he would write, and she would write, "What's that got to do with anything?" and he would write, "Everything," and she would write, "All I'm saying is, there's no difference between you and me," and he would write, "I don't bite people!"

They moved through cycles like this often enough. Somebody would get too close or too mean or too something, and the other would say, I need a break—this is too much. Sometimes a week would go by; sometimes a day would go by, usually with Claire writing an email that began with, "Okay, I'm weak."

He tries now to put her out of his mind, but sometimes that is impossible late at night, when he is awake in his bunk, staring at the inside of his eyelids and making a game out of the images he sees in them: a thousand blinking fireflies, a stone dropped in a purple pond rippling outward, a red mouth—hers—opening for him.

Trevor is still talking, sitting cross-legged on the floor and spitting sunflower seeds into an empty Coke can. The wind moans and snow skitters. When Patrick stares too long, when the night grows long and exhaustion overtakes him, he sees things. Darkness can have the same effect as the sun. When you look at it too long, it scorches into you. Blackened shapes play across your retinal screen. He imagines rock outcroppings into lycans, a pocket of shadow as a pool of blood.

He imagines tunnels beneath the drifts and terrible things moving through them, burrowing toward them. And he imagines his father. His father, out there in the darkness, watching him.

One of five MIA, the other seven in his squad killed. Lost to an ambush. Gone since November. Seven months. Seven months is a long time. Too long to hold out hope. This was his base, Combat Outpost Tuonela, same as the mine, same as the valley. Patrick requested to be stationed here, among the five platoons that inhabit the armory and hangar and dorms and latrine and maintenance bay and sump building and medical hut and laundry station and chow hall and Morale, Welfare and Recreation center (MWR), where they can lift weights and box and play hoops and poker and pound out miles on treadmills and Skype and check their email, all of these concrete buildings encased behind concrete walls encased in Constantine wire sharp enough to cut to the bone.

Some call him Patrick, but most call him Miracle Boy. He couldn't escape that, and with his shaved head and his uniform and his constant supervision, he cannot help but feel lost, known by another's name, another's clothes, another's orders. His father is the only thing that keeps him centered.

Movement.

He goes tense as he spots something beyond the

floodlights, moving toward the base. He says shut up and Trevor goes quiet. "What?" he says and when Patrick doesn't say anything he scrambles upright from his place on the floor and nearly knocks his rifle from its purchase as he takes position. "What?" he says. "What?"

There are more than one of them, a small black wave of them coming up the hill. Patrick has been here four months and during this time the base has been attacked only once by a single lycan who strolled up with a grin on his face and stood outside the gate and would not respond to their commands to halt. He wore an explosive belt and the blast ripped through a jacket lined with stainless-steel balls that peppered the concrete perimeter. There wasn't much of him left.

Patrick lines up his rifle and tries to glass them with his scope, but they're moving too fast and he keeps losing them in the dark. He peers over his scope and adjusts an inch to the right, an inch down, and there they are. Wolves. A pack of them. He can hear them chattering now, as they close in on a white-tailed deer that stumbles through the snow, slipping and clumsily righting itself.

He hears the click of Trevor thumbing off his safety. "Don't," Patrick says, but it's too late. Trevor rattles out five shots and lets out a whoop. Patrick instinctively closes his eyes, and when he opens them again, the deer is bounding away and the wolves are scattering, leaving behind one of their own, panting and bleeding in the snow.

The radio crackles to life. "Post Number Three. We hear fire. Report." Then another voice talking over the last, "Corporal of the guard, Post Number Two, we hear fire. Report."

Patrick shakes his head, knowing that the CO and half the camp are sitting up in their bunks right now, knowing that his squad will be punished for this, knowing that instead of rotating into patrol and heading out past the wire, they will be in for a week of bitchwork, washing dishes and burning the shitters. "Fire, Post Number One. That's us. No alarm. Nothing but wolves. Wolves at the door."

CHAPTER 34

CLAIRE IS LATE. Ten minutes late already for her nine o'clock class. Normally she wakes at dawn without any need for an alarm and goes for a run and drops by the cafeteria for a bagel or bowl of peaches and cottage cheese, but last night Andrea stumbled into the room after midnight wanting to talk about some boy and then ended up vomiting in bed, and by the time Claire stripped the sheets and cleaned Andrea up and Febrezed the smell of bile and rum from the air, it was after two.

She pushes through the entrance to Carver Hall, a three-story concrete structure with tall, slitted windows, and tries to calm her breathing and quiet her footsteps when she approaches the open doors of the auditorium.

This is Lycan History, a three-hundred-student lecture, mandatory for all freshmen and offered in the fall and spring by Professor Alan Reprobus, who calls himself an old hippie and refuses to use email or PowerPoint. There is a chair and desk onstage, but he never sits at it, instead marching back and forth with his hands seemingly cuffed behind his back. He wears jeans and faded T-shirts and motorcycle boots. He is broad shouldered and pot-bellied, with a trailing white beard and a wispy bit of hair ringing his spotted bald head. Over the past few months he has lectured, only occasionally glancing at his notes, on the origin of lobos, the intersection of biology and culture, the early communities and rituals and folklore, the genocide and near extinction of the race during the Crusades, westward expansionism, and World War II.

The course meets as a lecture twice a week and then on Fridays breaks out into thirty-student sections led by a TA, hers a senior named Matthew Flanagan. He's tall and thin and goateed and wears his hair spiked in front. When in class, his expression is brooding and he wears khakis and collared shirts with the sleeves rolled up, but she's seen him around campus looking less formal, one time playing Frisbee on the central green, and when he reached up to snatch the disc from the air, his shirt lifted and she could see his stomach, the way it dropped between his hip bones in a muscular V.

Today he is stationed by the door, handing out photocopies. "You're late," he whispers, and she says, "I know," and hates him a little for scolding her. From the very first time they met as a section, she has resisted the authority of someone only three years older than she, never challenging him outright but never raising her hand and only reluctantly answering questions when he cold-called on her.

She snatches the photocopy from his hand and it makes a snapping flutter and the professor pauses in his lecture and glances upward and catches her in the doorway. “Ms. Robinson?” he says, his voice booming through the high-ceilinged room.

She freezes on the steps, not only because she didn’t know he knew her name, but also because everyone has turned in their seats to stare at her. Jackets rasp and desks groan with shifting weight, and though she keeps her head down she can feel the pressure of their eyes. Reprobus says, “Would you mind staying after class?”

She nods and finds the nearest empty seat and waits for the lecture to continue and the students to return their attention to the front of the room before unzipping her backpack and withdrawing her notebook. For several minutes she is too upset—alternately despising her roommate, her TA, and her professor—to tune in to the buzz of the lecture or write down anything except for the black hash marks of what must be a jailed window or a game of tic-tac-toe that will never be played.

Then her face snaps up and her pen tears through the paper at the mention of a name, Balor.

She has missed the context, but the professor

is talking now about the lycans—or skinwalkers, as they were known—among the nineteenth-century Native American population, and how they refused to acknowledge the U.S. occupation of the American West. The raids on settlements and presidios, the thousands killed or bitten, the use of the media to spread terror, the flamboyant acts of violence against soldiers and civilians alike, the scalps woven into blankets, a young girl half-eaten and hung from a tree by a meat hook. "In many ways," Reprobus says, "very little has changed, the tactics of Geronimo repeated in the tactics of sixties revolutionaries like Howard Forrester and modern-day freedom fighters like Balor."

Her father. Howard Forrester. Her pen falls to the floor with a clatter and her professor's eyes flit toward the noise and settle on her for a long moment. She has her hand over her mouth and tries to feign a yawn. She feels like a fool. His involvement in the Resistance is no surprise—it's just so surreal hearing about him in the context of a college classroom. She needs to be more careful. Her only excuse is her lack of sleep. The professor is still watching her, his mouth open. He seems on the verge of saying something to her but doesn't.

A hand goes up near the front of the room and distracts him. "Yes?" he says. "What is it?"

A boy in an Oxford shirt with a carefully parted

head of yellow hair straightens in his seat. He says he's interested in the professor's choice of words. "You called Balor a freedom fighter."

Reprobus tugs at his beard. "I should have said *so-called* freedom fighter."

"I know you were involved with the Resistance in the—"

Reprobus dismisses him with a wave of his hand and talks over him. "My history, outside of my academic credentials, has no place in this classroom." He continues his lecture as if it were never interrupted. The boy with the parted hair raises his hand again, but after he goes unacknowledged for a minute, he drops it and slumps into his seat.

Claire feels headachy and distracted and can't keep her eyes off the clock hanging above the emergency exit to the right of the stage. The long hand winds its way to the top of the hour and the professor excuses the class and the students rise in a rush and the room is noisy with zipped backpacks and cell phones chiming with texts. Claire waits for the students to swarm up the stairs and then makes her way down them, to where Reprobus squares a pile of paper before fitting it into his leather satchel. She has never been this close to him and is surprised to discover they are the same height. "Oh yes, Ms. Robinson. Did I embarrass you? Calling on you like that?"

She shrugs and tries to keep her expression impassive.

"You seemed surprised," he says, and she isn't sure what he refers to, the moment when he pointed out her tardiness or the moment he spoke her father's name.

He smiles at her and his beard and teeth are yellow from coffee or the pipe tobacco that she can smell puffing off him. His jacket hangs on the back of a chair. It is horribly outdated, suede with leather fringe hanging from the arms. He pulls it on with some difficulty and throws his satchel over his shoulder and says, "You'll be on time from now on, I trust?" and when she nods, he says, "Good, good. Because there are things about your history you don't want to miss."

Jeremy Saber does not know how much time has passed since his arrest. He has no clock, no calendar, and his fourteen-by-fourteen cell has no window, so he cannot keep track of the hours, the days, the weeks and months, all of it a maddening blur punctuated by the occasional cold shower and meal of tacky oatmeal or chicken and rice drowned in gray gravy. He knows, because of his mental fog and his inability to transform, a strong dosage of

Volpexx must be ground and mixed into the food. He has tried not to eat, tried to hold out, but eventually his hunger possesses him. The lights remain on day and night and music pipes in at top volume so that he cannot sleep or think. His room is featureless except for a steel slab of a bed anchored to the wall and a stainless-steel toilet that sits in the corner. There is no sink and the lid of the toilet cannot be removed without a screwdriver, and he has on more than one occasion cupped his hand into the bowl and drank greedily when it seems as if days have passed without any food or water and the pit in his belly had to be filled.

His thoughts are like clouds. He cannot sharpen them, cannot concentrate. Sometimes he talks to himself. Images float around him. His daughter throwing rocks in a river that sparkles with sunlight, plucking a dandelion and handing it to him, smearing her face with a red beard of spaghetti sauce. His wife, naked in the shower, smiling and looking over her shoulder when he pulled back the curtain. His wife with fireflies woven into her hair. His wife brushing back a strand of hair with a hand gloved in dirt from gardening. His wife curled in a ball in bed with a stone-cold expression on her face.

He vaguely remembers his capture. He was at the safe house in Sandy—a farm set back from a county road, ten acres of oaks and firs and blackberry brambles and barbed-wire fences and rotten outbuildings and alfalfa fields gone to weed. Two days had passed since the Pioneer Courthouse Square bombing, and since then, he and his fifteen men had done very little except surf online and watch the coverage on TV and drink whiskey out of paper cups and toast to the memory of Thomas, who had so courageously sacrificed himself at the wheel of the van. That night, the giant Magog was supposed to be on sentry, but he offered no warning when the agents whispered through the tall grass and encircled the farmhouse and simultaneously rammed open the back and front doors and stormed through the rooms and slammed Jeremy to the floor and flex-cuffed him and tranquilized him before he could shake off his dreams, before he could transform.

Then he woke in this cell. Whether a gun was fired that night, whether the others were killed or arrested, he does not know. He does not know a lot of things. Like where he is being jailed. And by whom. And why they haven't questioned him. And whether the media know of his capture, and if so, how he is being portrayed.

None of this matters to him now. He has made his mind purposefully blank. For the past few hours, Britney Spears has played on repeat over the loudspeakers, and he has developed several techniques for escaping the noise and brightness of his cell, for avoiding the trapdoor of madness he senses underfoot. One trick is to recite the alphabet forward and backward. Another is to create designs and patterns in the air bubbles hardened into the concrete walls. Another still is to imagine himself on a path in the woods and approaching a gnarled pine tree and pulling down on its branch like a lever so that a door swings open and then stepping into its shadowy interior and descending a coiled staircase to a muddy root-tangled room with a pond full of glowing fish and peeling off his clothes and going for a swim.

That is where he is now, swimming in that underground pond, while at the same time sitting on his bunk, his body bent in half, his hands smashed against his ears. The fantasy dissolves when he realizes the music has stopped. He isn't sure when this happened, maybe five minutes ago, maybe five seconds. His palms peel away from his ears.

He startles when he realizes that someone is standing in his cell. Not one of the dead-faced buzz-cut guards, who bring him his food and who escort him to his shower and who will not respond to his pleas or questions and who wear uniforms that match the tons of concrete that surround him. This man is different.

He is so tall that he must have ducked his head to enter the cell. His face is glossy with burns and his nose slightly upturned so that its tip appears to have been snipped away. He has no eyebrows, but the places where they ought to be hook upward like question marks.

Behind him the cell door opens and two guards enter carrying aluminum folding chairs. With a clatter, they set the chairs up facing each other as if across an invisible card table. The man extends a hand, indicating that Jeremy should sit, and after a moment he slowly walks from his bunk and takes his seat and feels little surprise when his arms are seized and wrestled behind him and cuffed to the chair. Then one of the guards departs the cell and the other stations himself against the wall with his eyes trained on Jeremy.

The Tall Man sets down his briefcase and then he does not so much sit as fold himself into the chair. He sighs and crosses his legs and knits together his hands over his topmost knee, and Jeremy notices that only a few of his chalky fingernails remain. "I'm sorry I haven't come to visit you sooner," he says. "I've been busy hunting, you see."

Jeremy feels an itch on his cheek and goes to scratch it and forgets about the cuffs and the chain rattles when his arm stops short.

The Tall Man offers him a sympathetic smile.

"Now that you've had some time alone to think, I believe we're due for a little talk." He uncrosses his legs and leans over and sets the briefcase on its side. It yawns open to reveal a padded interior filled with gleaming instruments. His hand floats over them and then decides upon a pair of pliers.

For the next hour they talk. The Tall Man tells him that he never wrote a book, that *The Revolution* was in fact a bound copy of blank pages. That he never led a faction of the Resistance, never had a wife or a child. The planes never went down. The bomb in the square never detonated. It was all in his head. The person he thought he was and the life he thought he built and the followers he thought awaited him did not exist. "You have been in this room your entire life and you will remain in this room the rest of your life. This room, this fourteen-square-foot room, is your universe. And I am your god. And as your god, I dictate that your purpose is pain. That is your existence. That is the only word of your vocabulary and the only sensation you are capable of experiencing. Pain."

Five of his fingernails are now gone, peeled away by the pliers. Jeremy thinks that after his fingers the pliers will go to his toes. He thinks that after his toes he may lose his teeth. He thinks that after his teeth there are so many places, so many pink and vulnerable places to slide a blade, rub salt, apply a jolt from a live wire. He thinks, maybe, the pain will never end.

Claire knows the off-campus mail—the credit card offers and spring break flyers and fashion catalogues—normally whispers into her box around two o'clock. She arrives a few minutes after, the mailroom a crush of students who tap messages into their cell phones and call loudly to each other over the din about test scores and coffee dates. She feels so still and silent among them. She opens her mailbox to find a J.Crew catalogue, a solicitation from MasterCard, and a nine-by-twelve manila envelope.

Once again, no return address and a Seattle postmark. Once again, the name Hope Robinson encased by quotation marks. She hardly notices she is walking toward the exit until it opens in front of her and the wind comes through like a great gasp.

It is the boy from class, the one with the tidy part in his yellow hair and the neatly pressed Oxford pinstripe. She thinks his name is Francis. He is heading into the mailroom, but she is hurrying her way out, so he steps aside and holds the door open, an obligatory politeness. His chin is rashed over with acne. He doesn't say anything and she barely whispers thank you as she moves past him.

The sun cooked away the fog by noon and now the sky is bright blue and the snow-dusted mountains are visible in the near distance. She starts toward her dorm but guesses Andrea is still lounging in the room, napping off her hangover or watching YouTube or instant-messaging about some crushable boy, some dreamed-of love, so she changes course to the library.

Aside from the union, it is her second-favorite building on campus, a blend of Old and New World architecture, a modern glass-walled addition built onto a columned building made from red sandstone. She keeps busy with her classes—mostly prereqs, Calculus, Comp, Poli-Sci, and Lycan History. Her free time she spends in the library. Avoiding Andrea, avoiding everyone. Conversation is impossible for her. During orientation, she learned, when she faced the weeklong barrage of bonding activities with her fellow freshmen, that after learning your name and major, everyone wants to know where you are from, who you are, who you will become. She has no way to respond. Her history has been erased; her future is uncertain. So she hides in the library, where silence is the norm.

She takes the elevator to the fourth floor and

walks down the line of carrels until she reaches a shadowy corner. She pulls her laptop out of her backpack and while it hums and bleeps to life she runs a finger along the top of the envelope and shreds it open. Another DVD falls out. She fumbles it onto the tray.

On the screen she sees a grassy field with blacktop trail running through it. A park, she realizes. There is a bench along the trail. A picnic table along the tree line. The sky boils with clouds and the camera lens is spotted with rain. The grass and the dandelions gone to seed shudder against a mild wind.

A few minutes pass and then the woods spit out a runner. Miriam is wearing a black tank top and matching running shorts and she is sprinting, her arms chopping the air, her legs scissoring. For a moment, Claire worries that something will emerge from the woods behind her, chasing her. Then Miriam slows and brings her hands to her hips and breathes heavily and kicks her legs, kicking away the lactic acid. She walks in slow circles for a few minutes, then goes offscreen and the camera jogs left, following her to an empty playground structure. Beyond it Claire spots another asphalt trail snaking off and disappearing into a wall of willow trees. Miriam stretches her arms and then leaps up to grab hold of the monkey bars.

She hammers out a set of ten pull-ups, her head rising neatly between the bars, her muscles surging and the wings tattooed on her back seeming to rise and fall and help lift her weight from the ground.

Then a hand suddenly appears, the hand of whoever holds the video camera. It rakes the air as though clawing at Miriam and then retreats from view. It is visible only for the flash of a few seconds. Claire can't be certain she sees what she thinks she sees. So she leans forward and drags the recording back and hits pause and captures the hand midswipe. There it is, blurred but clear enough, a hand that from this angle appears as big as Miriam and ready to gobble her up. A three-fingered hand, curled like a talon.

Puck.

Every hour, from eight a.m. until ten p.m., a shuttle—colored gray and purple, the school's colors—leaves the union and drives the ten minutes to Missoula. The university is isolated, and though it makes an effort, with its markets, coffee shops, bowling alley, bookstore, and bar—the shuttles are almost always full. There are three drop points: the mall, the Safeway, and downtown.

Claire heads downtown—not for the bars or the restaurants, like most of the other heavily perfumed and cologned students that pack the seats around her—but for Café Diablo, a red-walled coffee shop with ironwork chandeliers and black cracked-leather chains. She comes for the free Wi-Fi. All incoming and outgoing messages on campus are monitored, Miriam warned her, so she should never attempt to contact her except from a remote server. Claire created a special email address for this express purpose. Not gmail. Miriam didn't trust the way they scanned their messages for direct advertising. They used Yahoo instead. Lost.girl76@yahoo.com was her address. When Claire wrote it down on a piece of paper, Miriam rolled her eyes and asked if she might consider changing her username to drama.queen.

They have exchanged only a few messages since the school year began. They do not use names. They do not speak in specifics. "Things are good," Claire wrote when she first arrived on campus, her hands hovering over the keyboard, so uncertain as to what she could and could not say. "I made it here fine and the location is prettier than I imagined." Miriam demanded that Claire not make any reference to William Archer or her classes or anything that could pinpoint her identity, in case their accounts should be compromised. She was told, too, not to use her debit card when at the coffee shop—cash only—so that no one could coordinate her presence with this email filtering through that particular Internet port. Claire told her she was being paranoid. "Maybe," Miriam said. "But people are looking for us. We're invisible until we give them something to see."

She was here yesterday. She has been here every day since receiving the first DVD. She hurries her green tea to a chair with a round-topped side table and splits open her laptop and taps her feet hurriedly against the floor and glances around at the few people reading newspapers and novels and chatting over a glass of wine or mug of cappuccino. She calls up her browser and logs in to Yahoo and discovers her inbox empty except for a message from Patrick. "Yesterday I saw a woman with hair the color of honey. She had her back turned to me. Thought it was you. Nearly called out your name. Were your ears warm? Thinking of you."

What might have made her smile any other time makes her frown now. Nothing from Miriam. Four days and still no response to her four emails.

Claire punches out another message. "Another video arrived today. You in the park. On a run. It's the little man. He's alive. PLEASE RESPOND IMMEDIATELY to let me know you are okay!!!" She reads it over twice, making sure she hasn't revealed anything critical, then hastily writes, "Love,

C," at the bottom. They have never used the word before, but it feels right.

She tries to make sense of what is happening. She doubts they are stalking her—what use is she to them? This is about psychological torture. Puck toying with her, maybe trying to draw her west, like the spider that plucks its web to make a song. She wonders if the same can be said of Miriam. Maybe Puck hasn't captured her yet because he is afraid, because he is studying her habits, waiting for the right moment to strike—or maybe he is delaying his attack like a kind of foreplay to heighten his pleasure.

She remains in the coffee shop until right before the last shuttle arrives, trying to do her homework but spending most of her time hitting refresh, refresh, refresh on her browser, waiting for a response that never comes. Finally she punches out an email to Patrick. "Not doing well," is all she says.

Two months ago, Miriam gave her a gift, a Glock, along with two bricks of ammo. "Keep it close," she said. After Claire returns to her dorm, after she checks on Andrea—who lies in bed breathing heavily, her eyelids fluttering with sleep—she slides open her desk drawer and removes her pistol and climbs into bed with the safety on but her finger curved around the trigger.

CHAPTER 35

THE OTHER NIGHT Patrick dreamed about his father. He was standing outside the gates of the base. His cammies hung off him in tatters. Bruises coiled around his wrists and his ankles, and his bare feet were blue in the moonlight. A crow perched on his shoulder and when he opened his mouth to speak, his voice was the bird's high, rusty cackle.

This was around the time when the cold snap hit, when the arctic wind came wailing through the valley, dropping the temperature forty degrees in a matter of hours. Several pipes froze and burst and shut down the latrine. A crew has been working on the problem ever since, with some luck, but in the meantime, everyone is using the Porta-Johns.

There aren't enough of them. A dozen. A dozen shitters for the attachments and engineers and medical personnel and mechanics and cooks and five platoons of thirty Marines who at every meal stack their trays high with chow and who take great pride in the size and frequency of their waste.

Someone has to burn them once a day, and that someone is Patrick, along with the rest of his squad. All the platoons work in two-week rotations on whatever tasks keep the base running. The personal security detail (PSD) escorts the company commander and any other visiting brass to the towns and the Tuonela Mine. The quick reactionary force (QRF) is always locked and loaded, ready to react, to depart the base with a minute's notice in case of an attack on a patrol or forward operating base (FOB) or uranium mine or battle position. The presence patrol drives around in four-hour shifts for movement-to-contacts, trying to draw out the baddies, or for knock-and-talks with locals, trying to make peace with the locals and hand out candy to the kids, most of whom are happy to see the soldiers, happy for the security, happy for their jobs at the mine.

Then there is security and bitchwork. Always assigned to the nonranks. Manning the posts. Washing dishes, folding laundry, sweeping, mopping, scrubbing, polishing, stacking ammo, hauling and knifing open the endless parade of conex boxes full of toilet paper, bags of rice, cans of beans. And burning the shitters.

His entire platoon remains on security and bitchwork for the next rotation, but every platoon is made up of three squads of twelve soldiers, and their sergeant makes certain it is Patrick's squad who get the shitters. Thanks to Trevor.

They strap four shitters into the bed of the MTVR, along with a stack of tongs and muck-encrusted rebar, a pile of welder's gloves, several gallons of diesel. Then they drive five miles down-wind from the base to a basin blackened and reeking from years of burned garbage and excrement. They unload the shitters and unhinge their back doors and tong out their depositories and splash them full of diesel and spark a match and step back as the flames and black smoke coil out of the half-frozen mess within the barrels. After a minute they step forward, into the stink, into the heat, to stir the barrels with the rebar. Day after day of this, and with the showers down, no amount of scrubbing at the sinks can get the smell from their skin.

Patrick stands there, leaning on the rebar as if it were a cane, his eyes watering, his mouth razed with the taste of charred shit, while next to him, Trevor, oblivious to their situation, blathers on and on about how he and his pals used to go noodling for catfish in the bayou. Over his helmet he wears the pelt of the wolf he shot, its head draped over his, its body and tail dangling down his back like a second skin. The smoke swirls and the shit hisses and bubbles and pops and the snow around them melts away to reveal a ten-foot circle of browned grass.

This is not how Patrick imagined his time in the Republic.

He imagined himself in a Humvee, in the machine-gun turret, rolling through trash-strewn streets and lighting up anything that moved. He imagined himself at a battle outpost, hurling a grenade and ducking down to jam his hands against his ears. He imagined himself cracking the butt of his rifle against the face of a bearded man and flex-cuffing his hands behind his back and dragging him to base to reveal, in a shrieking confession, the whereabouts of his father. And he imagined, finally, kicking down the door to a compound and surprising people in bed or watching television who would lift their arms in surprise when he made their bodies dance with bullets, and in a back room he would find his father, blindfolded, his wrists and ankles duct-taped, starved and beaten, but alive. He imagined it would be more like a video game, more like the movies. And he imagined, too, that he might find a saner, more stable version of the community he felt with the Americans.

Instead he found himself in a country of frightened people who only wanted to be left alone, their way of life threatened by the extremist rebels who called them cowards and the U.S. military rapists, raiders.

Patrick's first night at the base, his staff sergeant joked that he couldn't be killed and put a pistol to his head and pulled the trigger, the chamber empty, the bunkhouse full of ugly laughter. This was Dave Decker, the E-6 in charge of his platoon. His head was shaped like an egg on its side and he wore thick, square glasses that made his eyes swim. He was muscular but had large buttocks that seemed all the more prominent due to the way he stood, bent forward at the waist. He walked around with his mouth open, like a shark. He holstered his pistol and clapped Patrick painfully on the back and said he was just joking of course but that the boy ought not to expect any special treatment.

The first few weeks, Patrick tried to ask about his father, but the base had gone through a major rotation that summer, the twelve-month deployments turning over. Few knew Keith Gamble besides the brass, who considered the Guard units the shit-sucking bottom-feeders of the military and couldn't understand why a pretty-boy media-fucking darling like Patrick was here at all and what he wanted to prove and how he had a target on his back and why in the hell he, a green bitch pussy motherfucker fresh off the plane, thought it was okay to talk to an officer like an officer was a friend. Every now and then somebody would talk to him, but what they said didn't tell him anything: "He was a good man," and "Sorry for your loss," and "He made a hell of a beer, I'll give you that."

Patrick soon learned the mandatory distance between the ranks and nonranks. They were different animals. The CO and gunnery and lieutenants and captains did not go out on the wire. They did not often leave their quarters. They dealt with intelligence and set up missions that the grunts on the ground then carried out. "Do you understand what you are now?" Decker told the platoon one day during a drill. "You are part of the death machine."

The death machine. He isn't sure what Decker meant by that. The Marines or the military. The base or the Republic. Or maybe life. Maybe life was the death machine, a big nightmare with jacked-up wheels and chainsaw mandibles that never stopped mowing down bodies, never stopped eating.

That certainly seems possible now, as he stands in this basin, its sloping walls and charred debris and smoky exhalation making him feel like he has never been closer to the underworld, the trapdoor to Hades beneath his feet. He curses himself and his situation, disgusted by his powerlessness, and gives his barrel another stir, too rough this time, knocking it over, the burning sludge oozing across the ground. He curses again and hurls his rebar like a spear. It lands a few feet away and coughs up a divot of black earth and emits a strange crunch.

He looks over to see if anyone noticed his little

tantrum. But Trevor has the ear of another private, the two of them stirring their barrels like cauldrons while debating who would be a better lay, Angelina Jolie or Cameron Diaz.

Patrick approaches the rebar and pulls it from the ground and in doing so uncovers a jumble of bones. He crouches down and sweeps away with his gloves what could be the skull of a dog or a wolf. He withdraws it and it sheds big chunks of earth and he blows the black dust from the eye sockets and then notices all around him, poking out of the dirt and patches of snow like some dead garden, bones, dozens of them.

CHAPTER 36

CHASE WILLIAMS is in the green room. Which is actually the basketball coach's office in the boys' locker room at Redmond Senior High School. He sips a Monster Energy Drink and sits in a swivel chair at a desk cluttered with team rosters and handouts on offensive strategies. He wears a suit coat and pressed Wrangler jeans and Justin boots polished to a glow. All around him hang 4-H calendars, team photos, banners and pennants for the Panthers.

He used to be one of them. Class of '85. Long time ago, but he can still remember color-saturated images: driving that white Dodge pickup to school during the week and during the weekends into the pasture, tossing an M-80 into a garbage can and watching the belly of it jarringly distend, snapping his arm and spiraling the football perfectly from his fingers and losing it momentarily in the haze of the stadium lights, branding and castrating and feeding and deworming and vaccinating cattle, taking the boat out on the reservoir and skinny-dipping with girls whose bellies were tanned as brown as beans.

A knock at the door makes him swivel around in his chair. Before he can respond with a "Come in," Buffalo is already in the room, moving toward him, the knock like somebody clearing his throat, telling you to look his way and be ready. He smiles widely and his cheeks dimple like the thumbprint cookies his mother used to make. Buffalo always does that, Chase has noticed, when he first walks into a room. He begins by smiling, showing off all his teeth, and then his smile fades and his mouth tightens and his eyes grow fixed, as though he is very hungry and debating his next meal. "You ready?"

"Bring it."

In a few minutes, he will join the Republican nominee and the Democratic incumbent in the second of three presidential debates scheduled before the November 6 election, each at a location of the candidates' choosing. He has nicknamed his competition: Herman Munster, the former governor of Massachusetts, with his stiff black hair and freakishly rectangular face and toneless advocacy of pro-life, capital punishment, tax cuts; and the incumbent, the Incompetent, whose middle-of-the-roadness translates to constant compromise and never taking a stand on anything. Chase doesn't feel nervous about tonight so much as he does sick and tired. He wishes they could quit all this talking and put each other to the test in some other fashion, maybe a footrace or cage match.

He imagines grabbing the Incompetent by the ear and using it as a handle as he peeled away a long ribbon of skin. He imagines what his blood would taste like. Like cherry cough syrup. His tongue runs along the ridgeline of his teeth. He can't help it. He has learned to stop hating himself, hating what he has become. It would be like hating the whorl of his fingerprint, hating the sun and the moon's rotation in the sky. Some things are the way they are and there's no changing them.

Buffalo is leaning against the desk with his arms crossed over his belly. "Did you read those foreign policy books I gave you?"

"Pretty much."

"You either did or didn't."

"Why do I need to read what I've already been briefed on by the policy wonks? I read some, skipped some. Books. Jeez. I just wish they were all as good as that *Freakonomics*. There's a guy who can tell a story out of one side of his mouth, give a lesson out the other."

"I am not trying to entertain you. I am trying to educate you."

Chase swivels his chair in a slow circle. When he comes to a stop, Buffalo uses his middle finger to push his glasses farther up his nose. "You know you can't control these debates the way you can control a town hall meeting. You know you're coming across as cocksure but empty-headed, a single-issue candidate. You know you're too complicated right now as an Independent, neither fish nor fowl, seeming to agree and disagree with everyone on everything. It confuses people. We need something that distinguishes you. Cowboy and war hero will only get you so far."

"You got my candy?"

Buffalo studies him for a few seconds and then reaches into his suit coat and tosses Chase the bottle of Volpexx. His body pulses at the sight of it and he feels an immediate ache, a need as basic as thirst. He catches it with a rattle and shakes out on the desk a few pills. The container is a mix of Volpexx and Adderall, white moons and blue jellybeans that will at once dull him and sharpen him. He uses a coffee mug to mash them up and a credit card to cut the powder into lines and a dollar bill to snort.

He is lost for a moment in a weird gray buzz. Then he feels Buffalo's hands. Fitting the earpiece into him until it is invisible. Lifting his coattails and clipping the belt pack to the small of his back. He remains hunched over the desk, his eyes closed, until Buffalo pats him on the shoulder and tells him he's all set.

After the bombing, his left ear recovered immediately, but the ringing persisted in the other for two weeks. He wondered what he would hear, if anything, when it faded. Not much, it turns out. High voices are better than low, all sounds registering as if run through a cotton filter. "Did I get the right one?" Augustus asks and Chase says, "Yes," and touches his damaged ear.

The bombing of the courthouse square secured his run for the presidency. Three days after the event, after he had been discharged from the hospital with a concussion, third-degree burns, and a ruptured eardrum, Buffalo arranged for an AP photographer to visit the governor's mansion and shoot him bruised and bandaged, but very much alive, sitting at a desk with pen poised over paper and a phone pressed to his ear, unstoppable. He became the victim as well as the aggressor, someone people could sympathize with and rally around. He met with the president and provost and board of regents at the University of Oregon. Soon thereafter the Center for Lobos Studies became a reality, and for the first time since the mid-twentieth century, vaccination became a possibility. Within a week, dozens of lawsuits had been filed and he was on the cover of *Time* magazine in military dress and with half his face cast in shadow. The donors soon followed. Among them Alliance Energy, given his support of nuclear energy and the continued occupation of the Republic.

Buffalo has arranged the rest, including his running mate, a bright-eyed NRA-endorsed fundamentalist constitutionalist senator from Arkansas named Pinckney Arnold. They don't know each other really—they hardly see or talk to each other outside campaign events—but Pinckney is a fine choice, soft-spoken and articulate and humble and God-fearing, a nice counterweight to Chase and his swinging-dick persona. So says Buffalo.

Chase swigs again at the Monster Energy Drink. It tastes chalky. He heard somewhere that all energy drinks include that chalky flavor, not because it's an active ingredient, but because people expect it. They expect anything high-octane to taste a little bad. Maybe that has something to do with why people tolerate his behavior, why he so suddenly emerged as the dark-horse contender of the election. He doesn't try to come across as puritan like the rest of these chumps. Onstage, he scoffs, rolls his eyes, and once stormed off in annoyance. He interrupts and calls bullshit. He curses so much that the networks televise with a thirty-second delay. He hurries to tell an off-color story—the reason no one should stand behind a sneezing cow, the time he got frostbite on his doohickey during a pee break on a subzero patrol—and folks believe in him because of that. "He's like us," they say. "He's ordinary people."

There is a knock and the door cracks and a young man with sideburns and a clipboard says, "Ten minutes."

Buffalo thanks him and tells Chase to stand up and makes a twirling gesture with his hand. "Let me look at you."

Chase does as he's told and Buffalo picks away lint and smooths wrinkles and says, "You're going to be listening to me, right?" He taps his ear. "Right?"

"Always am. Always listening."

"Good. Hear me out now. We're going to surprise people tonight. You're going to announce a visit to the Republic. Two weeks from now, right before the election. Tour the bases and the mines, meet with the troops and hear their concerns. Four years and the president hasn't been there once."

"So I make him look like a total chickenshit."

The dimples rise in Buffalo's cheeks again. "Doesn't matter what else you screw up on tonight—that's what people are going to remember. That's what's going to distinguish you."

"I like it," Chase says, when in fact he feels chilled and unsteady, as if he has stepped out onto a frozen lake and watched the ice crack beneath him and the water rise like sudden black creeks.

The Republic. He talks about his time there often enough, but it's been more than ten years, and now it's become less a place and more a story. And he can't help but feel repulsed at the idea of moving among the crowds of soldiers, who will smile at him hopefully and grab hold of his hand not knowing it is a paw.

There comes another knock at the door and Chase feels something warm on his upper lip.

Buffalo's face creases with concern. "Here," he says. "Let me get that." He pulls out a silk handkerchief and dabs Chase's nose with it before returning it, spotted with blood, to his breast pocket. "Perfect."

CHAPTER 37

OUTSIDE THE FITNESS CENTER, a massive concrete block of a building, the line of students stretches through the propped-open double doors and trails along the sidewalk. They are not here for a basketball game or volleyball match. There is no sports program at William Archer, except for intramurals, since lycans are not permitted to play in any collegiate or professional division, the hazards of blood and adrenaline and litigation too great.

In the gymnasium, after showing their IDs and filling out a form, the students are led to one of a dozen nurse's stations, where they sit on a folding chair next to a table topped with plastic sheeting. The nurse, wearing a long-sleeve apron tucked into latex gloves, asks how the student is doing and the student says fine, thank you, and then the student's thumb is pricked and squeezed, a blood sample collected. The nurse then hands over a bottle of Volpexx along with the student's choice of a Tootsie Roll or a Dum Dum sucker. This is how it is the second Friday of every month.

The gymnasium is crowded with students, whose

sneakers squeak against the hardwood basketball courts and whose voices rise to the rafters to flutter and die—it sounds like game day—and that's a little what it feels like to Claire, a game.

Her family asked her to never tell anyone—*any*one, not ever, not unless she wanted to see them all in prison—about the doctor who falsely reported their monthly tests, and she didn't realize how lucky she was until she stole a pill from her friend Stacey's bathroom, taking it with a glass of water later that evening and feeling so knock-kneed and woozy that she couldn't keep her eyes open through *American Idol*.

Volpexx, like alcohol, affects everyone differently. Some walk around in a fog. Some counter the meds with high doses of caffeine or Adderall or Dexedrine. Some develop a tolerance over time, and some avoid it altogether by way of bribery or family connections.

She supposes it is an improvement over the way things used to be. She has heard stories about lobotomies, the long steel spikes driven into the brain to sever and deaden what the doctors referred to as the aberrant circuitry of the lycan's mind. *Lobos*, which means wolf and which means the lobes of the brain. And *tomos*, which means to cut. Cut the wolf, kill the wolf, and make the patient once again human. Beginning in the 1930s, the psychosurgery was largely successful and widely prescribed, not only among criminal lycans but for those suffering from schizophrenia and bipolar disorder. Among the psychiatric community, lobos was discussed as a mental illness, an unchained id with physiological symptoms. It wasn't until the 1970s that the procedure was discontinued—replaced by quaaludes—less out of humanitarian concern and more for the rising number of incapables that became wards of the state and a burden to taxpayers.

She doesn't have the luxury of a sympathizer doctor anymore. Miriam arranged through some black market a collection of blister packs—the blood within them O positive, same as Claire's, and laced with Volpexx. They are flesh colored and about as big as a quarter and after she affixes them with spirit gum they are nearly invisible. Still, she always comes to the gymnasium late in the day, after the nurses are glassy-eyed from so many students, so much blood.

She thanks the nurse and takes a Dum Dum sucker and by the time she returns to her dorm sucks it down to the stick.

The room is hers. Andrea is gone for the afternoon, working at the Victoria's Secret at the mall, where she seems to spend half her paycheck, coming home always with a new top, new eyeliner, new heels. Most of the shorts she wears say PINK across the butt.

Claire spends the next four hours at her desk, reading her way through a pile of books. It's difficult to concentrate—with the video images of Miriam spinning through her mind—but midterms are approaching, so she forces down the sentences. Her mind wanders to Patrick.

Their emails range from favorite movies and books to guessing the lines to songs to ranting about the best fast-food hamburgers to issues of greater seriousness, the loss of parents, the occupation of the Republic. Sometimes their messages are feverish, sent every minute or two over the course of three hours, and sometimes they settle down, not because they don't have anything to say, but because they don't need to say anything, like some couple drinking iced tea on a back porch, watching the stars, comfortable with the silence and the feeling of warm nearness between them.

She takes off her glasses and rubs them mindlessly between thumb and forefinger, cleaning them of spots that aren't there. She needs to stop. Stop thinking about him. He takes her out of the moment. She can't live in two worlds at once. She needs to focus on the present. *Focus.* She drops the blinds and bends over her work and bleeds her highlighter through so many pages.

Reprobus has assigned a seven- to ten-page midterm paper due the next class period. She has decided to write about her father. His legacy in the battle for equal rights. She knows this is dangerous. Looking backward. When most people think about their history, she expects, they have a sense of the vertical, like a ladder pushing upward, through the clouds, some of the rungs rotten and unpainted, but otherwise substantial enough to bear their weight. But for her, there is only the rung she hangs from, the clouds below her dark, jagged with lightning.

On her laptop she scrolls through an article, downloaded as a PDF and originally published in the *Chicago Tribune*, about the Struggle, about the Days of Rage. There is the familiar photo of her father. Standing on the steps of the federal courthouse. Throwing back his head in a howl. Clutching an American flag half-blackened with a tail of flame. Rather than reading more, she lingers for a long time on the photo, double-clicks to maximize it. She tries to put herself there, to step through the screen and into the past, and for the first time she notices other details about the image. The three stone archways yawning in the background. The sun slanting down and making every reflective surface shine as bright as the flaming flag. The windowed entry revealing a muddled reflection of hundreds gathered in the street. The mustached policeman, with one arm outstretched and the other on his holster, moving toward her father. And then, in the foreground, an out-of-focus body, shot from behind, only some of him visible, an upraised fist and two long Willie Nelson braids.

She scrolls down and pauses at another image, and then another, and then another. Dead bodies in the street with rubble all around them, the aftermath of a bombing. A woman who could be pleading or could be fighting with the paramedics who try to help her, her naked torso reddened with what appear to be bites. Close-ups of protest signs, two fingers raised to the sky in a V, claw marks, a gunshot chest, a mug shot of her father defiantly jutting his chin and staring directly into the camera.

On each of them she lingers. In the photo of the dead bodies on the street, she notices the high heel blown off a thick-ankled woman, the way her panty hose melted in places like a rotten spiderweb. She notices the ambulance turning down the street. She notices the man on the curb holding a handkerchief to his bleeding forehead. She notices the mailbox on the corner and the pigeon perched atop it and the man standing nearby, observing the chaos in the street, a man with long braids.

The man with long braids. She scrolls back and squints at the earlier photo of the protest. No doubt many wore their hair long then, but the length appears the same, as does his stocky build.

She returns to some of the other articles—other demonstrations, other cities, other times—and finds him in a few more, this man with the braids, never the focus of the shot, always appearing in the back or foreground of the picture like a chair or tree, something half-glimpsed.

"Who are you?" she says.

She decides to clear her head with a walk around campus. Outside the sky is the same golden hue as the leaves that spin from the trees on the central quad. One of them catches in the hair of a girl who sits on a nearby bench. She doesn't notice, too caught up in the taste of her boyfriend, their eyes closed, their mouths mashed together.

"What do you think about chemistry?" That's what she wrote Patrick in an email not long ago.

His response read, "I think, every now and then, you meet somebody. And everything clicks. Everything feels right. You know? Like you've plugged into some current. It's like electricity."

"I don't understand electricity," she wrote back.

The pathways are messy with leaves and she can

hear footsteps crunching behind her. She doesn't like the feeling of being followed and slows so the person will pass her. The footsteps slow to match hers. For a minute she allows herself to be paced—and then spins around.

Matthew catches himself midstride and stutter-steps. He holds up his hands as if she might strike him. It is the closest they have been.

"Hey," he says.

"Hey yourself."

She starts walking again and he jogs up next to her. He is a whole head taller than she is. He has changed since this morning, out of his TA uniform and into scuffed Dr. Martens, frayed jeans, a pullover fleece. "Where are you going?"

"Home." She has never thought of her dorm that way, but she supposes it's the right word, for now the only home she has.

They walk in silence. She tries to focus her attention on anything but him. A gray squirrel worries over a pinecone. A leaf blower whines in the distance. A football spins through the pale blue sky and drops into some boy's outstretched hands. And on the asphalt trail they follow, Matthew's shadow falls across hers.

"Don't ask me about anything related to lycan history," she says.

"I won't."

"Good. I'm sick of it."

Through the cluster of pine trees up ahead she can see her dorm. She quickens her pace and Matthew falls behind and she feels she has shrugged off an invisible leash. Then his voice calls out to her, "Hey, are you in some kind of trouble?"

She stops in the shadow of a pine. Browned needles rain around her. She turns and tries to read his expression—eyebrows raised, lower lip tucked beneath his teeth. "What does that mean?"

He peers around as if afraid someone might overhear him. "I was at the registrar yesterday. Signing up for my spring courses. There was a man there. Some suit. Everybody behind the desk seemed nervous about him. He had a list of names he was cross-checking. You were one of them."

"I don't understand."

"I don't either. I just thought I'd let you know."

Her dorm room is unlocked. She holds the knob in her hand and looks both ways down the hall. Empty. A bad lightbulb sizzles in and out of shadow. Several doors are propped open and music filters from them. She reaches a hand into her pocket to grip the knife there. Slowly she pushes open the door. A rusted hinge screeches.

Failing sunlight falls through the window. No one is in the room, not under the beds, not in the closets. Her hand releases the knife. She closes the door and shrugs off her backpack.

She nearly cries out when a second later the door opens and Andrea walks in, her flip-flops snapping, her body cocooned in a towel. She brings with her a cloud of mint shampoo. She sets down her shower-spotted tote and withdraws a pick from it and flips her hair forward and begins to rough out the damp tangles.

As much as Claire hates to admit it, she needs her roommate. It would be easy to write her off as a complete idiot, but Andrea is bewilderingly smart with computers and graphic design. During orientation, she said, "Give me that piece of shit," and stole away Claire's laptop and spent the next two hours uploading software along with an extensive collection of music and videos, much of it pirated. She runs a blog called *PinkGrrl*. She does web consulting for a firm in her home city of Chicago and writes code for her computer science course while instant-messaging friends, and virtually every evening somebody knocks on their door asking a question about Linux this and Kerberos that.

"Andrea?"

"Yeah." She twists her body and looks at Claire

sidelong and flinches as she rakes through a painful kink.

"Remember what you were saying the other day—about if there was anything I ever needed, to let you know?"

"Course."

"I need help."

She has to clear away the mess on the floor to drag her chair next to Andrea's. They sit side by side at the desk, their faces lit by the glow of Andrea's iMac. Claire doesn't know much about computers—Microsoft Word, Internet Explorer, and iTunes are the limits of her technical savvy—but she has heard Andrea brag about this one, its quad-core processor and advanced HD graphics and FaceTime camera. Desktop Nirvana, she calls it.

Andrea transfers the files from the laptop to the desktop with a thumb drive and opens the articles into so many windows the screen looks like a mess of playing cards. She then clips away the images from each PDF and formats them into Photoshop. All this with a rapid-fire series of clicks Claire can barely keep track of.

When Andrea squints at the images and asks, "What do you even care about this old crap for?" Claire says, "It's just a history project."

She wonders if Andrea can sharpen up the pictures, zoom in on this figure in the background—there and there and there—pointing at the screen.

"No prob."

Claire isn't positive what Andrea does next—the mouse moves too swiftly, the windows open and close at shutter speed—but it appears to have something to do with the density of the files. Here is the photo of the bodies on the street. "Nasty," Andrea says and then zooms in and clarifies, zooms in again and clarifies. "Best I can do." The face is blurry and somewhat pixilated, like rain-smeared newsprint, but they can tell he has a beard.

The same for the other two photos. Andrea calls up the image of the federal courthouse, the image of her father, and they study the back of the man in the foreground. "I guess there's nothing to be done on this one," Claire says.

Andrea shrugs her apology and then answers an instant message that pops up before returning to the photo. "Maybe, maybe, maybe," she says under her breath and then drags the magnifying function over the entryway to the courthouse. A glass revolving door with the sunlight brightening it. Andrea drags it closer and closer still. She changes from color to gray scale and then messes with the lighting to dampen the glare. Clarifies again.

The pixels rearrange into the reflection of the man with the braids. Not perfect, but focused enough to clearly observe him from the waist up. His face half-hidden by his beard. His jacket, leather fringe. Professor Alan Reprobus.

CHAPTER 38

MIRIAM HAD NO ALLIANCES—everyone an enemy, no one a friend—and that was a difficult way to live for anyone, let alone an eighteen-year-old girl. She had to protect Claire. That was what her brother wanted and that meant keeping her in the dark and pushing her away, saying goodbye, no matter how difficult it was to let her go. The farther away, the better, the safer.

In the parking lot outside the train station, she closed and locked the door of the Ramcharger and sagged down on the bench seat so that no one could see her, and cried. She did not tremble—she shook completely. She permitted herself five minutes of this before straightening up and roughing away the tears and driving off without snapping her seat belt into place.

It was time to get to work.

Miriam had been doing her research. The articles she read about the raid—following the courthouse bombing—implied cooperation between local police and federal authorities. No names were released. The location was listed as outside Portland, but she knew the safe house was in Sandy.

She visited PSU and walked around campus until she saw a girl of the same approximate build and appearance as her and approached her and smiled broadly and shouted, "Cynthia! It's so good to see you!"

The girl wore a hiking backpack that turtled her with its weight and size. "I'm not Cynthia."

"You're kidding me. I'm so embarrassed. You know, you look exactly like her. I'm going to have to tell her she has a double." She laughed in a high, shrieking way. "What's your name?"

"I'm Kirsten. Kirsten Packer."

"I'll tell her to look for you. It will be like looking in a mirror. This is so weird. Sorry, Kirsten."

Kirsten gave her a perplexed smile and adjusted the straps on her backpack and trudged off to class and Miriam pulled out her pay-as-you-go phone and dialed the number for card services and said, with a panicked voice, that she had lost her purse and would like to report her student ID card stolen. "Kirsten Packer," she said. "That's my name. Can you help me?" They assured her they could print up another, no problem.

The building was a five-minute walk. She pinched the skin around her eyes to swell and redden her expression. Then she stared at the sky for thirty seconds until her eyes watered before pushing through the door. A kid with a short Mohawk was working the counter. "That sucks so bad," he said. "I hope everything works out for you."

She tucked the card into the back pocket of her jeans and said, "It will."

She stopped by the campus bookstore and bought a pink PSU sweatshirt and drove the twenty minutes to Sandy, to the police station, where she said she was a criminology major at PSU doing a report on police raids and wondered if she might view some reports.

She made herself look younger by pulling back her hair in a ponytail and pretending to chew gum. She had a spiral notebook in one hand, her ID card in the other. A woman with jowls and her hair done up in a jet-black helmet looked at the card, looked at Miriam, and said of course, so long as she signed in and paid the administrative fee.

Within twenty minutes, she had the information she needed. Ten names. All local police.

She made phone calls, fiddled around on the Net, drove through a few neighborhoods, before narrowing down her prospects to Ernest Hobbes, an inspector in Sandy; and Dennis Hannah, a SWAT team member with Clackamas County. Both single.

In Hobbes's home office, she finds a large stash of gay pornography, so she turns her sights on Hannah, a thick-necked man with a mustache who wears jean shorts and changes his own oil and drinks at the Tip-Top Tavern every Friday night.

She drove to the mall and browsed the stores and bought high heels from JCPenney and a lace push-up bra from Victoria's Secret and a short skirt and skimpy top with a scoop neck and a jangly necklace and earrings from Maurices. She circled the cosmetics counters at Nordstrom. The women who worked there all wore white coats as if they were doctors and when they looked at her plain face they twisted up their expressions in sympathy as if about to give a difficult diagnosis. "Can I help you?" one of them said and Miriam said, "Get me whatever lipstick, foundation, blush, and eyeliner you think matches my complexion. And whatever perfume you think smells good. Now."

At home she laid everything out on the bed in the shape of a woman, the invisible woman she planned to become.

Apparently she has a small head. She bought a blond shoulder-length bob at the Wig Gallery in northeast Portland. Even their smallest size kept slipping out of place. So she held it with her hand, as though it were a hat, when walking from her truck to the ramped entry of the Tip-Top Tavern. The day was cold, but she wore no jacket.

Once inside, her stiff posture loosened into a slink. The juke played Johnny Cash. Somebody tossed darts in the corner. An Oregon Ducks clock glowed green and gold on the wall. She spotted Hannah at a high, round table, sharing a pitcher of light beer with a friend. She took her time approaching the bar, making sure everybody got an eyeful. She ordered a ginger whiskey and climbed onto the stool and crossed her legs.

It didn't take long. She sipped her drink and watched the Trail Blazers on the TV hanging over the bar. She sensed him before she heard him, the man in the brown leather jacket with the American flag patch sewed onto its shoulder. He was leaning against the bar only inches away from her. "Buy you a drink?" he said.

She lifted her whiskey and gave it a little twirl.

"Can I buy you another drink?"

She shook her head, no.

He said something else, but she was already sliding off her stool, leaving the bar, approaching Hannah. He and his friend had their eyes on her and their pint glasses half-raised to their mouths, frozen by her approach.

"Do you mind if I sit here?" she said. "That creep won't leave me alone."

"By all means," the friend said. He was older, squarer. Black polo shirt and jeans. Badge and pistol clipped to his belt.

"What did he say?" Hannah said and peered over her shoulder with a hard-eyed expression. "Do we need to teach him something about manners?"

"It's fine," she said. "I don't think he'll bother me anymore now that I'm with you two. You two look pretty tough."

When Hannah smiled, she saw the gap between his teeth she didn't know was there.

Two pitchers and two hours later, she is in his car, a Dodge Challenger parked under a skeletal oak tree with a few browned leaves still clinging stubbornly to its branches. She has his zipper undone and the hard muscle of his cock in her hand. In the tavern, they talked about the shit economy, about the Trail Blazers, about her cousin who died of cancer, about her job as a hairdresser—and then she asked what they did anyway.

Condensation dribbled from the pitcher and pooled at its base and Hannah dipped his finger in it and touched her on the back of the hand. "We're cops."

"No!"

"We are. We really are."

"Tell me, is it like in the shows? Like that *CSI*?"

They laughed and shook their heads and said the shows were good fun, but real police work was a little less glamorous and she'd be surprised by how much Hollywood got wrong.

"Tell me something badass you've done," she said. "Something dangerous and heroic." She made her tone half-mocking and half-daring and Hannah wiped the foam off his mustache and grinned at his friend and said, "Oh, we've got some stories, don't we, Paulie?"

"Yeah, we do."

It wasn't long before Hannah brought up the raid on the lycan safe house. He talked about working with the prick feds and stalking through the grass and ramming open the door and charging through the house and finding it empty except for one guy. Who turned out to be *the* guy, the one who wrote that banned book that pissed a bunch of people off. "Weirdest thing," he said. "Him all alone like that. It's like he had been left for us."

She let her jaw drop lower and lower as he spoke and said she couldn't believe it. "That was, like, in the news."

"I know," he said. "It was some seriously serious shit."

Now, in the car, she can tell from his breathing and from the short little hip thrusts that he is close to finishing. She leans toward him and nibbles his ear and says, “Where did they take that guy? The one from the raid?”

“What?” His eyes are half-shuttered with pleasure. “What do you care?”

“Just curious.”

“Keep going. Please.”

“Where is he?” She gives him another pull and his whole body arches toward it. “Where is he?”

In a rush he tells her FDC SeaTac, he’s at FDC SeaTac.

She releases him and slaps him with the same hand and says, “What kind of woman do you think I am?” and pushes open the door and leaves him there with his mouth and his pants agape.

CHAPTER 39

AUGUSTUS KNOWS all about the eugenics programs. The Americans, from 1907 to 1960, sterilizing hundreds of thousands of lycans and homosexuals, the poor, the physically and mentally disabled. The Germans, during the 1930s and '40s, trying to create an Ubermensch, a perfect Aryan, while at the same time playing God with the Jews and Gypsies and all those with what they called inferior blood, sometimes sterilizing, sometimes exterminating, sometimes experimenting—injecting patients with chemicals and diseases, exposing them to mustard gas, sewing together their bodies, immersing them in cold water, forcing them to sexually engage with dogs, striking their skulls with hammers to study head trauma.

And he knows that the ACLU and a handful of congressmen and the demonstrators outside the White House are accusing him of the same. He tries not to give interviews—he needs Chase to remain the mouthpiece—but the other month, a reporter sprang out and stuck a microphone in his face and he couldn't stop himself. "Everyone needs to realize that what we're talking about here comes down to public health, public safety. All medical efforts are in support of that. AIDS is not a person. Mad cow disease is not a person. Swine flu is not a person. And lobos isn't either. It's a dangerous pathogen." A certain segment of the population seemed to be in denial of this, as if lobos were a dangerous truth they preferred not to believe in, like an X-ray spotted with tumors.

But he knows that he is correct. Knows without a doubt. That is one of his more upstanding qualities, he thinks. Absolute certainty. This certainty enabled him to muscle private and corporate donors into his corner, convinced the University of Oregon to risk the lawsuits they knew would come and then fast-tracked their endorsement of Neal Desai's search for a vaccine and allowed him to manifest a research team in a semester's time and named him the director of the Center for Lobos Studies.

And now—only a hundred yards away from where he stands—the bulldozers and dump trucks and concrete mixers and men in hard hats and orange reflective vests are building the five-million-dollar Pfizer extension of the research campus.

Neal's team is presently working out of an old laboratory, the tile floor the sickly green of an old hospital ward and the benchtops—as everyone called the counters—black and impervious and covered in plastic-backed paper held down with colored tape meant to define territories. Upon them sit boxes of pipette tips, pipettes, Sharpie pens, personal centrifuges, a spectrophotometer, water baths, glassware, latex gloves, Kimwipes, inverted microscopes, safety glasses. Lab coats hang from hooks. Computer terminals glow in the corners. An industrial refrigerator—double sided, with an open glass front—hums next to a liquid nitrogen tank that registers –170 degrees.

Augustus helps adjust a decapitated dog's head—a German shepherd—into a vise on the stainless-steel counter. The fur prickles through his latex gloves.

"Thank you," Neal says. His oscillating saw whirs to life. It whines when pressed into bone, slowly circling the skull, which he then pulls off with the soft pop of a bottle top. He stares at the brain, blackened with prions like an old walnut.

Neal believes he is here to say hello, tour the lab, pick up another carton of Volpexx. And he is. But he is also here to convince the good doctor to join Chase in the Republic. "Privately as his medical assistant. Publicly as an emissary."

"I need to be here to help with my family."

"Last I checked, your lycan daughter enrolled in a rehab program. Sounds like she's getting all the help she needs."

"No."

"You'll pose for a few photos, give a few speeches. You'll meet with Alliance Energy representatives—"

"No."

"—who, may I remind you, are one of your corporate donors."

"My work is here," Neal says, though his voice has lost its resolve. They both know it: he is no longer needed in the lab. He has more than enough people to carry out every duty—thirty of them altogether—the secretaries, the professors, the postdocs, the grad students. But this is what he loves most—the work—his eye pressed to a microscope, the smell of formaldehyde scorching his nose and the talcum powder from the latex gloves whitening his knuckles.

"I don't want to tell you what your work is," Augustus says. "But I will if I must." Neal always puts up a fight, but Augustus always wins, and these past few months the doctor has more often than not found himself behind a desk or on a plane or in a fluorescent-lit boardroom meeting with politicians, meeting with donors, meeting with faculty from other universities wishing to interface with their research.

Then there are the interviews, him stationed on a couch alongside Chase, thanking the governor for his support and trying to explain, in layman's terms, some version of the following.

This is how you make a vaccine.

Step one: Identify the infection. In the case of rabies, it's the dog frothing at the mouth, the bat that swoops down from the attic rafters and savages a hand reaching for a light switch.

Step two: Isolate the bacteria or virus. Kill the dog. Kill the bat. Cut off its head. Find the negri bodies, the black spots in its brain that look like rotten grains of rice.

Step three: Purify and replicate the virus. You have one bullet but you need to make more. Through the gene splicing of the DNA and RNA in your infected specimen, you build your arsenal.

Step four: Inject the virus into a healthy animal and see if you get the same symptoms.

Step five: Once the virus is confirmed, you know that within this gattaca, this particular pairing of DNA, is your killer.

But only a very small portion of this composition is actually dangerous. The rest is merely the shell, the snake that surrounds the venom. So in further replication you excise the venom and keep the snake. This is what is known as a live modified, and once injected into the body of a healthy specimen, it harmlessly mimics the virus. The immune system then launches an attack and retains a history of that attack so that it can never be invaded again.

Zoonotic diseases are infectious agents that affect both animals and humans. They come in the form of fungi, bacteria, viruses, parasites, and prions, and their names are familiar to the newspaper headlines: AIDS, anthrax, mad cow, E. coli. There are nearly fifteen hundred pathogens that can affect humans, and 61 percent of them are zoonotic, among them lobos.

Lobos is a prion infection. Prions are an infectious agent made up of misfolded proteins so similar to normal proteins that the immune system does not fight them off. They contain no DNA or RNA, so the standard practice of isolation and sequencing is not possible.

"So what are you doing?"

Neal smiles. "Top secret. Let's just say I had a breakthrough a few months ago."

Augustus only knows that it takes forever. He calls Neal regularly for updates, and he can hear the frustration in the doctor's voice. He had to isolate different groups of mice—those with low antibodies and those with high antibodies—and gauge thousands of results. Then he had to redesign the vaccine so that it could be used on dogs and wolves. Now he is in the process of testing thousands more subjects, and once that is done, he will have to redesign the vaccine once more for humans. Then there will be the months lost, at least three, to manufacturing and packaging and distribution.

Chase often says, "Why can't he just hurry this whole thing up?"

But it can take anywhere from three to ninety days for someone to show symptoms of the disease, and the center must by law wait four hundred days to know for sure whether the agent manifests itself.

Of course they do not have forever—with the election looming.

"So it's settled, then," Augustus says. "You're coming. We'll arrange a plane ticket. Make sure your passport is up-to-date."

Neal shares the lab with three thirty-something postdocs who address him as Dr. Desai no matter how many times he tells them it's perfectly all right to call him Neal. They are all hovering around a laptop in the corner of the room. One of them turns to look at Neal. Adam. Carrot-orange hair and a wispy beard that grows mostly along his neck. "Something's happened," he says.

"In a minute," Neal says and rubs the bridge of his nose. "I really don't want to go."

"Come on," Augustus says. "It'll be a hoot."

"It's cold there. I hate the cold."

"Dr. Desai." Adam calls out his name again, and Neal says, "Yes, one moment."

Neal scribbles something into a lab notebook on the benchtop. He and Augustus peel off their latex gloves and soap their hands and remove their safety goggles and walk past the incubators and the fume hoods and the centrifuges and join the grad students.

"Dr. Desai, you should see this."

"Yes, yes, yes."

Adam steps nervously away from the laptop. Augustus squints at the black rectangle in the middle of the glowing screen. "What am I looking at?"

"It's everywhere," Adam says. "CNN, AOL, Facebook. Look." He toys with the mouse and taps a button and Augustus realizes the black rectangle is a paused video that now comes to life.

A face fills the screen. An old man's face. His head is not shaved or misshapen. His skin is not ravaged by scars or tattooed with skulls or snakes or barbed wire. His voice is not booming and poisonous. He looks like a nice old man. The light is dim and his eyes are mostly lost to shadows and his face hidden beneath his long silvery hair, parted in the middle and curtaining his face. His dagger of a nose is otherwise his most definitive feature. When he speaks, his voice is calm and strangely accented, some mix of singsong Swede and boarding-school British. "The United States has fed on us long enough," he says. "Now we feed on the United States."

One of his eyes, Augustus can now tell, is discolored like an eggplant. The old man breathes heavily, as though on the verge of hyperventilating, a serrated whistle sharpening every exhalation. There is nothing else to hear except the faint electrical whine of the recording. His head shakes. His mouth trembles. The breathing, the breathing, in and out, so pronounced it seems sexual. The old man leans forward and his face goes momentarily out of focus.

Then he lurches back. The camera wobbles and readjusts. His face is creased with wrinkles. His eyes blink rapidly, tearing up with blood. He shows his teeth in a damp red scowl. He blurs away from the camera and the camera refocuses. A poorly lit room. A pitted concrete wall. At the base of it lies a soldier in cammies. A young man with his buzz cut grown out and his skin darkened by bruises. His wrists and ankles bound, his mouth taped shut. He is struggling like a worm to move away from what is moving toward him, the old man, the lycan, visible again at the edge of the screen.

There might be a growl. There might be a short-lived scream muffled by duct tape, but it is hard to tell. Soon the soldier stops struggling and the only sound is the sound of feeding.

"Balor." Then Adam brings his tremoring hand to the mouse and pauses the video. "They're saying his name is Balor."

CHAPTER 40

PATRICK ROTATES onto knock-and-talk and then rotates again onto patrol. Sometimes they would drop off crates of Volpexx in the barrows. That's what they called the outlying tenements, the barrows—where the welfare cases lived—the rows and rows of concrete apartment buildings with trash stacked up on the curbs and music thumping behind windows and figures shrinking back into doorways and corpses lying frozen in alleyways. Every two weeks, on street corners, the convoy unloaded several dozen shrink-wrapped cardboard boxes, each filled with one hundred bottles rattling with one hundred pills. The lycans are given the choice—that's what the commanding general says—they are given the choice as to whether or not they will control their disease. The military enables that choice. And the choice, for some of the lycans, is to crush and snort the drug and drift off into fog-filled dreams and become hollow husks of the people they once were.

As far as Patrick could tell—from his mother, from Claire, from many of the locals here in the Republic—lycans can control their symptoms just fine without the help of meds. Sometimes his unit would drive through the fishing villages and visit with families. Meet-and-greets or knock-and-talks, they called these trips. They would crouch down and hold out Kit Kat bars to cautious children and say, "Come here, come on," as if they were dogs. They would accept invitations into homes and stand sweating in their gear and watch women with big pillowy arms rolling dough in the kitchen and old men smoking pipes and mending fishing nets and young children playing dominoes on living room floors. Eating sandwiches and drinking coffee at all hours of the day. Their houses are small, sometimes one big room, lumber and pipes and sleds and skis stored in the ceiling beams. The smell of grease and fish hanging in the air. Tools and belts hanging near the door along with jackets. Fishing poles hung from the walls like artwork alongside dreary gray-smeared paintings of the sea. They would eat cookies that seemed made of nothing but butter and flour and that sucked all the saliva from his mouth. They spoke Finnish. They spoke French and Russian and German and Chinese and Spanish and English. They said how thankful they were for the military, for the mine. "You keep us safe," they said.

Occasionally Patrick would ask, on his own or through an interpreter, a question about his father, but no one knew him—they could only shake their heads and hand him another cookie and ask him whether he liked the snow. Rarely did their squads encounter any young men, and when Patrick asked about this, Sergeant Decker looked at him distractedly and said, "Because, you fucking idiot, they're the ones we're fighting."

And sometimes they would, when on patrol, drive into a fight. The sky was often heavy with clouds and the air thick with snow, and when machine guns rattled and RPGs blasted, the orange-and-yellow flashes and the thunderous explosions that followed gave the impression that a summer thunderstorm had descended upon them.

He misses this.

After a couple of two-week rotations on the base, he feels like the concrete and cinder block and Constantine wire are contracting, closing around him, and soon he will have nowhere to go; soon they will rip through his flesh. He feels like he is getting soft. He feels like time is slowing down. He feels like he has lost another month to what he realizes is a failed hunt for his father. The lycans win. He might as well accept that. It's no use.

He has just finished sweeping and mopping the National Guard bunkhouse. He slops the mop into the brown-watered bucket and stands over his father's old bed. He has been here many times before, but this is his first time alone. Gray light comes through the windows. The air smells of bleach. A spider crawls from under the mattress and across the sheets and comes to rest on the pillow. Patrick hurriedly flicks it off. His hand hovers above the pillow a moment, and then he strokes the hollow where a head has rested.

He sits down. The frame creaks. He waits a minute in silence and then swings back his legs and lies where his father once did. He wonders if a part of him is still there, dissolved into the sheets and floors and walls of this place, watching him.

He stares at the spring slats of the bed above him. A honeycomb design. He notices something then. What he first thinks is a tag, the kind that you see stapled to mattresses, the kind that warn of your arrest, or something, if you scissor them off. But the quality appears more brittle and yellowed along the edges.

He reaches up, and sure enough it slips against the pressure of his fingers, slides through the grating. A piece of paper folded once and once again. He sits up in such a hurry that his boot hits the mop bucket and it rolls a few paces away and sloshes loudly and he checks the room to make certain he is still alone.

He doesn't know what he expects. Certainly not this. Not a paper scribbled over with hieroglyphics.

He recognizes the blocky slanted handwriting, but he can't make any sense of the notes about cell concentration, viability, vitality, yeast strain, yeast propagator, hemacytometer, methylene blue, pH, yeast slurry, flocculation, dissolved oxygen, yeast nutrient, or the word that comes up most often, metallothionein.

Then he sees a sentence that makes him blink hard and remember the pit full of blackened bones. *Lobos subject #14: two days of improvement and then death.*

The platoons rotate again, and Patrick is assigned to the QRF. He will be out on the wire soon enough. Finally. He has been working nonstop with the glass cleaner and floor polish. After an eight-hour shift, no matter how hard he scrubs off in the showers, he can't shake the ammonia and bleach smell. Nobody knows when—the schedule classified for security reasons—but presidential candidate Chase Williams will be visiting the base at some point in the near future and the CO wants the place photo-op ready.

But that's no longer Patrick's problem. Yesterday he sat through a briefing. In a clearing next to the armory, Lieutenant Colonel Steve Bennington, an ash-haired West Point graduate, stood before a vast diagram constructed from snow, mounded and carved to mimic the surrounding landscape. It was twenty meters in circumference and captured one hundred klicks of territory. He used food coloring—blue for water, green for military, red for enemy—and stepped over hills and trudged through valleys as he indicated various problem areas they would likely attend. Chief among them: Ukko, a combat outpost seventy klicks from here and home to a company of soldiers from the 1/167th Battalion. They had come under repeated mortar attack and expected more trouble in the coming week. "The pressure system changes tonight. We're in for a warm spell," Bennington said. "And warm weather means trouble."

This morning, Patrick wakes to the sound of water dripping from the eaves. He pulls on a fresh pair of camo pants, olive-drab shirt, shoulder-patch knit sweater. He clips a radio to his belt, mandatory for all assigned to QRF, so that when the call goes out, everybody comes running.

The ground is a sticky mix of snow and mud when Patrick heads over to the MWR. The line for the computers is always long, and this morning it takes him more than thirty minutes before he's stationed in front of a Dell with a gasping fan. All around him keyboards tick and people yell and cry and joke their way through Skype conversations with their families. Every now and then they glance around embarrassedly, knowing they are being overheard. More than they know, Patrick thinks. He once talked to his mother and later that afternoon received a visit from the lieutenant. She was a registered lycan and communicating with her so freely compromised base security. No matter if she was his mother. He could send her letters.

He checks his email first and opens a message from Claire. "Just wanted you to know," she writes. "These emails matter to me. They mean that I matter to someone. And that means I actually exist."

He reads it twice. Then begins to peck out a message about how he remembers when he told her he was leaving. They were on the porch of the cabin and he wishes very badly he could go back to that moment. He hasn't lived long enough to know for sure, but he guesses in the end life adds up to one long string of regrets like this. Memories of should-haves and might-have-beens that will sneak up on him when he least expects it, when he's soaping his armpits or driving a nighttime highway. There is no going back. The trick is looking ahead, anticipating and remedying the mistake before it occurs.

He writes that *this* is what he would do if he

could go back. When she stood from the bench and stomped across the porch and slammed the door on him, he wishes very much that he had told her to stop. And when she turned, he would have taken her face in both hands. To kiss her, yes, but first to memorize her. He has thought about it many times. Then there would have been a physical marker to tether them all this time.

He sees it now. Sees the mistake he made. Letting her walk away. "If you offered me a million dollars right now or a kiss," he writes, "I'd take the kiss." He isn't sure whether this qualifies as a good line or a bad one, but he means it. He really does.

He hits send and heaves a sigh, then takes the piece of notebook paper from his pocket and unfolds it and flattens it on the desk beside him. He calls up Google and plugs in the word his father kept using: *metallothioneins*.

Every webpage takes a maddening length of time to load, the images staggering downward like a stiff set of blinds. Eventually he finds what he is looking for on bestenbalt.com, an entry that tells him metallothioneins are presently in virtually all forms of life. Their function is not entirely understood, "but experimental data support participation of metallothioneins in regulation of Zn and Cu, detoxification of toxic metals like cadmium, silver, copper, and mercury, and in protection of cells against reactive oxygen species and alkylating agents."

He reads this three times and slumps back in his chair. He doesn't know what this means, but it means something. He hits print and folds the paper into his pocket.

The Tall Man visits regularly. Sometimes he asks Jeremy questions—about the Resistance, about addresses, about email and phone communication, about money and management and infrastructure, about Puck, Miriam, Claire, and a hundred other names—and sometimes he removes a small black notebook from within his suit coat and jots a few notes down in it.

But mostly he hurts Jeremy. That is their primary mode of communication: suffering. The Tall Man electrocutes him with live sparking wires. He pulls out clumps of his beard, and then his armpit and pubic hair, with a pair of pliers. He makes him eat a live scorpion. He burns him with cigarettes. He rubs salt into his eyes and open wounds. He drowns him in cold water and scalds him in hot.

At first Jeremy coped. He left behind his body and escaped into his mind and found himself, day after day, walking down that same dirt path in the forest and approaching the gnarled pine tree and pulling down on its lever of a branch and stepping into the dark yawning entrance that led him belowground. That was his safe place.

Then it became too much—the vast, intricate networks of pain that seized every nerve so that his attention became singular with the injury coursing through him. It was not like something on a television program. The Tall Man would not ask a question and then prod Jeremy to receive an answer. Instead, in silence, he would torture Jeremy for hours—just watching, his eyelids never seeming to lower—pleasuring in the screams, the flash and curve of his many tools. Then he would slump back in his folding chair and unscrew a bottle of water and gurgle a swallow and smack his ruined mouth and say, "What do you think? Do you think you're ready for a break?"

The break lasts only as long as he talks. These days, Jeremy is always ready to talk, always ready for a break. Though he once clung stubbornly to his silence, that time has passed. His old life and loyalties are so far removed from his current situation that they seem like a story he once read. When he talks to the Tall Man, he is simply recounting a plot, somebody else's fancy, the information harmless, meaningless.

Sometimes he talks about his daughter and the

way the bomb tore her into many meaty pieces that he collected in a black trash bag. Sometimes he talks about how, when he was a student at William Archer, he was called into the office of Alan Reprobus to discuss a paper he wrote about violence as protest, a paper the professor called brilliant and incendiary, a paper that would go on to become the first chapter of his book *The Revolution*. Sometimes he talks about how the professor would hold late-night meetings at his house during which they would discuss political issues and plan protests and design flyers—mostly harmless—but once in a while Reprobus would take a few of them aside—the trusted ones, he called them—to design an act of terror: mail a bomb, slash brake lines, trash a construction site. Sometimes he talks about the semester he spent abroad in the Lupine Republic—building houses and teaching English—and how the Master sought him out during this time. That is how he refers to Balor, as the Master, and the Tall Man is very interested in the Master, very interested indeed.

And sometimes, when Jeremy runs out of stories, he invents new ones, anything to keep the Tall Man from growing bored.

If his father was brewing, he had a workspace hidden somewhere on the base. Patrick feels stupid for not realizing this earlier. Months ago, when one of the lieutenants mentioned in passing that his father made a hell of a beer, Patrick figured he was a fan of Anchor Steam. He has a few off-duty hours to spare and spends them searching.

He checks behind the mess hall, thinking the cooks might have hooked him up with space and supplies. He checks the storage rooms at the rear of the MWR. He checks the maintenance bay, the hangar, the armory.

Outside the latrine, he turns a corner and spots Sergeant Decker marching along with that half-stooped posture of his. Patrick ducks back the way he came and knobs down the volume on his radio and waits for the footsteps to fade, and then his eyes settle on the middle distance, past the melted ruins of Lieutenant Colonel Bennington's snow diagram, where he spots an old toolshed near the east guard tower.

He has glanced at it dozens of times without really seeing it. And now there it is, like an old book on a crowded shelf that suddenly announces itself when your fingers trail across its leather spine. The wood is dark, weathered. Vines have overtaken it, gray with winter, like dead veins. There is a padlock on the door. None of his keys work—but a rock does. He splinters it away from the rotten wood.

The lightbulb sputters to life, and its dim orange glow seems to bring more shadows than light. He drags the door closed behind him. He can smell the yeast coming off the twenty-five-gallon drums stacked in the corner for propagation. A waist-level bench is built into the wall. On it, Patrick sees a close cousin to the mess of his father's workspace at home. Beakers, vials, droppers, jugs, and jars. Petri dishes. A rusted microscope. The lightbulb sizzles and then dies. He has only the winter light streaming through the window.

On an overhead shelf, black binders, notebooks full of his small, square handwriting, the penciling faded and smeared. He flips through page after page and reads meaningless entries about yeast cells and blue cells and regions and dilution factors and slurry. He discovers among them a printed email correspondence. He only glances at them, their contents impersonal, a garble of chemical terminology. He folds them up and shoves them in his pocket to study later.

He spots a moth perched on a table and touches it, and it crumbles to dust. He picks up a glass container next to it, filled with a powder that has long ago hardened. A strip of masking tape reaches across it on which is written "Metallo" in black pen. He sets it down and picks up another bottle, this one plastic with a childproof cap, and whatever is inside it jangles. He spins it in his hand until he can read the label, Volpexx.

Something snaps drily beneath his boot. He steps back from the workbench and peers into the shadowy space beneath it and there observes the desiccated corpse of a wolf or a dog—it's difficult to tell—the body sunken, the fur falling away in patches, the bone of its hind leg split by his weight. Around its snout is a muzzle and around its neck a chain leash bolted to the wall behind it.

One thing is certain: his father wasn't just making beer.

He hears something then. A chewing, spitting sound. He looks down and his eyes settle on the radio. In a panic he knobs the volume to high and a static-filtered version of Decker's voice assaults him. "All QRF squads report, all QRF squads report for immediate departure!"

He has no time to think further about his father. He can only run. As he does—mazing his way through the barracks, every step sending up a splash—he joins other soldiers who pour from alleyways and doorways and pound toward the four-truck convoy waiting for them.

It is Ukko, as expected. The gunfire and RPGs started at dawn and haven't let up. They need backup.

Patrick throws on his gear. He checks the crew-served weapon systems: the medium and heavy machine guns, the rockets and TOW guns. Checks the head space and timing on the .50 caliber to make sure the weather hasn't made it swell or shrink and thrown it off by a few clicks.

They line up next to their vehicles—four fire squads, two Humvees, two armored trucks—and Decker walks the length of them and knocks them each on the helmet. "Death on a pale horse, gentlemen. Let's roll."

Today the Tall Man leans into Jeremy until his face is the only thing. It is an expressionless face, a dead face, the skin glossy and colored different shades of red and pink and yellow and tan. "You're wondering. But you're afraid to ask. You're wondering why I look this way?"

The Tall Man asks questions and Jeremy answers them—that is their routine—but in this case he does not know how to respond. Will he be punished for a wrong answer?

The Tall Man exhales through his slit-like nostrils, a long, deflating hiss. "It happened a long time ago. You weren't even born yet. At the time I was a police officer in Chicago. My first year on the job and I was assigned foot patrol during the Days of Rage. You know all about the Days of Rage, don't you, Mr. Saber? I've read your book. I found it a very interesting piece of propaganda. I am the other side of that propaganda. I am an asterisk in one of your chapters. I am what happens when an animal tries to play human games and gets itself into mischief. As you know, on October 9, 1969, a bomb went off in front of the capitol building. It injured and killed many people and drew many more police and spectators to the scene. I give the lycans credit for that. It was a clever bit of bait. I was there, dragging an injured woman from her car, when the second bomb went off. We were standing in a lake of gasoline." He opens his mouth and blows into Jeremy's face. "Poof!"

He leans back and crosses his legs. His knees appear sharp enough to pierce the black fabric of his slacks. He might be smiling, though it is hard to tell. His tone is conversational. They might be old friends fondly remembering a moment from years before. "You might not believe it," he says, "but I was once a handsome man. And you'll like this. You'll like this a lot. Your estranged and deceased brother-in-law is responsible for my condition. It was him. He was responsible for the bombs. Yes. That's right. He was. He was never prosecuted for it, but he came to justice all the same. I made sure of that."

He seems ready to say something more when the door clangs twice. Somebody is knocking. Before the Tall Man can turn in his seat, the lock slides and the door opens, held by a guard who says, "Augustus Remington is here to see you, sir."

Before the Tall Man can respond, a short, pear-shaped man sneaks past the guard and into the cell. He wears a light gray suit and a red tie. His glasses and bald head swim with the light thrown by the overhead fluorescents. "There's our boy," he says, nodding at Jeremy.

The Tall Man rises to his full height and side by side the men appear like funhouse distortions. They do not shake hands. Nor do they greet each other. Jeremy cannot tell if that is because of a mutual comfort or discomfort.

"The trial is set. It's going to be a military tribunal."

"Military? This doesn't have anything to do with the military."

"Act of war. That's what they're calling it. A week from now. I did everything I could to delay things further, but no dice. Somebody in here has been talking. Reporters are on it. ACLU is crying foul. Unfair imprisonment, prolonged solitary confinement, suspected abusive interrogation tactics, and blah, blah, blah. All that human-rights-violation crap."

"The Patriot Act exists for a reason."

"You don't need to defend yourself to me. I'm just telling you that whatever information you've pulled from him, you're going to run into a lot of inadmissible evidence since you've never assigned him a lawyer."

"This has never been about building a case."

Augustus goes silent for a moment and his eyes flit from the Tall Man to Jeremy to the open briefcase on the floor, the instruments within it polished and gleaming. "Well, I hope you've had fun, then. But the fun's over. They're going to make a martyr out of him."

The Tall Man walks to the other side of the cell and stares at the wall as if there is a window there. "I wonder who leaked this to the press."

Augustus seems not to hear him. He stations himself in front of the empty chair across from Jeremy and tugs at his pant legs and sits with a huff of difficulty. "As I understand it, he's going to be indicted tomorrow on eleven counts. They'll be shipping him off to the supermax in Colorado."

The Tall Man continues to stare at the wall, his

back to them. After a moment's pause, he says, "I wonder, too, about a trial timed alongside the election. I wonder about that. I wonder about it very much."

"Wonder all you want." Augustus peers into the open briefcase. His fingers scrabble the air like a spider. He ends up selecting a scalpel and testing its weight in his hand and smiles at Jeremy. "May I?"

CHAPTER 41

CNN IS HER HOMEPAGE. Every time Claire opens her browser, she scans the headlines for news about the Republic, the Resistance. Every now and then an article pops up about a roadside IED ripping through a Humvee or a mortar attack on a combat outpost—and her finger always hesitates above the touch pad before scrolling down, checking the battalion number, blowing out the breath she didn't know she was holding.

Today she does not hesitate. Today, hidden away in her library carrel, there is no doubt. She knows the content of the article before she reads it. Under breaking news—in white text on a red banner across the top of the webpage—"Resistance Leader Indicted on 11 Counts."

Denver—Jeremy Saber, alleged mastermind behind the 8/3 plane attacks and the Pioneer Square Courthouse bombing, was indicted on eleven counts today, among them conspiracy to use a weapon of mass destruction, use of a weapon of mass destruction, destruction by explosives, and first-degree murder.

Since late November of last year, Saber has been detained for questioning in a federal facility in Seattle, Washington. The secrecy of his imprisonment, defended by the Patriot Act, recently came under fire when an anonymous source leaked to the press information reporting alleged torture, including waterboarding, starvation, and months of solitary confinement. The ACLU filed a lawsuit against the FBI and ATF for human rights violations, including unfair imprisonment without a trial.

Saber has since been extradited to Colorado, where he will stand trial before a military tribunal in Fort Collins, a surprising and widely criticized move that will make any appeals and stays impossible if the death penalty is elected. Federal authorities declined to comment except to say that the military has designated the plane attacks and courthouse bombing as acts of war.

On her way back from the library, she keeps her hood up and her head down, busy with her thoughts. Following the courthouse square bombing, several articles ran about raids and arrests, but for so-called security reasons, the FBI was withholding names and any further details that might compromise its investigation. There were other attacks—a car bomb that ripped through a Christmas parade, a ten-gallon plastic drum of diesel and detergent that detonated at a Methodist church and flamed and clung to everything it splattered—but the courthouse square attack was the most dramatic and resulted in the most casualties, and several cameras captured it from beginning to end and made the rest of the country feel as though they felt firsthand the impact of the van shredding open, the tree igniting.

At that time, she and Miriam cleared out the cabin and moved to a room above a bar called the Weary Traveler, where they paid their rent in cash by the week. Miriam said she needed to do some digging and abandoned Claire for several days and demanded she remain in the apartment. She watched Christmas specials and stared at the snow falling out the window and listened to the music thumping from the bar below and worried about Patrick.

When Miriam finally returned, standing in the open door, the snow melting in her hair, she said it was Jeremy. Jeremy had been arrested.

"Only Jeremy?"

"Only him."

"How is that possible?"

"Feds received an anonymous tip from a scrambled cell. He was the only one in the safe house when they arrived."

"It was Puck," Claire said. "It had to be."

"Puck is dead." She closed the door behind her and leaned against it.

Claire asked what she was going to do, and Miriam said there was nothing to do—Jeremy had gotten himself into this mess—and then she locked the door with finality.

This was the beginning of Miriam's reluctance to share. Whereas before, Claire had felt like a pupil, Miriam now treated her like a pampered niece. In the months that followed—after they visited several credit unions and banks to withdraw and redeposit money, after they moved into an apartment in the Hawthorne district of Portland, after Miriam secured her admission to William Archer, after they browsed Powell's Books and shopped at REI and ate barbecued pork kebabs from the Korean carts and hiked Forest Park and stood in the rain at the memorial erected at Pioneer Courthouse Square—whenever Claire would ask questions, Miriam would shrug them off and say, "Don't worry about it." Claire would wake sometimes in the middle of the night and catch Miriam staring out the window or scrolling through websites about the courthouse square bombing and know from the stiffness of her spine that the kidnapping had changed something between them.

These months were a gift, the gift of normalcy, and that gift would expire as soon as they said good-bye at the train station. Then Miriam would begin hunting.

Little did she know she would become the hunted.

Claire is not worried about Jeremy. She is worried about Miriam. His indictment—along with the discovery of Reprobus in the old newspaper photos—has simply fed into this almost cyclonic gathering panic Claire feels. The sense that things are coming together and at the same time spinning out of control.

Enough fucking around. She needs answers.

Night has fallen. The clouds are low. In the distance she can see the yellow lights of Missoula reflecting off the overcast sky. Reprobus holds his office hours late. She goes to Carver Hall and spots the yellow square of his office and stands below it until it goes dark.

A minute later, she spots him at the entrance, easing himself down the steps, then walking along the sidewalk with the hunched mosey of an old man with plenty of vigor still in him. Many of the faculty and staff live in Missoula, but Reprobus talks often about his morning stroll to the office, which means he lives in Campustown, the small village of university-owned property available for staff and faculty housing.

She tries to keep fifty yards between them but panics every time he disappears behind a building or into an island of trees. She takes off her boots and jogs with them in her hands. His footsteps clunk along the pavement, but hers barely whisper. She comes around a corner and finds him stopped in the path ten yards before her. She panics—and then sees a spark of flame, a puff of smoke. He continues walking and she follows, pleasuring in the smell of cherry tobacco from his pipe. Security lamps and streetlights throw puddles of light that she avoids, sticking to the shadows.

She could simply call out to him. But what would she say? Did you know my father? She needs to be certain. A pixilated image from several decades ago can only tell her so much.

His house is one of many of the same design, all boxy cardboard-brown split-levels built in the seventies with a small square patch of lawn in back and a smaller square patch in front. She hides behind some hedges across the street and watches the windows of his house brighten with light—and waits another hour for them to go dark—and another hour after that before she tests the back door and finds it unlocked.

* * *

The antique clock ticking on the wall makes her think of a bomb, and she feels like she is racing to defuse it, her hands careful but her heart hurried when she opens and closes the drawers of his desk, rifles through the papers and tries to read them in the dim moonlight streaming in the windows.

After an hour, she feels beside herself, ready to give up. Since she doesn't know what she is looking for, she forces herself to go through everything. Receipts, tax reports dating back twenty years, instruction manuals—a lawnmower, a microwave, a laptop, a fax machine.

A laptop. Reprobus was a professed Luddite who refused to exchange email with students, so she hadn't been surprised to find his office desk topped by an old typewriter. But here was the instruction manual for an HP Pavilion, along with the Costco receipt, dated two years ago. She searches the office again—and then the living room—and finds nothing. It must be either in his university office or upstairs.

All this time she has kept her backpack on, not wanting to set it down and forget it. The weight of it, combined with the reek of pipe tobacco and mothballs, is bringing on a headache. The stairway is next to the kitchen and she goes to stand at the base of it. Out of the corner of her eye she sees a flickering blue light. The laptop—plugged in and resting on the counter. The phone cord snakes from the wall and into the machine. Dial-up.

She slowly opens the laptop and the processor whirs and the screen blinks twice and comes to life. He is too trusting or lazy or incompetent to password-protect. She guesses she won't be as lucky with his email, though. The taskbar carries an icon for Outlook and she clicks on it and it loads and a password request pops up. Her frustration passes a second later as she sees all of the email stacked up in his inbox and the three thousand messages listed in his trash bin. His security settings are minimal. By opting out of the password request, she can't download any new messages, but she has access to everything archived.

She spends the next thirty minutes scrolling and clicking and finding nothing out of the ordinary. She freezes when she hears footsteps overhead, the floorboards squeaking with weight. She slams shut the laptop and readies to run when she hears a stream of piss rushing into an upstairs toilet—then the roar of the flush—then the footsteps again and the faraway squeal of bedsprings. She waits in silence for several minutes until the sound of snoring again filters down the stairwell.

She opens the laptop and checks the sent box.

She is into July's messages and about to give up when she spots an address she recognizes: mairimiriam@yahoo.com.

She clicks open the message. "I promise," it reads. At first she attributes this to Miriam, then realizes it is a sent message. Reprobus promised her—what?

She scrolls down, past the top matter of the next message, and reads what Miriam wrote: "Promise me you won't let her get involved."

She can still hear Reprobus snoring. She could stand by his bedside, prod him with the knife to wake him. She stands at the bottom of the staircase. It is wooden and turns a corner, vanishing into shadow. She doesn't trust it. She has no sense of the upstairs layout, and in a house this old, every step could creak.

There is no indecision, no fearful desire to run. She is done with this. Tired of being left in the dark, tired of being treated like a child.

She goes to the living room and peels off one of her socks. Slowly she unscrews a lightbulb from a lamp and tucks it inside the sock. She crushes it with her hands. It makes a muffled ping and crunch.

At the base of the staircase she waits for another snore. There it is. Like cardboard tearing. She gently shakes out the glass from her sock onto the linoleum. The shards sparkle in the moonlight, thousands of tiny white teeth.

In the kitchenette, a round wooden table with a newspaper on it, the *New York Times*. As quietly as she can, she peels away the front page. Then she looks up at the brass chandelier, and next to it, the smoke detector with its winking red eye.

She goes to the kitchen and clicks on the gas stove and brings the newspaper to the flame. She hesitates a moment, the newspaper burning in her hand. She hadn't noticed the headline about Jeremy—"Soldier of Misfortune"—accompanied by a faraway photo of him dressed in a neon-orange jumpsuit and dragged from a black Chevy Suburban by men in black suits. She wouldn't have recognized him. Bald and worm pale and so thin he might break over a knee. But she recognizes the man beside him, the Tall Man gripping him by the biceps. She knows it is him, though his face is a smear, unrecognizable. The flames scare her back to reality—the fire licking its way through both Jeremy and the Tall Man, making their bodies warp and blacken. She hurries to the dinette and climbs onto a chair and holds up the torch until the tips of her fingers sear and the fire alarm screeches to life.

The newspaper's flaming remains flutter to the floor and char and curl and die. She ducks behind the counter and listens over the painful shriek of the alarm. She has made a bet. That he will rise out of bed bewildered and panicked. That living and teaching on campus all these years have made him soft. The unlocked door makes her feel confident this is true.

Directly overhead she hears a thud when Reprobus swings out of bed. He thumps down the stairs without caution, hurrying through the dark, still shaking off whatever dreams enchanted him seconds before. She wishes she had her Glock, but the serrated knife drawn from her pocket will have to do.

She hears the footsteps booming louder—he is almost to the ground floor—and then he cries out, a bark of pain. She leaps up in time to see him crash down, a mewling heap on the floor. Wearing a white T-shirt and white briefs. Clutching his feet, the blood black in the moonlight.

She hits the light switch—and with her knife out and the alarm still shrieking overhead, she approaches him.

He throws up an arm against the sudden light. The pain and confusion on his face transform to perverse pleasure when he observes her standing over him. "How can I help you, Claire?"

* * *

She cleans up the mess she made. Tweezers, blood-spotted paper towels. Bandages. A broom drawn from the closet, a dustpan tinkling shattered glass into the garbage can. He sits in the dinette, watching her, chuckling, saying how she certainly knows how to get someone's attention. He is still in his undershirt and underwear, a half-filled glass and a bottle of J&B on the table.

She feels as stupid as she does relieved. Somebody knows her, acknowledges her by name. She feels like a ghost who passes mournfully through walls suddenly marveling at the resistance of flesh. She exists. "All this time you've known who I am."

"How do you think you got admitted? Miriam was one of my pupils, you know."

"No, I didn't know. There's a lot I don't know. People seem to enjoy that. Me not knowing things."

He makes a pyramid of his fingers and through it she can see his smile. "I was under orders, you know. It's apparently what your father wanted. You not to know." His voice goes from playful to derisive in the space of a sentence.

She can ask him about that later. For now, she needs to tell him about Miriam and the videos. His smile fades when he listens. He combs a hand through his beard. "You have no way to contact her outside of email? And no indication of where she might be staying?"

She shakes her head, no.

"I want to say she can take care of herself. I believe that. But still, this is disturbing news." He tells her to get a glass from the cupboard and she does and he pours her two fingers. He raises his glass in a toast and she hesitates a moment before reciprocating with a clink. She drinks and twists up her face. "Tastes like smoke."

"That's from the fire it lights inside." His eyes are kind but rheumy. His belly bulges beneath his shirt. His arms, thin and spotted. His legs, pale and hairless—fat at the thighs, twiggish at the calves. His voice is his power. His voice, low and booming and roughened at the edges from pipe smoke, is what commands an auditorium full of students, is what intimidates her even now, despite the frailty of his appearance.

"I need to know what you're hiding me from," she says.

He nods at her pocket, the outline of the knife there. "Will you cut me open if I don't tell you?"

"Maybe."

"I almost believe you. You're like your aunt, a good bully." He finishes his Scotch. A few drops bead his beard and his tongue darts out and finds them.

"Tell me."

He glances at the oven clock, its green numbers reading a few minutes after midnight. "Are you up for a walk? They should still be there."

The shattered lightbulb peppered his feet, his right foot worse than the left, a blade of glass toothing open a gash in his arch. She helped him pull on two pairs of socks, but he still limps a little when they take the short walk to the rec center.

"Sorry," she says, and he says, "You should be. Abusing an old man."

A quarter moon cuts the sky like a sickle. They walk past bare-branched trees and dark-needled hedges. The campus is quiet except for the buzz of the occasional lamp. Reprobus points out two does grazing along the edge of the quad. "They're on the move this time of year. They can feel the winter coming."

They walk around the rec center. It is built into the side of a tree-studded hill and the ground slopes downward to reveal the lower stories of the building. The trees thicken around them and block out the sky and at first Claire doesn't see the gravel path that curves off the sidewalk. She follows Reprobus a short distance to a steel maintenance door, a side entry to the rec center. He fumbles out his keys and jangles them until he finds the right one. He jams in the key and swings open the door. "Here we are."

The smell hits her before her eyes adjust to the light. An animal's den. For a split second she worries about what she might be walking into, worries she has given herself over too easily to Reprobus. She is so hungry to trust someone that she didn't think to question his motives in bringing her to this place. She is standing in the doorway, half in, half out, when he grabs her by the wrist and drags her forward. "Hurry."

Music is playing from some unseen stereo. Thrash metal. A voice hollers, a guitar screams, blast beats pulse. The walls are windowless, the floor concrete. The ceiling reaches twenty feet above them. From its steel rafters hang thick, braided climbing ropes and chains from which dangle heavy bags ripped open in places and repaired with duct tape. Old gymnastics equipment—balance beams, sawhorses, vaults, parallel and horizontal bars—has been arranged strangely around the room. She sees what she thinks is a shredded log set upright in the corner. The floor is smeared with what appears to be blood old and new.

In the flash of a few seconds, she takes this in, before feeling their eyes on her. Then she spots the lycans. They are all men and all naked. Standing next to a punching bag that sways and creaks on its chain. Hanging halfway up a rope by one arm. Crouched on top of a sawhorse. Their mouths are red and gaping. Their bodies thick with hair and muscle. Watching her. Slowly, with the music charging and raging in the background, the one next to the punching bag begins to creep toward her.

His abdomen sinks and expands as if he is inhaling her. His eyes close and his body quakes. He cries out in obvious pain, falling to all fours and arching his back and lowering his head. When he lifts his face to her, she recognizes him, Matthew. It takes him a minute to rise from the floor and straighten his long body and quiver out a breath.

Nearby is an industrial sink, a coil of hose, a pile of towels. He splashes his face with water and towels off the blood and sweat. Someone shuts off the music and in the sudden quiet he looks at her and says, "Hi."

She tries to focus on his face, not his body, when she says, "What is this place?"

He ties the towel around his waist. "Basically it's where we go apeshit."

"Or wolfshit," Reprobus says. She has forgotten about him. Now he lays a hand on her shoulder. "You're among friends, Claire."

CHAPTER 42

THEIR CONVOY HEADS down the hill. The MRAP trucks are slow moving, mine resistant, ambush protected, but Patrick is in a Humvee. It has been up-armored by the mechanics, with greater suspension and ballistic-resistant glass, but he has seen their black carcasses trucked in and knows an IED can crisp and cut metal as if it were paper.

Patrick has been on base so long—walled in, enclosed—that the snow-scalloped field out the window makes him feel untethered, as if the Humvee might lift off the ground and float into space. Then, in a blink, the woods are all around them and the trees shut out most of the sky except a few fingers of light and he feels oddly comforted.

They drop down the valley and through the town of Hiisi—first the neighborhoods where the mine workers and fishermen live in their modest, square homes—and then into a narrow labyrinth of rotting buildings, some of them high and some low, many ruined heaps of wood and stone, all of them close and crumbling into each other except when a fire charred a cavity. They pass a motorcycle with studded tires, a group of children who do not wave, a brightly colored jingle cart carrying goods to a market.

In the windows and doorways, he can sense eyes watching him. Shadows shift. The inside of the Humvee keeps fogging up, so they have the windows cracked and he can smell the reek of sewage and garbage and sour-sweet decomposition.

At the edge of town they pass a graveyard outpaced and overrun by bodies. Some graves are marked and some are not. Some bodies are buried and some are not. Mounded in barrows of snow or laid out in the open air or blanketed with rocks. Half-decayed blackened bodies. Skeletons the color of old ice. A dog trots out carrying a femur in its mouth like a stick. Every now and then a man or two or three will rough a shovel into the stony, frozen soil and dig a fresh grave, but they can't always keep up with the death, and when spring comes, when the weather warms and the rain falls, decayed flesh will muddy the ground and flies will gather like storm clouds.

He watches this all with passing interest, but his mind's eye turns inward. He can't stop thinking about his father and his shed, the notes left behind and what they might tell him. Because of this, the busyness of his mind, he doesn't feel as nervous as he should. Trevor sits next to him—the wolf pelt still attached to his helmet and draped down his back, a meaty smell puffing off it. Every time Trevor tries to speak, the squad leader tells him to shut his hole. For this, Patrick is grateful.

They drive north out of the valley and then east between two low, flattopped hills, the roads deteriorating further with every passing mile. They skirt the edge of a fjord and a flock of seagulls surrounds the convoy briefly, screeching over the engines, beating their wings outside the windows, before drifting away. Then striped canyon walls surround them and they head up into a narrow winding passage that will bring them into the next valley, where the combat outpost is located.

The sun is directly in front of them—aligned perfectly with the chute of the canyon—and blinding when reflected off the snow. Patrick squints even with sunglasses. The afterimage of the landscape singes into his eyes, the whiteness seeming to infect him so that whiteness is all he sees, nothing distinguished, everything running into the next thing, as formless as spilled milk.

Decker is at the head of the convoy and Patrick hears his voice squawk over the radio. "Slow down. Trouble ahead." The canyon opens into a U-shaped clearing five hundred meters long and half as wide. At the far end of it, where the road again narrows through canyon walls, a rockslide has blocked their passage.

Trevor curses when he tries to drink from his canteen and the Humvee brakes to a sudden stop. “Goddamn do I have the worst luck,” he says and swipes pointlessly at the spill dampening his chest.

There is a tinkle of glass when the bullet rips through it. Trevor’s head whips to the side. His eye has vanished, replaced by a hole from which blood leaks. His canteen drops to the floor, sloshing and gurgling as it empties between his boots. He shakes, as if in an epileptic seizure, then tips over and lays his head on Patrick’s shoulder.

Patrick isn’t sure how much time passes. Maybe a few seconds, maybe a minute. He is too caught up in the sensation of blood warming his shoulder, the pressing weight of Trevor’s head there. An explosion wakes him from his daze, so powerful that the windshield cracks and the Humvee rocks. Near the front of the convoy he can see a black wraith of smoke twisting upward, blotting out the sun. He is about to ask his squad leader what to do when he realizes he is the only one left in the Humvee. The driver and passenger door are open and the air outside crashes with gunfire. Men scream.

He scrambles for the door handle when another bullet sings through his window and embeds itself in the seat next to him. Because of the way the

Humvee is angled, he realizes he is on the battle side of the vehicle and will end up ribboned by bullets if he steps out. He hears another bullet ping and ricochet off the door and he curses and ducks down and clutches his M4 and climbs over Trevor's body to the opposite side of the Humvee and falls out the door and flattens his body into the snow.

He hears a voice screaming, "Squad vee, squad vee!" Two fire teams forward, one fire team back. Somehow the drivers reacted as they should and the Humvees and MRAPs have parked at a strategic diagonal rather than a straight line against the fire zone.

He peers around a tire and sees one Humvee blackened and broken. Whether destroyed by an IED or RPG, he doesn't know. He spots three soldiers in the snow, their bodies still and sprawled out, their blood so bright against white. Another dangles backward from the gun turret of an MRAP.

The lycans have positioned themselves against the sun. Patrick is blind to them. He tries to visor his eyes with a hand but can make out nothing outside of their gunfire flaring like sunspots. They seem to be above and below, on top of the canyon walls and dug into the rockslide, how many of them he cannot say, whether a dozen or dozens.

Fish in a barrel, he thinks. That's what we are.

He recognizes Decker toward the front of the convoy. The sergeant positions a SMAW on his shoulder and steps around the nose of the MRAP and launches a rocket. It spits flame and emits a firecracker hiss when it travels fifty meters through the air and impacts the canyon wall.

There is earsplitting thunder. A giant fist of flame erupts. Rock rains down on the lycans. Patrick tries to remember his training. Firing from rubble, firing from barricade, fighting from prone supported. Alternating between slow and rapid fire so that he might analyze each round and determine a hit or miss. Locating the target by hasty search and if hasty search fails, employing a systematic examination of the terrain with an overlapping strip method, fifty-meter sweep, hundred-meter sweep, one-fifty-meter sweep. All of this and more, clotting his brain, paralyzing him for the space of a few seconds.

Not this. Not again. The fear. The familiar fear from the plane. Calcifying his arms, palsying his legs, choking his breath. Every part of him a tangled mess of nerves that he cannot control. He crouches frozen behind the Humvee even as he despairs of his inaction. His body seems to be caught on hooks.

He hears a dripping and looks down to see the

blood pooling from the open door. The blood of Trevor, uncorked by a bullet. It melts the snow into a red slushy pattern that reminds him of those Rorschach inkblot tests. What does he see? The fate that awaits him if he does not act.

Abruptly, like a cracked knuckle, he feels relieved of the tension that seized him—and he loops the sling of the M4 high on his arm and snaps off his safety and forces the butt against his shoulder and swings up and rattles off twenty rounds in the general direction of the rockslide before dropping behind the Humvee again and reminding himself to breathe, breathe, the big gulps of air he takes now hot and sullied by smoke.

He can feel a grenade shake the canyon walls and reverberate through his bones. He can hear a spray of rounds, from one side, and then another, like thunderclouds calling to each other. He can hear the *whang* of bullets ricocheting off metal. He can hear Decker calling his name, telling him to assemble forward. He waits until his breathing settles and then bursts from behind the Humvee. He moves his legs as fast as he can, but he cannot sprint in the snow, every step a sliding uncertainty.

At the top of the canyon, near the blue cutout of the sky, he observes what looks like a lightning bolt. He takes three more steps before the thunder catches up with him. The ground opens up—a volcanic burst of flame that makes snow into steam. Patrick feels like a child picked up and hurled through the air. The strength of the explosion rips off his helmet and one of his boots. The world jars black when he hits the ground ten feet away and then fades back to white.

For a long time he lies there, loose limbed, unable to move. He sees the sky and he sees a snow-mantled cliff and he sees upon it what he first believes to be a tree, the inky spill of it against all that blue. He wonders vaguely how it has survived on such a barren purchase.

Then the tree moves. It lifts not a branch, but an arm, signaling to those below—and then draws away from its vantage point, vanishing from sight, the tree that is not a tree, a lycan clad in black, a smear of darkness on a sunlit day.

The gunfire continues—for how long, Patrick doesn't know. He does know that it will all be over soon. He knows, too, that if he is still alive in a few minutes, and if the lycans choose to survey the bodies and rummage through their pockets and salvage equipment, then he will be dead. His rifle is nearby but he cannot reach for it, cannot even feel his hands, cannot muster the energy or the will to flop his arms in the direction of the weapon. Something is wrong with his shoulder. He feels something hot and red there and imagines it as a planet, a spinning ball of toxic gas.

He registers in flits and flashes the cold creeping into his skin and the smell of blood and gun smoke all around him. Shock. That's what this is called, but recognizing the word does not antidote him. His vision wobbles. He believes he might have a concussion, though the letters won't come together properly in his head and he thinks, concession, commotion, conception? He has a conception?

His mind grows blurrier by the minute, like a window frosting over. He wants to tell someone, anyone, *see,* see, not such a miracle anymore, am I? But he has no audience. At one point, he realizes the canyon is encased in shadow, the sun lower in the sky. Getting close to night. Night is when he sleeps. At the threshold of waking and dreaming, his last thought is how pillowy the snow feels and how much he would like to have a little rest.

CHAPTER 43

EVERYTHING IN western Washington is draped in moss and smells of earthworms. Rain falls more often than not. Cars are rust flecked from the salt breeze coming off the ocean. In September, Miriam found a motel outside Tacoma that didn't ask questions and let her pay by the week in cash. The walls were paneled with pine and the carpeting stained and the overhead lamps darkened with dead moths. Smoking was permitted. Lawn chairs and Old Smokey grills sat outside of three of the seven rooms. This was a place people lived, among them a toothless man she suspected of cooking meth and a whore with dishwater-blond hair who wore the same purple miniskirt every day.

The federal detention center is located twelve miles south of Seattle. No fencing surrounds it. No guard towers loom along its perimeter. Because the inmates remain indoors, in total isolation. It is located in an oddly public place, nearby a Rent-A-Wreck and the Bull Pen Pub and an All Star Grocery where she regularly parks her Ramcharger and sits looking at the FDC, an institutional gray building that resembles nothing so much as a medieval castle that could not be stormed.

There is a Starbucks on every corner of the city and she taps into their free Wi-Fi and does her research. The facility was built in 1997 and meant to accommodate 677 prisoners. Some are sentenced and some are awaiting sentences. Their crimes range from crypto-anarchy to wire fraud to aircraft theft to bank robbery to domestic terrorism. A phone call from a pay phone revealed that Jeremy was not listed as an inmate, but that means nothing.

She does not trust and does not have the patience for the red tape she will have to go through to request blueprints, so she researches the architect and finds him easily through a Google search and one night breaks into his firm and steals the plans along with three computers to make it look like a proper robbery.

She unrolls the blueprints on her butterfly-patterned bedspread and weighs them down with her mud-caked sneakers and paperback detective novels bought from grocery stores. She does not like what she finds. Every hallway and stairwell has alarm-triggered lockdown doors. The heating ducts are built with bars staggered through them to prevent the possibility of a crawl space. Every floor has a checkpoint, including the two that run belowground. The cells here are windowless and labeled high security. That is where he will be found.

Her mind plays through so many different scenarios. She imagines walking through the front door with a shotgun pressed to the throat of a hostage. She imagines short-circuiting the transformer to kill the electricity and then lighting a fire in the furnace ducts and sneaking in with the firefighters. She imagines following a guard home and duct-taping him to a chair and interrogating him about the layout and procedures of the center before donning his uniform and hoping she can somehow bluff her way inside.

She exercises every day—getting ready for what exactly, she doesn't know. She only knows that she owes it to her husband, whom she no longer agrees with but of course still loves, to try to set him free. She has no doubt he is being tortured. She has no doubt he will be put to death. She thinks of him when she runs the hiking trails that thread the woods and when she dons a wet suit to swim in Puget Sound and when she uses the play structure at a local park for pull-ups—wide arm, close grip, underhands—and leg-lift crunches.

She can't shake the feeling that she is being watched and carries a knife or a gun on her at all times and pauses often in doorways and on street corners. At night the motel window is like a liquid black eye that peers at her, and she draws the curtains over it and sleeps with a shotgun in the bed beside her like a lover whose oily smell and indention linger on the pillow.

One day the meth-head calls her sweetie and she gives him the finger and he calls her a cunt. The next morning she finds the Ramcharger's front left tire slashed and she walks directly to his room and kicks open the door and finds him tweaking in the bathroom and smashes his face into the mirror and brings down the lid to the toilet tank on his back and tells him if he ever fucks with her again he will die.

She parks at the All Star Grocery and rolls down the window and studies the FDC, not knowing what she is looking for but not knowing what else to do. She imagines her husband somewhere in the belly of the building. The first thing he ever said to her was that he liked the way she smelled. It wasn't a line. It was how he felt, his nostrils flaring. He has always been like that, direct and aggressive and hungry and pursuant. That is what made him such a good leader and a bad husband. She has followed him all these years. Even now she follows him, his priorities her own.

One time, when they were still dating, still students at William Archer, they were tangled up on a futon and he said he was going to make love to her and there was nothing she could do about it. She said to him, "Do you always get what you want?" and he said, "Most of the time," and she said, "Me too," and grabbed him by the shirt and dragged him toward her.

When he spoke at rallies or gave lectures, she felt as she did when he made love to her—as if some glowing ball of energy was swelling inside her, heating her—and from the rapture in everyone else's eyes she knew they felt the same. Sometimes, though, she tired of the ideology. Sometimes she pined for a normal life, normal conversation—paint the porch this and mow the grass that—soccer games and park playdates, backyard barbecues with neighbors. When their daughter died, that ball of light inside Miriam, that glow that sustained her over the years, unraveled into many strands that went black like burned-out lightbulb filaments.

Today she goes for a ten-mile run. A light rain mists the air. Wind comes off the sound and carries the smell of algae and dead fish. Crows gather in a tree barren of leaves and make its branches appear heavy with some black, poisonous fruit. They depart when she runs beneath them, their wings stirring the air, their shadows swirling all around her.

When she finally makes her way home to the motel, her lungs hot and her legs heavy, she keys the lock and checks the dusting of talcum powder on the floor. She keeps a tin by the door and every time she leaves she gives it a few shakes to see if anyone has tracked their way inside. Nothing.

She peels off her track pants and sweatshirt and stretches naked for a moment before walking to the bathroom and staring at her red-nosed reflection in the mirror. A hot shower will scald the chill out of her. The curtain is the same dark orange color as the carpeting. She drags it aside to crank on the water—and the tug of her arm reveals the giant crouched figure of Morris Magog waiting for her.

☽

She is an old woman, a lycan, though it is hard to tell beneath the gray cover of her long coat and head scarf, her appearance more like a twisted branch or crooked pillar of stones. A few stray white hairs have escaped her trappings and blow around her face. She is slow moving, some of her steps crunching through the snow, some of them carrying her on top of the hardpack. She carries a quiver of arrows and an ash bow crossways over her shoulders. A large dog follows her—thick necked and long legged, with the sharp snout of a wolf—dragging behind it a sled mounded with snowy white rabbits, their bodies soon to be skinned and gutted and cooked, every last ligament and ribbon of meat harvested. They were killed by arrows or by snares and their bloodied furs match the battlefield that makes the woman pause and the dog whine.

She comes from a side channel that spits into this canyon and stands for a long time at its exit, surveying the wreckage. The Humvees and the MRAPs are still smoldering and she knows that whatever happened here happened not long ago. The canyon walls are pitted from bullets and RPG blasts, halos of black imprinted on stone. The wind shifts and the dog whines at the smell of cooked flesh, burned rubber. There are many bodies, a junkyard of broken bodies, all of them so still.

She goes to them. The snow glimmers with ejected shell casings. She withdraws a knife from some secret fold of her coat. At one body, and then the next, she does not bother struggling with buttons and snaps. She draws her sharp blade through nylon and canvas and hurries her way through pockets and belts, tossing some things aside and placing others in the sled. Bullets, matches, knives, first-aid kits, wipes, belts, canteens, binoculars. One soldier is missing half his head. Another seems to be smiling, with his belly and chest shredded by bullets. Another has tried to crawl to safety and a thick viscous slug's trail of blood follows him to his resting place thirty yards away.

One of the soldiers lies flat on his back. The dog whimpers and huffs and paws at the snow near his head. His face is obscured by blood and soot and sunglasses. A boy. His shoulder is torn up—whether by a bullet or shrapnel, she doesn't know. His helmet is gone. So is one of his boots. She crouches down and removes her mitten—leather, lined with rabbit fur—revealing a skeletal, leprously spotted hand. She snatches off his sunglasses. His eyes are half-lidded, telling her nothing.

She digs beneath his high collar and touches his neck to see if she can find a pulse. Right then his eyes snap open and closed so quickly that she would have missed it had she not been searching for some sign of life. She stands and looks around, looking to see if anyone is watching her. The sun flashes off her knife.

CHAPTER 44

NEAL STANDS in the open doorway of the toolshed. Everyone keeps saying that the day is unseasonably warm, that he should be grateful, that the winds in the Republic are sometimes so severe that a minute of exposure can freeze a finger and snap it off at the knuckle. To him, thirty-five degrees is cold enough. His eyes peer out beneath a wool hat with a pom-pom on top. Otherwise his body is wrapped completely in a down parka and scarves and mittens and boots. Chase tells him he looks like the Michelin man.

Chase is always calling him something. Tubs. Doc. Captain Curry. Neal wouldn't mind stabbing the fool in the eye with the syringe he keeps in his pocket—capped, but ready with a 30 cc dose of sodium thiopental strong enough to knock Chase out. Just in case his emotions get the best of him and the pills can't contain the animal. That's what Neal is here for—to take care of a man who can't take care of himself. Everyone calls him doctor but here he is merely a nurse. It is insulting, and he would not have come except for two men he is indebted to: Augustus, his leering benefactor;

and Keith Gamble, his longtime collaborator, his friend.

They arrived several days ago and his mind still hasn't adjusted to the time change, his days feeling like nights, his nights days. He checks his wristwatch—he is always checking it to ascertain the time, as if he has trouble believing in the sun's place in the sky. Another hour and their convoy will roll out of the base and head to the Tuonela Mine, where he and Chase will meet with diplomats and executives before holding a press conference.

He steps out of the wind and into the shed's dim interior. A lightbulb hangs overhead, but when he pulls at the string, nothing happens. His eyes adjust and he spots the desiccated carcass of the wolf that makes the workbench above it appear like a squared shrine.

The lab conditions are laughable. But the value of Keith's work has always been conceptual more than practical. So many conversations with him began with the phrase *What if?* Kirk and Spock. That's what people called them, and that's how they dressed up one Halloween. Keith was the dashing rogue and Neal was the wearying bore. Wearying bores did well in biochemistry. Wearying bores could tolerate the endless stream of data, the endless pile of grant applications, the political hurdles, the pompous lunacy of academics—everything Keith referred to as bullshit. When his friend first became a brewmaster, Neal told him it was a waste, a waste of his great talent. But he was wrong. This—Keith's death in the Republic—that was the waste.

There is nothing of use to him in the toolshed. He is here to say good-bye. He pulls off his mittens and slowly fingers the beakers and vials, flips through the notebooks, the binders, their pages yellowing along the edges. Everything is coated in dust that his fingertips streak through.

"It's just like you described it, old friend."

☽

There is another video circulating online. The second Balor has released. Augustus clicks on it eagerly. He has watched the other—with the door to his office closed and the sound lowered, as if he were indulging in some pornographic fetish—more than thirty times. He can play it in his head now—can see Balor, the tic at the corner of his eye, the rise and fall of his shoulders as he breathes heavily—can hear the screaming and meat-mouthed feeding—as if it is happening to him.

He cannot say why he is so fascinated, but when he stares at the screen, he grips the mouse tightly in his hand and from it a tingling signal seems to run up his arm and into his chest and rush the blood through his body. This is his enemy. This is what Augustus has committed thousands of hours to eradicating. Balor believes the video empowers him, but Augustus believes the opposite: every new hit and post might as well equate to a vote for Chase Williams. The video strengthens them, fortifies their posture.

A part of Augustus cannot help but wonder about the soldier Balor tore to pieces. He was not a person—he was food, though not even that, since hunger was secondary. The man was an implement and Balor was using him. He does not see Chase in quite the same way—they are friends, after all, the closest of friends—but the connection does not escape or bother him.

The wall behind Balor appears paneled with wood. There is no overhead light, what must be a table lamp throwing shadows sideways across his face. An insectile hum, maybe a generator, nearly swallows his voice. A hint of a smile plays across the corners of his mouth. He is smiling at Augustus. He is smiling at everyone who stands in his way as if ready to swing a scythe through them. "Do you know how much money it would take to destroy the United States? I do not mean to interrupt or injure the economy. I do not mean to blow up a bridge and make people feel sorry for those who died or blow up a landmark and make people feel hot with patriotic fever. I mean destroy. Do you know how much money it would take?" Here he runs a tongue across his lips. "It would take thirty thousand dollars. I will show you. Soon. Soon."

"Bring it on," Augustus says and starts the video again.

Chase doesn't eat much for lunch, not because the chow hall is serving Jell-O and green beans and gray mushy chicken cubes, but because his nerves have left his stomach in a twist. He excuses himself and waits outside, next to the convoy of Humvees parked and idling in the mud like prehistoric beetles. The cold air hones him, chases away the nausea.

He knows what the media are reporting. The Patriot Act amendment, the vaccine hearings. The hard-line, no-compromise rhetoric. The pending trial of Jeremy Saber. The good-gosh down-home campaigning of his running mate, Pinckney Arnold, who drives from small town to small town and gives stump speeches and kisses babies and shakes hands and sings "God Bless America" with his hand over his heart. The publicity photos of Chase and Neal roaring across the Atlantic on a Curtiss Commando transport with several hundred newly deployed soldiers. All of it has worked. Just like Buffalo promised.

Every smear campaign has failed—because Chase admits to everything, the groping, the drinking, the fighting, none of it illegal, all of it tied into his platform: brutal honesty. The election is a week away and every phone poll lists him as the front-runner. Chase doesn't respond to the soldiers calling him Mr. President, doesn't feel as excited as he ought to, the Republic distracting him from every emotion except fear, sometimes alternated by remorse and guilt-absolving defiance.

That morning, when he arrived at the Tuonela Base, when the CO invited him into his office, he made an offhand comment about the weather, saying how nice it was, how warm. The CO—a gray-haired toad of a man with no neck and a broad, fleshy mouth—said he'd take negative forty over this any day. "Keeps the mutts in their pens." Two days ago, an ambush wiped out an entire platoon. "A real dick up my ass. And now you're here." He sipped his coffee and choked a little on it. "Don't think they don't know. They know. Which means some shit is bound to happen." The CO mentioned Balor then. Chase asked what they knew about him. He has seen the videos, he has read the articles, he has been briefed by Buffalo—but what does the CO know that he might not?

"What's there to know you don't already know? Might say he's the alpha of the pack. Been in the computer for years, more than two decades. Worked for us—bet you didn't know that—though you might soon. Some fucker at *The New Yorker* has been sniffing around about us supplying him and a few other mutts with arms in the eighties to drive out the Russians. Now he's turned the crosshairs on us. Now he's gone from low level to big shit. He says something, the rest do it. Whoever gets his head on a pike will get so many medals pinned to them their tit will fall off."

"What's wrong with his eye?"

"Fuck do you care? Fuck am I supposed to know?"

"Just curious."

Now Chase scoops up a handful of slush and packs it into a ball of ice that he lobs like a grenade toward the high wall of the perimeter fence. It falls short. He is joined a minute later by the lieutenant who will be serving as his PSD escort to the mine. Nathan Streep, a twenty-four-year-old with a boyish face that doesn't look like it's ever needed a razor. A scar curls from his upper lip like a worm. He pulls out a pack of Marlboros and knocks out two cigarettes and offers one to Chase and they light up and smoke in companionable silence.

The day is bright but the sun seems to warm nothing. A shadow slides across the ground and a few seconds later Chase hears the boom of a jet streaking overhead. He knows they are always overhead, easy to hear and hard to spot, as gray as the surrounding hills, their missiles sometimes giving them away, sun silvered at the tips. But he can't help it: he covers his head and lets out a whimper. Most people, he knows, are unable to imagine their own death. They can worry over a grandparent, choking on a half-chewed bite of ham sandwich or slipping in the shower and snapping a hip; and they can worry over a child, imagining a pigtailed girl toddling after a ball and being crushed by a passing car, the bloodied tread of the tire imprinted on the asphalt until the next rainstorm—but their own death remains a denial, and then a vague possibility, and then, only in those final foggy-eyed years, an inevitability. He is not sure quite how this happened, but ever since he was bitten, he has felt age settling over him like a black blanket, and for the first time he feels death is not only foreseeable but also imminent.

He straightens up as quickly as he can, thankful the photographers remain inside. The lieutenant watches him curiously. Chase can't tell if it is a smirk or if the scar makes his lip naturally upturned. "You all right there?"

"Fine."

"How long has it been?"

"Near eleven years." In his pocket he carries the pocketknife his father gave him, the one he carried through all his time overseas, and he squeezes it now.

"Not so long."

Long enough for the anchor-and-eagle tattoo on his shoulder to fade to the color of a bruise, but not long enough to shake off memories as vivid as last night's nightmare. He remembers the tracer rounds and mortar explosions, the thunderous pulse making his ears pop, the dripping chandeliers of white and yellow and red light making him pause and marvel at the beauty of it all. He remembers the rattle of a chain gun and the rotor wash of a Blackhawk and the hushed air that seemed to hang around bodies zipped into black bags. He remembers attacking a cave system—a hive, the CO called it—and the lycans that came rushing out of the dark at them. He remembers lighting up a woman with a flamethrower—the same woman who visits him sometimes at night—and the way she kept coming even after her eyeballs burst and her skin crisped to ash so that he had to unholster his pistol and drop her with a shot to the head.

He takes a deep breath and can hear his cigarette sizzling at the tip and flicks it away in a sparking arc and nearly gags on the smoke.

He realizes, when the convoy starts down the hill, that he doesn't know the name of anything here. He knows the valley, the mine, the base all share the same name that now escapes him. He eyes a stunted evergreen, a bush bright with red berries, a deer as big as an elk darting between the trees. He likes knowing the names of things. Without them, he feels lost, as though he hardly knows who he is.

Ten minutes later, when they push out of the woods and into town, they brake next to an apartment complex under construction. A forklift drops a pallet of rebar with a boom. A welding torch glows blue. A saw whines. The workers, in orange hard hats, stare at the convoy until it departs. A few blocks away, they pass a building carved out by a bomb. It was the same old story when Chase was here—their mission unclear: building and destroying.

They drive through an alleyway busy with murals to commemorate a World War II battle in which hundreds of Nazis were killed by lycans—and then the convoy parks at a nearby square, where a crowd has gathered. "Check it out," the lieutenant says. "Some unfriendlies are hosting a potluck." A gnarled leafless tree rises in the middle of the square and a straw effigy draped in a U.S. flag hangs from it. A group of young bearded men stand around it and stab it with pitchforks and then cut it down and finally throw it on the fire they have kindled nearby. The smoke darkens and the flames lick upward and everyone lets out a cheer. In the weak sunlight, a lamb is spitted and two teenage boys crank it around and around over the fire. Men roll cigarettes and drink hard cider from jugs, while women arrange plates of sausage on a folding table. Children run among their legs, playing tag and pretending themselves into wolves.

Chase tries to smile off the pitchforks—but can feel, with every thrust, an imagined prick scraping between his ribs, into his heart. Neal sits in the seat behind him. He leans forward and rattles a container of Tic Tacs in his ear. "I think you need two of these."

They aren't breath mints at all, but Volpexx. The doc is here to make sure he chokes them down when needed. He rattles some into his palm and dry-swallows.

"Hey, my breath stinks," the lieutenant says. "Can I steal one of those from you?"

"No," Neal says and tucks away the bottle. "They're ours."

Chase will need every one of them. Just as he needs Neal to dole them out slowly. Because the first pill leads to a second and then a third and then he tends to lose count and sometimes slips into the black fuzz of those beer benders that defined his twenties, after which he would rise feeling as though he had sawed himself in half.

The mine grows larger and larger with their approach, its smokestacks and blackened metal making it look like a factory where nightmares are made. The fence line begins a long way out—reaching on for miles and miles and miles—surrounding a strip mine so cavernous that the dump trucks trundling along its bottom might be toys. He imagines the millions of tons drawn from this crater, bored by drills and chewed by dynamite, and can't help but think about the tunnels within his own body that house a poisonous ore.

They pass through a security checkpoint with undercarriage mirrors and tire shredders and a reinforced steel gate and after a brief questioning drive for several hundred yards before they arrive at a parking lot, the distant fence line necessary so that no RPG fired or bomb detonated at the checkpoint can damage the facility.

The escort for the reporters is held up another ten minutes as the guards search and chemical-reactant test their bags and camera equipment. Chase can feel the Volpexx deadening him—the equivalent to a three-beer buzz—and closes his eyes and rests his chin on his chest and watches the clouds of colors play across his retinal screen.

When the reporters arrive, when their Humvee parks alongside his, he takes a deep cleansing breath and climbs out and approaches the Alliance Energy representatives who now wait on the sidewalk edging the parking lot with smiles on their faces and hands extended for a shake.

CHAPTER 45

PATRICK IS AWARE, first, of the sphere of pain in his right shoulder. If he stays still, its heat remains focused, but if he moves—if he so much as sighs heavily—the sphere cracks open and sends hot, nauseating knife twists of pain into his chest, down his arm.

He lies on the floor of a one-room gray-wood house. Wind rasps through the cracks. The roof creaks under the weight of snow. The floorboards are soft and squawking beneath him. The logs in the woodstove collapse into embers. The whole place struggles to stay upright. The air reeks of fish and onions. Herbs and jerky hang from the rafters. Old dusty spiderwebs—jeweled with the husks of flies—thread the corners. Pots bubble on the woodstove.

He does not notice this all at once, but in one-eyed glimpses as he rises intermittently from a sleep that won't let go. He feels out of focus, outside of himself. He can't tell whether he keeps fading in and out due to his injuries or whether she has drugged him. She, the lycan woman.

Her back is hunched, her breasts flattened by age. Her neck is as thin as a wrist. A cluster of long white hairs hang off her chin and tremble when she sucks at her toothless mouth. When at first she does not respond to the English or the little Finnish and Russian he uses on her, only stares at him with that mummified face and those eyes dulled by cataracts, absent of any curiosity, of any emotion altogether, he figures her deaf or senile. Or maybe he never says anything. Maybe he speaks to her in his mind, his tongue unable to find traction enough to form words.

He dreams about his rifle shuddering in his arms. He dreams about a lycan staggering back and hitting a rock wall and smearing it with a frond of blood. He dreams about the old woman standing by the window, her pale mottled skin appearing translucent so that he believes he can see her blood and sinews coursing and surging, like some dark presence living beneath the surface of her. He dreams about her sucking on a pipe, the smoke coiling around her, as she studies him sharply, with suspicion glowing in her foggy eyes. He dreams—or maybe he is awake?—about a wolf watching him from a shadowy corner.

Then she crouches next to him with a pile of rags, a pan of steaming water, and a pair of needle-nose pliers. "Your fever won't break and your skin is going dark," she says, her voice like a rusty hinge. "Need to get that metal out of you."

She speaks. She holds a knife between them. He does not agree or disagree. He just turns his head away so that he doesn't have to watch her work. He supposes, if he were on an operating table, he would be strapped down. But he doesn't have the energy to arch his body, to flinch away, when he feels the probing sting that turns into a hard jolt of pain. The sphere explodes. He hears the *tock* and *pick* of shrapnel hitting the floor and feels a hollowed-out relief in his shoulder—and in the flash before he passes out from the pain he thinks of his father and finally makes the connection.

He wakes in a daze, not knowing how long he has slept but knowing it has been a long time. It is dark outside, but it is dark so often here that the hour could be four in the afternoon or four in the morning. Outside he can hear the chattering and howls of wolves, whether natural or lycan, he is not sure.

He feels better, somehow lighter, as if the shrapnel weighed so much it was pressing him into the floor. He sits up for the first time and realizes he is naked only when the pelts that cover him roll away from his chest and pool in his lap.

His shoulder is sticky with a mudpack that smells

fungal. A woodstove roars in the corner, giving off waves of heat, but the air is otherwise cold enough to crystallize his breath. On a three-legged table small enough to be a stool, a candle sputters, its dim, flickering glow the only light in the cottage. He is alone. A few feet away, his uniform is folded neatly next to his boots.

He rises naked from the floor. The room spins, then settles. His muscles are tight and unused to movement. He keeps his bad arm tight against his side when he creeps to his clothes. He finds them clean, smelling of pine soap. He almost pulls them on and then remembers his final thoughts before passing out.

He fingers through his pockets until he finds it, the sheets of paper—some printed in the MWR, some pirated from the toolshed. He unfolds them clumsily with his one hand and carries them to the candle.

He was being poisoned by the metal, infected by it. The old woman saved him, as if knifing away a bruised section of peach, by excising it from his body.

In the flickering light of the candle he flattens the wrinkles from the paper. Some of the ink has splotched and warped, but he can still read the words. The protection of cells, the regulation and detoxification of metal, such as silver. Silver. One of the principal components in Volpexx was silver. Some of the old mythology was true: the metal was septic to a lycan. The two largest suppliers in the country come from Alaska, he remembers reading, the Red Dog Mine and the Greens Creek Mine producing somewhere around three hundred metric tons a year, with Pfizer as their majority stockholder.

Keith Gamble lost his wife more than fifteen years ago, but all this time, he was still trying to save her. He knew he couldn't kill the wolf, but he thought he could kill the drug. The metallothioneins would somehow detoxify the Volpexx, Patrick guesses, allowing for a positive blood test without the emotionally deadening side effects.

He wonders in how many different ways and over how many years his father has been chasing some kind of cure. At home, his father often worked in his shop, built onto the garage, a room with a sloping floor and central drain, stainless-steel tables scattered with vials and tubes and decanters, like some mad scientist's laboratory in the midnight movie. He kept it locked except when working in it and allowed Patrick to observe him only if he didn't speak and remained seated on a stool in the corner. He said he was working on home-brew recipes. But Patrick can clearly recall the gleam of syringes on the counter—and can remember, too, the many dogs he had as a child that died so often of "cancer" he stopped making up new names and just called them all Ranger.

He looks at the other sheets. The University of Oregon emails. Ndesai. Ndesai. Ndesai. Over and over again. Correspondence traded back and forth for what appears to be two years. Neal. It was Neal, the old college friend his father was always talking about, always chatting with on the phone, always telling Patrick to visit. The footer at the bottom of each email identifies Desai as a university professor and the director of the Pacific Northwest Regional Biocontainment Laboratory in the Infectious Disease Research Center. He would be hearing from Patrick as soon as he could get to a computer.

At that moment the door creaks open and reveals a black rectangle. A snow-caked animal, what could be a dog or a wolf, trots through it—followed by the old woman. A cold wind rushes inside and gutters the candle and freezes Patrick where he stands. The dog shakes off a cloud of snow and ducks its head and flattens its tail and growls. The old woman shoulders the door closed and secures the latch. She carries three bloody white rabbits by the ears. She uses her free hand to unwrap her shawl. She stares at Patrick a moment—her eyes dropping from his face to his body—and only then does he remember his nakedness. He tries to cover his crotch with the paper. The wind rises to a whistle outside. Then her face breaks into a smile with no teeth.

She turns away from him and peels off her mittens and kicks off her boots and shrugs off what seems more like a robe than a coat and arranges it all near the fire to steam. It is an odd dance, her undressing and him dressing. She is slowed by age—and he by injury—and they finish around the same time and look at each other across the room as if to say, what now?

"You're hungry," she says, not a question. She knows he is. Terribly hungry, aching inside, as if he has been pitted.

He watches as she skins a rabbit. Yanking out its guts and splatting them on the floor for the dog to gobble up. Peeling away its pelt to reveal its candy-red musculature. Fingering the meat from the bone, knifing it into cubes, tossing it into a pot filled with snow and roots and bones that boil down into a stew on top of the woodstove. Together they sit at the table and she clunks a steaming bowl before him and he says, "Thank you."

Claire feels, no other word for it, happy. Buoyant even. As though, if she opened her window and spread her arms, the wind might puff her away. For the first time since arriving on campus people know her by a name other than Hope. For the first time she has a sense of community. For the first time she has friends, if that's the right word for it, someone to sit with at the cafeteria, wave to across the quad. Were they her friends? Would they say the same of her? She thinks they might.

She barely notices the election signs that pop up all over campus—signs that read VOTE NADER or IMPEACH WILLIAMS. She barely registers the conversations about the vaccine program under way or the spike in voter approval ratings for the Oregon governor now that he has departed for the Republic.

She knows it is irresponsible of her, but after months of gut-tangled anxiety, she has momentarily lost herself to pleasure. She feels as she did, so many years ago, when traveling a nighttime highway with her parents. One minute they were tunneling through the black, listening to NPR—and the next minute, her father was wrenching the wheel, screaming, "Son of a bitch!" Out of the darkness tumbled bicycles. Dozens of them. Claire didn't know this at the time, but up ahead, at seventy-five miles an hour, a trailer hitched to a church van on its way to the Northwoods had come undone. When it flipped and crashed against the asphalt, bicycles spun every which way. Her father cranked the wheel hard right—and then left—dodging a pink Huffy, a white Trek—some of the bicycles skidding along with a trail of orange sparks, others bouncing wheel over wheel, haloed by their headlights only a second before vanishing. The red flash of a reflector. The dark rush of pavement. Their screams turned to laughter, when they swerved their way down the highway, thrilled and enchanted and somehow unscathed—alive!—after so many near misses.

The past week, she has joined them every night in the gym. The three men, all teaching assistants for Reprobus. The Pack, he calls them. They wore clothes at first, unsure how she would feel, but after two nights she said, "Can I trust you?" and Matthew said, "If we don't have trust, we're no different than the pure breeds." She was fairly certain this was a line stolen from Reprobus—who was always muttering platitudes and prophecies that felt somehow half-baked and devastatingly true—but if so, it was a good line and one worth repeating, because that was one of the things most lacking in her life, trust.

She stripped naked and they did the same. A guttural rumbling filling their throats. She knew, if she was going to be all college textbooky, that modesty was a by-product of human intelligence, irrelevant when the animal took over. Transformation was all about tapping into impulse, forgetting about what was outside you. She knew this. She did. But she still felt, with her clothes in a pile at her feet, as if she might throw up.

The hours spun away on the wall clock as she ripped at the heavy bags, leapt over sawhorses, swung from ropes, eventually stumbling away from the gym feeling languid and frayed and emptied, as if she had just screamed her way through the greatest orgasm in world history. She has forgotten the goodness of letting go, unleashing herself. How the adrenaline rushing through her feels like the hit of some delicious drug. How coordinated every sensation becomes. She remembers reading, in an anatomy and physiology course, about how the senses operate at different speeds—the mind processes light more slowly than sound—and then tastes and smells, slower still. That does not feel true any longer, every signal seeming to spark her brain at once.

Does she think of Patrick? She does. But not so much, not anymore. He is part of another world, and this is her world. Matthew is right now, right here. When she thinks of Patrick, she wonders whether she was simply starved and knows that the starved, with no standards of taste, will hunger for anything—dirt, a browned banana, a half-eaten sandwich pilfered from a garbage can.

Waking up is difficult. So is completing her homework. Her joints feel full of ground bits of glass. Her toothbrush comes away from her mouth bloody, so she sticks to mouthwash. She tells Andrea she has met a boy. Every morning, a few minutes before class, she rolls out of bed and pancakes her face with makeup to hide the bruises, then rushes off.

For this reason she misses the news about the Howling Bill.

It isn't until she walks through the light snow that has fallen overnight and makes the campus sparkle like white fire—it isn't until after she kicks off her boots and enters the auditorium—it isn't until after she looks for Matthew and spots him conferring at the front of the room with Reprobus—that she notices the upset buzz of conversation around her. It isn't until she takes her seat and unzips her bag and observes Reprobus climb to the stage and cross his hands over his belly and address them in a solemn voice that she realizes something terrible has happened.

"We are at an interesting juncture," he says and waits for silence to settle over the room. "History is being made. History that will one day be taught in this very course, assuming this university continues to exist, which I very much hope for but very much doubt all the same. Yesterday, Congress rushed the bill, an amendment to the Patriot Act, using a procedural trick normally reserved for noncontroversial laws. They made significant changes from an earlier version, never making the new draft available for public review prior to the vote. Only two representatives voted against it. The bill now goes forward to the Senate, where it is expected to pass."

The snow in her hair melts and drips to her shoulders and lap. She takes out her pen but there is nothing to write, so she holds it like a knife.

Reprobus says this comes in the wake of last week's raid on a Florida terrorist cell, an entire apartment complex full of lycans busted—dozens arrested and a large cache of weapons discovered. With the security level at red for two years now, with new threats discovered every week, the government has decided new steps must be taken to keep the country safe.

She writes down *safe* in her notebook and then scratches it out.

He explains what this means. With the new year, all IDs will note lycan status. The lycan no-fly will remain in effect indefinitely. A database, accessible to anyone online, will list every registered lycan, along with their addresses and photos. Antidiscrimination laws will be lifted: it will be legal for a business to deny service and employment to a lycan, because the government has determined that, in light of recent and repeated attacks, lobos is now a level-one public health and safety threat.

This is the gateway, Reprobus says, to impoverishment, to ridicule, to attacks. The gateway to vaccinations proposed by the idiot cowboy running for president.

"I refuse to bear it. That might mean a fine or that might mean imprisonment. That might mean my job. I don't know. I don't care. When I was your age, I made a lot of noise. I have noticed your generation doesn't make much noise. I find you disgustingly polite. I would encourage you to take to the streets. I would encourage you to be rude and obnoxious. Make yourself heard. Howl."

And then he excused them.

CHAPTER 46

HARD BITS OF ICE fall from the sky and bite his skin and patter his cammies. His radio is broken, shattered by shrapnel or a bullet, but his GPS still works. Patrick panics when he realizes it is switched on, a button accidentally pressed, the battery half-drained. He has the coordinates for the base saved and keys them in and sees he has more than forty miles to travel. To save power he will have to check his placement every few hours and hope that he can eyeball his bearings and not wander too far off course.

An hour ago, when he opened the door to leave, she grabbed him, her fingers bony but strong, pressing painfully into the meat of his arm. She handed him the pistol that she had kept hidden from him. He thanked her and holstered it, but she did not let him go. He could sense, in her trembling face, that she wanted to tell him something. He waited—expecting her to warn him or wish him well—but the words never came. She let him go and gave him a push and closed the door. He stood there and faced the empty country ahead of him and felt the deepening cold, like the breath of a cave where there is no cave, already creeping under his clothes.

He grew up in the country and at night often sat on the porch with a Coke watching for shooting stars. He knows darkness unadulterated by the glow of a city. But out here, on a night lit by a half-moon, with thick clouds smearing away most of the stars, he feels gone. So gone that when he hears a chopper—the rotor like a flopping saw blade—and guesses it is twenty or more miles away, he doesn't bother trying to spot it, to spark a flare and wave his arms. There will be no more help for him out here, no more miracles: he used up all his good luck on the old woman.

He trudges through the snow, every step a loud crunch, like a big dog toothing its way through a brittle bone. He would worry about the noise if everything didn't seem so empty. He looks behind him and sees the trenches his footsteps have gouged through the snow and knows that if somebody or something comes looking for him, they won't have much trouble finding him.

He can feel his heartbeat in his shoulder. He tries to concentrate on something else. A cluster of stars. A knob of ice. The piney woods that spill from the hills he must cross, east of here, where for a long time dawn has been coming. A faint green glow creeping across the sky. He is on a rise when the sun finally breaks with a white flash. He goes momentarily blind and loses his footing and goes sailing down a hillside with a wave of snow coming with him, going fast, nudging against a few rocks but otherwise feeling weightless as he's buoyed along, leaving his stomach behind him on the ledge.

His shoulder feels bitten and he worries that the scab has broken. He flexes his fingers and toes, making sure he's otherwise uninjured, and then kicks his way out of the cold, thick blanket that surrounds him, nearly whooping with excitement and relief.

His cries are cut short by the tracks he spots all around him. Boots. Fresh, the details of the tread not yet erased by blowing snow. He crouches to study their imprint. It matches his own. The tracks, at first separate and then twining together, head into a pine forest a hundred yards away.

He wants to sprint through the snow, follow their passage, call out for help, but something roots him in place for a long minute. He does not understand what a group of soldiers—maybe six of them, as best as he can tell—would be doing out here, far from any road, far from anything. Maybe special ops, maybe choppered or parachuted in, maybe to destroy some terrorist camp. Or maybe something else.

Just then the woods erupt with a high, plaintive yowling. They, the wolves, sound excited. Something has excited them.

He is barely aware of drawing his pistol, barely aware of lifting his feet and letting them fall, hurrying across the last snowy expanse and pushing into the cover of the woods, trying not to trip over the roots and fallen branches that knot the ground.

It is easy to find them because of the noise they make—at first howling and then yapping and clacking their teeth and disturbing the underbrush—so much noise that they do not notice him when he stands near. But it is not easy to make sense of them—to make sense of what he sees—a clearing full of men, dressed in cammies, dancing around a moose that struggles weakly to rise. The snow is stamped down and dappled with bright pools of blood.

Its antlers are a thorny basket, and the moose rakes them one way, then another, when the soldiers dart toward it and stab its haunches and its belly with spears—yes, spears—ten feet long and whittled into points. The moose's legs don't seem to be working, one of them bent at a sharp angle. Its eyes roll back in fear and it releases a deep-throated moan that is cut short by a spear piercing its neck.

The men throw back their heads and bay raggedly and before Patrick can stop himself he lifts his pistol and fires it into the pink, brightening sky. There is a cracking boom. The sun flames at the top of the trees.

Some of the men swing around and some flatten to the ground and some dart into the trees. A holy silence settles over the forest. Patrick lets his arm slowly fall until the pistol aims at the ground.

Then one of the soldiers separates himself from the others and starts toward Patrick. At first he appears misshapen—hunchbacked, two-headed—the kind of monster that pursues a child in a fairytale forest. Its crunching footsteps are so loud, like teeth chewing ice.

Patrick feels a pressure around his heart. He recognizes that this is not one man, but two, the second upon the other's back, riding there like an infant in a leather harness. Legless. Deformed or war wounded.

The man who serves as a carrier stands at an angle, so that both can observe Patrick. They each wear cammies—torn and muddied and patched and ice-caked, as if stripped from a scarecrow—and they each wear beards that cannot hide the blunt snout of a lycan, their eyes rimmed with blood the color of the dawn. They may as well be the same man for their appearance.

Then the one in the harness begins to speak. What first sounds like a growl mellows into a string of recognizable words. “Patrick,” the lycan says, “Patrick? Is that you, Patrick? Is that really you?”

It is hard to see, with the sun half-risen and the forest soaked in shadow, and it is hard to believe, with so much time and so many miles between them, but Patrick gradually comes to understand that he is looking at his father.

Chase is always so tired. During the day, he can more or less deal with the pepper-belly stress, chewing down another tablet, calling Buffalo for advice on what to wear or say, studying a speech until he has more or less committed it to memory, choosing to relish or ignore the possibility he will very shortly be elected president. But at night, once sleep overtakes him, he cannot contain any of his anxieties, and so they pound through him like black bulls escaping a ranch without fences. So he doesn’t sleep, not as often as he should.

He used to sleep like a baby, like a rock, like the dead—that’s what he always told people. He would nap every afternoon and wake up with a half smile and pulse-slamming erection, ready for whatever needed conquering. No longer.

And the lack of sleep is beginning to catch up with him, so that, like a drunk, he can only patch together memories, a few shards gone missing from every moment. Sometimes he will be telling a joke or a story—the one about the priest and the sheep, the one about the time he punched a grizzly sniffing around his tent when camping the back-country at Glacier—and his audience will smile but he can tell from their shifty apologetic gazes that he is repeating himself.

That's how he feels now, at the Tuonela Mine, where the air smells like sulfur and the lung-blackening exhaust of a tractor-trailer. He feels like he has been here before. He feels like he must have worn the same clothes yesterday. He feels like he keeps saying, "Great, great," but can't stop himself from repeating it no matter what anyone tells him.

The tour guide, Mason, is a squat-bodied American with the black wiry hair of a nostril who speaks with expansive hand gestures and who wears a gray shirt wrinkled like foil along his broad back.

Mason leads them first through the business center, a hive of narrow hallways and square concrete offices without doors in which sallow-faced black-tied men hammer keyboards and square stacks of paper and drink from disposable cups of tea. He walks backward when he can, occasionally jarring a shoulder into a doorframe, while talking to them about uranium mining and refinement, telling them how the ore is generally low concentration so that the extraction has to be high volume. He tells them, with his fist smacking his open palm, that 20 percent of the world's uranium presently comes from the Lupine Republic. "Twenty percent," he says. "Ten thousand tons. Quite a bit of which was drawn from the ground beneath your feet. That's a whole lot."

He talks about how the ore is processed by milling it into particles and he talks about how it is then treated by chemical leaching to extract the uranium and he talks about how the yellowcake is the result of this, a dry powder sold on the market as U_3O_8. "And that's what you see blasting out of here on train after train after train."

Chase knows most of this—he's been briefed extensively on the mines and forced to memorize all the talking points that make nuclear energy the key to powering the States through the next century—and he pays more attention to whether he is slouching, whether his gut is sucked in, as the reporters snap so many photos of him that he sees the bright burst of a flash even when his eyes are shut.

The tiled hallway is wet and Mason tells them to be careful and they skate around a corner, where they surprise a black-haired janitor with a tumor like a cauliflower growing out of his neck. He wears gray coveralls and he hunches over his mop and he says, "Oh!" when he sees them and retreats against the wall and says how terribly sorry he is, his eyes flitting between Mason and Chase, how terribly sorry.

They step outside, into sunlight so bright it makes them shield their eyes, onto an observation deck with the snow recently scraped from it, to take in the view of the open pit mines, one of them half-full of yellow ice, and the other, carved out layer by layer, the walls sloping gradually inward, so that it appears a pyramid was drawn upside down from it. Dynamite claps like thunder. Loaders and diggers rattle and beep, their drivers in iron-sleeve suits and enclosed cabins with the very best filtration systems, which protect them—"Mostly," Mason says—from radiation and airborne dust.

Inside, they stomp the cold out of their feet and put on safety goggles and yellow plastic helmets before heading into the refinement facility, where they clamp along ironwork planks and up and down stairwells and pass by milling machinery stained with rivers of orange rust wherever there is a scratch or a rivet or a screw. Geiger counters and radon detectors seem to hang from every wall like a clock collection clicking its way to doomsday.

They take a juddering elevator with graffiti notched on its walls and gum stuck to its floor to some dim lower level full of access shafts from which cool, musty air gusts like the breath of a buried beast. There are grated fans everywhere, sucking out the radon-poisoned air and blasting in filtered air from outside, and Mason has to yell over the top of them to be heard. He tells them about sunken shafts and ore veins and crosscuts. He talks about tunnels known as raises and as winzes meant for extraction.

A miner with a headlamp walks past their group and smiles, his teeth flecked black, and says something to Chase in Russian. He holds out his hand and Chase takes it and pumps it even as the security force closes in around them. He knows that everyone who works for the mine must succumb to a monthly blood test, that any who do not test positive for Volpexx are immediately terminated. "Don't worry," Chase tells them and adjusts his body to face a flashing camera. "You worry too much."

When they climb into the elevator again, Mason leans in to Chase and snickers and says, "Hey, is it true you once threw a ball of hamburger at a vegan protester after touring a meatpacking plant?"

"That's not true. She was a vegetarian."

He tries to laugh along with Mason, but the laughter feels stale in his mouth and the memory of packing and hurling the handful of ground beef feels like somebody else's memory, and he can't help but think, and not for the first time, that he is a fool. Then the elevator doors open and the grated walkway they cross looks down upon another grated walkway, and another and another still, and when Chase drops his head he feels a momentary uncertainty as to where he stands.

At one point Neal hands him a phone and he retreats to a quiet corner and hears Buffalo on the other end, already talking, telling him about Jeremy Saber: *60 Minutes* was pushing for a death-row interview—and the media want access to the execution. "We don't want him to have a camera. We don't want him to have a microphone. We don't want him to do any more damage than he has already done, and damage is what will come if they allow the media to film the execution. Cameras make martyrs. Cameras stir up the crazies. The LA riots would not have happened if not for the Rodney King footage."

Chase says okay, okay, and asks if there is anything he can do.

"You can shove a towel into his mouth and pour the Mississippi over his face. Then you can cut off his tongue and dick with the same pair of scissors. Then you can snap his neck and toss him in a coffin and fill it with concrete and shoot it with a cannon and watch him shatter into a million pieces."

"Why are you calling, Buffalo?"

"I'll need audio from you by tomorrow. How dangerous it is to give a terrorist a media platform. How a dog should be put down behind closed doors." He blows out a sigh that translates to static. "Otherwise, just checking in."

"You miss me, don't you?"

"Fuck you, I miss you."

"You sound upset."

"There's kind of a lot on the line here. Maybe I'm the only one who recognizes that."

The press conference will take place in a room with an angled ceiling and three concrete walls, the fourth made from floor-to-ceiling windows that glow with pale winter light and look out onto a snowy field that stretches to the chain-link perimeter. A plastic ficus tree anchors every corner, and five rows of aluminum folding chairs have been positioned before a podium.

Fifteen minutes before the press conference—after the mike check, after the Republic and U.S.

flags are hung, after the video tripods are arranged at the rear of the room, after the diplomats and dignitaries, hair-sprayed and cologned and wearing dark blue suits, begin to arrive—Chase says he will be right back. He needs to hit the head, lose a cup of coffee.

One of the executives—a thick-shouldered man with a porcupine of a beard—says, “I will show you.”

“Don’t bother. I can hold my own prick.”

Sometimes Chase doesn’t know he’s made a joke until someone laughs, the laughter now uncomfortable and following him from the room and down the hall. He pushes into the bathroom, tiled yellow with two naked bulbs screwed into the ceiling. There is a sink and a stall and a urinal, all of them marbled with veins of mold. He unzips and lets loose a pungent orange jet of urine. The Volpexx affects him worse than asparagus.

The speech will roll on the teleprompter, but he has never been good with tracking, so he always tries to remember as much as he can. He recalls some of the key phrases—*strategic energy planning*, *uranium is the new gold*—and so barely registers the door creaking open behind him. He shakes off and tucks himself in and observes in the tile the reflection of a man sliding toward him with his arms out.

Chase jerks around in time for the man to impact his chest. What he sees next is like a deck of cards tossed upward. Black hair. Teeth gnashing, bubbling with blood. The ceiling tilting back, the lightbulb flaring. Sharp-nailed fingers scrabbling toward him. A tumor bulging out of a neck. Somewhere, amid this flash of images, he remembers the wet floor they skated across earlier that afternoon, the janitor clutching his mop and edging against the wall to let them pass. And somehow—as he falls, in his seemingly endless descent—Chase manages to cry out, "I'm one of you!" before slamming against the floor, his head cracking the concrete and dulling his mind.

The lycan is on top of him. He can see his panicked reflection in its eyes, can smell its bloody breath playing over his face, can feel the fingers lacing around his neck, squeezing. He feels as though he is sucking air through a straw. His vision blackens at the edges; just before it collapses altogether, the bathroom door swings open and the lieutenant comes in with his hand already at his zipper.

He keeps his hand there but does not pause in his approach, hurrying forward to swing a leg and kick the lycan in the ribs. There is a sound like sticks snapping. The lycan yelps and releases his grip and Chase drags in a few ragged breaths through a throat that feels like it has been struck by a dull-bladed guillotine.

By now the lieutenant has drawn back his boot again—and kicks the lycan in the temple. There is no yelp this time. Only a damp thud. The lycan rolls off Chase and lies still a moment before scampering to the corner, a whimpering ball.

The lieutenant is by his side now, touching him all over as if his hands could heal. "Did he get you?"

Chase tries to speak and can't. He swallows hard. "Nope." His voice toadish. "Good."

The lieutenant does not say anything. His forehead is pleated with deep lines. He is studying Chase's hand. There is blood there. The heat of a wasp's sting. Chase brings it to his face. There, along the meaty bulge below his thumb, the clear imprint of teeth, as if he were some soft candy tested and disliked.

There is no arguing with the lieutenant. He has been bitten. He will need to be treated and tested. And when the blood work comes back positive, everything will be different; all of this will be over. He sits for a long time, staring at the wound, before rising slowly from the floor. His throat feels collared by hot iron. There is a sound in his head, a sputtery hum, like an electrical short.

"Gun," Chase says and holds out his hand.

"What?"

He gestures impatiently. "Gun!"

The lieutenant unholsters his pistol and offers it butt-first to Chase, who holds it in his hand a moment and observes on the black barrel the vanishing whorl of a fingerprint.

Chase thinks about how easy it would be to bring the pistol to his mouth, whistle a breath, pull the trigger, and end all of this. The secret of his infection, the static that fuzzes his thoughts, and the disquieting sense that the more powerful he becomes, the less he controls and desires. He should just shoot himself. He should just shoot himself and make it all go away.

The idea is short-lived.

He raises the pistol and fires into the lieutenant's face and observes the scar along his upper lip twitch in surprise before the top half of his skull opens up and blood slides from it and churns down his face and neck like a red snake before he topples to the floor.

Chase has only a few seconds now. They will have heard the gunshot. They are already coming. They are almost here.

He goes to the lycan, and the lycan, run through with adrenaline, remains transformed. A pink mess of blood and tears dampens its cheeks. It holds up its hand—and the hand trembles as if controlled incompletely. How fragile it looks, how slight of wrist and thin fingered. It is hard to imagine its cruel strength, wrapped around his throat a moment before, squeezing. Then Chase looks closer and notices the nail, yellow and long.

Chase keeps the gun steady and imagines what he looks like from below, from the lycan's vantage point, his body stepping forward now, blotting away the lightbulb overhead. The pistol swings enormously into view, allowing the lycan to observe the black, gaping maw of the chamber. When he squeezes, the trigger will give with a snap, like the striking of a match. And then the pistol will jump back and a bullet will leap from the muzzle, but the lycan will never see it move, already elsewhere.

CHAPTER 47

THE VIDEO INSTANTLY goes viral. Somehow, someone snuck a smart phone into solitary confinement, and Jeremy Saber has recorded and uploaded a five-minute rant. He is barely recognizable—in part because of the grainy image and in part because his hair has been shaved down to stubble and his face appears sunken, black hollowed; he is a wraith of a man. "I have nothing to lose. I have no political office to gain, no money to make, no power to attain." His voice is whispery and interrupted by a cough—but resolute. "So please listen to me when I say that you must resist. You must. You cannot roll over. You cannot obey. You cannot play the bad dog they want you to play. Do you know how many lycan attacks occur in the country every year? Eleven. Less than a dozen. More people are attacked by sharks. But that's not how they're treating us. So we might as well live up to their expectations. Fight back. Bite back. The public registry and the abolishment of antidiscrimination laws are equivalent to hate crimes. They are crimes against humanity. Lycans are human. We are *human*."

The T-shirts appear soon thereafter. They are handed out in malls, on street corners, in schools. They are handed out at William Archer—in the post office and cafeteria—and they read HUMAN in black lettering across the chest. Posters and evites and chalked sidewalks announce that everyone should gather on the quad at noon. Claire does not have a Facebook account—Miriam forbade her from opening one—but Andrea shows her how everyone has changed their profile picture to a raised fist and updated their status with a single word, *Solidarity*.

On the horizon, banks of cement- and plum-colored clouds boil and blur the air with what must be snow or sleet, but the sky over the campus is clear when Claire and Matthew join several hundred students on the quad.

There is something different about him, Matthew. It is less the way he looks and more the way he carries himself: he is less unfinished than most of the other boys, more a man. Her heart whirs when he touches her, as he does now, guiding her by the elbow into the mass of students. She feels protected by him. And with threatening packages appearing in her mailbox and strange visitors asking about her on campus, when she knows she is being watched but not by whom, protection is what she wants.

The day is cold and their breath steams from their mouths, like something boiling over. The media are waiting for them. Similar protests are going on all over the country—in parks and town squares—but the William Archer organizers sent an announcement to every major news outlet, and they have responded and the focus is here. Dozens of reporters corral the mass of students. Their cameras and microphones carry the logos of NBC, CBS, ABC, Fox News, CNN, MSNBC.

There are no chants, no speeches. There is no march. The students simply stand in place—in relative silence—while the reporters thumb in their earpieces and chatter into their microphones. Claire can hear the *rip-rip-rip-rip* of cameras firing off shots at shutter speed, can hear people coughing, stomping their feet to kick the cold out of them, can hear a boy she recognizes from her calculus class—long hair, Birkenstocks, ankh tattoo on the back of his neck—talking to a reporter with a video camera aimed at him like a cannon.

"We just want to be ourselves, you know. We just want to be ordinary and treated like anybody else. You can't let the few define the many. Jeffrey Dahmer and John Wayne Gacy didn't make the world turn against all thirty-something white males as a bunch of crazy-ass serial killers. We're not a bunch of terrorists—we're just people."

"You don't think you're dangerous?"

"I think *people* are dangerous. Period. I'm not going to bite anybody. I don't want to bite anybody. Why would I want to do that? That's messed up. You'd have to be crazy to do that, just like you'd have to be crazy to shoot up a school or bomb a building. It's just a matter of being human. Some of us are mean. It's like my professor was saying the other day—humanity is a flawed creation—all of us are all different kinds of fucked up."

"Who is your professor?"

"Reprobus. Professor Reprobus. He's the *man*."

"Did he have anything to do with organizing this?"

The student goes silent for a beat before saying quietly, "No."

Through the wall of reporters, on the steps of the union, with the bruised banks of clouds gathering overhead, Claire spots the blond boy from her class. Francis. He is more than sixty yards away but easy to recognize with his standard uniform of a collared shirt and chinos. He is looking in their direction with a cell phone pressed to his ear. His mouth is moving, the hole of it black, as he tells someone about them.

At a protest in Berkeley, on the central green of the campus, the police gather in a long line. They wear riot gear—black body armor that exaggerates and squares their musculature—and they hold their batons two-handed, at their sides and aimed forward, like the spears of some ancient army. One of them lifts a bullhorn to his mouth. It squawks. His voice booms through it when he says everyone in the area must immediately disperse and anyone who remains will be arrested and anyone who resists arrest will be dealt with accordingly. Then he drops the bullhorn and waits. One person gathers up his backpack and takes off running. The rest of the two dozen protesters remain in place. They hold homemade signs made of cardboard boxes and wobbly poster paper that read ENOUGH! and ALL MEN ARE CREATED EQUAL and THIS SHIT IS FUCKED. They cross their arms. And they remain in that posture even when the police begin, in a line, to march toward them.

At a protest in New York, in Central Park, near the zoo, one hundred people have set up a tent city. They—lycans and nonlycans alike, many of them twenty-somethings with ratty beards and wool caps and army surplus backpacks—will occupy the park until their demands are met. "What are your demands?" a reporter asks them, and they say, "An end to second-class citizenship," and when the reporter asks them to be more specific, one of them says, “I haven’t seen my family for seven months because I can’t get on a plane,” and another says, “I’ve been told to look for new work in the New Year,” and still another says, “I ordered a burger and a beer at a bar the other day, and when they saw my ID, they asked me to leave.” When the squad cars roll up, flashing their red-and-blues, the protesters form a seated circle around the tent city and link their arms. The cops give them a thirty-minute warning, and when it expires, they pull on their goggles and shake their cans of pepper spray and calmly walk around the tent city and soak the faces of those seated along its perimeter—one by one by one—until their bodies wither and the air sharpens with screaming.

At a protest in Oxford, Mississippi, in the shadow of city hall, two groups assemble: demonstrators on either side of the issue. They yell at each other, spit, shove. The police have laid construction cones between them but otherwise remain separate from the gathering, leaning against their squad cars, their thumbs hooked into their belts, watching. And they continue to watch even when someone lobs a brick, a bottle, when a fistfight breaks out, when the crowd surges one way, then another, when a man falls underfoot, when blood is spilled.

On C-SPAN, a Democratic congressman from California speaks on the House floor about the precedent of the past. "Have there been unprovoked lycan attacks? There have. Every year there are a few. Usually someone who is unstable. Off their meds. They bite somebody. And then? Does that person, once bitten, go wild and bite somebody else who bites somebody else who bites somebody else? Of course not. We do not live in a world where some crazed wolfman is going to jump out of the bushes. The infected seek help. They solve their problem. They control the disease that can lead to harmful impulses. Nothing needs to change. The system is not broken. A few terrorists have made us believe otherwise. They are the problem. We need to hunt them down and bring them to justice. That should be our focus. Not these measures we are taking, which will not increase our safety, which will instead provoke an otherwise nonbelligerent, law-abiding people." He pauses here, waiting for applause that does not come.

And in Tulsa, Oklahoma, an older woman named Mattie Spencer scratches out a grocery list on a slip of paper and puts on her favorite purple jacket and gathers her purse and punches the garage door opener and there they are. Maybe twenty of them. She clutches her keys and they spike between her swollen knuckles like a weapon. The figures are wearing black ski masks and they are scattered across the driveway and the lawn and the sidewalks and the street, as still as statues.

She feels her expression shift along with her heart as she feels confusion and then recognition and then horror. A trembling runs through her body and her voice when she says, “What do you want?”

One of the men—they are all men as far as she can tell—says, “We saw you on the website. Saw you on the registry.”

She thinks she recognizes the voice and the build of the man and says as much, “Joel? Is that you, Joel Rawlings? You’ve seen me most days of your life and never had a problem.”

The man takes a step back and looks up and down the street.

She shakes her keys at them. “You come after me, threatening me, and what does that change?” Finally she says, “Well?”

They don’t know what they’ve come for—except to lash out at something—but maybe seeing her now, with her round face and shivering dimpled chin, makes them realize she isn’t what they are looking for after all.

“Bunch of fools,” she says.

Slowly she retreats to the back of the garage and

hits the button and the door jars down, and when it does, none of the masked figures make a move to stop her.

Later, at William Archer, after the students disperse, after the six o'clock news airs, after rolled-up rubber-banded newspapers thump onto front porches, a long line of pickups come barreling up the hill and through campus, revving their engines and blaring their horns and flashing their lights. They hurl eggs and beer cans out their windows. They slide around corners with blue smoke rising from their tires. They rock over curbs and do doughnuts in the grass. They run students off the sidewalks before tearing down the hill again, the smell of exhaust lingering like a fired gun.

Claire watches this from the patio of the union. The tables are empty and barnacled with ice, a black cavity at their center from the sun umbrellas long ago tied off and toted to storage. She and Matthew, drawn outside by the noise of revving engines, hold paper cups of coffee steaming in their hands. They watch the fleet of pickups, jacked-up Dodge Rams and Ford F-150s with floodlights along the roof, until their coffee has gone cold, the bitterness pronounced.

They return inside to gather their things, to return to the dorms, and Claire says she wants to first stop by the PO. They pass a few students wearing HUMAN shirts and whispering harshly to each other—otherwise, they are alone, their footsteps echoing down the marble hallway.

She kneels at the bank of mailboxes and spins the dials and hears the tumblers fall into place. She yanks her box open. Above her a light flickers on and off with an insectile buzz. Her mind is elsewhere, so it takes a moment to register the manila envelope crammed into the slot. It catches and tears when she draws it out. She fits her finger into the tear—noting the postmark, noting the name, "Hope Robinson," in letters that look slashed by a sword—and rips open the package. There is an odd weight to it and a bulge at its center. When she reaches inside, she does not understand at first what she has, a quart-size ziplock bag rolled up, and within it, something red and familiar.

And then she understands. And then she begins to scream.

CHAPTER 48

PATRICK HAS NO CHOICE but to do as they tell him. Right now that means kicking through ice-scabbed snow that sometimes softens and rises into belly-deep drifts. They have been trudging along for more than an hour. The sun makes everything a blinding white. His legs throb along with his shoulder. He feels feverish despite the cold. Every now and then he scoops a handful of snow to his mouth and chews it down to water.

This morning, when the sun flamed pink rafters across the sky, when his father called out to him, the lycans wrestled away his pistol and patted him down and then left him to stand there dumbly while they gutted and quartered and skinned the moose, severed the head and tossed it aside. This took more than an hour, and during this hour, he and his father sat on a log and looked at each other, simply looked at each other. At first his father smiled, marveling at their reunion, and then the smile died and he took on the startled, resigned expression of a man leaning over his own child's coffin. "I've wished all this time to see you," he said. "And now I wish I hadn't." In the clearing the carcass steamed and the blood stained the snow and made it appear as though they were wading through a red pond. The steaming pile of viscera, purple and red and green, drew crows that cawed and busied the ground with their spinning shadows.

Now the lycans drag two sleds made of branches lashed together with rope and sinew. They use their spears as walking sticks. One of them carries an M57 over his shoulder. Another carries Patrick's father. They wear their uniforms, but they are not soldiers, not anymore. They do not walk in formation, but in a huddle the shape of a dog's paw, with Patrick at the center.

Eventually, along a wooded hillside crowned by a granite and gneiss cliff, they enter a bombed-out village made mostly of stone and cement houses with the roofs collapsed in. The snow here is packed down, threaded with footsteps, stained with urine and blood and feces.

From the base of the cliff grows a church, square and built from blocks of granite. A broken cross rises from its roof. A crow roosts on it and departs when they draw near. A splintered door rests against the entryway, no longer hinged, and they drag it aside and then pack snow onto the meat and heave up the sleds to carry inside.

A stone cistern for holy water lies cracked on the floor. The pews are gone—smashed up for kindling, Patrick guesses—and the roof has collapsed in places and snow has fallen through these skylights and made slick the slate floor. Roots break through the walls and cling to the stone.

They walk past the pulpit and through a doorway that leads to a rectory with candled recesses in the walls and a skeleton in the corner with a moldering Bible in its lap. The light is dim and the lycan carrying his father sparks a Zippo to an iron-handled torch and continues down a hallway and Patrick hangs back and watches the light swirl away like water down a drain before somebody gives him a nudge and he starts forward.

They walk through a crypt stacked with skulls and femurs threaded with cobwebs and rotten gray cloth. The tunnel then opens into a wider passage and they pass over a chasm on a wood bridge with iron trappings, maybe ten feet long, that Patrick can feel bow in its middle.

On the other side, they enter a high-ceilinged chamber with a small skylight far above and with some heathen altar at its center and with bedding along the floor made from animal skins and pine boughs. A fire pit glows orange with embers and the lycans throw more wood on it from a tall stack along the wall. The flames soon rise and pock their faces with shadows and make their expressions seem to move even when still.

They pull off their shawls. They are all windburned, their skin darkened in patches from frostbite and brightened in others by burst capillary rosettes. Their breath floats around their heads like lost souls while the flames gather higher and higher and the cavern comes into flickering existence around them. The ceiling is blackened from the smoke of so many cooking fires and from the hundreds of bats that roost there. The walls are smeared with murals depicting men killing animals and animals killing men, battles fought yesterday and today and tomorrow, a battle that has never and will never cease, killing for hunger and killing for thirst, the special sort of thirst slaked by blood.

The floor is black sand clotted with guano. There are sitting stones around the fire pit and the bleached skull of some giant animal Patrick does not recognize, and he sits upon its crown. His father is set down beside him. His legs end in stumps at the knees, so that he appears half-buried, half-lost to the underworld.

Patrick studies each of their faces. A black man named Jessie with half his teeth missing. A Mexican named Pablo with a dent in his forehead as if somebody jammed a thumb into mud. A white guy with a beard and a flat face with bulging eyes that seem never to settle anywhere more than a second.

His name is Austin. He is the one who stripped Patrick of his gun, who laughed when Patrick embraced his father and said, "Well, isn't that the sweetest fucking thing."

In the clearing his father explained what happened to them. The ambush on a routine patrol. An IED ripped through their convoy—the day bright blue one moment, red with fire the next—and before they could register what happened, out of the roiling smoke came what must have been ten or twenty or thirty lycans. "We sprayed off all our ammo," his father said. "We made a storm cloud out of the street, but there were too many of them. They wanted to bite—that's what they wanted. To bite us. And they bit us, some worse than others." He unrolled his sleeve then and held out a forearm branded with scar tissue. "Mission accomplished."

Five of them came out alive, all of them bitten, one of them without any legs. The blast shredded them, and the men cut away the remains and cauterized the ruined flesh with a hubcap they stuck in a roaring fire until the metal glowed orange.

Austin broke into their conversation. "Everybody talks about the *what if* moment. What if you get dog bit? Some say put a bullet in your head. Some say make do with life as an infected. We all got wives, kids. MIA or KIA and your family keeps the stipend. Go home a lycan? Then fucking what? Discharged. Divorced. Doped up and ruined." Behind Austin, in the clearing, the moose sobbed and tried once more to struggle upright, and he used Patrick's pistol to fire two rounds into it and the moose dropped as if a string had been cut. "Fuck that."

Now, in the cave, Patrick says nothing but watches the lycans and listens to their voices echoing and their footsteps hushing through sand and their knives sharpened over stone. They unload the meat from the sled and stack it on the altar and begin to carve away at it with the knives that flash in each of their hands. Some of the meat they eat raw and some of it they slice into steaks and chops to then pack with snow into a recess in the cave wall, what looks like an old tomb. The air smells of blood and body odor as tangy as sour wine.

Patrick keeps wanting to ask why. *Why* had his father not escaped these men, why had he not reached out to Patrick, assured him he was alive? He already knows the answer—he is no longer their staff sergeant, now their prisoner, the same as Patrick—but it's the wrong answer.

Pablo kneels by the fire and reaches into it to light a cigarette. His hands are gloved with blood and his mouth smeared with it. The dent in his forehead carries a black shadow. He makes eye contact with Patrick and drags hard on the cigarette and blows a cloud of bluish smoke and says his father is a good man.

His voice is high and Patrick realizes then how young Pablo is, how young they all are, only a few years older than he. But the weather has scoured age into their faces. "Sorry as hell you had to find out about him like this. But hey, at least he's living, right?"

Austin stands at the altar and thrusts and saws with his knife. He pops a ribbon of meat into his mouth and speaks around it. "Call this living, I'd rather be dying."

Pablo takes another hit off his cigarette and flicks it at Austin and it sparks off his cheek and Austin swipes at the burn and bugs his eyes and tromps over to where the M57 leans against the wall and racks a round in the chamber and holds it to Pablo's head. "Do that again."

"Only got a few cigs left or I might."

Austin keeps a bead on Pablo, aiming for the hole already begun in his forehead. Then he says, "Fuck yourself," and lowers the rifle and returns it to its place against the wall and once again snatches up his blade and goes to work on a haunch striated with bands of fat.

Patrick looks at his father, and his father looks at

him, then drops his eyes, defeated. He has no say among these men, no power to keep the peace, offer any direction, save his son.

One of the sleds sits near Pablo and he leans over and rips away a fist-size section of meat and jabs it onto a spear and swings it toward Patrick and says, "Hungry, man?"

"Don't give him that," Austin says.

"It's Keith's kid, man."

"Don't give him that spear."

"Four of us, one of him. How big you think his balls are?"

Austin looks at Patrick, talks to Pablo. "He can eat. He can't have the spear."

Pablo lets the spear hang in the air a moment more—so that Patrick could reach for it if he wanted—and then drags it back and balances it on his thigh and hovers the meat near the coals. Blood drips from it, sizzles. "You know your old man tells some crazy stories."

"Yeah?"

"Telling us stories how he dropped acid in Yosemite once and went on a hike. Tripping balls and thought, for some reason, might be a good idea to take off his clothes. So he does. So he's hiking along naked except for his boots. Then he comes across this woman wearing, like, some gauzy white outfit. Most beautiful woman in the world, he said. He touched her and she turned to ash when he touched her and blew away with the wind."

"That true, Dad?"

His father does not respond. His head is bowed and he is rubbing his hands along his thighs to their rounded ends.

Patrick smiles because it seems like the right thing to do. Even if he doesn't feel happy, he doesn't feel sad either. He doesn't feel much of anything except cornered. He doesn't think he has room for anything else inside his head except escape. He studies his purplish knuckles, the blue-veined backs of his hands, as if they might hold an answer for him.

The black man, Jessie, says, "Why you telling him that?"

"Trying to make conversation."

"You're supposed to be telling him some heroic shit. Not about some drug trip. Nobody wants to hear that about their dad." Then he says he needs some rack time and settles onto some bedding and rolls away from them.

The meat begins to char and smoke and Patrick eyes up the M57 leaning against the cave wall, only ten feet away but on the other side of the fire. He doesn't know how many bullets are in it, but he guesses there are enough. His eyes jog to Austin, who remains hunched over the altar, shirtless now, his arms sleeved in blood up to the elbows. Their gazes lock. There is no negotiating with him. There is no escape either. If Patrick tries to leave, he will be dead or infected. He can see the sharpness in Austin's stare and knows it is only a matter of time before he tells the others to hold Patrick down and gnaw on his thigh or take him up the ass.

☽

After Claire ripped open the envelope and held the ziplock bag in her hand and recognized the two fingers sliced off neatly at the knuckle and dropped the mess of it to the floor and retreated until her back hit the wall, it took a long time for her to stop screaming. Matthew at first tried to comfort her, whispering that it would be all right, and then clamped a hand over her mouth and dragged her outside, where the cold snapped her into silence.

She could not be alone—and she could not face Andrea, who would have too many questions Claire could not answer—so she would go to his room. "Is that okay?" he asked and she nodded until he stopped her chin with his hand and said, "Okay." He retrieved the envelope from the floor of the mailroom and shoved it in her bag and she felt sick with the weight of it when they set off into the twilight gloom.

In his room, a single, he apologizes for the mess and kicks a pile of dirty clothes into his closet. His shelves and desk are overflowing with textbooks and papers, coffee cups, a hacky sack, a half-eaten bag of Fritos, a troll doll with wild hair. Over his bed hang two posters, one of *Star Wars*, the other of Che Guevara. A minifridge hums in the corner and from it he pulls a bottle of springwater for her to guzzle, dried out as she feels from so much crying.

In the window sits an iPod dock and a globe that lights up from inside. She goes to it and snaps it on and it projects its colorful design onto the window, the walls, their faces. She twirls it and the room spins with color. "Where do you want to go?" he says and she slams down a finger, and when they see where she points, their faces fall with disappointment: the Lupine Republic.

She leans into him then and he wraps his arms around her and she studies their reflection in the window. Her eyes strain to focus on him, her mouth opening and closing, as though she is struggling to read in dim light. She can't quite tell if he's looking back at her or past her. They remain this way for some time and later retain much the same position in bed.

* * *

The next morning's sunrise feels like an ignition. She has to leave. It is impossible not to leave. Not with what she knows. She slips out of bed and shoulders her backpack and clicks shut the door, and five minutes later creeps into her own room, where Andrea still sleeps.

Claire sets her suitcase on the bed and flops it open and begins to empty her drawers. She will depart on the next train to Seattle. No good-byes. No regrets. Before, she chastised herself for her preoccupation with the past, thinking of it as a weakness. Now she feels furious at herself for being so neglectful. Her past is all that matters—and Miriam is the only part of it that remains.

She checks her bureau, checks her desk, making sure she has everything she needs, and finds there a paper graded by Reprobus. The paper about her father. She received a B-plus on it, and in his end comments he wrote, "More sources next time. Interested in hearing from others besides you alone. The wolf, remember, is only as strong as the pack."

She leaves her suitcase yawning open on top of her bed.

* * *

She has come to learn his habits. By seven o'clock every morning he has already gone for his morning stroll and picked up his coffee from the union and will now be in his office reading the paper or grading essays and readying his next lecture.

The door is half-open and she can see him at his desk—an old library table, he once told her, crosshatched with ink and anchored by a Smith-Corona typewriter—with a newspaper spread before him and a dead pipe clamped in his mouth. The walls are lost behind bookshelves and old protest posters ragged and curled at their edges. The overhead light is off, but a jade-green desk lamp glows next to him and pools the room with shadows and brightens his glasses, which turn to observe her now.

Her stomach is an acidic pit of indecision. She knocks at the door even as she steps through it. He lowers the paper until it crinkles in his lap. "Miriam," is all she has to say, and he brings a finger to his lips.

He pinches a pencil from a coffee mug full of them and scratches down on a piece of paper, *Not safe. Not here.*

"Let's go for a walk," he says.

* * *

The morning is still shadowy; the sun hasn't won the sky. And the campus buildings, in this early wrap of winter, appear the leached gray of tombstones. A few students and professors wander about, most with coffee steaming in their hands, but otherwise, the campus is empty, the ground salted with snow and the grass frozen in white blades that crunch beneath her boots when she strays off the pathway, trying to walk beside Reprobus but finding it difficult because of his size and his meandering gait.

Minutes before, when she handed him the envelope, when he studied the fingers with the bit of bone peeking out of their bottoms, she wondered if he would cry or shout or swing a fist at the air helplessly—his expression was difficult to read beneath his beard—but he only handed her back the package and sparked a match to the bowl of his pipe and blew out a sigh of smoke.

"I'm going to leave," she says. "I'm going to find her."

"What makes you think she's alive?"

She can't say, not for sure. A sense. For so long Puck has wanted her. Now, at last, she is his. Like a man on the verge of sexual rapture, he will want to prolong his satisfaction.

Reprobus looks straight ahead when he says, "And then what?"

Again he bullies her off the path and she nudges him back with her shoulder and says, “I haven’t figured that part out yet.”

His pipe tobacco sizzles with every breath. The sun passes between some clouds and their shadows blink in and out of sight before them. “Something is happening,” he says. “I’m not sure what. Scrutiny and suspicion of William Archer as an institution is nothing new. But there have been government cars in the east parking deck, men in suits wandering through Admissions, Accounting, IT, the provost’s office.”

There it is again, the urge to run. There is a battle to fight here, and another to fight for Miriam, and she can’t get caught up between the two. “I’m sorry, but right now it’s hard for me to care about any of that.”

“I understand. But remember—this moment is bigger than you and bigger than Miriam. We’re under attack. We, as in the university. We, as in you and I. We, lycans.”

The frost crumbles beneath her boots as if she were walking on a fragile shell, and the lights begin to blink on in the buildings around them as students crawl out of bed and professors boot up their office computers and janitors collect yesterday’s garbage.

“What do you think I should do?”

"You don't know where Miriam is?"

"I think she's in the Seattle area. Based on the postmarks. Otherwise, all I have to go on are these videos."

"What about email? You mentioned that you've been in email contact?"

"They don't mention anything about where she is."

"I was watching a television program the other night. One of those police procedurals. In it, they were able to find a runaway by an email she sent. Some sort of code hacker thing." He holds out his hands and pretends his fingers are typing—the same way her father might have—the universal code of old men everywhere for the computer. "Do you know anyone who knows anything about that kind of stuff?"

She wakes Andrea by cracking a can of Diet Coke next to her ear and then handing it to her when she groggily props herself up in bed, one eye still shut and mascara smearing her cheeks. It takes another five minutes of half-answered questions—Where was she last night? What's with the suitcase?—before Claire can get to explaining what she needs.

"No problem," Andrea says, her hair in a tangle.

She crushes the now empty can and lets it fall to the mess on the floor.

Claire opens her laptop and calls up the email and forwards it to Andrea. She remembers Reprobus's hesitation to speak in his office—she remembers what Miriam said about the Wi-Fi network on campus—but at this point, as she sees it, there is nothing to lose.

Andrea has powered up her computer and pulled back her hair into a ponytail. She pinches her mouth now into a button when Claire asks what she's going to do. "So let's say I am at Taco John's and tapping into their Wi-Fi. That means I get an IP address from them. I then send an email from Taco John's—and you get it. To figure out where it came from, you can just go all the way down the email and figure out the first received. That's the one that's farthest down. So I can look at that IP address—in this case 75.402.157.195—and it will correspond with the location."

"So do it."

"I was about to. Until you annoyingly made me explain all of that."

"Do it."

"I'm doing it." Her hands hover over the keyboard.

"What?"

Her tongue makes a hesitant clicking sound

against the top of her mouth. “Of course, if the person didn’t want to be found, they could easily spoof this without trying too hard. It’s like a pay-phone analogy. Telecom can tell you the incoming number and where the phone is with that number as far as their records know. Doesn’t mean I can’t unbolt the pay phone and call from some other place in town.”

“How do we know if it’s a spoof?”

“I can tell you whether this IP exists or not, and if it does, you can tell me whether the location makes sense.”

She opens up a website called IP2Location and plugs in the address and a Starbucks in Tacoma pops up.

“That’s it,” Claire says. “That’s the right location.”

Andrea asks if Claire has anything more and Claire says not really. “Just a video.”

“Show me.”

Andrea downloads both the discs and converts and compresses them through a program called Prism and opens them in two small windows and watches them simultaneously, dragging her cursor across them—pausing, jogging back, jogging forward, pausing again.

When Puck's hand appears in the foreground of the video and rakes the air, she says, "That's really fucking creepy."

She asks repeatedly for more information and Claire tells her she can't. Not because she doesn't trust her, but because if she shared any more, they would both be in danger. "Right now, you're just helping me decipher a video. Nothing illegal about that."

Andrea stares at her for a long few seconds. "Look at you, all black ops and shit." She readjusts her scrunchie. "Fine."

She opens up Google. Plugs in "Tacoma, motels." Dozens of listings pop up. She switches over to maps. The screen turns half-blue with Puget Sound, the Tacoma area fingering into it, lined white and black with roads. Orange dots indicate the many motels sprinkled throughout the city. "She's near freshwater. So we can eliminate most of these."

"How do you even know she's near water?"

Andrea drags the bar at the base of the video and halts on a still frame of Miriam pumping out a set of pull-ups on the playground equipment. She jacks up the zoom 300 percent and drags the screen until it fills with a mass of sagging green branches, one of many weeping willows that edge the park. "Duh."

Andrea says her aunt looks ripped but still probably wouldn't run more than ten miles at a time, right? Not in this kind of weather?

Claire says she can't say for sure. Her aunt is an unusual woman.

"We'll start there anyway." Andrea narrows the motels down to eleven based on their nearness to rivers and lakes, almost all of which butt up against parks. She switches over to satellite view and drops down to street level. Here is a motel called the Dew Drop Inn with a concrete porch and yellow-brick walls. Then the Tacoma Inn. The Rainier Inn. The Cascade Motel. No, she says. No. No. Nope. She rushes up to a cloud's point of view and then down to a sidewalk so quickly, trampolining from address to address.

In this way Andrea eliminates every hotel except for three that don't have satellite feeds. "Guess we'll do it the old-fashioned way."

She switches her iPhone to speaker and plugs in one phone number, and then another, asking the clerks how many rooms they have—seven the number she's looking for—unless they have more than one building?

Claire realizes her teeth ache from steadily clenching her jaw. She is ready to give up when Andrea calls the last number, the Bigfoot Motel.

A voice clawed out by cigarettes answers and Andrea asks how many rooms they have.

"Available or total?" the voice says.

"Total."

"Seven."

Claire feels something come to life inside of her then, like those ink-wash clouds flickering with electricity that sometimes hung over Wisconsin and boiled into something significant or dispersed into a wash of gray tendrils.

"What does your motel look like?"

"What do you mean what does it look like? It looks like a motel."

"Is it brown?"

"Yeah, it's brown. What do you care what color it is?"

"I love brown motels, okay? They're awesome. And you're near some woods?"

"Yeah. You love woods too?"

"Yes, I love woods. Can you by chance list off who is staying with you presently? Pretty please?"

"No."

Claire leans in to the phone and says, "Has anybody checked out on you unexpectedly? Like, in the past week or two?"

"That happens so often I can't even tell you. You want a room or not?"

Andrea severs the connection and highlights the address. "That's it. Bigfoot Motel."

Claire reaches out a hand, open palmed, and Andrea slaps it. The sound hangs in the air and then they say, at the same instant, "Thanks," and "You're welcome."

"You know I used to think you were dumb?" Claire says.

"You know I used to think you were a prude snob bitch monster?"

Claire smiles, but the smile dies, any good humor distracted by a yellow ignition within her no different from lightning. Everything suddenly feels like a double: the two fingers, the two videos, the two names she answers to, the sun and the moon, the infected and the uninfected, the United States and the Republic, the president and his contender, Matthew and Patrick, Reprobus and Miriam. She feels—the world feels—split down the center.

CHAPTER 49

PETER DRIVES TRUCK. Most of the time he works for Amazon, hauling containers packed tight with books and DVDs and clothes and whatever junk people buy online, but sometimes he does independent contracting and sometimes that means hauling from the trains or the docks. A few years ago, for forty-four grand, he bought his own truck, a 2007 Freightliner, a Columbia 120, big white dinosaur—dwarfs his house when he parks it out front—with gray smoke tendrils stenciled along the side. Ten-speed transmission, air-ride suspension, double-bunk sleeper, 515 horsepower, and rear-axle capable of hauling forty thousand pounds. He's got more than half a million miles on the odometer, mostly statewide miles, but the thing looks brand-new. He waxes it, even talks to it sometimes when running a rag along its monstrous grille, picking the bugs out of its teeth.

They called him. Said they found his number on the independent truckers site. Said they wanted him to haul a container due on the docks November 1, day after the trick-or-treaters scuzz up the streets with their candy wrappers and the pumpkins on porches sink inward like old toothless men. Drop-off point, an Olympia address, maybe 120 miles roundtrip. Yeah, he could do it, no problem.

It was an easy job, they said, and they were right. Funny thing was, they didn't pay like an easy job. Three Gs for three hours' worth of work. He was quiet after he heard that, and the voice on the other end of the line, as high-pitched as the shriek of an air brake, said, "We would appreciate your discretion." He knew not to ask questions. He could use the green. That's why he got into the independent contracts after all, sometimes putting in sixty hours a week or more. He had his eye on one of those HD LCDs at Walmart. The picture on those things, better than real life.

But a part of him can't help but wonder, when he latches onto his rig the orange rusted container still smelling like the ocean, when he raises a hand through the open window to wave at the controller, when he grumbles up to speed and passes the squad cars always waiting outside the security checkpoint for random screenings, if he might be in over his head. His GTW was under ten thousand pounds, a light load. He could be hauling a bomb; he could be hauling whores; he could be hauling a hundred bricks of black-tar heroin for all he knew. And if he got pulled over? His ass.

He snaps off the CB so that he can think and lays

down the hammer, hoping to get this job done and the bird home to roost before *Monday Night Football*. This is the end of the day—just after five, just after the docks close down for the night and the union foams up the bars with their beer pitchers and whiskey chasers—and the sun has already sunk from the sky. The wind picks up, and when the wind picks up, he feels it, the truck knocked around by the big gusts so that his wrist starts to ache from constantly readjusting the wheel.

He's got GPS in the rig but called up the address on MapQuest earlier, a gravel lot near a wrecking yard out in the boonies. The voice warned him about the chain-link fence but promised him the gate would be unlocked—and it is, the deadbolt yanked open, the hook of it like a talon. The place is maybe a quarter acre, the wrecking yard to one side, thick woods around the rest of it, trash caught up in the fencing, empty except for a few trucks and cars parked with the weeds growing up around them. He bumps through some puddles from yesterday's storm and decides here is as good a place as any.

He kills the engine, climbs out of the cab, shoves his fists into the small of his back and massages the hurt, like a bunch of watery marbles shoved between the chinks of his vertebrae, that grows steadily worse year after year and sometimes makes getting out of bed in the morning a goddamn curse. A sodium-vapor lamp buzzes over near the wrecking yard. The air is unseasonably warm, fine for a T-shirt, maybe even a little sticky. The pressure system has shifted; something is blowing through, which usually means trouble.

It's then that he hears—or thinks he hears—a shifting in the container. Though it's hard to tell, with the wind gusting and the weeds rattling and the gravel crunching under his boots. He pauses where he stands and leans toward the container and waits a long minute.

There it is again, a rasping, like a file drawn across metal.

He's read stories in the papers about sex workers shipped over from Russia asphyxiating into a tangle of swollen blue bodies. He hopes he's not part of something like that. He hopes he hasn't gotten himself into some shit.

He knows he should gun his way out of here, put the container in his rearview, but his curiosity gets the best of him. He makes his way to the rear and unbolts the lock. His hand grips the handle for a long, white-knuckled thirty seconds and then he says fuck it and swings open the door and inside finds tall stacks of cardboard boxes.

Their labels, from a medical supply company, read IODINE. A narrow corridor inky with shadow runs down their middle. He calls out, "Hello?" and feels like one of those idiots from the horror movies who ends up descending into the creepy basement when really they ought to be running to their car, slamming the locks, smashing the accelerator.

He keeps a penlight on his key chain and he clicks it on now. It gives off a weak white glow. He hoists himself into the container and works his way forward. He walks sideways, sucking in a pillow-size gut, and still barely fits, his body rasping against the cardboard. As he guessed, the container has a false wall, maybe ten feet short of the end. He knocks his fist against it and it makes a hollow bong and again he says, "Hello?" He doesn't like how big and tinny his voice sounds in here, like it belongs to somebody else. He jogs the flashlight along the wall and peers around the boxes and spots to his left a slight square recess, what he believes to be a sliding door.

Part of him feels creeped, but another part of him feels convinced that on the other side of that wall he's going to find a cabin full of sluts like he sometimes chats with online, all tattoos and purple lace underwear and dark roots showing beneath their blond dye jobs and stretch marks marbling their double-D implants. This is enough to motivate him through the next five minutes of hoisting boxes—each at least twenty pounds and rattling with what sounds like pills—to the open end of the container. He breathes hard, soaks his shirt through with sweat, and scolds himself, as he does every day, for not getting more exercise. Maybe with the rest of the money he'll buy one of those Bowflex things from the infomercials, set it up in front of the new big-screen, rip out some sets while watching *SportsCenter*. He imagines himself with the etched, veiny body of one of those actors on TV and he imagines next to him, staring at his new figure admiringly, one of those Russian sluts in purple lace that might be waiting for him beyond these few inches of metal.

A space has been cleared; the waist-high door has been revealed. He can hear his breath whistling through his nostrils and tries to calm it. He slaps the door twice, waits. When he hears no response, he crouches down and presses his ear to it. The metal is cold against his cheek. Maybe he hears something, but maybe it's just the wind gasping outside.

He gives the door a tentative push. It gives way and creaks open. He smells something feral, like deer pellets and wet dog hair and ditch water gone stagnant. At first he can discern only a black square. He holds out the penlight and tries to battle back the shadows. Then he hears a shuffling as something advances, a figure that looks, moving from darkness into light, as if it is emerging from a half-developed photograph.

"My God," he says. It is the last thing he ever says.

The light sputters out. Thunder mutters. Wind hisses. It carries the smell of Puget Sound, the reek of algae glopping the docks and the seaweed strewn along the rocks like clumps of hair pulled from drains. Somewhere, a rusty hinge cries out, a door slams. A plastic bag twists by, skittering along the gravel and then hurled into the sky, where clouds churn. The world seems to be vibrating.

A black Ford Expedition has pulled into the gravel lot and Jonathan Puck and Morris Magog have stepped out of it. Puck stands with his arms crossed and Morris holds by the hook a freshly tailored suit that next to him appears as if it might fit a child. His long red hair and his black leather duster sway with the rising wind.

They can hear a noise. The noise of something moving in the container. Footsteps that against the metal floor bang like hooves. And then the figure appears—a man, an older man—naked and painted in blood. But he does not grunt wildly or cover himself modestly. He appears perfectly in control of himself when he drops down and walks toward them with his posture erect and a smile beginning to form on his face. One of his eyes is ruined and the other unused to the light, the pupil dilated, black like a speck of ash. “At long last,” he says.

Puck bows his head slightly when he says, “Master.”

CHAPTER 50

PATRICK SITS upon the skull, as solid as stone. A few minutes ago he finished eating the gamey meat cooked to a char by Pablo and now he can think more clearly. He did not come halfway around the world and sign away his life for four years to die or become indentured to a mutt like Austin. His father is not capable of helping him. He is broken in more ways than one. That is clear to Patrick, and for now their roles have been reassigned: he will make the decisions.

So though he might want more than anything to shrink himself down to a black speck absent of any thought or will and let the wind carry him away to some other location where he might take root and start over, he knows he needs to act. He thinks about running, bolting from his seat, seeing how far he can make it, but he realizes that beyond the reach of the fire, inside the cave, where days become one endless night, other senses take over—smell, touch, especially hearing—and these men know the dark and know this space and will pursue and overtake him readily. So he will have to find another way.

"Dad?"

His father does not shift his gaze from the fire when he says, "What?"

"I know about Mom."

"I figured that might happen."

"And I know about what you were doing."

His father looks at him then, and his eyes seem to brighten, though it could simply be the fire's reflection.

"How far are we from Tuonela, Dad?"

His father's voice hardly registers as a whisper, and Patrick isn't sure if he says, "Not so far" or "Not so fast." He reaches into his breast pocket then and fumbles out a black moleskin notebook. "Here. Take this."

Patrick tucks it into the same pocket that holds the printed, folded-up sheets he brought from the base. "If I could help, Dad. What else could I do? What should I do? To help?"

His father leans toward him, but jerks back when Austin says, "What are you talking about?" He sits away from the fire, his back propped against the wall, a ceramic jug resting beside him. "No secrets." His mouth hangs open and a filament of spit hangs between his lips. "No secrets, not here."

Patrick stares into the fire and feels something combust inside him, as if his chest were a wet bale of straw with smoke billowing from it. Soon he will be ablaze.

Austin clears his throat with a cough. He is filthy, yet he neatens the wrinkles out of his sleeve now and plucks from it a hair or a pine needle. "You're not going anywhere, you know."

"I won't tell."

"Maybe, maybe not. Can't risk it."

"I won't tell."

"Saying it twice don't make it true."

"I can take my father off your hands. I can send word to your families that you're still alive. You can trust me."

Austin uses two hands to take a pull from the sloshing jug. Spirits likely stolen from some outbuilding or back porch. "Can't trust nobody. The world is a sewer of lies. We're all up to our necks in the sweet shit of it." Here he raises his pointer finger and his voice takes on a high, halting quality, mimicking the current president. "We're rebuilding a road—we're bombing a compound. Lycans can live responsibly if given the chance—lycans must be choke collared and medicated and treated like the dogs that they are. All men are created equal—but lycans are not men. They are and are not of the same species, so the same rights do not apply."

"Letting me go would be the right thing to do."

"Your father always said you were never a good listener. This is what you need to start getting through your head: we're in the same hole now. I didn't invite you here. You showed up."

Patrick can think of a hundred wrong things to say but doesn't. For a minute the only sound is that of the fire snapping and pitch pockets popping. Ash spins upward and Patrick follows it with his gaze and sees that the skylight still glows. He could have been here an hour or a hundred hours for all he can tell.

Pablo says, "You going to hog that thing all day? Pass the jug around, show some manners."

Austin takes another pull and rises with a double snap of his knees. He tries to hide it, but Patrick notices him stagger on his way to the fire. His clothes droop off him as if he were a hanger. The seat of his pants has been mended with a wide patch of fur and it gives him a diaperish look.

Patrick takes a quick inventory of his surroundings. His father is watching him. The black man's chest is rising and falling with the rhythms of sleep. The M57 is tilted against the wall with no one there to guard it. Austin plops the jug into Pablo's lap and announces he's going to take a leak and trips twice on his way to the edge of the chasm with the bridge reaching across it. A moment later, the sound of his piss splattering into the void.

"Patrick?" his father says.

"Yeah."

Pablo guzzles from the jug and scrunches up his face and shivers away the taste.

"You want to help?"

"Yeah?"

"Do what I've been telling you all along. Find Neal."

Pablo wipes his mouth with his wrist and passes the jug to Patrick. The jug is ceramic, the size of a milk jug, a two-toned brown spotted with guano. Its mouth is as wide as his own and the odor of spoiled potatoes comes from it. He feels sickened. He feels the snow of the Republic weighing him down and he feels the darkness of the grave pressing around the fire and infecting his vision so that there seems to be no separation between the living and the dead, a child born with a mud wasp's nest for a heart and its eyes already pocketed with dust, ready to be clapped into a box and dropped down a hole.

Patrick asks, in as calm a voice as he can muster, whether he can bum a cigarette.

Pablo fingers the pack in his pocket. "I don't know, man. Only got a few." Then he hands one over anyway.

Patrick burns its tip in the fire and then pinches it between his lips and sucks until the cherry brightens, taking care not to breathe in any of the smoke, knowing he will cough.

He looks at his father then, who nods and reaches down to claw his hands into the black sand. "Hey," he says, "get a load of this," and when Pablo looks at him curiously he flings two fistfuls into his face.

Pablo bring his hands to his eyes and Patrick grips the jug by the neck and leaps over the sitting stones and stumbles ten paces to where the M57 waits for him.

His father is dragging himself around the fire, toward Pablo, trying to get to him before it is too late. But it is too late. Pablo blearily reaches for his spear and lashes out with it, catching Patrick's father in the face with it, then the base of his neck, then his chest, stabbing, stabbing. His father, who has seemed all this time an apparition, now bleeds and screams, terribly alive in this final moment.

But Patrick cannot stop. He can hear the footsteps pounding toward him and by the time he pulls the rifle to his shoulder, it is almost too late. Austin's face is a rictus of startled fury, his teeth bared and already bleeding. He does not move smoothly, the transformation shuddering its way through him, as if he is succumbing to some toxin. His arms are outstretched to draw Patrick into the kind of crushing embrace that would snap his ribs and branch them through the pink pits of his lungs.

If the safety were engaged, Patrick would have been dead. But Austin is no longer subject to protocol. The trigger snaps. The rifle quakes. Orange light spits from the barrel. Two rounds knock the lycan back just as he reaches the end of the muzzle. The cave fills with a thunderous crack that bottoms out into a fluttering rush that Patrick at first mistakes for the blood rushing to his ears.

But he is wrong. It is the bats.

They have been startled from their slumber and now darken the air and make a wind with their wings. Their high-pitched screeching is all around him. They are everywhere, an unstable shadow fallen from the ceiling, and he tries to fight his way through them. They batter his body and scratch at his skin and he ducks down and hurries forward. In his panic he nearly hurls the jug and fires the rifle wildly into them. He thinks he is headed for the bridge but feels lost in a black current, uncertain which way to swim to find the surface. The cave floor is uneven with bones and bedding and the occasional ankle-turning stone. He can hear the scuffling and low-throated screaming of the others and guesses that they pursue him and knows that if he faces them they will no longer be men.

He nearly steps into the chasm. At either end of the bridge, two ironwork poles jut from the stone and anchor it in place. He walks directly into one of them, the impact like a fist to the gut that sends him reeling sideways, and there it is, the edge, the yawning darkness beyond it. He steadies his balance and clambers onto the bridge and though it pains his shoulder he hurls down the jug and it shatters and splatters its foul contents across the boards.

Somehow he has managed to keep the cigarette nipped between his lips this whole time. He steps back to the swaying center of the bridge and, with the bats now swarming above and below and to either side of him, he hurls the cigarette and prays, prays, prays for the spark and the *foomp* that finally comes and spreads with a great gasp of blue flame that sends him staggering back. The bats churn away with a collective shriek, some of them too late, their bodies alight and crisping to ash even as they try to outfly the burn.

At the far side of the bridge, Patrick turns back just in time to see that the timbers and the ropes have caught and risen into a chest-high door of fire. Through it crashes a lycan, Austin. One hand is pressed to his chest where blood pumps and the other steadies his balance against the blazing ropes that he seems not to feel. Fire creeps up his legs, up his torso, but the anger or the adrenaline masks the pain and he continues forward until Patrick empties a round into his face. He collapses and the charred boards crumble against his weight and his flaming body continues downward with a comet's tail into the chasm that turns out to be four times as deep as it is wide.

This evening a pile of dead dogs burns on the central quad. Three men wearing pillowcases over their heads unloaded the carcasses, splashed them with gasoline, and set them aflame before tearing off in a pickup with no plates.

Claire can see the heap of blackened remains—and the groundskeepers surrounding it—from the dormitory laundry, a first-floor room with six machines lining the walls and a tile floor slippery with spilled soap and two windows looking out into the darkness with snow falling like translucent shreds of rice paper.

She has her earbuds in and listens to an NPR podcast about how the lycan demonstrations will affect tomorrow's presidential election. Darrell West, a political analyst, predicts record turnouts and a rout for Chase Williams. "He's got it. I think he's got it. And I also think we need to be very, very careful about the backlash that could come of this—from both sides. *Some* lycans may be pushed into aggression—and *some* nonlycans may feel they have been granted permission to, to, to—let's say—behave unkindly."

She does not understand people—whether infected or clean—for their capability and appetite for violence. No other organism besides a virus seems so hungry to savage everything in its way. Violence defines humanity and determines headlines and elections and borders, the whole world boiled down to who hits whom harder.

She hates how poisonous she has become in her thinking. But these past two days, since she received the package, she has felt her vision blacken at times to a level only the blind would comprehend. Everything seems overwhelmingly dark, as if her side of the world has spun away from the sun and paused in its orbit. She might go mad if not for Matthew.

He will not let her go unless he goes with her. To this she has agreed, with reluctance but also with the sweet relief of someone starved biting into a pie. He needs this day to get his affairs in order. They will leave the next morning. Now she is doing their laundry on the lower floor of the dorm.

Only five thirty and already full night. It gets dark so early now. She misses the sun. Despite the ugliness of her circumstances she finds herself smiling slightly at the sight of their colored clothes mixed up in the wash with a scoop of detergent sanded over the top.

She lets the lid to the machine fall with a bang and at that moment a shadow slides by the window. She only catches a sideways glimpse but it is enough to make her put a hand to her mouth.

Slowly she approaches the window. Behind her the washing machine hisses full of water and then gurgles and lurches alive. Through the weakly falling snow she sees him, maybe ten paces away, his back to her. Spotlighted by a cone of yellow light thrown by a security lamp. He is watching the groundskeepers as they chip and dig at the dogs with shovels, load their remains into black plastic bags.

It is him. She knows it is him. She doesn't understand why—she can't understand what she has that he wants—but after all this time, he has found her. In her mind's eye, she sees him where he stands—wearing a black knee-length peacoat dusted with snow along the shoulders, his hatless head an inflamed pink—and as he was more than a year ago, a lean black outline stenciled against the night her parents died.

He stands as still as the lamppost beside him and she feels certain that any second now he will turn on his heel and observe her framed in the window and reach into his coat and withdraw a pistol and from it bullets will blast and trace through the black air with lines of light like gold wires.

Instead he reaches down and scoops up a handful of snow and packs it into a snowball. But instead of throwing it, he takes a bite of it, as if it were the peeled white pulp of an apple. Then continues along the path toward central campus.

She blinks and breathes for the first time in a long time. Maybe he is not here for her after all. Maybe he is here for all of them—like some black-hooded specter shredding a scythe through wheat. Either way, she should run.

She retreats to the washer and lays her hand on it for support and feels its shushing and whispering work its way up her arm and all through her, the whispering of her parents ripped through by bullets, the whispering of Miriam, who holds out a mangled hand absent two fingers, and of Jeremy, who paces in his cell, ready to take a needle full of poison, the whispering of everyone who huddled in the central quad and stared into the cameras and dared the government to crack down on their rights. She hears the whispering and it tells her to chase the Tall Man down and knife his spine or neck. Open him up and spread him around.

But he is twice her size and she knows his breast bulges with a nylon holster.

Still, she cannot stay here, cannot simply hide. Every nerve in her body says no, but she ignores good sense. She needs to know why he has come. If for her, and that must be the reason, then at least she will know. She will know where he is and she will know what he wants. Knowing will make her more powerful than cowering in her room.

She leaves the laundry and pushes out the door, where she loses her breath to the cold and almost turns back for her coat upstairs. She doesn't have the time, she knows, so she hurries forward in sneakers and sweatpants and a hoodie, pulling the hoodie over her head for warmth and camouflage. She keeps her face down, pretending to look at her feet, though her eyes strain upward, tracking him, waiting for him to sense her and swivel on his heel. She imagines him pointing at her, his mouth widening, an alarm blaring from it—and from all around campus droves of men in black Kevlar will swarm toward her.

No stars. The sky churns with big-bellied clouds that look as if they might snow soot. It is early evening and the walkways are busy with students heading to dinner. When he threads between them,

Claire expects them to turn and look at the Tall Man, recognize the enemy among them, but they seem not to notice. A suited adult on a college campus is nearly invisible—a professor, an administrator, an irrelevance.

She isn't sure, but he might be whistling. The farther they walk, the more she regrets following him. The more she feels as if she is underwater. She feels as if she is underwater in a dark river and a current is muscling her deeper and deeper, an undertow that will press her against the muddy bottom and hold her there until she dies. What can she possibly accomplish—an unarmed girl in sweatpants?

There is a windmill stabbed into the hillside over campus. She can see it now, its red light blinking through the snow. It belongs to William Archer and she remembers during orientation hearing something about how it supplied six million kilowatt-hours of energy, nearly a third of what the campus needs every year. She walked up there once, just for the sake of walking, and at its base she could hear the electricity coursing through the stanchion.

She slows her pace when he takes a sharp right onto the walkway that leads into the administrative building, Skinsheer Hall, a limestone rectangle with a domed rotunda. He climbs the stairs two at a time and swings open the heavy oaken door, which sends the snow whirling and thunks closed.

She approaches the short stone stairs that lead into the building. In the snow she can see his footsteps leading to the door and stands where he did a moment ago. The tip of his toe reaches another five inches beyond hers. She pauses here, uncertain how far she is willing to go, when one of the windows darkens briefly with a silhouette.

She makes certain the walkways are empty, then climbs past the hedges and tries to ignore the snow that bites and numbs her ankles. She creeps up to the window that glows with orange light. She is just tall enough to peer in between the two rich red curtains that frame the glass.

She sees a tall wooden bookshelf neatly arranged with leather-bound volumes and curiosities such as an antique train and a shiny brass clock and a magnifying glass with what looks like a polished bone handle. And then a face appears before her so suddenly she almost screams.

It is Francis, the blond boy from her class. She is about to run when she realizes that he cannot see her, that the light inside reflects off the window, making it into a mirror. He is studying his reflection. She stands perfectly still when he leans into the glass and picks at a pimple on his chin. He stubbornly works at it until it bursts and bleeds.

With a look of contentment on his face, he wipes at it, smearing the blood.

Then he startles and turns. He has heard something, a knock at a door she cannot see. He vanishes from his place at the window and now she can take in the rest of the room, a wide wooden desk squatting at the far end of it and facing outward. Here sits a man—one of the deans, she realizes, a short, white-haired man who always wears brown suits that bunch at the ankles and billow loosely around his middle—and he stands now to hold out his hand.

The Tall Man steps into view and the two of them do not shake hands so much as they grip each other forcefully. Then the dean pulls his hand away and tucks it into his pocket. They begin to talk. She is not certain what they say, but she can guess, from their stonelike expressions, from the way the dean seems to shrink inside his own skin, that it is nothing good.

Francis passes by the window again, still fingering the popped zit and speaking now on his cell phone. She does not feel particularly surprised at his presence here: he has always felt to her more shadow and bone than flesh and blood. He is an informer. She can hear his voice more clearly and makes out the words *imminent* and *campus shutdown*.

That is enough to send her racing into the night. Midway across campus she observes the windmill. Even now, from several hundred yards away, she can hear the hum, along with the blades *whir-whir-whirring* as they cut the air. A red light blinks a warning.

CHAPTER 51

THE EXECUTION WILL take place at eight p.m.—the very minute the presidential polls close.

The tribunal that convicted Saber deliberated less than an hour before recommending he be put to death. The defendant's remorseless courtroom monologue—in which he questioned who the real monster was and demanded that lycans rise up against the American war machine—only convinced the tribunal that they made the right decision. The judge was permitted to reduce the death penalty to life without parole, but he did not. He imposed the sentence—and now, on this November evening, with ice in the air and stars in the sky, with no possibility of an appeal or stay of execution, the sentence will be carried out.

After the verdict was imposed, Jeremy was transferred thirty miles south of Denver, to the supermax detention center, a white-roofed, brick-walled structure with a lake of asphalt around it that spreads into brown-grass plains.

The crowd began gathering earlier that day, soon after the president released a statement that said, "Saber met the fate he chose for himself nearly a year ago. The matter will soon be concluded, and then our country can move on." At first a few dozen people appeared, and then twice as many, and then twice as many more, every few minutes another vehicle pulling in, until the visitors' lot was full and the cars and trucks began to park along the road they followed in from US 67. Some wore William Archer sweatshirts and some carried signs that read RESISTANCE NOW and BETTER DEAD THAN DRUGGED.

By lunch the guards had arranged themselves in a wall between the protesters and the facility. They wear riot gear—black hard-shell armor, goggles, helmets, pistols at their belts—and they hold their rifles diagonally before their chests. And by dinner a long line of squad cars, with their blue and red lights flashing, pressed through the crowd and parked in a defensive line and asked everyone, through a loudspeaker, to disperse. No one did.

At seven thirty, they begin to stomp. One foot and then the other. As if they are trying to kick their heels through the asphalt they stand upon, as if they are trying to crack the very shell of the earth. They know the noise can be heard for many miles, can be heard through the cement walls, can be heard by Jeremy Saber when he is escorted by the priest and the two guards down the long hall to the glass-walled execution chamber, his ankles and his wrists bound by hinged cuffs. Their stomping keeps its cadence, like the drumbeats that precipitate war, and when a few minutes later Jeremy is strapped into the chair and a stream of drugs is administered through a needle in his right leg, the noise will still be in his heart.

He found them online. Or maybe they found him. He was mouthing off in one of those Internet chat rooms when he got the request for a private chat and then one thing led to another and here he is, however many months later, piloting a Cessna single-engine Skyhawk through a rain-swept sky. It is a little hard to process.

His name is Marvin. No one ever remembered his name. He hated that. Hated that he was so forgettable. "You look like the most ordinary person in the world." That's what a girl named Tiffany once told him. He remembered her name. He hated her and for a long time imagined different ways to kill her—pushing her in front of a school bus, slamming her head repeatedly into her locker, strangling her with an athletic sock. He hated her and he hated school. He hated his stupid teachers and the stupid students and the stupid books in which the letters kept moving, crawling all over each other like ants.

But they remembered his name. They treated him like he was somebody. They gave him things. An Xbox, they gave him that. They gave him a gun, a Hardballer .45. For his eighteenth birthday, they gave him a woman. That was nice. Except that she wouldn't kiss him even though she would let him do everything else. So he ended up just putting his mouth over hers and breathing into it. There have been many since then, most recently a black-haired woman whose sharp face makes him think of a bird. They keep her wrists and ankles handcuffed to a steel frame bed. He doesn't mind that she spits, that she tries to bite him when he lies with her. He doesn't mind that at all.

He trained for two months—the medical exam, the forty hours of flight time—and when he learned that it cost three thousand dollars he said he couldn't possibly pay for that and they said not to worry. They would take care of him. He would never have to pay for anything again. That was nice. He had trouble reading the books, so they read the books to him. That was nice too, being read to. It made him feel like he was their child, like they were his parents. He could remember what he needed to remember—about ground check and throttling to two thousand rpm and checking your magnetos and suction and oil pressure and all that—but he had trouble putting the letters down. They had a copy of the test and they made him practice it over and over again until he got it right. When he got it right, they told him he was smart and he liked that. It was nice. He had never smiled so big in his whole entire life.

Everyone talks about Balor. Balor this, Balor that. He isn't sure what to believe, but he likes to believe it all. That Balor punched a hand through a chest and tugged out a heart and took a bite of it like an apple. That Balor could rip a tree from its roots. That Balor could see things with his dead eye that others could not, could see right into your soul and know whether you believed or did not believe, so you had better believe. And he, Marvin, believed.

The engine whines and the propeller spins in a gray blur. He cruises along at eighty ktas with his hands tight around the yoke, trying to hold steady and correcting against light turbulence, keeping his eye on the directional and elevation, everything thrown off by the heavy payload he's carrying. Yesterday, they unbolted the seat and filled the belly of the plane with C-4. A postdoc chemist made the $C_3H_6N_6O_6$ in their basement lab, where they mixed the powder with water to make a slurry and then polyisobutylene to bind it and then they sucked out the water by drying and filtering and then added a plasticizer to make it gummy and the end result wasn't so different from a bunch of gray Play-Doh. Marvin watched all this and understood it because science is something he understands so much better than those dumb novels and poems and plays his dumb English teacher is always assigning and talking about breathlessly as if they mattered and people didn't spend all their time watching TV anyway.

At the moment of ignition, the C-4 releases nitrogen and carbon oxides that expand at more than twenty-six thousand feet per second and knock flat and rip to pieces anything and everything within its reach. Less than a pound of C-4 can reduce several people to meat. A little more than a pound can open up a truck like a soup can. In the fuselage behind him, he has more than five hundred pounds of clay. That's a lot. That's enough to tear a hole in the fabric of the universe.

They taught him all of this. They taught him so much. They taught him how to veer off his flight plan—from SeaTac to Tri-Cities—after about twenty minutes, when he neared the Columbia River, the timing such that the explosion ought to correspond roughly with the execution. They taught him to cut his lights. They taught him to ignore air traffic and snap off his radio. They taught him to bring the plane down to ten thousand feet and then five thousand and then two thousand feet and press the nose downward and aim for the black mouth of the Columbia Generating Station, at the Hanford nuclear reservation.

They taught him to ignore the fear that might take hold of him—his heart crashing, his body like a drum—and to remember that it would all be over soon. And then he would be in the newspaper. Then he would be a hero. Everyone would know his name. Even Tiffany.

The explosion will have two phases. First, the gases will expand like a terrible wind, but in doing so they will suck everything out of the heart of the explosion, which makes a vacuum. Second, after the initial blast, everything will rush back and create another energy wave. He likes the idea of that. He likes the idea of everything rushing toward him. All that energy channeled inward. For the next few days, months, years, he will be the center of the world.

He asked if many people would die, and they said yes. And he asked if even babies would die, and they said yes. "Sometimes," they told him, "terrible things must be done." Did he understand? He did.

He banks left and makes a yawing motion with the rudder and tries to eyeball the red blinking lights of the power plant over the nose of the plane. Once east of the Cascades, the rain lifted and he can clearly see the Columbia, a great black snake, and the gridwork of electricity next to it, the Tri-Cities, and then, closer by the second, the tiered stacks of buildings and the six steaming cones of the reactors that squat like giant mushrooms. He pitches the nose and reduces power and steadies the throttle as he heads toward them.

They are headed toward darkness. A black bank of clouds piles up on the Cascades. Though it is a moonless night, Claire can discern them from the way they blot out the stars. This is November 6, Election Day, and the clock reads 7:50 and a crumpled Burger King bag lies at her feet and she and Matthew are a few hours out of Spokane, just north of Yakima, crossing the scablands of eastern Washington on their way to Seattle. When she thinks about what is ahead and behind her, when she thinks about Jeremy's execution, the burger she ate goes sour, and she fights the urge to empty the surge in her stomach.

"Why are you doing this?"

"You're in trouble. I want to help."

"Is that your thing? Girl in danger?"

"Maybe."

She makes a show out of rolling her eyes, though he can't see her except by the glow of the dash.

She remembers one time, on a road trip to northern Minnesota with her parents, along Lake Superior, she squatted behind some dunes to pee. After she zipped up she noticed that three white butterflies had already drunk from the moist spot she left in the sand. They were beautiful, but as they drank greedily she wondered if their wings shuddered from pleasure or from poison. She cannot help but feel this way about the two of them, about whatever it is they have, which can't possibly be sustainable. She is toxic. No good comes to anyone close to her.

He keeps jogging through the radio stations, mostly sermons and country songs, hunting for something about the election or the execution. She feels torn in too many directions at once and can only concentrate on the road ahead, on Miriam, on the possibility of finding her. She hears something over the radio, the buzz of a horsefly. Somehow it has survived the cold and stubbornly clings to life. It drones past her head, a greenish blur, and batters the windshield, looking for a way out. Matthew leans forward in his seat and swats at the windshield, missing, sending the fly into a wild buzzing panic. "Leave it," she says.

Outside the window she can make out a browned-grass ditch and then miles of shorn wheat fields punctuated by the clustered lights of farms. The state is so divided, like Oregon, the high desert soon giving way to rain forest, where mushrooms and ferns press upward from the mossy earth. She looks forward to getting there, the greening of a world otherwise gone dun and gray. She reaches out and takes his big hand in hers. “Tell me things are going to turn out okay.”

“Things are going to turn out okay.” He squeezes her hand—and the pressure seems to send all the blood to her chest.

It is then, in a white flash, that the horizon explodes.

Part III

CHAPTER 52

PATRICK IS LOOKING for the woman named Strawhacker. Her eyes are scarred with cataracts, so gray they might have been spun by spiders. But she can see—that's what people say. She can see things others cannot.

This is March—along the Idaho-Oregon border—where Patrick has been stationed the past few weeks at an FOB devoted to cleanup. Nearly five months have passed since, in the Republic, he came staggering back to Tuonela with his boots full of numbing snow, only to find most of the soldiers already departed. "Pack your ruck," the guard told him. "We're going home."

"What?"

"The war is at home."

His first assignment: a Nebraska tent city, outside Omaha, one of hundreds set up to accommodate the newly homeless and to quarantine the newly infected, many of them jeweled in sores and vomiting blood. Then the dead bodies started piling up. Then the riots began. For obvious reasons he hated it there, but the Nebraska sky bothered him more than anything. With no mountains to interrupt it, he felt blotted out, weighted down by its enormous size.

He requested a transfer into toxic cleanup and got it. It was the assignment no one wanted. They sent him home, to Oregon, to the place everyone else had fled, to join more than a hundred thousand cleaners already there. That's what the military called the microbiologists and doctors and botanists and cleanup and construction crews: the cleaners. Many of them—some ten thousand—have since died from radiation poisoning, the gamma-ray intensity and the long-term exposure about as healthy as a shot of mercury to the jugular. Many more have vanished beyond the perimeter, presumed dead from lycan attacks.

This is where he needs to be. This is where he will find what he is looking for, what his father was looking for.

Tonight, in the high desert, the temperature hovers above freezing. Rain falls. Mud sucks at his boots when he tromps the streets of the FOB. The three-acre base was built around a deserted community center outside Ontario—fortified by Hescos and wrapped in hurricane wire—and he is headed outside the gates to a bar called the Dirty Shame. This is where he will find the woman, Strawhacker, who deposits herself there every evening to nurse whiskey and tell the fortune of any who seek her out.

Patrick feels like a fool but cannot help himself. Along I-84, near the security checkpoint, there is a gray-slatted barn that has become a billboard for the lost. Thousands of sun-bleached photos have been tacked to it. They streak in the rain and they flutter and tear away with the wind. People have written across them, in neat block letters, *Need to find my daughter* or *Have you seen me?* or *Worked for Nike* with emails and phone numbers listed. Patrick stapled a note there, too. *Missing*, it read. Beneath this are two names. Susan Gamble is one, Claire Forrester the other.

He has scanned the faces of the survivors—many of them lycans, sick from radiation or disenchanted with the Resistance after several months of living off the grid—who day after day still stagger through the checkpoint. He has tried calling his mother but only gets a recording that says, "This number is no longer in service." He has tried emailing them both, but his messages go unanswered. He is not surprised. With few exceptions, once you step inside the Ghostlands—that's what the media are calling it, the Ghostlands—you can no longer rely on electricity or phone service.

The wind rises and the rain blows sideways and he ducks under the dripping eaves of twenty plywood structures of the same boxy design, workspaces of the clerks, liaison officers, battalion, and company staff. SWA huts, GP tents. Then he passes the mess hall, as big as a barn, built as an extension off the community center kitchen. He can hear the KBR contractors inside, clattering pans, tocking their knives across cutting boards, getting ready for tomorrow's breakfast. He holds his breath when he passes by a long row of Porta-Johns. They are stacked next to a tan tent the size of an RV, lit up from within, rowdy with laughter. He hears the snap and riffle of playing cards. Most of the sleeping quarters are like this, canvas topped with rows and rows of racks inside them, rucksacks and weapons littered everywhere. Generators groan. Lights sputter in the community center, home to the labs, offices for tactical planning.

He signs out at the gate and splashes a quarter mile along a heat-cracked county highway to the Dirty Shame, a tavern built into the side of a hill, a long windowless rectangular box of railroad ties with a sawdust floor and a mirror behind the bar with a bullet hole in it. The electricity here can no longer be relied on, so the meager smoky lighting comes from lanterns and candles that sputter and dance when he creaks open the door and peels off his poncho and shakes away the rain and hangs it from an iron hook.

Shavings cling to the mud on his boots. The oven-warm air smells like the creosote and formaldehyde the ties were treated with, the smell powerful enough to make everyone dizzy, along with the beer foaming out of mugs and curling down wrists, the whiskey shots lined up on the bar and slammed back with a gasp. There are thirty or so people drinking tonight, some soldiers, some civilians, who in this tight space give off a lot of heat and noise. He works his way through them to the bar, where he orders a beer and pays without any trouble. ID doesn't matter in a place and time like this.

So many of the rules no longer apply.

Not very far from here, the perimeter fence begins, nearly three thousand miles of hastily constructed hurricane fencing that is practically useless and encases most of Oregon and Washington, some of Idaho and Montana, the length of it staggered with checkpoints and FOBs. Beyond the perimeter, the noise of traffic roaring, televisions blaring, cell phones ringing, Muzak trembling from shopping-center sound systems, all of it has ceased, leaving behind a scary silence.

Coyotes slink through the aisles of Safeway. Elks plod along the streets of Portland. In the fields and in the streets are semis and tanks and planes, rust cratered, the grass growing around them, looking like dinosaurs, fallen and decaying.

The lycans have carved out their own country, abandoning Volpexx, denying the xenophobic laws that in their collective choke collar felt more constrictive than all the prisons in the world, or so they said.

Patrick leans against the bar and drinks, hoping the beer will warm the chill from him. The bartender seems to have no neck, his head balanced atop his rounded shoulders. He wears a moth-eaten cable-knit sweater with the sleeves pushed up to reveal his meaty forearms. He collects two empty pint glasses and wipes the counter with a filthy rag.

Patrick looks beyond the bartender to the mirror behind him. Sometimes he hardly recognizes himself. Head shaved down to skin. Skin as brown as the high desert soil. Body lean, muscles sculpted like carved rock. He looks like a man even when he feels like a kid. He uses the mirror to study the faces around him. A woman with dreamcatcher earrings and a high, shrieking laugh. A weak-chinned man in civilian clothes but with the standard-issue high-and-tight buzz. A Mexican with a handlebar mustache and cheeks pitted from acne. He spots a huddle of men standing around a corner booth, laughing, speaking to whoever sits there.

Patrick asks if that is where he will find the

woman named Strawhacker, and the bartender says indeed it is, and Patrick wipes the foam from his lip before taking a closer look.

The light is so dim that at first he cannot see into the shadowy booth. Then the woman leans forward. Her face is as wrinkled as an old tissue, and her nose filamented with tiny red and purple capillaries. Her gray hair is cut boyishly around her ears. But her eyes are her most striking feature—milky puddles that seem with every blink ready to stream down her cheeks. On the table before her, a whiskey tumbler and a stack of tarot cards.

She is playing some sort of game with the men who stand around her. One of them pulls five dollars from his wallet and lays it on the table. Then he draws a card from the tarot deck, the middle of the pile, and holds it up for the others to study. Strawhacker goes rigid and licks her lips and finally says, “The Magician.”

The men gasp out their laughs and shake their heads and curse good-naturedly and Strawhacker steals away the five dollars and bids them good night and they leave her.

Strawhacker then sips her whiskey and looks at Patrick. They are ten feet apart, and Strawhacker has no eyes, but nonetheless Patrick can feel her dead gaze. His skin tightens into gooseflesh and he takes a step back.

"Where are you going?" Strawhacker says. "Please. Come here. Stay awhile."

Patrick approaches the booth with his beer held like a pistol. The door creaks open as the four men depart the tavern, and he startles at the noise, some of the beer fuzzing over the rim of his glass to chill his wrist. A blast of wind hurries inside and makes the candle flames dance before the door slams shut.

"How did you know what card that was?"

"Just luck, just luck," Strawhacker says and shuffles them with a riffling snap, neatens them into a pile. "Or maybe something more."

The booth, too, is built from railroad ties, every inch of wood scarred from knives, people carving out their names and the names of those they love. There is a chair at the end of the booth and Strawhacker indicates that Patrick should sit there and he does.

"Some people come to me for games and some come to me for reasons more profound. I try to give people what they want." She sweeps the stack aside. "You're not here for games."

"I'm supposed to believe you can see things?"

"You've come here, haven't you? Part of you must believe. Yes, part of you must."

"I don't know what to believe."

"It's hard to know what to believe anymore.

These are strange times. What I've discovered about myself is this: there's a muscle in my brain that stretches open, like an iris maybe, yes, some diaphragm of muscle, and images soar through. It has no discernible real logic—but that's my best explanation—it's a spot to start from."

"You talk like a crazy teacher."

"You talk like an insolent boy." She lifts her face in defiance, her chin protruding farther than her nose. Her voice is lower when she speaks again. "You want to know if I can see? I can see. I can see you colliding with another boy in center field after chasing a pop fly, can see the bone swell that made you limp for three weeks after. I can see you fingering a girl behind your middle school and then not washing your hand for a whole day to preserve that mysterious, intoxicating smell. I can see you shooting your first deer and putting your thumb into the kill wound and tasting the blood. I can see your father running out into a lightning storm to grab your teddy bear forgotten in the yard while you watched from the window. And I can see him now, a dead man in a faraway cave with bats roosting over his bones." Flecks of spit fly from her mouth. "And if you want more from me than that, you're going to have to pay up, like every other asshole."

"God."

"He won't be able to save you. Not where you're going." Then her expression softens and her head tilts, as if she hears something. "What's that book you've got in your pocket?"

Patrick can feel the weight of it now at his breast, his notebook, the one salvaged from the Republic. His father's. He keeps it always in his breast pocket, over his heart, to touch now and then. It seems to pulse, as if made of nerves and muscle. He has always turned to his father to know what to do. Now the book tells him what to do.

"There's something in that book, but I don't understand." Strawhacker holds out her hand, the fingers long and bony, the nails rimmed with dirt. "What's in that book?"

"Shut up about the book. I came to ask you about two people."

"Tell me what's in that book and I'll tell you what you want to know."

Patrick pulls out a wadded-up five-dollar bill and lays it on the table and it vanishes into Strawhacker's hand. "These two people. You want to know if they're alive or dead. One of them is, one of them isn't. That's all I know."

"Some fortune."

"You're planning something. You are. You're going to do something incredibly stupid, aren't you?" She reaches out a hand for Patrick. "What is it you think is waiting for you out there? Beyond the fence? Tell me. Please."

Her hand scrabbles closer and Patrick slams his fist down on it as if it were a spider.

Strawhacker cries out and the tavern goes silent and so many faces swing toward them and the bartender yells, "Hey!" Before anybody can ask a question, Patrick stands and snatches his poncho and shoves his way out the door and allows in the wind that extinguishes all the candles in one rushing breath.

The storm is stronger now. The rain lashes at him, pattering his poncho and needling his skin. He looks over his shoulder often, seeing if anyone follows, half expecting to see the long silhouette of the blind woman loping after him, the silken orbs of her eyes hatched, spiders spilling from the sockets.

He reaches for the book twice, reassured by the weight and pressure of it, as if it might have been snatched away after all. He has learned much from it. First that his father was experimenting with more than a neuroblocker for Volpexx. There are slips of paper printed from websites full of passages about neurodegenerative conditions associated with prions—everything from Creutzfeldt-

Jakob disease to fatal insomnia to lobos—and how they are spread: the consumption of meat, the administration of human growth hormone, and sexual intercourse. There is no cure for prion infection and the pathogen is difficult to destroy, resilient to heat and enzymes.

And there are pages crammed with his small, square handwriting about stock cultures and select agent organisms and the CDC and sodium hypochlorite and on and on, like a language Patrick didn't speak.

And then there was the very last page, ripped almost entirely, only a frayed sleeve of it remaining, on which is written half his Gmail address. His father, he knew, was paranoid. He wouldn't correspond with Patrick through his military account because he thought someone would read their emails. And he constantly changed the passwords on his credit cards, frequent-flier programs, and other accounts because he was certain someone would hack him.

At first Patrick thought nothing of the email address, but something drew him back to it. Then one day, after peeling off his rain-soaked clothes, he noticed that his socks left the red imprint of their stitching on his clam-white foot. He stared at it for a long time before retrieving a pencil and opening the notebook to its second-to-last page and rubbing the graphite softly across it. There were the words already printed there, and then there were other words scarred over the top of them, the residue of what his father had scribbled on the other page. Patrick at first thought this hopeless, the graffiti twist of letters, but then he made out a stack of words with *X*s through them: beer, yeast, California. Passwords. His father couldn't remember his passwords, so he wrote them down. The final word in the column, the only one not crossed out, was his name, Patrick. Patrick was the password.

He had tried to email Neal Desai after he returned stateside, without success, the doctor missing, presumed dead. And he had tried to get the military and Google to hand over his father's email accounts—but they wouldn't until he was confirmed dead and Patrick named his inheritor.

Now he had the password—and it told him what he needed to know. It told him what he needed to do.

He turns again to check the road behind him and this time sees headlights cutting through the rain and steps off the road so that he won't be struck. The vehicle—a van, he can now tell, one of the vans the nurses and EMTs have been using for medevac—slows as it nears him, and he throws out an arm, sticks up a thumb.

Lightning flashes and colors the world a pale

blue. With the afterimage in his eyes and the rain pelting his face, he can hardly see a thing when he yanks open the door. He hears a woman's voice yell, "Get in already," and then, when he shakes off his poncho and pulls back the hood, "Oh."

It takes him a minute. The darkness. The baggy uniform. The rain-swept confusion of the night. And then he notices her red hair, the color of a poisoned apple, chin length and tucked behind her ear. And she smiles, and he knows her, Malerie.

"You," he says. He is halfway into the cab already, his foot on the railing, his hand on the dash, and he pulls back now and steps into the rain. "Second thought, I'd rather walk."

Maybe it is the way she chases after him, maybe it is the way she fiercely apologizes and calls herself stupid, the stupidest person in the world, maybe it is the torrential downpour or the grumbling thunder or his general loneliness or the sick-scared feeling that has followed him from the bar, but he finally says all right, *all right*, and lets her give him a ride back to the base and an hour later he has her propped up on a bathroom sink and is fucking her while staring at his reflection hard in the mirror.

CHAPTER 53

CLAIRE HAS SWEAT through her clothes digging his grave. Now she sits cross-legged against an oak and stares at the hump of dirt with the shovel stabbed into it. The shade offers no relief from the heat. Neither does the canteen of water she gulps, splashes her face with. A cloud of humidity hangs over everything, like the breath of the reactor. A bluebottle fly buzzes languidly through the air and orbits her head before settling on her wrist to drink from the sweat beading there. She watches it a moment, then crushes it with her palm, a smear of blood and black twitching legs.

She could have buried Matthew anywhere—a park, a backyard—but she chose a graveyard. With all the disorder in the world—helicopters stuttering overhead, cars rusting in the streets, neighborhoods burning, birds falling dead from the sky—she liked the order of the place and the act. Burying him here, among his fellow dead and the tidy granite headstones, felt good, felt right.

She found a place on a hill, an empty spread of grass, and stomped the blade of her shovel into it. She took her time—pressing down with her foot, leaning into the handle, sinking the blade into the soil with a slow scuff. Sweat trailed down her forehead and stung her eyes and blurred her vision of the hole growing larger and larger beneath her. The loamy, overturned earth mixed up with the smell of his pungent body. Her hands first blistered, then wept, then bled. After three hours, she had gone three feet. She tried not to look at his body when she dragged it to the edge of the hole, rolled it in with a thud. But she could see, out of the corner of her eye, that he landed facedown, his arm bent at an unnatural angle behind his back. She couldn't let him lie like that for the rest of eternity. She dropped into the hole and, with some difficulty, flopped him over, folded his arms over his chest, where his heart was hidden. The day was hot, but he was as cool as the exposed dirt, and she fought the temptation to shove a gun in her mouth and lie down beside him. She looked at him then—saw his skin graying and swelling around the edges, saw half his face missing as if someone had taken a bite out of it—and the urge passed and she only wanted to cover him up, to forget.

Sometimes Chinook choppers buzz the sky like hornets. Sometimes they drop cartons of Volpexx and sometimes they drop bombs. Sometimes soldiers spill out of Humvees and staple posters to telephone poles and storefronts and garage doors, posters about amnesty and contamination, about what will happen to those who choose to remain behind: imprisonment, a slow death from radiation, a swift death from execution should they engage with any military personnel.

She doesn't need a poster to tell her this. The reminders are everywhere. Bodies sit on park benches. Bodies are buckled into cars. Bodies are curled up on sidewalks. Some of them with blackened skin the wind dusts away, their carcasses nothing more than dried-out husks encasing a bundle of bones. Some of them, more freshly dead, gunshot or clawed up or bright with sores and missing clumps of hair and stinking so badly that she rarely goes a day without retching between her feet.

It is because of Matthew that she is alive and it is because of her that Matthew is dead. Five months ago, when the sky lit up, he drove them directly to the Seattle REI and hurled a rock through the window and ignored the alarm blaring while he shrugged on a backcountry pack and she did the same to fill with iodine tabs and Clif Bars and knives and matches and tents and sleeping bags and aluminum blankets and rain gear. They even got a bicycle rack and two Treks, and when she yelled, "Why?" over the alarm, he said, "For when there's no more gas." He understood it all so clearly, as if their story were a novel and he simply flipped to the end to see what would happen.

They should have left—with the millions of others who sought escape from a ruined world and treatment for their ruined bodies—but they hesitated. Within a day, the gas stations dried up, the freeways gridlocked, clogged with cars, many of them abandoned. The whole world deafened by sirens and horns, gunfire. Soon it was too late: she could not make it through the checkpoints the military established. Matthew could have left but he did not.

Now she is alone. Now he is dead. Now he is buried beneath a mound of black dirt with a shovel stuck in it. She does not cry. Though sweating feels like a kind of crying, her clothes soaked through, her hair plastered to her forehead in damp whorls. When her hair started to grow out blond again, he touched its roots and said, "Why did you hide that from me?" He called it the color of beaten gold, and she called him an English major. When it was long enough, he helped her scissor away the dyed sections of her hair so that she looked like one person, not two.

It happened yesterday. Here in Monmouth. They came from the coast, where Matthew had the idea to steal a boat and sail it north to British Columbia. The beaches were strewn with the reeking carcasses of crab, halibut, sharks, whales thickly netted with flies, poisoned from the Columbia's outflow, and she could see the cutters and battleships floating several miles out that would intercept them.

On the road they met another couple—Ella and Sam, who were like them; there were many like them, lycans who didn't want any trouble, who only wanted to be left alone—and they spent the past week together, sleeping in an abandoned house, a brick ranch, nothing conspicuous. They drank gin and talked books and politics and smoked hand-rolled cigarettes. One morning, while Claire slept off a hangover, Matthew and the others were sitting on the front porch, drinking coffee and reading old magazines, when a chopper passed overhead.

Choppers were always passing overhead and they ignored it. But it didn't ignore them. It spotted the three of them—then lit them up with a chain gun. Target practice. She woke to the rattle of gunfire and then the rotor wash banging closed the front door.

She blames herself for not being beside him. She blames Matthew for being so careless and arrogant. She blames the soldier who manned the chain gun, blames the pilot who hovered the Blackhawk over the house, blames the brass for sending squads into an irrecoverable wasteland, blames the entire U.S. war machine for fencing lycans in, here and abroad, and expecting them to tuck tail. But most of all she blames the Resistance. She blames Balor. Because of him everyone believed that lycans are feral, are capable only of raw animality. Because of him her world has become one big grave.

She pops a few iodine pills and glugs them down with a long pull from her canteen. She knows the iodine can only do so much to defend her, to fight the radiation. She knows that, given enough time to work its way through her system, the radiation will bloom into yellow tumors.

There are other unmarked, freshly dug graves here in this cemetery. And there are unburied bodies, too, maybe the remains of those who dragged themselves here to expire. Again she considers joining them, opening up her head with a bullet. This isn't a new impulse. She thinks often about suicide. A rope around her neck knotted to a garage beam. A dive from the top of a building. A long swim into the ocean. After a momentary discomfort, there would be no more hunger, no more fear, no more running and running and running.

The shovel she used still has a neon-yellow

$19.99 price stickered to it. She was in a fog when she roamed the store, a Bi-Mart at the end of the block, not looking for anything except what she needed: a wheelbarrow to transport his body, a shovel to bury him. She left Ella and Sam where they lay on the porch. She could muster the energy for only one funeral. Now that is done. Now, she supposes, she needs to return to the store. Several times a day she pumps up her back bicycle tire and needs a patch kit for the leak. Ammo, if she can find any. Nuts, granola bars. A new jacket, the one she stole from REI rotted through from the toxic rain.

Finally she stands. For a long time she wavers in place, like a risen corpse, before stumbling down the hill. It feels good to have a job. A purpose. It makes her not think about killing herself. It helps clarify her mind, propel her body. She will leave the graveyard. She will collect her supplies. And then she will, to the best of her ability, find Balor and put a bullet through his eye.

She is near the gated entrance to the cemetery when she hears it—the distant noise of dogs barking accompanied by a high-pitched and unmistakably human scream.

She gave up on her Glock after it jammed twice.

She prefers the reliability, the heft and power, of the .357 Smith & Wesson she pried from a corpse at a kitchen table, a suicide outside Portland, his hand curled so tightly around the stock she had to break his fingers. Everywhere she goes, she takes the revolver with her, carried in a belt holster so that she has a yellow callus along her hip. She withdraws it now.

The graves—marked mostly with crosses, rounded and squared headstones, punctuated by the occasional crypt—rise up the hill. At its summit she spots movement. Someone running. A girl. She wears a white T-shirt several sizes too big, so that she at first appears a billowing phantom. She darts between the graves, zigzagging down the hill.

The barking grows louder. Claire spots them, a tide of dogs—white and gray and brown—plunging down the hillside, chasing the girl. The distance between them closes. Thirty yards, twenty yards, ten. The girl is almost at the bottom of the slope when she risks a look over her shoulder. The dogs are nearly upon her, their barking more frenzied, maddened by the near taste and smell of her.

She realizes the futility of running any farther and clambers up the side of a marble crypt. A Doberman launches itself into the air and snaps its jaws at her dangling feet. But she is too quick. The crypt is six feet tall and topped by a crouching angel and the girl climbs onto its winged shoulders.

This whole time Claire has remained statue still, as if her exhaustion or apathy has created an unbridgeable separation between her and the girl. She came here to say good-bye. Not for this. Not more trouble. But the sight of the girl, maybe ten years old, long black hair falling to either side of her head, surrounded by yapping dogs that tense their hindquarters and flatten their ears and howl for her blood, makes her guts boil with anger. She cannot stop herself. She throws herself toward the crypt, pumping her legs, cocking her revolver.

Now that the girl is out of reach, she watches the dogs calmly, as if they are stuffed animals and not something she needs to fear—until one of them, a big standard poodle, stands up on its hind legs as if to push the crypt over. She screams.

This sends the dogs into convulsions, exciting them even more. They jitter and prance and wag their whole bodies and bawl like some kind of mob hungry for an execution. Claire counts twenty of them—Rottweilers, Dobermans, German shepherds, Labradors, even a wiener dog. Their coats are knotted and filthy and speckled with burs.

Claire skids to a stop ten yards away. "Hey," she says. "Hey, dogs!" At once the whole horde turns to look at her, panting, hesitantly wagging their tails. She wonders if two instincts—loyalty and hunger—fight inside them like a Siamese monster. She doesn't know what to say, so she says, "Bad dogs."

At this some of them peel back their lips, showing their teeth, while others whine and stutter-step forward, as if she were an old friend they hardly recognize.

There are more dogs than there are bullets in her revolver, Claire realizes. She wonders if she can summon the strength, the desire, to transform. She doubts it. With the sweat drying on her skin and her back spasming and her nails rimmed with half-moons of dirt and Matthew only an hour in the ground, she feels impossibly empty.

The poodle, a mud-caked mess of hair, moves toward her, looking at once ridiculous and terrifying.

"Sit," she says. "Sit. Stay. Roll over." But the poodle keeps coming.

She lifts the revolver. It feels incredibly heavy in her hands. The poodle lowers its head and begins a hunch-shouldered charge. Saliva swings from its teeth when it opens its mouth to bite her. She puts a bullet in its leg and it screams in a terribly human way before collapsing and rising again and limping fast and far from her, leaving behind a trail of blood.

At the sound of the gunshot—a whipping crack

that bottoms out and echoes away—the other dogs scatter, diving down rows of graves. They bark and yowl as they thread their way back up the hill, disappearing into the trees that thicken toward its top.

The wiener dog is the only one who lingers, peeking from behind the crypt. Claire holsters her gun and lifts her arms and says, "Yaaaaah!" and the dog releases a tiny stream of pee before trotting off to join its pack.

Claire looks at the girl and the girl looks at her, looks away, and then gets brave enough to maintain a stare. Brown eyes, broad cheekbones, skin the color of upturned earth. Under the giant T-shirt she wears jean shorts, Velcro tennis shoes. Claire raises her hand—the universal sign for *hey*—and the girl does the same. They each manage a small smile. "Speak English?" Claire says.

Her expression does not change and Claire sees in it the same thing she saw in the wiener dog: a mixture of fear and loneliness that at once makes the girl want to rush forward and back away.

"Down," Claire says. "*Abajo*." Or is it *derriba*? She can't remember. High school seems ten thousand years ago. She motions with her hand. "Down. *Down*. Before they get brave and come back."

The girl doesn't move, except her eyebrows coming together to form a silent question: is Claire dangerous?

"*No estoy peligroso*," she says. "No kidding. I'm a good guy. *Yo estoy su amiga*."

"I'm not stupid," the girl says with a soft accent. "I can speak English."

"You a lycan?"

The girl gives her eyes a theatrical roll and says, "I'm Latina," and Claire thinks, *this* is why I hate kids.

"We need to get going."

Except to sneeze into her hands, the girl does not move.

It would be so much easier to walk away, to abandon the girl. Why should she care? Why should she even go on breathing? A part of her wants to whistle the dogs back and lay bare her neck for them to maul.

"Where are your parents anyway?" Claire immediately regrets asking and in her chest gets this jab of dread when the girl scrunches up her face and starts breathing heavily like kids do before they really lose it.

"Forget it." Claire holds up her hands and twiddles her fingers and says, "Come on. Come on already."

After a hesitant moment, the girl scoots her butt toward the edge, dangles her legs, and falls into Claire's arms.

CHAPTER 54

THIS IS WHAT HAPPENED in the seconds after the plane exploded in the belly of the Hanford nuclear facility. The electrical circuit board surged and spit fire. The turbines ceased spinning; the coolant water stopped flowing. The heat spiked. The power surged and caused a steam explosion that caused the containment vessel's caps to evaporate. The control rods and graphite insulating blocks melted. And the radioactive core ignited, creating a blast as powerful as two nuclear bombs that mushroomed upward and pinwheeled cars through the air and burned to ash anything living within a hundred miles and made the moon glow an angry red.

The president declared the Pacific Northwest, and then the West Coast, and then the Plains, a state of emergency. He ordered the citizens of Oregon, Washington, Idaho, and western Montana to evacuate. He did not acknowledge that the polls had just closed, that the media had called the race hours ago. That he had lost. For the moment, that was an irrelevance, as freeways clogged with people driving as fast and as far away as they could.

Clouds boiled over the open reactor. Helixes of flame played across the sky. Lightning uncurled and lashed the ground like white whips. A hot wind blew east and spiked the atmospheric radiation as far away as Michigan.

The same night as the explosion, a video was released on the Internet. In it, Balor and the Resistance claimed responsibility for the attack and declared the Pacific Northwest their own sovereign territory. Lycanica, he called it. He asked others to join them there. And he asked all lycans already in the region to savage their neighbor and in doing so make them a fellow citizen—and to remain in Oregon, despite the radiation, for the greater good.

Five months later, an estimated five million are dead.

Everything has gone splendidly. Everything has gone exactly according to plan. Because of him. Because of him, a new nation has been carved out—with November 6 its Independence Day. It does not bother him that he is surrounded. Fencing, studded with military bases, corrals the borders of Washington and Oregon. Battleships patrol the coastline. Drones knife across the sky with a cut-paper whisper. Bombs sound like distant thunder. They reduce water towers, power stations, to smoldering craters. This is to be expected. So is the economic crisis—the S&P double downgrade, the stock market diving more than four thousand points—that will soon enough result in the retraction of the military. The Ghostlands, they must realize, are a lost cause. The Ghostlands, they will accept, are his.

He debated a long time where to headquarter. The capitol building would be too obvious, a mall or skyscraper too difficult to defend. They considered the Rajneesh compound in Central Oregon but decided it was too far from any resources. They considered a correctional institute in Salem, a squat, mustard-colored building, but he did not want any of his men to read into this a metaphor for what their life had become. He needed them happy. And he needed a city to loot. And he needed a defensible position. And that is why they chose the Pittock Mansion.

It is a twenty-three-room chateau—built in 1914 by Henry Pittock, the publisher of the *Oregonian*—in the West Hills of Portland. Forty-six acres surrounded by wrought-iron fencing that contains the sheep and goats and cattle that now wander the grounds. The walls are made from sandstone and will withstand gunfire. The fireplaces will keep them warm in the winter, the high ceilings cool in the summers. The outbuildings serve as storage for the gasoline they have harvested, for the iodine pills they crush into their meals and water to fight the radiation that brings sores to their skin.

He rolls down the hill now as part of a convoy—three black Expeditions tricked out with brush guards and bulletproof windows followed by a semi hauling a trailer. Despite the heat, he wears a tailored charcoal suit from Brooks Brothers. No tie. His long silvery hair carefully parted down the middle and tucked behind his ears. Next to him sits the giant, Morris Magog, crushed behind the steering wheel. The backseats have been folded down and upon them rest flats full of beans, rice, salsa, candy, granola bars, bags of chips, piles of fresh muskmelons to be distributed to all those who attend this afternoon's gathering at Pioneer Courthouse.

He knows what they say about his eye. That he was wounded by shrapnel, that he was bitten by a snake, that he was poisoned by the military, that he was shot and the bullet passed through his cornea and nested in his brain. The truth is, when he was a boy, his vision began to fog over. Headaches plagued him daily. His mother took him to a doctor in his village, who examined him and told them it was a tumor and he did not have the ability to operate on it. His mother took him to a military hospital and begged their services. They turned her away, and when she would not leave, they struck her face with the butt end of a rifle and then kicked her when she fell. “But he will die,” she told them and they told her, “We know.” That was when his mother began to pray. She prayed when dawn broke and when night fell. She prayed before meals. She clasped her hands together and sometimes held him against her breast when whispering words he could not decipher, some desperate incantation to fight the nosebleeds and then the darkness that eclipsed his eye. One night he woke to find a white figure standing over his bed. There was only a smear where a face should have been. There were only tendrils where fingers should have been. It reached for him—it reached into him, into his face—and there he felt a needle jab of exquisite pain. When the hand retreated, it gripped something black and squirming. He believed this an extraordinary nightmare until the next morning when he woke and could see. Not perfectly, but he could see, his left eye like a dirty window. The doctor told him the tumor was gone. “I do not understand,” he said. “I must have been wrong.”

“By the will of God,” his mother said. By the will of God he lived. He was the will of God. He does not share this with others. He keeps it hidden, like the statue of a saint buried upside down in a backyard. It does not matter that his men believe in God—it only matters that they believe in him.

The Expedition follows the road down the hill and out the gates and through neighborhoods of tightly clustered bungalows, their yards waist-high with weeds and grass gone to seed. He spots snakes sunning themselves on the blacktop, bees swarming out of an open mailbox, a red-tailed hawk picking apart the purplish remains of a cat. He has helped make this happen: the world returning to its natural state.

When a deer bounds out between two houses and skitters to a stop in a driveway, he lays a hand on Magog's wrist and tells him to stop. "Slowly." He unholsters the 9-millimeter at his belt. The window hums when he opens it. He rests his elbows on the sill and closes his dead eye. The deer, a buck with the mere beginning of two velvety horns, stares back at him, twitches an ear, then startles backward when he fires. It makes it ten feet before collapsing. Its legs continue to kick as if dreaming their way to escape. He watches the animal until it goes still. "Throw it in the back," he says. "We'll spit it over the fire." The giant swings open his door and climbs out and the vehicle shakes with his abandoned weight.

Balor holsters his pistol and closes the window and cranks the AC. He feels a pleasant heat spreading through him, a rush of endorphins that makes his mind buzz and his skin prickle. The equivalent, he supposes, of sex. He does not hunger for it the way the others do. He has never visited the woman they keep in the basement, though he is glad she is there to satisfy the others. He gratifies his appetite in other ways. The letting of blood, for him, like the letting of semen. An impulse that satisfies his hunger and his need to dominate and infect, to multiply.

Several hundred of his children will be in attendance today. He knows there are thousands of others spread across the Pacific Northwest and more trying to sneak their way past the border every day. He knows they are afraid. He knows some of them are sick. He knows that they are uncomfortable and inconvenienced by the lack of electricity and running water. He will tell them that their discomfort is only temporary. He will tell them his plans. He will shake every one of their hands and he will look into every one of their eyes and he will tell them not to worry for this is only the beginning.

CHAPTER 55

THIS SIDE OF THE MOUNTAINS, in the high desert of Eastern Oregon, dogs roam freely, broken glass sparkles in the streets, front doors swing open and shut with the wind, freezers leak lines of blood, bodies lay about in various states of decay, as rounded and wooden as their own coffins. As a cleaner, in a radiation suit straight out of Buck Rogers, Patrick and his squad clear roads of abandoned vehicles, drag corpses into piles and light them up with flamethrowers. The reasoning is unclear, the area uninhabitable. But orders are orders.

As is the case with Chernobyl, a concrete sarcophagus now encases the Hanford site, but the damage has been done. Radiation will cling to the Pacific Northwest for thousands of years. Whether a hundred or a thousand or a million years, the president says, it doesn't matter: the United States will reclaim Oregon and Washington one town at a time.

Nobody wants to go out on the wire. Everyone wants sentry duty at the Ontario checkpoint. Keeping the curious and the crazies and the lycan sympathizers out, treating with chemical showers all those who travel within. Hurricane fencing stretches off into the distance. The interstate leading up to the checkpoint is stacked with concrete blockades so that cars must crank their wheel one way, then another, then another, slowing to a crawl before reaching the first security post, twenty yards out. Exiting the Ghostlands takes four stages. First, every vehicle is searched, and then everyone, after which time they are photographed, fingerprinted, questioned—then sent to a dosimeter crew for radiation and blood tests—followed by several hours of detainment in a chain-link pen while their case is considered.

There was a time when the line of cars stretched off into the desert haze, but these days, most everyone who wants to flee has fled, except for the occasional lycan disenchanted after living too long without restaurants, Internet, electricity. Sometimes two or three days go by when no civilians pass through the checkpoint at all.

Everyone likes it this way, likes how peaceful and predictable sentry duty has become, with plenty of time for bullshit and magazines, darts, card games, almost like a vacation, the world so empty here, with the sagebrush flats stretching off into the distance. It is a stark, beautiful landscape, untroubling because it is composed mostly of nothing.

This has made the soldiers on sentry duty lazy, so Patrick is certain he can get away with his plan. And Malerie is going to help him, though she doesn't know it yet.

From his father's email account, he patched together hundreds of pages of correspondence with Neal Desai. He already knew they had gone to college together at UC Davis, both biochem majors, but that was the extent of it. He learned that his father had enlisted around the same time Neal began applying to graduate programs, that his father had taken the job at the brewery around the same time Neal accepted a postdoc fellowship. His father had been experimenting on dogs in his garage while Neal was training a lab of technicians how to inject prions into the brain of a rat. Their children—Patrick and a girl named Sridavi—were around the same age. And both men had a personal stake in their research: they loved the infected.

In one of their emails—which dated back almost two years—his father wrote, "I was thinking about that time we tried to buy beer. You remember that? We glued on beards we bought from the Halloween store. The guy at the liquor store took one look at us and said get lost. We were so depressed. We were so sure we were going to be able to pull it off. I can't stop thinking about those beards. Those stupid glue-on beards. What if the body doesn't have the same careful eye as that guy at the liquor store? We know it doesn't."

To stimulate an immune response, to get the body to recognize lobos as an infection, his plan was to develop a vaccine that attaches prion proteins to a live modifier, an altered and attenuated strain of salmonella.

Neal took it away from there, and Patrick saw that the "Breakthrough!" message his father sent him corresponded directly with the first successful inoculation of an infected dog.

The vaccine is ready. It has not gone through human trials, but it is ready. Waiting for him in the Ghostlands.

Malerie has that special shade of hair, sometimes red and sometimes brown, depending on the light. Back in high school she was good to look at, but out here, with nothing but men and wild dogs to keep everyone company, she is beautiful. She has apologized to him endlessly over the past few days. "I've done a lot of growing up since then," she says. So has he. Those were different times, and he can't help but feel inclined to forgive her and enjoy the hard bud of her body, her Eastern

Oregon drawl like a mouthful of honey, their conversations about everything—about love. "I thought I loved Max," she says, "but I was wrong. I don't think I've ever really been *in* love. Like, movie love. Like, can't-think-straight head-over-heels love." She has not seen Max since graduation, and good riddance. After the courthouse square bombing, she says, he became even more dangerous, obsessive.

"How about you? You ever been in love?" she said.

"I don't know," he said. "Maybe."

In the barracks, in her private quarters, a square concrete cell with a sink and a bed and a bookshelf, she lies on top of Patrick, naked. He is bigger now, strapped with muscle, and he jokes that he might put her in his mouth like a piece of candy. She fingers the gummed-up scar along his shoulder. She lays an ear to his chest so she can listen to his heart. "Everybody always says they want life to be like in the movies," she says and rakes her fingers through his chest hair. "Now it is. Now life is like a movie. But it's the *wrong* movie."

He says, "You said it," but he isn't really listening. He is too busy with his own thoughts, all mangled in his mind. He runs a finger up her spine, into her hair, then back down to her lumbar vertebrae, where her shoulders narrow into her neck.

He circles the spot and she hums and says, "I like that."

He wants to say, "You shouldn't," but doesn't. This circle he traces is a sort of bull's-eye. Here you put your knife if you want to paralyze someone. As much as it horrifies him, every part of her body he considers both a soft, curved, perfumed thing—and a target. Which gives him a sick feeling at the bottom of his heart he recognizes as both the beginnings of affection and the opposite of it.

"Sometimes," he says. "Sometimes I feel like I've got this filter, and all the stuff that's supposed to go in and out, between the world and me, it gets muffled."

He has never told anyone this before, but it is true. He doesn't know whether it is the death of his father, his time in the Republic, the impossible devastation of the Hanford explosion, or some combination of them all, but emotionally, he hasn't felt anything in a long time. A song on the radio that might have nodded his head, tapped his foot—or a scene in a movie that might have jacked up his heart rate—nothing. Food is filling and sex is emptying.

Malerie traces a fingernail around his nipple until it hardens into a point. "I need you to do something for me," he says.

She pinches the nipple and he swats her hand away and she says, “Anything.”

Normally, in a combat zone, he only gets nights and weekends off, but to keep morale up, the brass is handing out liberty time. “I’ve got a few days libo coming up. I want you to sneak me into the Ghostlands.”

She sits up in bed; her breasts swing. “What on earth for?”

“That’s my business.”

“Fuck you, it’s your business.”

“Hey, you owe me, right?”

“I don’t owe you that much.”

“You owe me. You said it yourself. You owe me.”

“You’re going to end up dead or we’re both going to end up in the brig.”

“You owe me.”

CHAPTER 56

OF COURSE THERE ARE other ways into the Ghostlands besides the perimeter checkpoints. Looters have cut the wire fencing. Undocumented Mexicans too. Like pioneers following a trail west to begin anew and take whatever there is to take from the place, mine the ground, plant their crops, hammer together structures to protect them from the elements, to shelter them when they bear their children.

Then there are the freedom fighters—like Max and the Americans—who have tunneled under the perimeter so that they can go hunting. Max writes a blog called *AngryAmerican*. On it he posts music videos by Toby Keith, rants about closed borders, the effectiveness of torture, the need for lycan internment camps, the worthlessness of the dollar next to the euro. His bio reads, "I'm pissed." His contact info is listed and every now and then he will receive an email calling him a villain or a hero. Some want to know how to join the fight. Some want to prove him wrong, to convert him. He loves how violent the liberals can get with their language. “I want to see you hang,” one wrote, “alongside the president. And as your faces turn blue and your eyeballs burst and dribble down your faces, I will laugh.”

Then comes the message from a man who wishes to remain anonymous and who works for the government and who wants to help Max in any way that he can. “I know,” he writes, “that you abhor the government for its interference and legion inefficiencies. As do I. I am not a politician, nor am I a bureaucrat. I am more like a missile or a handgun. I come to you as a weapon. And as a friend.”

Now, a few weeks and a few dozen emails later, here they are, in an abandoned Methodist church in the small town of Dorris, along the Oregon-California border. This is where they have been headquartered for the past two months. There was a time when Max believed that writing a letter and handing out flyers and speaking at farmers' markets and marching on Washington made a difference, but that time is over. He believes in action. He believes in doing.

He has a dozen men who believe the same. They sit in the pews around him. Their heads are shaved. Their shirts are white, their pants khaki, their boots polished black. They do not cuss. They do not drink or smoke or befoul their bodies. They spend several hours a week throwing weights around and riding stationary bikes to thicken their bodies with muscle and ready them for the long-distance running and hand-to-hand combat sometimes necessary in the Ghostlands. The backs of their hands are inked with silver bullets.

A homemade banner hanging from the wall reads FELLOWSHIP. The stained-glass windows glow faintly with moonlight, all their fragmented colors reduced to blue. A kerosene lantern shines on the communion table. The candelabras—lit and set about the room—sputter.

In the basement, through the cinder-block wall, they have built a tunnel fifty feet long and six-by-six-feet square, the sidewalls framed by two-by-four studs. It runs underneath the perimeter fence. It is big enough for them to roll their dirt bikes through to the other side.

In the basement there is also a Ping-Pong table and they have laid upon it their instruments of change: shotguns, machetes, chainsaws, gasoline and matches, baseball bats with spikes nailed into them. Next to it, on the wall, where a quilt once hung, they have hammered scalps. Fifty at last count. Of every color imaginable, but all reddened along the edges. Their own kind of craft.

The Tall Man stands before them now, in a

black suit, with his arms held out, like some ghastly preacher. He has brought them supplies. Grenades, Glocks, M4s and M16s, a Heckler & Kock PSG1 sniper rifle, and so many crates of ammo, which an hour ago they hauled rattling down the stairs. There is more where this came from. And there are of course conditions to their little arrangement, as he calls it. They will not advertise their presence in the Ghostlands and they will not speak out about any governmental assistance. Their discretion is of course very much valued. And should he call upon them, and he may or may not call upon them, but if he should, they will do as he says. He may have a target, some concentric circles drawn on a paper map he might send them toward to slash through, or he may not. Only time will tell.

His voice is a slow baritone, every word clearly enunciated and separate from the next, notes sprung from a bassoon. "For now, you need not worry about whether what you're doing is legal. You need only worry about whether it is right. And it is right. I would not be here otherwise."

Max sits in the front pew, his elbows on his knees, his hands knotted in front of his face, a position of prayer. "Every now and then we get a call. Otherwise, we keep doing what we're doing. And you're backing us."

"You are doing good work. I want to help you to continue to do good work."

"No government interference?"

"In this uncivil twilight, we make our own choices, we wear our true faces." And what a face he has, like chewed gum mashed onto a hot sidewalk, a face Max finds equally disturbing and reassuring—reassuring because what you see is what you get. He wears, like he says, his true face. The world would be easier if everyone wore their true face. That's why he likes John Wayne movies. The villain wears a black hat; the good guy wears a white hat. You know where you stand. But anybody can be a lycan. Your neighbor, your cousin, your waiter, that girl giving you the eye at the post office. They fool you. They wear masks that hide how hairy they are on the inside. Now, at least, they are caged. The perimeter fence cages them. In that way, the Ghostlands might be the best thing that ever happened to this country. The soldiers are turning people away, but Max says let them in, let them all in, and then shoot them where they stand and burn them and scatter the bones.

He wants the Tall Man—who appears to be grinning, though it is hard to tell, his mouth hanging open and swallowing a shadow—to leave. Leave them, leave the weapons. But the Tall Man does not. For a long minute he studies Max with his lidless gaze.

"We good, then?" Max says.

At that the Tall Man tucks his hands in his pockets and gives them all one last assessing look before saying, "Go raise some hell."

CHAPTER 57

NEAL DESAI NOTES the time on his wristwatch, 3:20. Seven hours since the generator coughed out. The green glowing face of his watch fades to black. He wonders how long it will be until its battery runs out, until time goes still for him as it has for so many others. He wonders how many clocks stopped at the minute of the blast and how many melted until the numbers were indecipherable. He hopes that his wife and daughter died like this—quickly, in a time-stopping flash—rather than winding down slowly, like him.

He is so hungry. He is not sure when he last ate. Two days ago, three? When he let the last of the rations dissolve on his tongue. His body feels as though it is eating itself. His wristwatch and his belt are notched as far as they can go, his belly concave beneath the canopy of his ribs.

He is not alone. He can feel the thing sitting on the counter, feel it as if it were alive. The vial. He hates it. It is the reason he spent so many thousands of hours in the lab. It is the reason he did not put a gun in his mouth and pull the trigger when the ground shook and the sky lit up and the alarms sounded, when he realized what had happened. It is the reason he has been holed up beneath the ground, waiting, waiting—for what, he no longer knows—his thoughts no longer coming together, frayed at the edges by hunger and isolation.

His whole life people have been telling him how smart he is, but he feels dumb now, too dumb to do it, to end it. For so long Sridavi has been his reason for living—the hours in the lab devoted to her, not to humanity, not to the alleged well-being of the nation, not to any political cause, or so he tells himself, now that she is gone. Now that he lives for the vial, the vaccine.

He was watching television when it happened. Jet-lagged from his time in the Republic. Weary of talking to reporters about the assassination attempt on Chase Williams. He only wanted to tune out. But every station played news of the election and no matter how many times he flipped the channel, he saw the same stupid smirk, heard the same celebratory speech. The idiot had been elected.

This was good for Neal, good for his research—he knew that—but he could not help but feel like an accomplice in some fool's magic act, part of the illusion everyone wanted to believe in. The American people had sent a message—that's what the talking heads said. The American people wanted change. The American people wanted to feel safe. Chase Williams meant security and—

From outside came a flash of light, as if a passing truck had clicked on its brights. Then the picture on the television lurched and froze and collapsed into darkness. Three lightbulbs sizzled, then exploded. A teacup shuddered off the counter and shattered against the tile.

He hurried out into the yard in time to see the moon lit red, like some new sun swung into orbit. The sky to the north churned with what could be clouds or could be smoke. His first instinct is to call out for his wife and daughter, but they are gone. Gone to Washington. The direction of the blast. Where Sridavi was supposed to be safe, to heal. He was alone.

By the time he discovered what had happened, by the time he shoved his revolver into the waist of his pants, by the time he packed some food in a duffel and ripped the cords from his computer and hurled them both into the car, it was too late.

The streets were jammed with cars. The night chaotic with honking, screaming. He heard gunfire. He saw pillars of smoke rising from fires lit by arson or short circuit. He didn't have far to go—the lab only five miles away—but the streets were impassable and he had not filled up on gas, as he meant to the other day, so he worried his quarter of a tank might not be enough to get him through the gridlock. Brake lights colored the night red. He was laying on his horn—trying to blast the traffic unstuck, though he knew it was pointless—when he saw the first lycan.

Neal did not recognize him immediately for what he was. The man seemed drunk or mad or injured because of the swaybacked, loose-limbed way he moved. The streetlamps were dead, so it wasn't until he stepped into the road, into the sweep of headlights, that Neal noticed the hair, the blunt snout, the blood-bathed teeth. He ripped open the door of a canary-yellow VW bug and climbed in to join the passengers, who flailed their arms and struggled too late with their seat belts.

Neal hit the door locks and glanced suddenly around him. He was in a commercial area and the sidewalks and parking lots were busy with people clustered in groups and hurrying along, all their faces dark and impossible to decipher. There was an alley up ahead that cut between a sandwich shop and a bookstore and he cranked the wheel and pounded the car up on the sidewalk. People dodged out of his way, some of them cursing him, throwing up their arms, knocking a fist into his windshield—and then he was in the alley, rushing past the Dumpsters and splashing through puddles left by yesterday's rainstorm. His side mirror struck a pipe and ripped off.

When he cut through the other side, to a side street full of saltbox houses with chain-link fences, he spotlighted a long-haired lycan—whether man or woman, he couldn't tell—hunched over a girl and feeding on the bowl of her belly. He took his foot off the brake and mashed it onto the gas and gritted his teeth against the heavy thud, the rise and fall of the left front wheel when he rocked over and crushed both their bodies.

He saw, in the labyrinthine route he followed to the lab, many more lycans tearing off their clothes and scrabbling about on all fours and tackling passersby. He cranked the radio dial and the few stations that came through told him what he already knew: this was an uprising. Later, the world would learn that many lycans were as afraid as Neal, as eager to escape, but right now there was the overwhelming sense that the world had gone feral.

The radio told him that the blast originated in the Tri-Cities area, that by all accounts the reactors were in a state of meltdown. He accepted then that his wife and daughter were dead—lost to a blast as severe as the sun's breath—but did not have time to mourn them, all of his energy focused on the five feet of road unspooling ahead of him.

The Center for Lobos Studies was a galaxy of light. The emergency generators had kicked on when the blackout hit. The parking lot, as expected, was empty. Even the security guards had abandoned their posts, the booth at the gates vacant and brightly lit, a paperback novel laid open to the page its owner thought he would one day return to. Neal drove into the entry lane, his grille nudging the crossbar, before killing the engine. In the sudden silence he noticed he was breathing as if back from a hard run.

Over the past few months, there had been protests staged in the parking lot. Virtually every day, security ended up hauling someone away, someone waving a gun, a knife. More than once, Neal was evacuated due to a bomb scare. Some of them were animal rights protesters and some of them lycan sympathizers and some of them lycans. If this was an uprising, then the center would be in their crosshairs. Neal didn't think he had much time.

He had been working out of the old lab for the past few months, while construction continued on the five-million-dollar Pfizer-funded extension. It was a massive round-roofed building that looked like a whaleback rolling out of the earth. Last he heard, they were to begin moving their equipment next week, the exterior finished, the interior electrical, tile work, and painting still under way. One of its features: a safe room in the basement with coded locks, refrigeration units, a separate well, filtered air, and generators with enough fuel to last six months.

He hurried the two hundred yards, first with his duffel and computer, a stitch in his side so severe he felt as if a knife had run through his ribs. He keyed open the building and tromped down the stairs and rounded the corner to where the door was waiting for him, as unassuming as a closet except for the steel-tooth keypad. He punched in the code, his birthday, and it swung open with the cold breath of a crypt.

He dumped everything he carried and then ran back upstairs and exited the building and staggered more than ran to his lab, where he unlocked a storage cabinet and grabbed as many vaccine vials as he could fit in his pockets. He nearly took them from the fridge and then decided he couldn't trust the power, so chose the vials full of lyophilized powder that were sterile and must be reconstituted with diluent before injection. They were stable enough to survive harsh conditions.

He hurried his way outside again. When he plodded along the pathways that snaked between the buildings, the vials clinked and jingled. He realized he was sweating heavily, despite the night's chill. He could not seem to get enough air—and his chest ached in time with his pulse. He leaned against a building as long as he dared.

He wanted to lie down in the grass and rest. It looked so soft and he was so tired. But he couldn't. The cranberry glow of the sky reminded him of that.

On trembling legs, he started forward, not jogging, walking, knowing he would collapse if he wasn't careful. A cold wind blew and the bare-branched trees shook like things half-alive. He was twenty yards away from the Pfizer Lab when he heard the roar of engines, saw headlights smear across the glass-doored entry. He tried to turn and as he did so his knee popped, buckled. He fell into a heap.

He felt a sharpness and heard a sharp chiming at his side. He had crushed some of the vials. He lay there a moment, willing himself to move, gulping air down a throat that felt blistered, as if he had been sucking on a hair dryer. There was something wrong with his knee. It felt loose, unbound. And when he tried to move it, he felt a sting, as if a wasp had burrowed into the joint. He struggled into a seated position and then managed to stand upright. His knee nearly gave way, but he had no choice except to put the pain far from his mind. He dragged himself forward—a few feet at a time—lurching and resting, lurching and resting.

He heard glass exploding. He heard wood splintering, metal banging, plastic shattering—and he could picture clearly the desks overturned and file cabinets knocked over and computers hurled against walls, their wiry guts spilling everywhere. Then he heard footsteps padding along the concrete pathway.

He groped for the revolver at his waist. It was slick with sweat and lost in the fat of his belly. By the time he retrieved it, the lycan was almost upon him. A woman. Her hair dreadlocked. A hemp necklace the only thing she wore. He did not get a closer look than this because she did not pause in her approach, a blur of hair and muscle. He fired. The bullet shouted. She squealed and fell and curled up on herself.

Once the gunshot faded, howling replaced it. They would close in on him soon.

Somehow he managed to shoulder his way into the building—to thud down the stairs—to drag the steel door closed behind him—before they found him. But find him they did. He put his hands over his ears when they threw their bodies against the door, again and again, a thundering that seemed like it would never stop. Until it did.

* * *

That was five months ago. Sometimes he doesn't know whether he is waking or dreaming. Sometimes he talks to himself. Sometimes he shits and pisses freely on the floor. Once he woke and thought a lycan crouched over him, its face only inches away, its mouth open to reveal the serrated edge of its teeth. Neal issued an animal cry and scampered to the far corner of the room and huddled there in a ball. "Stay away from me," he said. "You stay away from me!" But of course he was alone.

Still, he can't help but keep his revolver close, tucked into the back of his pants, so that the skin there is thick with callus. The generators are still humming, but the lightbulbs burned out a week ago and now he spends his days alone in the dark, the pace of his breathing the only conversation.

Only one of the vials survived; the rest shattered in his escape. It sits on the counter, along with his laptop, his papers. Waiting.

There is a sink in the corner. This is Neal's toilet, washbasin, and drinking source. He tries to fill up his belly on the water from the tap. His hands shake when he fumbles for his glass, a beaker. He fills it and brings it blindly to his mouth and starts with a thin swallow. But that is not enough. He swings it back. The water sloshes and bubbles. His neck convulses when he swallows. He drinks and drinks until he chokes and coughs and vomits and then drinks some more.

Many years ago, he went on a no-carb diet and lost fifty pounds in a month. His skin sagged off him as if he were melting. "I don't recognize you," people said. That was because he was no longer himself. He was meant to be heavy. And now he is moving further and further away from what he is meant to be, the fat gone from his body, his bones pressing through his loose skin. He is now at the point where he has nothing left to lose.

He remembers, what feels at once like ten minutes ago and ten years ago, watching a show on the Discovery Channel. It was about identity. At one point in the episode, a scientist posed a question about what made you feel like you. Suppose, say, he was to steadily replace every cell in your body with a cell from Ronald Reagan. When would you cease to be yourself? Could a single cell, somewhere in the middle of the transfer, make all the difference? What if you retained your body but your brain was transplanted? What if you descended into a coma or succumbed to dementia—when do you cease to be? What is the line that distinguishes you from not-you? With his daughter, he could point to the precise moment when everything changed, when she was and was no longer his little girl. As for himself? There is a stainless-steel paper-towel dispenser above the sink. Before the lightbulbs burned out, he would study his ghostly reflection in it. Toward the end, he did not recognize himself—bony and sallow skinned as he is—but he wonders if the stranger he sees might have come to life some time ago, long before the day the world exploded.

He opened the door once. The hallway was pitch-black and he coughed at the smell of smoke and when he thought he heard something shuffle and scrape toward him, he slammed the entry shut and pressed his back against it.

What chance did he have out there? How could Neal keep himself alive, keep the vial safe? His knee was ruined—he could barely drag himself across the room. His only choice is to wait. Someone will come. Someone has to come.

If someone doesn't, he will die. He is dying. His body is eating itself. And if he dies, everything will have been a waste. His years in the lab. His daughter's suffering. All this time entombed beneath the ground, this room like a black hole awaiting its dead. He cannot let that be true. He must live. For him to live, he must eat.

Sometimes he thinks he hears things outside the door. Whispers. Claws gently teased across the steel. But now, when he presses his ear against it, he can only hear his own stomach—gurgling, whining. Hunger is his only voice. He doubles over until the cramping passes and then he reaches for the doorknob and clamps his hand around it and says to the darkness, to the vial, “I’ll be right back. You’ll see. I’ll go and I’ll get us something to eat.”

CHAPTER 58

CHASE WILLIAMS tells the women to take off their clothes. There are two of them, an Asian and a blonde, both as slender waisted as wasps, and they do as they are told. The Asian wears a long red sweater with a black leather belt and knee-high boots to match. When she bends down to unzip the boots, she turns around so that her ass peeks out, the purple thong dividing it. The blonde wears a black thigh-length dress that falls around her ankles in an inky pile. She kicks it aside, along with her heels.

He tells them to touch each other. He tells them to give him a show. No music plays, but they move as though they hear something, tossing their hair and jutting their hips, as their hands roam along a thigh, a breast, the long scoop of a stomach. They snap the bands of their panties. They gaze hungrily at him through the veil of their mascara-clotted lashes.

On the walls of his suite hang two portraits—Andrew Jackson, Teddy Roosevelt—squared by gold-leaf frames. The décor changes with every president. He requested these two men specifically—the two men he often referenced on the campaign trail, not Lincoln, not Reagan, not all the old standbys. They seem to stare dispassionately at the women along with him. They were, Chase has always said, the right kind of assholes. Everyone calls this place the People's House, instead of the White House, and he likes that, likes the way the term looks past the sculptures and polished woodwork and museum-quality hush and acknowledges instead ordinariness, the possibility of weakness, dirty little secrets.

Though he does not tell the women to do so, they slowly gravitate toward the bed, knowing that this is where he will want them. They cannot simply fall back on it—they have to climb up. The bed is massive—a king-size that rises three feet off the ground—with wooden corner posts that twist upward into snakes. When the stylist asked if he would prefer a queen instead, he gave her a deadening glare and said, *no*, only a king would do.

He does not join them there. He sits in a wingback chair in the corner with his legs crossed. He wears one of the many navy blue suits that appear in his closet as if by magic, all perfectly tailored. A round wooden table beside him carries a brass lamp and a stack of paper-clipped documents from the briefing he attended that morning. He will never read them. The more he reads, the more he feels he doesn't know.

The women begin to keen and writhe. They unlatch their bras and their breasts tumble out. Their mouths open and their tongues dart out to taste each other. They keep staring at him, waiting for him to tell them what to do. He snaps off the lamp beside him so that he falls into shadow. He wants to look—he doesn't want them to look at him.

He heard somewhere that presidents age faster, that they go gray and wrinkle suddenly in office. That certainly seems the case. His hair is thinning away from his forehead. His skin is the spotted brown color of a dead leaf. His muscles are soft, his belly bloated. When he gets out of the shower, he doesn't towel the steam from the mirror. His reflection disgusts him. He no longer has the energy to exercise—he only wants to eat, to sleep. It is strange to think how young he was once, a baby at his mother's breast, a teenager with a football spiraling from his fingertips, a twenty-something with a throbbing hard-on, and that this person remains curled up inside him somewhere like a worm.

There was a time when the sight of two women rolling around in bed would have sent him into a state close to seizure. That time has passed. He feels curious, of course, but not awakened. He tries to will all the blood in his body to his groin, to pump himself into a state of arousal. Maybe today will be different. Maybe today will be a good day. Because he has two women who will do whatever he asks them. And because so far nothing bad has happened. The absence of a negative. That is a good day. How pathetic he has become. He tries his hand now, tries undoing his belt, massaging what feels like a dead slug. Nothing.

The portraits on the wall now seem to stare at him, their expressions souring, forbidding. He has let them down. One of the women—the blonde—says, "When are you going to come over here and fuck us?" She lies on her back with her legs spread and her hands cupped between them.

"It's been a long day," he says.

"What?" she says.

"You can go. You can both go. I'm tired."

The women sit up, their lipstick smeared, their hair tousled, and then the Asian slides off the bed and slinks toward him. "We want to stay. We want to make you feel good." She reaches out a hand.

He would retreat from her, but there is nowhere to go. "Get out," he says and zips himself up and swipes at the air and covers his face with a trembling hand. "Leave me!"

* * *

Once he heard a story from a man who worked in a bullet factory. He guessed that over the past ten years he had plated millions of hollow-points. Brass strips punched into primers. One hundred and eighty-five grains. Nickel-plated, copper-plated. All day long he stood at the press and every evening he watched the news and saw how some cop in Arkansas got shot in a routine traffic stop, some sister in New Jersey got a round through the eye when her brother was fooling around with a handgun swiped from a nightstand. He pulls a lever in a factory in Billings and two months and three thousand miles away somebody loses their life. One thing leads to another.

There are so many examples of this. You take a left instead of a right turn and miss a head-on collision that would have left you brain damaged for life. You tease a friend about his shaky hand and it shames him into going to a doctor who discovers a brain tumor just before it metastasizes. You decide to drop by the grocery store to pick up a bottle of wine and reach for a bottle of Shiraz at the same time as a woman with a switchblade smile who will bear you two children before running off with a bartender named Sasa. Think too hard about it and you never want to leave your house. The way one decision can domino through the rest of your life.

A plane packed with C-4 comes spiraling out of the sky. And then?

The Bonneville Power Administration, which markets the power generated at the Hanford nuclear site and thirty-one federal dams, goes offline. Its service territory covers all of Washington, Oregon, and Idaho, and western Montana, as well as small contiguous portions of California, Nevada, Utah, Wyoming, and eastern Montana. BPA's wholesale customers include public utilities, public utility districts, municipal districts, public cooperatives, some investor-owned utilities, and a few large industries such as aluminum companies. In addition to the transmission network within the Northwest, BPA operates large interregional transmission lines that connect to Canada, California, and the Southwest. Widespread brownouts and blackouts follow the explosion—followed by the collapse of the western grid. And then? What happens when the power goes out? When radiation spikes and the Pacific Northwest empties in a matter of days?

The loss of Boeing and Precision Castparts brings the airline industry to a halt.

The loss of Intel's largest fabrication center, where most of the world's computer chips are produced and designed, results in a major disruption in the computer and chip market.

Costco collapses. And other companies nearly follow suit, with their heads cut off—Nike, Columbia Sportswear, Microsoft, Starbucks, Cray Computers, Amazon, Safeco and PEMCO, Nordstrom, REI, Alaska Airlines, MSNBC, Nintendo, T-Mobile, Eddie Bauer, Expedia, Greenbrier, and Daimler Trucks.

Seattle's port, and Portland's to a smaller degree, brings in many of the products shipped to the U.S. from Asia, a capacity that cannot be covered by other harbors.

Even Facebook is affected, with one of its major data centers in Prineville shut down in an instant.

All of which causes panic and panic causes the collapse of the stock market and the collapse of the stock market triggers a worldwide depression, so that when January 20 comes and Chase is sworn into office in the middle of a blizzard, he knows he has been sentenced to carry the blame. He has virtually no public or congressional support. Partisan disagreements have twice created threats of partial government shutdowns and nearly caused a historic governmental default on their debt.

It is too much to bear.

After the women gather their clothes, after they whisper harshly at each other to hurry, after the door clicks closed, he leaps from his chair. He knocks the lamp from the table, sweeps the briefings to the floor. Before the snowstorm of paper can settle, he marches over to the portraits of Roosevelt and Jackson, ripping them from their hooks, hurling them across the room, one of them striking an antique globe that gashes the canvas. He chucks a pillow, drags the duvet off the bed, and feels sickened by the smell of perfume that lingers here like some contamination. He tears the curtains from their rods and moonlight spills through the windows and makes the suite the color of underwater. He punches the wall and curses at the pain and tucks his hand into his armpit and staggers into the bathroom and snatches a bottle of Volpexx from the cabinet and twists off its top as if breaking the neck of a bird.

The bathroom is windowless, a marble cell. He observes his shadowy image in the mirror. He appears a phantom. He has been close to death before, but it always felt like something that could be avoided, something that gave off an almost repellant force. Now the opposite seems true, as if it were an inevitability, a dark mouth drawing him in.

One thing leads to another. Cause and effect. If one person's choice to pack a plane with C-4 could open up a crater that the entire nation has collapsed into, then maybe he could make a choice too, one that might be similarly impactful. The choice to heal. He imagines something beginning here, in this moment, that would spread outward and affect everyone.

He breathes heavily when he stands over the toilet and shakes the bottle empty and flushes, knowing that if he waits another moment he might end up dipping his head into the bowl and palming to his mouth the pills already dissolving there.

He hears a knock. There is always a knock. That is the problem with this place. He can never be alone. Even here, on the second story, his residence, someone is always posted in the hall, always watching, always asking if he needs something, as if he were infirm or a child with a lost expression. He prefers Camp David.

A knock is never a good thing. A knock means more bad news about economic growth slowing to a crawl, about oil and food prices shooting through the roof—about how slashing interest rates has not helped after raising interest rates has not helped—about the S&P double downgrade, about inflation, joblessness, homelessness—about how angry everyone is, how very angry, his approval rating at 30 percent. This is all his fault, they say. Violence begets violence. If he worked more on integration, the Resistance would have nothing to resist. And now it is too late. And now a section of the country and the populace has been carved away as if by a knife. His efforts to reclaim the Ghostlands are pointless, a waste of money and resources. The other day the *New York Times* ran a column that referred to cleanup and antiterror efforts in the Pacific Northwest as "a lost battle. Like raking leaves in the wind."

Again the knock at the door. More of a thud really. As if someone has hurled an arm against it, demanding to be let in. Rather than answer it, he stands looking out the window. A guard with a German shepherd patrols the lawn. A cherry tree snows blossoms that appear in the moonlight as white as shredded paper. The moon hangs like a cool blue disc in the sky. He cannot see any stars, not with the glow of the city all around him, but he discerns a red light, what must be Mars.

Maybe the knock is not bad news after all. Maybe it is one of the whores back for a forgotten earring. Maybe it is an agent who heard Chase ripping apart his room, who wants to confirm the president is all right and ask whether he would like something, maybe a sandwich or maybe housekeeping to help him put everything back in order.

The door opens and Buffalo stands for a moment at the threshold of the suite and the light from the hallway throws his shadow clear across the dark room and makes him appear momentarily as tall as a giant. "Chase?" he says and fumbles for the light switch.

"Leave them off."

Buffalo's hand drops to his side. He lets the door swing closed behind him and squints into the darkness, his eyes unadjusted. "Something wrong?"

"Nothing," Chase says. "Everything."

Buffalo trips over the ghostly heap of the duvet. "I can't see worth a damn, you know that." He snaps on a floor lamp and then shakes his head at the spilled folders. He crouches down and then gives up on tidying them and retrieves the fallen lamp and sets it on the table again and tries to adjust its broken shade before illuminating it. His glasses glow gold. "We may have something on Balor."

"Go ahead."

"The Pittock Mansion. In Portland. We're not one hundred percent, but the satellites have picked up a lot of activity there." He explains the need to act. He says what he has already said a dozen times before: that *this* is their moment, following the containment of the territories and disablement of all infrastructure, to put maximum pressure on the lycans. "They're up against the ropes. If we keep up the pressure, we'll cripple them."

They have been through all of this before. How they need to make Balor their priority. How they need to cut off the snake's head. How the Resistance will convulse awhile, but then go still.

Now that Jeremy Saber is out of the picture, Buffalo tells him, their number two seems to be Jonathan Puck. From England. Twice deported. Twenty-seven convictions. Theft, assault, rape, narcotics, unlawful intimidation, possession of an illegal firearm. "And—get this—he's five-two. A little big man. No chance somebody with that kind of stature or temperament can lead or galvanize all those moving parts."

Buffalo could talk all night. Chase cuts him off. "Send our guy."

"I was going to suggest a missile strike."

"No military. They fucked up twice already. Blasting their way through that elementary school full of Mexicans. Bombing that dam and flooding a whole goddamn town of people."

"We're not talking about people. We can't think of the insurgents that way."

"News fucking chopper overhead with all those bodies floating around like cordwood. Quiet and clean. That's how we're going to do it."

"Are we?"

"Send him. End of discussion. I want a severed head to parade down Pennsylvania Avenue." Chase silences any further argument with a lashing gaze.

They both take a step away from each other, and they are heavy men now, so the floorboards whine beneath them. Buffalo observes him worriedly and removes a pen from his pocket and bites the tip as if it were a pipe stem. "Is everything okay?"

Chase remembers the roar of the toilet, the confetti twirl of the pills as they vanished down the drain. He thinks about telling Buffalo. Telling him he wants to get clean, just for a little while. Flush the system. See if the old Chase comes wandering out of the fog. But he can't. That's what Buffalo will tell him—he can't. And he is tired of being told what to do. "Everything is fucking awesome. Can't you tell?" Chase cannot meet his eyes. He studies the floor, where the lamps staggered around the room entangle their shadows.

"You should be happy. Be happy. This is what we've been working toward. All these years." His voice is small.

"This?" Chase says. "This is what we've been working toward?" He sweeps an arm to indicate the mess in his suite, the ruins surrounding them. "You can have it."

CHAPTER 59

THAT MORNING, before the sun breaks the sky, Patrick creeps out of his bunk and shoulders his backpack—stuffed with a poncho, canteen, a few MREs and Snickers bars, GPS, satellite phone, waterproof matches, iodine tabs—and hurries to the vehicle lot. Yesterday, outside the mess hall, Malerie confirmed her assignment and plate number. She and another nurse would be in a medical supply van crushed into a long line of Humvees and FMTVs, a cleaner convoy headed into the Ghostlands. In the vans, Malerie said, there is a hollow beneath the bench seat for extra storage. A hollow big enough for him to cramp his body inside.

He told her thank you and she said he better not fuck up and he said he wouldn't.

They stood in silence awhile and then he said, "Well, I guess that's that." It was as close to goodbye as he could get. He blew her a kiss.

"Missed," she yelled, like he was far away, not ten feet from her—and then, unsmiling, she crossed her arms and walked away.

It is here, snapped under the seat with a crossbar

pressing into his forehead, that he waits for the next hour, until the sun rises and the trumpet calls and everyone climbs out of their rack and voices busy the air and the doors chunk open and closed and someone settles onto the seat above him and the vehicles all around the lot roar to life. He cannot fill his lungs completely—that's how tight the space is—and his neck is already cramping from having stared to the right for so long.

The van makes a series of turns, braking at the checkpoint with the rest of the squad, then rumbling up to speed as they head into the Ghostlands. Patrick cannot see out the window, but he knows the drive and can imagine it clearly as they cross the sage flats, the blacktop edged by red cinder, rabbitbrush rising from sandy washes like so many broom heads. Clouds wisp the sky. Turkey vultures ride thermals. Juniper trees twist upward like skeletons in torment. Black-and-red cinder cones hump the desert. Canyons are lined with basalt columns like ancient churches.

He counts off the seconds as they pass and imagines a clock inside him, a clock with many red and black wires curling out of it, that will eventually click its way down to zero and explode. He wishes they would hurry. Already he feels like he is too late.

The convoy stops in Prineville, where they have

been ordered to sweep the east side of town for bodies, kill any insurgents, detain any illegals, and torch all markets and grocery stores. He mouths, "Come on, come on, come on, come on," and waits an interminable amount of time as the van parks and the engine quiets and the nurses climb out and Malerie double-taps the door to give the all clear before he clicks the seat upward like a coffin lid and snaps his neck left, then right.

He hurls the brick into the display window of the Harley dealer and stands there with the glass all around him like the thousand jagged possibilities waiting for him in the Ghostlands.

The Night Train is a big bike, sixty-three horsepower. He wants to hurry but can't help but pause a moment to run his hands along the curves of it, smear his fingerprints and fog his breath along the metal. He scores the keys from a hook in a locked office. There is a generator in the corner. He guns it to life. The shop has its own gas pump and he tops off the tank and fills four canteens he stores in the saddlebags.

Patrick left his hazmat gear back at the base. The full-body suit, gloves, and boots—made from a nano-composite material called Demron—shield him from gamma rays and radiation particles but slow him down, make him sweat. He will be gone only two days and he will pop iodine tabs every few hours to fight the radiation and he will stay away from the northern half of the state and hopefully the overall effect will be no more severe than him standing in front of a microwave for a few hours.

He rolls the Night Train into the lot, turns on the fuel supply, pulls out the choke, hits the ignition, sets the kill switch to run, releases the clutch. The growl of the engine has enough thunder to turn heads all over town. The cleaners will know someone is here. He has only a few minutes before someone comes hunting for him.

He wobbles onto the street in first gear—nearly stalling out—and then throttles forward. Once he gets onto Highway 126, he kicks his speed up to seventy, eighty, ninety miles an hour, and the world blurs into a smear of colors and makes him forget, just for a second, who and where he is.

Outside town, he can see weeds creeping through the cracks in the asphalt, deer bedded down in an overgrown golf course. Nature thrives. Patrick has heard it all. How at night Multnomah Falls glows a faint red, as if the earth is bleeding. How raccoons, as bald as babies, overturn garbage cans and clamber through cupboards. Mountain lions slink about with tusks like sabers. Pterodactyl-like birds silhouette the open guts of the moon. An albino bear as big as a garbage truck sharpens its claws on a telephone pole.

Then there are the dogs. They run now in packs. They live in the woods and in the abandoned houses, cozying up to the couches and beds they were for so long forbidden to dirty. They come for him now, outside Prineville, at the bottom of a canyon, his engine's noise drawing them from the juniper forest—ears perked, heads cocked—as if summoned. They give chase, wailing like demons, their dark shapes surrounding him. They pop their teeth and he kicks at them and nearly loses control of his bike. They keep pouring out of the woods—close to forty of them. He dodges their bodies like a halfback and zooms up and up and up the switchback highway that rises from the canyon, until he reaches its plateau, a viewpoint overlooking the dry basin of Crook County. He parks and gets off the bike, and sure enough, several hundred feet below him, gray and black and brown, the dogs race along the highway, following his scent.

Christmas is the last time he saw his mother. This was before he deployed for the Republic, and he spent a good deal of his holiday eating. Everything from cinnamon rolls to meatloaf to asparagus casserole, everything he could get his hands on and knew he would not taste outside a mess hall for a long time.

"Come back to me," his mother kept telling him. His last day before climbing on a plane to Los Alamitos, California, she pumped his hand furiously, as if to distance her affection, and then couldn't stand it anymore and drew him into a hug. When they pulled apart, she smiled a sad smile and touched his face. "Aren't you scared?" she said, and he said, "Course I'm scared."

And he was, but not anymore. That nerve seems to have been excised from his body. As much as he checks and checks, and keeps on checking, as far as he can tell, ever since he came back from the Republic, he has not been scared, not sad, not excited, not feeling much of anything, his numbness like armor.

Which is why he feels so surprised by the sour twist in his stomach when he roars up to his mother's home in a squall of gravel. He is—no other word for it—afraid. For a long time he stands at the front door, not knowing what to do, studying for clues in the wood grain. When he finally steps inside, he does so with care, to honor the tomblike stillness of the place and also to keep from stirring the dust.

He tours each room, certain he will find his mother in one of them, and when he doesn't, he feels no relief, only assent to his prolonged suffering, like a patient whose nurse cannot find a vein while repeatedly stabbing a needle into the crook of an elbow. He climbs on his bike and drives through Old Mountain, past the dump, to the wooded subdivision, where he discovers her at last.

They have been hanged, the doctor and his mother, his mother recognizable only by her clothes, her skin otherwise black or stripped from the bone by birds. The noose knotted around her neck rises seven feet to the thick branch of a juniper tree. She sways in the breeze and so does the doctor's head. It hangs beside her, like some ghoulish ornament, but his body has long ago rotted away from his neck and fallen to the driveway, an angular pile of bones draped in weather-aged khaki. The smell of decay still clings to the air like some terrible perfume.

Across the garage door, in black block letters, someone has spray-painted *Go to hell lycans*. And beneath it, in smaller script, *Sincerely, The Americans*.

Patrick tries to sob but can't pull it off, managing more of a cough. Then his face splits open as rocks do when water freezes inside them, and he begins to cry. He touches the corners of his eyes as if to push the tears back inside him. He hates how weak and helpless he feels. He hates it so much that he charges the juniper tree and kicks it and a loose branch falls and strikes his shoulder hard enough to leave a bruise that will take a long time to shrink and pale and vanish.

CHAPTER 60

THE LYCANS are not alone. There are others—Mexicans mainly—who live in the Ghostlands. Like Claire, most are here because they feel they have nowhere else to go. At the perimeter, once the military discovers they are undocumented, they will be jailed and then deported. They could always return to the States by following a coyote through a dirt tunnel and across the desert. But why? The invisible threat of radiation, the sores that fester on their skin, mean nothing compared to the overcrowding, the joblessness, the anemic economy, found everywhere else.

They do not have access to iodine. Their hair is falling out. They are covered in radiation burns. But they also drive Mercedes and BMWs and Land Rovers. They shop at the abandoned Nordstrom and Macy's. Some live in gated subdivisions, in five-bedroom homes furnished by Pottery Barn, but most have stuck to the farms where they once worked, where they know the land from which they can harvest their apples and filberts, lettuce and grapes, raspberries, carrots, eggplant, sweet potatoes. A sustainable life.

A week ago, Claire and Matthew happened upon fifty people hoeing and seeding fields. The way they were dressed, you would have thought it was a cocktail party. At the edge of the field an old man in a tuxedo rocked in a rocking chair, his beard as white as corn silk. When they turned off the highway and biked down the long clay road that led to the fields, the old man rose unsteadily from his chair, lifted what appeared to be a cane, and fired. A yellow carnation bloomed from the front of the shotgun, followed by the roar and spray of buckshot that from a good fifty yards' distance only stung their skin. They turned back the way they came.

This is where the girl comes from—a farm, she says—a farm outside Salem. Her name is Roxana. "Roxana Primavera Rivera," she says in a proud, careful voice like she might have once used in a classroom. She is nine and a half. She was in the third grade before the sky caught on fire, before everyone abandoned this place. She hates math but loves reading. That is all there is to do anymore, she says, is read. Besides work. She has the whole library to herself and loves sexy vampire books especially. Her parents are dead—shot by soldiers when on a supply run. Her uncle takes care of her now. He is a pretty scary man, she says, her *tío*. Everyone is afraid of him. "But he's nice to me."

She talks breathlessly while they ride their bikes along the back roads, Claire on her eighteen-speed Trek, Roxana on a Huffy with pink streamers that sizzle in the wind. They found the bike in Bi-Mart, along with a grandpa-style pocketknife, a box of bullets, candy bars. They have pedaled maybe ten miles when the girl asks why they can't just drive a car, and Claire tells her what Matthew once told her: "Because gas is hard to come by. And because in a car you can't hear what's coming."

Her voice is scolding and impatient. She wishes she'd never found the girl. She is just one more thing to deal with, to worry about. If she had died in the cemetery, she would have died in the cemetery. She would have been another body. As simple as that. But now, if anything should happen, her death will belong to Claire like a diseased limb. So she must deliver the girl safely back to her family even as other thoughts occupy her mind. She sees, in the prickle of grass, in the bunching of clouds, the knots on a tree, the vision of Balor, and she imagines how she might get close enough to him to drag a blade across his neck or punch a bullet through his body.

She knows he is here—in Oregon, in Portland—feeding and supplying those loyal to him, trying to build an army, declaring this their rightful sovereign territory. She has seen GOD BLESS THE RESIS-

TANCE graffitied across the capitol building, seen posters declaring this place Lycanica. She knows that's why drones and choppers buzz overhead, why missiles sometimes come streaking out of the sky to open up the earth. He is being hunted.

This winter she and Matthew met someone—a man with a ratty beard and soiled North Face jacket who came out of the night to join their campfire. He held up his hands and said he only wanted some company. "I'm cool," he said. "I'm one of the good guys." And he was. There were many in the Ghostlands Claire knew would slit her throat, rip off her clothes—and that's why she and Matthew always kept their guns at their waists—but the criminal element was offset by men like this—Robbie, he said his name was—political idealists and peaceable foragers more interested in lying low and living their own lives than getting caught up in a war against humanity.

He shared some whiskey with them that they drank out of tin cups. After they stared into the fire for a long time and bullshitted about their pasts, Balor came up. Robbie said he'd seen him. There had been a gathering at the fairgrounds in Salem and Balor fed them before taking the concert stage, speaking with an evangelical rise and fall to his voice about their country. That's what he called it, their country. And their country would grow.

Another few miles and the girl's bike begins to wobble. "My legs hurt," she says. The sun sinks lower in the sky and retreats behind some clouds and glooms the air. A part of Claire wants to tell Roxana to suck it up and keep pedaling. She feels the need to get as far away as she can from the fresh mound of dirt in the cemetery, the town that swallowed Matthew. But another part of her knows she needs to stop, and stop soon, find a place to hunker down for the night. On her own, she might ride until her muscles cramp or her tire flattens, not caring where she ended up, only wanting to move, to sweat out her sadness, her feet spinning in circles. But she has someone else to worry about besides herself.

Soon after Roxana says, "Now my legs hurt *and* my butt hurts," they find a farmhouse a quarter mile off the road and dump their bikes behind it and check the rooms for bodies, dead or alive, then sit on the porch swing and watch the sky darken.

Claire digs a Baby Ruth out of her backpack and asks if Roxana wants a bite. The girl holds out her hand and says, "Please," and Claire breaks off a piece and tosses it to her and she eats it with smacking openmouthed chews. She smiles, her teeth just a little buck, and Claire tries to make her smile as genuine as hers and cannot.

They take swigs from a Nalgene bottle—the water soured by iodine—and it is then, when the girl throws back her head and drinks greedily, that Claire notices the raw red necklace encircling her throat, like the imprint of a leash. "What happened?"

The girl screws the bottle shut and touches her neck and says nothing. Just as she said nothing when Claire first asked how she ended up separated from her family, only shook her head, hid behind her hair.

The house is thick with dust that makes them sneeze into their elbows. Claire snaps on her flashlight. It carves away the darkness. The kitchen has an apple theme—apple wallpaper, apple dish towel, apple hot pad—that makes her imagine a woman with a silver helmet of hair clapping flour off her hands and humming church hymns. Flower-bordered dishes mucked with mold remain in the sink. They walk a short hallway, to the living room, where her light flashes off the screen of an old Zenith television and then slides across an oak coffee table, a ratty recliner, a couch with a red-and-yellow afghan draped over its back. "You sleep there," Claire says and the girl asks why, why not on a bed?

"All the bedrooms are upstairs."

"So?"

"Only sleep on the ground floor. Better exit strategy. Just in case."

The floor isn't very comfortable, but that's not why Claire can't sleep. She can't sleep because of Matthew. She imagines the grayness of his skin when she flopped that first shovel of dirt on him. She imagines the worms tunneling toward him like so many eager tongues. She imagines what he looked like when she found him on the front stoop, wide-eyed and surprised, his mouth a black O. She wonders what the hot rush of metal felt like when the bullets pricked his skin, and then the internal blossoming of blood as flesh gave way and bone shattered, as the back of his head opened up and ejected what looked like a handful of rotten watermelon. Did he have time to hurt? Did he feel the wind whistling through his newly rendered cavities before he lost consciousness?

Every time she falls into dreams, the image of him emerges from the dark, and she wakes with an asthmatic gasp, squeezing her hands into fists so hard the fingernails cut little half-moons of blood into her palms. She recognizes a similar sort of haunting in Roxana. In her dreams she wails, sometimes softly, sometimes at the top of her lungs.

For a while Claire just lies there, listening. Then

she says, "Shut up," her voice barely audible, a quiet curse. Then she gets up and stumbles to the bathroom and pees in the empty toilet. She checks the locks on the doors, peers out the windows into a blackness that tells her nothing. Then she stands over Roxana and squeezes her shoulder and whispers, "Hey? You okay?" But the girl won't respond. She goes on moaning and Claire goes back to pacing.

After another hour of this, she wants so badly to silence and comfort the girl that she scoops her up and holds her in her arms, tight against her chest, rocking her, saying *shhh*. She doesn't know if the girl wakes up or not, but her complaining softens to a sort of purr and her muscles relax and after a good fifteen minutes Claire sets her down and covers her with an afghan and falls asleep kneeling beside her.

The next day, in the midafternoon, they find the farm without too much trouble. Roxana knows it is near a river, knows it runs up against a big woods she pronounces Aching Knee. Claire consults the map until she finds the Ankeny refuge—and now they circle the roads around it until the girl says, "*There!*"

A gravel driveway cuts through a wall of oak

trees. Beyond it are newly disked fields, the dirt as black and porous as the heart of a chocolate cake. The driveway is lined by what first appear to be decorative fence poles, every ten feet or so, with no barbed wire strung between them. These turn out to be pikes run through severed heads. Their mouths hang open. The sharp ends of the sticks sometimes peek out of their sockets or pierce the tops of their skulls like horns. Flies buzz and taste the rank flesh and explode like the spores of a black dandelion when Claire and Roxana pedal past them.

Her hand teases the brake. The bike coasts. “What the hell is this?”

Roxana says, “Those are to keep the bad people away. The wolf people.”

“Is that what your uncle said?”

“*Sí.*”

She did not ask for this. She did not want to help the girl. And now look at what she has gotten herself into. Everything in her body tells her to spin around, hammer away from here, but her feet and her mind spin alike when the bike carries her up a grassy rise on top of which squats the house—two stories, black shutters, white siding with the paint flaking off—like a mildewed skull. There is a faded red barn, a whitewashed cinder-block milk house, a pole shed for machinery, a woodpile, three grain bins. Claire can see people working the fields, maybe two dozen of them spread out over ten acres. Two trucks are parked in the driveway and Roxana drops her bike next to them and takes off running for a vegetable garden in which crouch two men and a woman.

She calls out to them and they stand and shade their eyes with their hands and then let out a cheer and embrace her one by one and then Roxana points at Claire and they study her and raise their hands in hesitant waves and cram together in a huddle and finally decide to approach her, slowly, nodding too much and smiling too big, as if trying to convince themselves she isn't a threat.

They wear revolvers and so does she. The gunmetal catches the light on this sunny morning, advertising the possibility of violence, but they only want to talk, telling her thank you, thank you, for bringing the girl back to them. "How is this possible?" says one of them, a broad-shouldered, broad-hipped woman with a gap between her teeth. "*Tú eres un fantasma.*"

They stand in awkward silence another moment before asking Claire in their broken English what news she has from the outside, if any.

"*No sé nada,*" she says. Which is true. She knows nothing. No Internet, no TV, no radio, the newspapers moldering on porches and in kiosks all dating back to November 6. Which sometimes makes it hard to believe that the world continues to spin, that a thousand miles from here somebody might be drinking a latte in a coffee shop and updating their Facebook status on their smart phone.

Once they realize she speaks Spanish, they all start talking at once, their hands gesturing, flapping like brown birds, which to Claire is what they sound like.

She says, "*Lento, por favor. Lento*." They are too quick and too complicated for her, but once they slow down, she can make out their halting queries about where to find food, gas, whether or not the military will hunt them down.

They don't seem capable of evil. They simply appear trampled. One is an old man whose sun-weathered face could use an iron and whose hand rests on his revolver as if comforted by it. The other is a young man—just a teenager, really—with lamb-chop sideburns and radiation lesions on his face. His arm is in a sling and blood-soaked gauze has been duct-taped around his biceps. He says his name is Jorge and when Claire asks what happened to his arm a silence sets in like after a dish drops at a restaurant. Jorge brings a hand to the bandage and says, "I try to save Roxana. When the wolves take her."

Roxana drops her gaze. The gap-toothed woman

makes a clucking sound and pets the girl. Now Claire understands. The bruises around her neck. The whimpering nightmares.

"You are not a wolf, yes?" the woman says. "*No es posible*."

Before Claire can say anything, a rumble comes from overhead and they all squint up into a sky filled with cirrus clouds that look like pale fish bones. Here they spot a fighter jet. Its sound strikes Claire as sad, something far away and going farther. A moment later the plane vanishes over the coastal mountains, its contrail dissipating behind it.

How safe and beautiful everything must look from way up there, Claire thinks, even if it's not.

"You are not a wolf," the woman says again. "You are not a wolf, no?"

Beyond the farmhouse, behind the barn, next to a grain bin, on a spread of pasture, there is a chapel of bones. The walls are made of skulls stacked one on top of the other, mortared together with cement, some of their jaws propped open in mute snarls. Femurs have been fitted into benches, heavily lacquered to a slick yellow color. Eyeteeth and molars and finger bones braid the pillars and crossbeams. In the corners stand candelabras made from tibias and fibulas. There is a pulpit made entirely of vertebrae, fitted together like some morbid puzzle. On it sits a communion basket built from a rib cage.

Claire has been told to wait here. Not asked. Told.

She tried to tell them she must be going. She tried to move toward her bike and pedal off before they could stop her. But their smiles dropped from their faces and their hands gripped their revolvers and they said no. She could not. She had to speak to Tío.

They have her backpack, all her weapons except a knife tucked into her boot. She should have left the girl on top of the crypt. She should have known better than to do good, to believe that any sort of moral code applied to a world turned upside down. Now she waits in a cage of bones and tries not to imagine herself ripped apart and cleaned and made into a chair.

She hears Tío long before she sees him.

At first she believes the noise belongs to another fighter jet, a sharp tearing, like a blade slicing the fabric of the sky. Then it grows closer and she can distinguish it as belonging to the earth—stones biting, soil grating—what turns out to be a dragged pitchfork, the tines scraping the ground. He appears in the doorway, blotting out the rectangle of sunlight. His head is shaved, his brow a swollen shelf beneath which two black eyes regard her. He steps inside and the pitchfork emits a sound that makes her skin tighten all over.

She stands in the middle of the aisle. He walks the perimeter of the chapel, circling the pews that surround her. He wears boots, jeans, but is shirtless and sweating, with pieces of hay stuck to his skin. He is thick, not muscled. Hairless except for a stripe running up his belly. A tattoo of a splintery cross reaches across his back. The tissue along his shoulder is raised, a lighter color, a scar in the shape of a mouth. She searches for more injuries and finds them: claw marks ribbing his belly. She can barely hear his voice over the pitchfork's screech when he says, "I am grateful to you."

"Funny way of showing it."

"You're not dead. Yet." The grating continues until he reaches the pulpit and pauses there to lean against the pitchfork. "For that you should be grateful too."

"Why would you kill me?"

"Because you're one of them."

She nods at the scar gumming his shoulder. "So are you."

He fingers the scar as if he wishes he could peel it away. "Not long and not by choice. I'm just sick. That's what I am."

"Plenty of us who don't believe in what Balor

believes. Even here in the Ghostlands. Not everybody lets the dog off the leash."

"Then why not leave?"

"Same reason as you. I'm trapped in this pen."

He starts toward her, not in any sort of hurry. There is enough room in the aisle for him to circle her, and the tines sketch a shape like a noose around her. She can smell him, the musk of his sweat. She imagines him swinging the pitchfork, skewering her. She has wished for death, but she always imagined it coming swiftly, her neck wrenched by a rope, her body vaporized by a missile. She won't die here—not like this.

"I'm going to kill Balor," she says, almost at a yell. Saying it aloud makes it feel real for the first time and not an idle fantasy.

Tío is behind her now. She can feel his breath gusting from his mouth, across her neck, when he leans toward her. "Do you know where he is?"

"Not exactly."

"I know where he is."

"Then you'll help me."

Again he circles her, his eyes crawling across her body, and then bullies up against her. His belly sticks to her arm. He pinches a lock of hair between his fingers and sniffs it. He whispers in her ear, "Who are you, telling me my business?"

"I'm the one who saved your niece, asshole."

She hears the damp crackle of his mouth opening and then the click of his teeth closing around her hair. He sucks on it a moment, tasting her, before stepping back, lifting the pitchfork, and stabbing it into the dirt floor. It shivers between them.

"Do you know what I noticed the other day?" he says. "That I do not pay attention to the things I used to pay attention to. When I used to walk down a street, you know what I would see? I would see houses or cars. I would think, *man*, look at that place. With that wraparound porch and that leaded glass and all those gables and shit. I would love to live there. I would think, look at that sweet ride, look at those rims, listen to those six cylinders thundering. I want one of those." He reaches a finger into his belly button as if feeding it. "You know what I look for now? Movement. My eyes are always hunting for movement. For animal life. All those things I used to care about no longer matter. What matters is hunger. Appetite. In this way I have become what I behold. Don't call me human. Call me animal. I no longer live in a world where people sit around the television like some cold fire that conjures images of what I supposedly need. What I need is food. What I need are claws to tear my food and teeth to gnash it."

She is convinced that this is her only chance, that she has only moments before he tires of her audience. “I’m going to kill him. Are you going to help me or not?”

“This is what you think when you are an animal. You think, am I predator or am I prey? Am I climbing into a mouth or am I widening my jaws?”

“Your niece—”

He yanks the pitchfork from the ground and holds it before his face and stares at her through its silvery tines. “I am widening my jaws.”

CHAPTER 61

MIRIAM KNOWS she is in a basement, but she does not know where. The room is twelve paces by twelve paces. The walls are concrete. When it rains, water dribbles from a crack in the corner. The floor is slick there from mildew. Light leaks from a shallow window made from glass blocks.

There was a short-lived time when they merely kept her locked in the room. She picked at the glass-block window until one fingernail broke and another peeled back. Then she swept off the mattress and wrenched up the frame and slammed one of its posts four times against the window, chipping it, cracking it, but by then two lycans rushed in and wrestled her down and taught her a lesson. That's what they call it: teaching her a lesson.

She never seems to learn. She bit the eyeball of one guard, blinded him. She crushed the windpipe of another with her elbow. That was when they began handcuffing her to the bed. First her hands. Then, when she scissored her legs and broke someone's nose, her ankles too.

She bucked her body and rattled the bed frame

and strained against the cuffs until they cut her skin. And the men would come in, one after the other, and teach her a lesson. Months pass in this way. She is a hole. She is a hole into which a knife fits.

Now her body feels as if it is collapsing inward. She stops spitting and yelling at them. Her eyes are dry but her bedsores weep. They feed her through a straw or with a spoon and she pisses and shits into a pan. She lies as still as a corpse. Her stare goes unfocused and settles on some middle distance beyond the drop ceiling. Every now and then she will hear the shrill voice of a mouse or the shuddering of a pipe or the groan of a footstep overhead. Otherwise, there is nothing to occupy her but the possibility of what exists high above and beyond the gray faces of these walls with mold vining across them—and how she might escape, how her life depends on fleeing this room, her future so much easier to study than a past in which crouch the shadows of her child and husband.

She hears someone enter the room but does not turn her head. She can smell him—the cologne applied thickly as if to hide some stink. And she can hear him—the openmouthed smack of bubblegum. Puck leans over her. She keeps her gaze unfocused even when he leans in and sniffs her.

He picks up her hand, lets it fall. The hand he sliced the fingers from. To make them even. This was more than a month ago, when he plugged an iron into the wall. Then pulled out a pair of garden shears. He opened and closed them, opened and closed them, making a rusty song. He was watching the iron. When it began to hiss and burble with steam, when the orange light on its handle blinked off and indicated it was ready, he took her hand and snipped off one finger, then the other, right at the knuckle. The blood sizzled and the flesh cooked when he pressed the iron to the stumps, cauterizing them. The wound has healed but remains an angry red.

He picks up the hand again and takes the thumb in his mouth. He sucks on it, then bites down. She does not react, though she wants to scream, to pull away from him. With blood on his lips, he says, "Just a taste of what's to come."

She is of no use to the Resistance. She has done nothing to terribly wrong them. Her capture and punishment have everything to do with this one man. This little man made big by his wretched desire. He tells her she is filthy. She is disgusting. She is so vile that he cannot maintain an erection. He tells her she is the reason—she and her wretched niece—they are the reason he is pocked with scars. Scissors, bullets, knives. All instruments of torture he will look forward to introducing her to. His voice softens when he says, "Don't think I'm going to kill you. That would be too kind. You're going to be around for a long time, my pet."

His face hangs over her for a long time, studying her, waiting for some response.

"I know you can hear me," he says.

A part of her can't, the part of her that no longer feels alive, and a part of her can, the part of her that remains coiled and ready to spring once given the chance.

☽

Chase feels extraordinary. He feels better than he has in years. For too long he has felt outside himself, as if he were watching a show on the television across the room, only distantly aware that he was the lead actor fumbling through his lines. Now he is so *conscious*, hyperattuned to the mottled texture of the wall, the pebble stuck to the tread of his shoe, the rank cloud of perfume trailing a woman down the hall. His belly has shrunk and tightened. The veins are beginning to rise out of his skin again. He grows a beard, despite Buffalo demanding he shave, telling him that the public believes a man with a beard is a man with something to hide. Instead of slumping often into a chair, he paces or runs in place or shadowboxes or pounds out push-ups. He cannot sit still.

The other day, in the West Wing, he met with the secretary of agriculture about food security. He had that dreamy glow about him that comes from two beers on an empty stomach, and he crossed his feet on the desk while she sat across from him smelling like honey and wearing a powder-blue power suit with a black lace bra blooming from her blouse. "The conversation so far has been about oil and uranium. Food and water need to be on the agenda. We've lost thousands of hectares of farmland in Oregon and Washington."

He held a pen in his hand—a big-barreled fountain pen—and he spun it and rolled it between his fingers. He knew she thought he was an idiot. Somehow she looked down her nose at him even when seated. And she explained policies and probabilities with the voice of a kindergarten teacher speaking to a special student, telling him China had 20 percent of the world's population, but only 7 percent of the arable land, their population outpacing their ability to be self-sustainable with grain production. The Chinese have bailed out Bank of America and Northwestern Mutual. Now they are ramping up their efforts at offshore land acquisition. They have purchased thousands of hectares in Africa and now want to do the same in the U.S. "Don't allow it," she said. "Enforce restrictions." And, on top of that, he needed to put forth a conservation act that would stop suburban sprawl and preserve that land. With fuel costs out of control, locally grown food was no longer a luxury; it was a necessity.

He nodded and smiled and somehow carried on a reasonable conversation with her even though he was about to propose to Congress a revision of the Foreign Investment and National Security Act of 2007 that would lessen oversight on mergers, acquisitions, and takeovers in its specific support of offshore land acquisition by foreign agricultural companies and even though he could only think about what her pearl earring would taste like if he took her ear into his mouth.

The pen spun over and under his fingers—from his thumb to his pinky and back again—and he said, "Thank you. Thank you very much."

They needed the bailout—he didn't know what else to do—with an acre of Iowa farmland up to twenty thousand dollars—and he needed to get laid—he could not think about anything else—even days later, during an autoworkers and union leaders rally in Dearborn, Michigan, when he tells the crowd about his 447-billion-dollar jobs package, about fast-tracking economy-boosting initiatives, rolling out infrastructure projects and cutting payroll taxes and social security taxes, taxing capital gains, limiting deductions for the wealthy, and while he speaks, he can only concentrate on the redheaded woman in the front row wearing the Harley-Davidson tank top, so that afterward, when she emerges from the crush of photographers and hand shakers, he allows her to get closer than the Secret Service agents permit, her hand around his neck, her mouth at his ear.

Buffalo has followed him to Michigan. They have three more stops over the next two days in Flint and Ann Arbor and Kalamazoo. In the limo, after the rally, Buffalo clicks on an overhead light and snaps open a copy of the *Wall Street Journal* and from behind it asks, "What did that woman say to you?"

Chase unstrangles his tie and unbuttons his long-sleeve and tosses them aside. He wears an old white T-shirt with deodorant-stained pits and a hole torn in the belly. Once he arrived in D.C., his wardrobe was no longer his own, his closet and bureau stuffed with pinned shirts and neatly folded triangles of underwear. He hasn't worn his old clothes for a long time, until now, and the smell of the shirt, of mildewy sweat, reminds him of the breath of some deep, dark place. He likes it.

"She said I was a fool. She said I was a wayward

knight. She said I was Don Quixote. She said all it took was somebody to appeal to my elevated sense of worth and importance and I would do whatever they told me to do even if that meant spearing windmills and calling them dragons. That was what she said."

The pages of the newspaper wither into a crumpled mess. "You just stood there? That whole time? And let her say that to you?"

"Well, to tell you the truth, it was sort of an interesting insult, so I thought I'd stick around to see how it ended."

"How did it end?"

The rally took place at the Ford Motor Company headquarters and the limo and the police escort leave its gates now and pass through the throng of protesters outside. Their screams can be heard through the windows and over the hiss of the air-conditioning. They make their hands into fists and their mouths into toothy ovals. Their signs read IMPEACH WILLIAMS and THE DEATH OF AMERICA. A noosed doll in a blue suit dangles from a streetlamp.

Chase feels that old familiar anger uncoiling inside him. He wants to kick open the door, break their signs over his knee, piss in their mouths. Instead, he puts his hand on the door as if it needs holding shut and snaps off a line at Buffalo: "She said I could be my own man if only I cut loose that fat leech attached to my ass."

Now they are past the protesters and cruising the empty, pitted streets of Dearborn, the sky as gray as the concrete stacked all around him. When Chase looks from the window to Buffalo, he sees that his adviser's eyes have narrowed into slits, his mouth into a white puckered ring. "I see."

Chase's anger fades all at once, as if he were a house whose pipes have emptied of hot water. The sight of Buffalo shrinking away from him is too much. His old friend. Maybe his only friend, who is only trying to help.

This past week, it has been difficult to keep calm, to control his pulse, his adrenaline. He nearly crushed a ringing phone with his fist. He nearly knocked over his chair and ripped off his clothes and leapt out a window during a briefing. He nearly pressed one of the interns up against the wall when he saw the way she fit into her skirt. He looks now from the stop sign on the corner to the smudge on his shoe to a fly battering the window to the brown sphere of Buffalo's eye. He is studying Chase.

Ever since he flushed the Volpexx, Chase has worried his secret would glow red hot and come sizzling out of his chest and reveal his risk, what would amount to betrayal, the possibility that he might come unleashed at any moment and alert the world to his condition. “Sorry,” he says.

At the center of the fountain is an elevated platform on top of which stand stone figures holding hands. Their faces are morose but resilient, chins raised, mouths pinched. Normally their empty eyes would gush tears and splash full the pool below them. But the memorial went dry a long time ago. This is Pioneer Courthouse Square, where the Christmas tree once burned like a torch and dozens lost their lives and where a few hundred lycans now gather.

Magog shakes bags of charcoal into the fountain until it is heaped full. Then he empties three bottles of lighter fluid and sparks a match. A circle of flame rises with the sound of a hundred fists striking a pillow. The high flames lick and blacken the legs of the stone figures before retreating to an orange glow among the whitening coals. Magog uses a shovel to stir them. Then he arranges several grates, upon which he lays venison and mutton and beef, steaks and chops, seasoned with a dry rub he scoops from a metal bowl and applies liberally. Meat sizzles. Smoke spices the air.

The courthouse square is edged by a long line of

folding tables. Here are stacks of plates, cups of silverware, bowls of chips and pretzels and candy. Soda. Beer. Apples. Muskmelons. Some of the lycans sit on benches or along the tiered steps. Others huddle in groups. Mostly men dressed in T-shirts, denim, their hair and beards long, their skin as tough and hard as roots. They wear backpacks slung over their shoulders. Their teeth gnash down on chips and snap into apples. Their throats surge when they guzzle Coors and Cokes. Maybe it is the hour of the day—with the sun directly overhead—or maybe it is the bodies all pressed together or the coals brightly burning in the fountain, but the square seems to grow warmer by the second. Their clothes darken with sweat. They drink and then they drink some more. Their conversations grow louder, tangled up with laughter. It has been a long time since they felt normal, since they stood in the open air without worrying about a plane rushing overhead or an arrow whistling from an open window.

All around them stretches downtown Portland, the streets like silent, empty canyons walled in by skyscrapers. The windowsills are mudded with swallow nests and the sidewalks spotted with bird shit. Pollen streaks windows. When the wind blows, dirt flies from sills and awnings like brown banners.

In the square, a drink is spilled, words exchanged. Two men circle each other with their arms out and their backs hunched. Their beards are as black as oil. They tremor into a state of transformation. They leap, drag each other to the ground. Fists thud. Teeth bite. Claws slash. No one makes a move to interfere. It ends soon after it begins, with the winner clamping his mouth around the neck of the other and chewing his way through it, the dying body quaking beneath him as if in a state of frantic sex. The quarrel is over. Laughter and conversation resume. The body remains among them, bleeding out on the bricks.

Balor knows that the Ghostlands are pocketed with good people, with farms and communes run by those who do not want any part of what he has built. And he knows they are not here today. He is surrounded by criminals, animals. Here for food and here for trouble. Which is why he feels no remorse for what will become of them. Soon.

By the time the meat is ready, the lycans are loose and drunk, nearly frenzied with hunger. They eat with abandon. Balor walks among them, shaking hands, grasping shoulders, laying his palm flat against cheeks. They ask him, won't you eat? And he says soon, soon, but he wants first to make certain everyone is satisfied.

Eventually he situates himself at the heart of the amphitheater and waits there with his hands held before his heart until everyone goes silent. He thanks them. Not only for coming today, but for making such sacrifices, for serving a cause larger than themselves.

A spearhead of geese glides through the skyscrapers that surround them. Their reflections glimmer along the windows and their shadows stream across the square. Balor squints after them and smiles and then says that he is reminded of a story. The story is about a mother goose and her goslings. They were paddling across a pond one day when an osprey circled overhead. It began to dive. At that moment, the mother goose separated herself from her brood. She splashed and cried out noisily, crooking her neck and beating her wings unnaturally so as to appear injured. The osprey changed its course and bulleted into the mother goose and tore her to shreds. The water went red. The goslings lived. The goslings lived because of her sacrifice.

He speaks slowly, letting each word hang in the air before moving on to the next, and by the time he is finished, the coals in the fountain have reduced to ash and most of the lycans in the square now lie silent in various postures of death. They clutch their bellies or their silverware or the meat-speckled bones they gnawed on only moments before.

"Thank you," he says, so quietly he can barely hear the words himself, "for your sacrifice."

Magog rattles open the door to the semitrailer, revealing its empty black bed, and they begin to gather and load the bodies.

CHAPTER 62

PATRICK BLASTS down the middle of the highway, following the meridian through Bend, Redmond, Sisters. He swerves to avoid a dead horse, abandoned cars, fallen branches, mud and scree the spring rains dragged down chutes and across the road.

He guides the bike up and over the Cascade Range and eventually the road levels out in the Willamette Valley, where streams cut through the woods and pool in lowland marshes that give way to blackberry tangles, birch thickets, farmland overgrown with alfalfa and vineyards tangled with weeds, busy with birds that delight in the grapes.

He sees corn growing in straight rows, sees men in the fields with hoes, sees a woman riding a horse, sees a tractor trundling along with a gray scarf of exhaust trailing behind it. At the perimeter he interviewed lycans who spoke about living off the land, who claimed no allegiance to Balor, but this is the first he has seen of it.

He sits straight backed at first and then learns to yield to the road, feeling the asphalt as if he were walking along it, bending his body around turns, the handlebars like an extension of his body. The bike—its beetle-black sheen, its rounded muscular frame, its snarly muffler, its engine humming between his legs, its rich oil smell commingling with the swampy richness of Western Oregon—is a beautiful machine.

He softens the throttle when he enters Eugene. He sees everywhere the face of Chase Williams—on billboards and posters, tacked to trees and telephone poles, taped to the sides of buildings—sun faded and wind ragged and rain blotched. Bits and pieces of his smile fluttering along the gutters. Patrick drives the streets and kicks up behind him mud and leaves and sticks now littering the asphalt as if his bike were a horse divoting the earth with the pounding of its hooves, the neigh and nicker replaced by the Harley's *pop-pop-pop* and grumble.

He consults his GPS one more time before finding the center and parking his bike on the wrong side of the street in front of a fire hydrant. Sometimes it feels good to be so wrong. He kills the engine. In the parking lot he spots the rag bundles of a few bodies he cannot decipher as male or female, gray-skinned skeletons.

Beyond the gate there is a mess of rubble from an office building carved out by what appears to be a bomb blast. From where he stands he can see into the building as if it were a rotten piece of honeycomb—gray, pockmarked—with birds buzzing in and out and with papers and desks and chairs spilling out of ragged niches and caverns.

He hears a *ping*. Something metallic—struck. He sees nothing and guesses it is a bird or the wind, a pebble knocked onto a car hood. Then he hears the noise again. And again. Coming together into a song he recognizes. He spots the man sitting at the base of an oak tree fifteen yards away. The man appears to grow from the nest of roots and he holds in his lap a guitar that looks as if it has been buried and then unearthed years later, the strings rusted and creaking like barbed wire strung across salt flats. He plays another minute, some country song, maybe Cash. When he stops strumming, when the notes still hang in the air, he stands.

"You don't look like one of us."

"What do I look like?"

"Like a big American hero guy."

"I'm not that either."

Patrick remembers his mother—he remembers Claire—he remembers the old woman who took pity on him in the Republic—he remembers that being a lycan does not automatically qualify someone as a threat. But this man's smile cuts through his beard like a razor blade. The guitar, dangling from his hand, falls with a hollow bong that trembles around the edges. He begins to shudder all over and rolls his head back and emits a groan.

Patrick does not wait around for him to transform. He tugs the pistol from his belt and fires a bullet into his throat. The man's hands rise to dam the blood pumping from him. An arterial spurt escapes his fingers. Patrick fires again, this time striking him in the chest. His body falls in a heap next to the guitar.

It is not Patrick's first, nor will it be the last. That is the way of things now.

When he walks through the gates, when he follows the rubble-strewn pathways and pokes his head into the burned and bombed buildings, the urgency and purposefulness drain out of him. He's too late. The air reeks of charcoal. And he cannot help but feel—with the heat of the Harley's exhaust pipes still clinging to him—that he might be smoldering along with the rest of this place.

Pointless. He has come all this way—risked his life, court-martial—for no reason. It's no wonder that vaccination, once a dominant headline, no longer makes the news or informs any political debate. They lost everything, probably the result of some institution remaining secretive with their intelligence so that they might secure a patent. His body aches from the long ride, his legs shivery, his lower back cramped. A fat black fly orbits his head and he waves it off in annoyance. He doesn't know what he expected to find. Not a vault harboring some ready-made syringe. But not this either. Not ruins.

Another fly finds him, landing at the corner of his mouth, and he spits it away. More appear, dozens more, buzzing lazily around him in the shape of a net. One lights on his skin and he swats at it. He looks back the way he came—brick buildings, overgrown grass with a narrow path cutting through and edged by maples—nothing that would attract so many flies.

They buzz around him and drown out every other noise in the world. He can feel the vibration of their wings just as he could feel the four-stroke engine trembling through his bones. The day is cloudless, the sun bright and at that afternoon angle that blinds. He holds up a hand to shade his eyes. He rounds the corner of a building and sees the body at the same moment he smells it.

Twenty yards ahead, in the knee-deep grass, in the shadow of a round-roofed building, Patrick can see a splash of dried blood the size of a quilt. In the middle of it lies the body, mangled, recently dead. When Patrick approaches, he smells the blood and the rotten matter of intestines and feels bile rising in his throat and tents his shirt over his nose.

The birds have disturbed the body. The face is

gone, as if peeled off, to reveal the gleaming bone beneath. His throat has been torn open, and ligaments, like piano wires, remain taut in their place even as the flesh has been stripped away around them. His button-down shirt is spread to either side of him like wings, revealing the carved-out place beneath his rib cage where something burrowed its snout or claws. Patrick does not brush away the flies that have tasted the body and now taste of him, even as they crawl along his skin with their prickly legs. Instead he kicks the corpse.

The flies rise in an angry swarm. In that moment, Patrick can clearly see the lariat around his neck and the security badge that bears the name, Neal Desai.

He tries to move quietly. Whatever killed Desai killed him recently. Maybe the lycan with the guitar, maybe not. But no matter how softly he depresses his boots, they still crunch through the thousands of shards that once made up the glass entry to the Pfizer building. The interior is cool, high ceilinged, draped in shadows.

He checks all the rooms on the first floor and finds them empty. No chairs, no tables, no equipment, no clutter on the counters or in the cupboards. The facility is so new it hadn't been inhabited. In researching Desai, Patrick vaguely recalls a photo popping up of him smiling, leaning on a shovel, some groundbreaking ceremony that must have taken place here.

He creeps down the central staircase. The sunlight dims. He pulls a mini Mag light from his cargo pocket and snaps it on and uses its beam to hollow out the darkness, to guide the bead of his pistol. A hallway stretches to either side of him. He can smell something down here—something that distinguishes itself from the smoke-scented air. A whiff of body odor.

He tracks the walls and doorways with his flashlight. Shadows move and lurch and he keeps waiting for one of them to come alive.

Ahead he spots an open door. He notes the keypad, notes the steel frame, a safe room of some sort. The smell is so tremendous he must breathe through his mouth.

He plays his flashlight around the room and spots a rumpled jacket in the corner—and then a laptop, a binder, a pile of manila folders and loose-leaf paper on the counter. He flips through them, noting dosage information, progress charts, chemical compositions that might as well be in a foreign language.

And then the beam of his flashlight reflects off

a silver-topped glass container, something that sparkles like a tiny star.

Patrick is flying—he is nothing but air. The road twists through the Willamette Valley, toward the Cascades. With the bike humming beneath him and the wind like a woman's fingers hurrying through his hair, bearing the smell of pine resin, damp loamy soil, he feels exhilarated. Everything he found in the lab is now in his backpack—including the vial, a vial full of powder, now wrapped up in his watch cap. The label on it reads: LOBOS VACCINE SAMPLE #342, 5ML, 10 DOSES.

Then he notices a gray cloud of smoke rising in the distance. Too big for a campfire, too indistinct for a burning house or field. And the cloud, Patrick realizes, is moving toward him.

He brakes and rolls onto the shoulder with a slurred crush of gravel. "Something's coming," he says to himself. Up ahead the road elbows into the trees. He focuses his eyes there, as if through the crosshairs of a scope, and the rest of the world falls away.

He senses, in a certain vibration of the air and the asphalt, engines. Lots of them.

His throat constricts, a lava-hot rush of blood makes his heart do a backflip, and deep inside him big chunks of black matter, stuff that has been lodged there forever, begins to melt away and infect him with a sick feeling. He has been numb for a long time. But this is fear. Unmistakable, remarkable fear.

Not for him, but for what he carries.

He blazes off the highway—into and out of the drainage ditch, its swampish bottom slippery, the bike almost sliding out from under him. He zigzags through the trees. Stiff weeds and clumps of scrub oak claw at the bike, screeching on its metal, and about thirty feet off the road—which seems too, too close—he brings the bike around a fallen tree and lays it on its side and starts covering it with branches.

The fallen tree is a Douglas fir, its needles a crisp brown, its bark interrupted by a jagged black vein made by lightning. When he pushes his way into its nest of branches, getting right up against the trunk, his hair prickles, his veins tighten. It is as if he can *feel* the residual electricity.

By now a faint reverberation is audible and he ducks down and listens to the noise get louder and louder still, and then around the corner comes a train of vehicles: motorcycles, jacked-up pickups, Cadillacs with red flames painted along their sides. All of them cough up oil like outboards, their ruined shocks and cracked mufflers and shrieking brakes rolling together to make a musical noise, like some junkyard circus, surrounded by a mystically blue exhaust that rises and joins the sky.

On top of one Cadillac, bodies are tied down like trophy stags. If they are not dead they are near it. Blood runs off the roof, down the windshield, where the wipers wipe it away. Patrick can see the man behind the wheel, hunched over and squinting through all that redness, smiling. A rosary swings from his rearview mirror.

Just five minutes ago the world seemed weirdly clean and calm. Now, in the drifting fog of smoke, engines mutter and horns beep and heavy metal blasts from CD players and tattooed men grin into the wind and for a second it's as if the meltdown never happened.

The caboose of the nightmare parade is a semi dragging a flatbed. On the flatbed are couches and chairs, arranged helter-skelter, with many men and women splayed out on them. Beer cans roll around their feet. Metal—maybe Pantera or Slayer—blasts from a boom box and nearly overwhelms the noise of the diesel engine. Five men circle a woman in a green bikini and dance—slightly off-kilter from drink or turbulence—their hands outstretched like Halloween scarecrows. They are dirty and they are excited. Several are in a state of transformation.

At the rear of the flatbed a shirtless man swings logging chains above his head. With his pistol, Patrick sights the man's chest, where excess flesh ripples down his rib cage, surrounding his guts, as if he has begun to melt after too long an exposure to Hanford's furnace.

Patrick's chest is a drum. Inside the drum, the fist of his heart bangs away and he feels clenched and jumpy and oblivious to the reckless stupidity of what he is about to do. His finger tightens around the trigger—in pure reflex—but before he can squeeze off a round, before the gun can jump in his hand, time seems to stop.

The music fades, replaced by several thundering cracks that make Patrick first look to his pistol and then to the cloud-swept sky, questioning their source. On the flatbed, a tiny red mouth opens below the big man's left nipple. Then another at his temple. He doesn't cry out or clutch his chest—he simply drops. He ceases to live. The physics of the impact work out like this: an ugly twist of limbs thrown from the flatbed, now baking on the hot pavement.

Then one of the rear tires rips apart and the rim gouges the asphalt with a fan of sparks. The semi grinds to a halt. One of the couches rolls off and spills its occupants onto the road. The woman in the green bikini somehow keeps her balance. She is screaming. She is painted with blood. One of the men near her sways in place a moment before falling at her bare feet. Another joins him. The others realize, too late, they are under attack.

Their enemy comes from behind, a dozen dirt bikes racing along the highway, their engines the high whine of a chainsaw. They are ridden by men wearing camo pants and American flag T-shirts and black backpacks. Their heads are shaved. Their outstretched arms carry pistols, shotguns. Puffs of smoke rise with every gunshot.

Patrick is not as surprised as he ought to be. He feels instead that he should have known. He should have known what they, the Americans, were capable of becoming. Their own militia.

They do not slow their speed when they approach the semi. Their formation splits and they fire from either side of the flatbed when they pass it. Bodies drop. Blood mists the air. A lycan leaps onto one of the bikes and drags its driver to the pavement and they skid and spin together for a good twenty yards before going still.

Soon everyone is dead except the woman in the green bikini. She has transformed and crouches on all fours and cries out gutturally when one of the Americans—Max, Patrick feels certain, from his bullet-shaped head and short, round stature—climbs onto the flatbed and approaches her. He runs a blade along her neck and then her hairline. Her scalp he shoves into a trash bag.

He is certain the clouds will break and the sun will glint off the Night Train's exposed muffler and one of the Americans will point a finger in his direction and yell, "There!" And that will be it—he will be dead—the vaccine will be lost. The Americans will surround him, as they did that day in the woods, and finish the job they started then.

But no, they climb on their dirt bikes and growl off into the distance, aware of nothing but themselves.

Nearby a bird shrieks the all clear and the forest returns to its business, twittering and chattering. With a gush of air Patrick realizes he has been holding his breath.

He is not sure what he expected to find at the labs. Answers. An answer may be what he has found. But what will come of this answer only makes more questions pour through his head like cement. His first impulse is to run. Escape to safety. But once he crosses the border there will be consequences. Consequences for him. And, if the military is able to draw from the vial something of value, there will be consequences of a much larger order. Consequences for all lycans. It's hard to know whether he is talking about wiping out a disease or an identity, what has essentially become its own race or species. Though at first Patrick felt elated, as if he found in the vial something given up for lost, his body now suffers some weird jolt—a power surge of fear—followed by a draining sensation.

The breeze picks up, and when he breathes it in, when he heaves a sigh, he can smell blood and gunpowder in the air. Plagues don't just kill people—and that's what lobos is, a plague—they kill humanity.

He returns his pistol to its holster and hauls up the Night Train and rolls it over to the road. He tries not to look at the bodies strewn across the highway, the blood pooling around them like oil slicks, when he gets on the bike. He lets the engine run for a minute, then guns the accelerator, spraying dust everywhere, his eyes black bagged and full of haunting questions, like the wounded who return home from a lost war. He needs to think. He needs to find a place to hole up and think this through.

CHAPTER 63

STORMS BREW, but no rain falls. Thunder mutters and lightning ripples and the air grows unnaturally dark and almost solid with humidity. Weather vanes and cell towers and mailboxes and doorknobs and flagpoles sizzle with blue electricity. The wind rises. On the porch of the farmhouse, a rocking chair rocks on its own. A chime dances, its reeds clattering out a skeletal song.

It is evening when Tío gathers the men in the chapel. Candles glow and sputter. Wind gasps through the cracks in the walls. The men sit in the pews and Tío paces before them, pausing only to speak in rapid-fire bursts of Spanish. The men hold bones in their hands, like drumsticks, that they clack together whenever Tío says something declarative, the same way one might offer up an *Amen!*

Claire watches this from outside, the ceiling of the sky occasionally lit by lightning. She hears a soft padding in the grass and discovers Roxana standing nearby, a blanket wrapped around her shoulders. Her eyes are prickling with tears. Her mouth is opening and closing without any sound.

In her face there is terrible fear and hatred. "You're going to kill some wolves with my *tío*."

"Yes."

"But you're a wolf."

"Yes."

"But you're not all the same."

Claire approaches her and reaches out and combs some pine dander from her hair. "No, we're not."

"Some are good and some are bad."

"Same as people."

"You're one of the good guys, right?"

"I think so."

"I ran away from them when they were drunk, when they were sleeping. But I wish I hadn't. Run away. I wish I had stayed. And killed them." The candles reflect off the girl's eyes, little gold sunbursts mixed into the brown pools. "I hope you blow all their guts out." Roxana says this point-blank, without a trace of humor or pity, and then takes a few steps back, as if to escape the memory attached to her words. Thunder grumbles overhead. Tío barks out something in Spanish and the men clack their bones.

Claire's father used to read westerns by Zane Grey and Louis L'Amour. In those wrinkled paperbacks, the heroes spend a lot of time seeking revenge. If somebody, usually a guy with a black mustache, kills a friend or a family member, it is your *duty* to pay him back in lead. It is the just and courageous thing to do, the *only* thing to do. Right now she feels this way about Balor, about the Resistance. Putting bullets and blades into them feels like the only thing to do. Tearing into them, one by one, reciprocating the pain they have caused. Even if she is outnumbered, *even* if her head ends up on a pike, she feels she owes it to Roxana, she owes it to Matthew, she owes it to Miriam, she owes it to her parents, she owes it to the hundreds of thousands displaced and ruined by the meltdown, herself included, seeking some sort of absolution.

She looks to the sky. The clouds have torn open in places to reveal stars. Some look to the sky and see wishes, heavenly possibilities. She sees a morgue bright with the glinting white of bones. She is ready to kill. She is angry, and the anger is good. It means there is something still flaming inside her. It means she hasn't yet gone to ash.

Inside, Tío's voice grows louder and the men clack their bones faster and faster until the sounds merge into one terrible war cry.

The low-slung sun smolders through the clouds as if they were a shriveling purply brown piece of hot plastic. Twilight rises from the mountains like smoke, fingering its way across the sky. Thunder sounds. Lightning flares. Patrick zigzags along some side roads and discovers, down the end of a long driveway, hidden in a thicket of trees, a cabin made of peeling gray logs. One bedroom, one bath. Only a few windows. No place anyone would ever want to live. Safe.

There is a stream nearby. The water is white with minerals and comes from the old glaciers way up in the Cascades. He strips off his clothes and climbs into it and grinds his teeth against the cold. When he bathes, when he dunks his head and scrubs his skin with sand, huge trout curl around him and dart all up and down the river, their rainbow scales glowing beneath the water. Sometimes the fish taste Patrick, taking his toes or fingers into their prickly mouths, chewing, and he finds the sensation strangely pleasant. For a moment he worries whether the water is cleaning him or dirtying him—the radiation washed right off the mountains and into his skin—but then he stops worrying. He has room in him for only so much.

Before locking up the cabin and dropping the blinds, Patrick stands on the porch to survey the night. Especially at this time of day, when darkness settles in and the towns no longer glow, the broken streets and empty buildings and burned-out cars as black as charred wood, the bats swooping and the frogs peeping and the Cascades a cutout against an ink-wash sky, it is easy for him to believe that all other human life has been extinguished.

He lights up the cabin with flashlights he finds in drawers, a propane lantern he finds in a closet. He eats an MRE, guzzles a canteen of water. A shelving unit in the living room is loaded with books—westerns, romances, science-fiction stories—and though he has never liked reading much, he paws through them now not just for entertainment, but also for the comfort of following smart people who say all the right things and in the end figure stuff out.

Fifteen minutes later he hasn't made it more than a few pages. Every time he tries to read a word, the letters scramble away from him. He ends up tossing the book aside and staring at the wall. There is too much in his mind, too many possibilities branching before him depending on what choice he makes.

A long time ago, every goal was so material: I want a fast red car, I want a sexy wife, I want a great job, I want a house with a field out back where I can play catch with my kid. Now every need has become an abstraction and he is left with a carved-out soreness he recognizes as homesickness. Not just the want to go back to California—

the want to spin the globe backward like a clock and rediscover that moment in life.

In the vial lies that very possibility. A cure for a sick world.

Any anxiety Patrick might have—about getting court-martialed, about handing over the vial—is laid to rest now. The world needs to move on, to heal.

He kneels beside his backpack and pulls out the satellite phone and hesitates only a second before punching it on and dialing the base. "This is Patrick Gamble," he says. "I am contacting you from beyond the perimeter. And I have located what I believe to be the lobos vaccine."

CHAPTER 64

CHASE WATCHES the fights from the concrete bleachers. This is at the fairgrounds outside Fredericksburg, Virginia, in an open-air building normally used for showing farm animals. The roof is steel; the floor is dirt. Some of the lycans grow their hair long and spike it into Mohawks. Others keep it short and shave lightning-bolt designs into the sides. Some grease-paint their faces into skulls, sneering demons. They wear outfits made from leather or spandex or polyester jeweled with rhinestones that catch the light and sparkle when they explode from doorways, hurrying through the applause, the jeering voices, the concrete bleachers and aluminum folding chairs, toward a dirt ring awash in fluorescent light.

It is a pit more than a ring. There are no ropes and there are no posts. There is only a concrete perimeter, a ten-foot-high wall that encases twenty square yards of dirt scratched and pitted and muddied with blood. Five black house-party speakers carry the booming voice of the announcer introducing the pit fighters with names like Wolfsbane and Hooded Justice.

The fights are hosted by Combat Zone, an indie circuit that promises ultraviolence. Chairs, ladders, thumbtacks, razor blades, light tubes, and barbed wire are standard weapons of the trade. So are teeth and claws.

The lycans leap into the air as if flying. They grapple with each other upright and on all fours. They crunch windpipes with their fists and snap arms behind backs and rip out clumps of hair and bite out hunks of flesh and seem to pleasure in the pain, both given and received, because the pain feels good. That's what Chase thinks. The pain feels good. Because it reminds you you're alive. Unlike the numbing fog of Volpexx.

A few weeks ago, he visited a lycan detainment center, one of a dozen established around the country for those accused or suspected of terrorist activity. Voices echoed down cement hallways. In the cells paced shirtless, hollow-eyed men whose ribs came together like claws above their sunken bellies. They pressed their faces against the bars and pleaded and spit and muttered nonsense. He felt bad for them. But he feels good for the lycans in the pit. Jealous even.

Chase cheers along with the rest of the audience. He wears jeans, a hooded sweatshirt, a ball cap pulled low over his face. He has not trimmed his beard in days and it has a mossy quality. He is flanked by two Secret Service agents who do their best to appear as civilians—wearing Redskins Windbreakers—but they are so obviously wooden and watchful that Chase has to nudge them with his elbow every few minutes and tell them to relax, lighten up. They did not want to bring him here. But he demanded it, threatened their jobs if they didn't do as he said. Special agents Trice and Houston. Those are their names. Tweedledee and Tweedledum, he calls them. He can barely keep anyone straight outside of a nickname. Secretary of the interior, secretary of commerce, the director of the Office of Management and Budget, the cabinet secretaries, the administrator of NASA, the Joint Chiefs, the court justices. Too many faces, too many names, all of them unified by their desire to get him to do something he doesn't want to do.

He has been working out three hours a day. Hitting the treadmill, hefting weights. His whole body feels like it is throbbing with pleasure every time he clips another hundred pounds on the bench press, every time he slams a fist into the speed bag, his body surging, exploding with the feeling of power.

Watching the men in the ring gives him a similar sensation. His hands open and close into fists. He pants more than breathes. His muscles jump. When he feels himself on the verge of losing control, when he tastes blood coppering his mouth, he leans in to one of the agents and says, "Time to go."

"Yes, Mr. President," the two agents say.

The recon site is south of Salem—a spread of pasture used regularly as a drop point for ground troops. A county highway runs alongside it. During the night, fog spills from the woods and ditches, filling up the world, making the air seem full of ghosts. The recon task force is scheduled to arrive at dawn, their point of contact now delayed until visibility clears.

For hours, Patrick waits. Moisture gathers on the Night Train like sweat. His clothes and hair dampen. The excitement and resolve he felt through most of the night have given way to paranoia. Sounds travel strangely in the fog, and at times the breeze breathes in his ear and makes him spin around. A pinecone falls. A squirrel chatters. A snapped stick makes him think of a charged rifle.

Earlier, when he drove slowly through the fog, a mule deer bounded across the highway and sprang into the air, so impossibly high, hurdling a barbed-wire fence with a white swish of tail, disappearing into the fog, where a milky hole appeared and then fused together.

"Did you see that?" Patrick yelled and then realized no one could hear him. "That was beautiful."

He felt so good then. Confident. Purposeful. He wishes he could bottle that feeling. It is unavailable to him now as his watch ticks its way toward noon and the fog disperses to filaments wisping around his legs. Last night he spoke apologetically to his lieutenant and then the CO. He did not barter a deal. He did not feel the need. They cussed him out, called him a damned fool, as he expected. What in the fuck he was thinking—following a hunch, risking his life, disobeying every rule in the book—they did not try to understand.

"Sir," he said, "with deference and with respect, I apologize, sir." He explained what he thought he had in his possession, and there followed a long silence, after which he was told the coordinates by which they would meet the next day. They were bringing him home.

Perhaps, he thinks, his efforts would not be commensurate with his rewards. Perhaps he was about to land his ass in the brig. Perhaps the vial was nothing but a vessel of glass and ash, nothing of value. He glasses the horizon with his binoculars. Clouds hang here and there in cottony clumps, but otherwise, the sun has the sky to itself. Hills roll over and become mountains, the sharp white tips of Hood, Jefferson, stabbing the blue. The choppers will come from the east, he guesses, two Blackhawks, maybe more. He runs his vision along hillside ridges, mountaintops. Nothing.

He drops the binoculars. The wind races through the forest and shakes the trees, hushing through the trunks and branches. And then it hits him, a warm wave that carries grit in it and blows away the last traces of fog. He closes his eyes and lets it play across his face. When he opens them again, it is just in time to see the line of trucks and Jeeps pause on the road that runs along the edge of the field, ten yards away.

The wind dies and he hears the engines, like the grumbling of a big animal. The doors swing open. Out step twenty men with glowering faces, Mexicans.

There is no point drawing his pistol. They already have several shotguns trained on him. He stares into their black bores and waits for the buckshot to come. He wonders if he will hear the gunshot that kills him. He hopes not. He hopes death will come quickly, every sensation wiped clean at once, silence, darkness, peace.

He flinches when he hears a word, "Patrick," as if it were a trigger's snap.

She pushes her way through the men. He recognizes her immediately, but the image of her standing before him now and the memory of her sitting beside him in his Wrangler come together in his brain like a constellation he can't quite figure out. They have a conversation with only their eyes. Their eyes speak of their confusion and delight. Their eyes say that she looks older, and he does too, as if the collapse of the world has knocked the youth from them, rushed them into adulthood. Their eyes say, *I can't believe it's you.*

"It's you," she says.

"It's me."

Before they can say anything more, the air grows busy with the stuttery whir of helicopters, and their eyes swing to the sky.

☽

Chase has not yet reached for the light switch—and the door has not yet clicked closed behind him—when a lamp snaps on across the room. In its orange nimbus sits Buffalo. His glasses are aflame with the reflected light. For several seconds his hand remains on the pull chain while Chase stands with his jacket half off. "Where have you been?"

"I've been out."

"Where?"

"Out."

Minutes ago, when he walked through the buzzing metal detector, when the usher approached him and asked for his jacket, Chase said to screw off. He could hang up his own clothes. Now he peels off his jacket and tosses it on the floor. "I had to get out."

Buffalo does not raise his voice when he says, "You are the president of the United fucking States. You don't go out." Chase hates him then. Hates the way his stern expression and forbidding eyes match the portraits hanging in the East Wing—all of them watching—all of them supportive so long as he behaved in a particular way, performed a particular job as they saw fit. He can't go anywhere alone—he can't make any decisions on his own. He wouldn't be their flunky; he wasn't their Mr. Smith. "I assume you're here for some other reason than to lecture me."

"Something has happened." His stillness is unsettling. "Something big."

Chase doesn't wait around to hear it. In the bathroom, he unzips, pisses, makes Buffalo wait for him or talk over the noise of the bowl. He takes his time washing his hands.

When he emerges from the bathroom, Buffalo remains in the chair, legs crossed, hands folded over his knee. He asks if Chase remembers Miracle Boy, the punk kid, the sole survivor, the one who made news for playing dead and later enlisting.

"How could I forget? That's when this whole mess began."

"He just pulled a stunt that could be a publicity dream. Or nightmare."

Buffalo tells him what he already knows. At the same time the Hanford site detonated, the Resistance torched the vaccination labs. Everything was lost. Other private facilities picked up where Desai left off, but they remained a year away from inoculation, and inoculation is precisely what this presidency needs. Miracle Boy claims to have found it. He went AWOL, snuck into the Ghostlands, discovered a safe room in the research facility. He found Desai, his papers, his laptop, and what he believes to be the vaccine.

"What exactly is the problem? This sounds like a wet dream."

"He's gone missing."

At first they do not move, as if the choppers might not notice them, should they stand as still as deer. The two Blackhawks circle the meadow once, twice. The grass flattens and the trees shake with the gusting rotor wash. Grit bites their faces. The choppers hover like wasps, black bodies with lean, long tails. Their stammering roar is such that Patrick can barely hear the voice that screams in his ear, “These your friends, GI Joe?” Before he can respond, someone grabs a fistful of his hair and yanks his pistol from his holster and shoves it into his throat.

All around him the Mexicans swing to the sky their rifles and shotguns—among them an AR-15—and begin to fire. Bullets spark the underside of the choppers. Glass shatters and falls in a sparkling rain. One of the birds banks hard and rises steeply. Its rotor blade clips the rear stabilator of the other Blackhawk. There is a sound like a fork caught in a garbage disposal. The four-blade rotor snaps, and one of its blades swings wildly through the air and impales a truck with a deafening screech.

The Blackhawk, destabilized, tilts into the line of trees walling the road. The remaining three blades slash through branches, embed themselves in trunks, and then crack and separate from the craft. The chopper smokes and whines when tumbling through the air. The nose falls first, the tail reaching upward like the fletching of an arrow. There is the terrible crunch of metal meeting stone. The impact does not open into a ball of flame. The aircraft simply screams onto its side. The engine winds down. Smoke and dust rise from the wreckage.

The sky is empty, the other chopper departed. Patrick is released, shoved to the road, where he batters his knees against asphalt. He looks for Claire and spots her among the Mexicans. She does not look horrified, as he imagined. She does not weep or cry out. She does not bring a hand to her mouth. Instead she stands there holding a revolver the size of a cannon, the muzzle still smoking. Her mouth is a white line as if she has bitten away any emotion.

A few of the Mexicans approach the fallen bird and try to yank open the carrier door. But it is smashed shut. So they fire into the windows and then reach through the holes they have rendered in the glass and finish off those still strapped to their seats.

☽

Buffalo explains the aborted rescue attempt, the downed helicopter, the suspected abduction, the signal traced from Miracle Boy's satellite phone, and he does so dramatically, his hands moving and making a kind of shadow theater on the floor, so that Chase can't help but imagine himself there, among those twisting shadows, caught up in the fight.

"One vial?" Chase says. "He has one vial?"

"That's it."

"Just one."

"Yes."

"How many doses are in one vial?"

"Ten, I believe. Maybe fewer. I'm not sure."

"We get our hands on it, we can replicate it."

"Hypothetically."

"How long would that take?"

"I can't say."

"One vial."

"Yes."

"Our magic bullet."

These past few weeks Chase has been dreaming again. When he was on Volpexx, his dreams were empty, a dying blackness overcoming him every evening. Now his dreams sometimes seem more wakeful and vivid than life. The woman—the woman with the charcoal skin and smoldering eyes—has returned. So have others. Last night he dreamed of the man he killed on patrol on a two-lane highway south of Niflhel. His platoon was clearing the road for a supply convoy, and in the dream he was there again, truly there, every klick of the road and every detail of the city familiar, as he drove past a sewage canal, decaying tenements, shacks sculpted out of tin and mud and snow, carts sloshing with half-frozen jugs of milk. They came across a man crawling along the side of the road in a state of transformation. His hair was as white as the snow piled everywhere. He was barefoot and wore only tattered slacks and a long-sleeve thermal. He seemed not to recognize the rumble of vehicles beside him. He stared straight ahead, blood drooling from his mouth and weeping from his eyes, while dragging himself forward one arm after the other. Chase got on the platoon net and ordered the other trucks to stop, then switched over to the battalion frequency, reported their location, a sit-rep. Sometimes the prions, in a later stage of development, made the brain bleed and gave the infected symptoms equivalent to dementia. "Think we got ourselves a rabid dog."

A few seconds later the order came down to kill the lycan.

Chase could have ordered his gunners to fire but didn't want to burden them with another death. He dismounted and crunched through the snow and sighted the lycan with his M16 but couldn't abide shooting him from behind. He called out twice. The second time, the lycan spun around and lifted an ice-caked hand feebly to claw the air or warn him away. He was old enough to be Chase's grandfather. Chase pumped a single round into him and then climbed back in the truck and left the body slumped in a snowbank. He felt wretched but at least the wretchedness was his and didn't belong to one of the red-cheeked, tattooed nineteen-year-olds under his charge.

That's what he wants now, an opportunity to cowboy up and take whatever pain or glory comes with it. And he knows he must. There is no other way to secure the vaccine for his immediate use. Without the help of medication, he can keep his condition hidden for only so long.

Buffalo is talking strategy—what needs to happen over the next twenty-four hours—and his voice slows when Chase begins to strip. He kicks off his shoes, then peels off his shirt, yanks away his pants, his socks and briefs, until he stands naked in the pile of shed clothes.

"What are you doing?" Buffalo says. It isn't time for bed. They need to call a meeting. They need to go to the Situation Room. They need to patch through the CO stationed at the perimeter. Buffalo has already ordered coffee from the House Mess.

"I'll go."

"You'll go where?"

"I'll go to Oregon."

Buffalo does not seem to know where to look. He uncrosses and crosses his legs. "You'll—what?"

Chase walks over to the chair and stands a mere foot from Buffalo. "I'll go. I'll go and find the boy." His stomach looks like stones stacked on top of one another. His arms are a root tangle of veins. His groin is pulsing.

Buffalo turns his head away so that he is staring directly into the lamp. "I don't understand—what are you—why do you think—"

Chase has been thinking long and hard these past few days. If he only did things himself—if he didn't simply tell others what to do—this could be a good line of business, a rewarding job. As it was, he only talked, never did anything. He needed to *do* something, and now something could be done. He thinks of all that land—those mountains rolling into hills that then leveled into sage flats gouged out by irrigation canals, Central Oregon a patchwork of brown cheatgrass and bright green alfalfa corralled by barbed wire, the bent-back skin-burned stage of his former life, his father's life before him, and his grandfather's before them both, a stage upon which they shot antelope and counted stars and raised horses and cattle and family, all of that stolen by the lycans, gone, nothing left but old wigs of sagebrush, fences kicked over and rotting into the ground. By returning there, he sees a chance to reclaim that part of his life, that part of him. And to own up to what people thought they were voting for. He has sworn the oath and invoked the name of God, but they were just words, spoken too soon, and words do not make someone a leader. People need to be reassured—they need him to instill the confidence he has lost. They need to see him doing a job to believe in him as president. He isn't sure, until now, that the title has been anything more than a costume.

Buffalo still stares at the lamp when he says, "Surely you're joking?"

"I am not joking."

"You're serious?"

"I'm seriously serious."

Buffalo compresses his lips and bows his head and then something seems to overtake him. He leaps out of the chair. When Chase moves to block him, Buffalo shoves him back a step. "You're not going. Of course you're not going. You think you're some rough rider. You're not. This is ridiculous and purposeless and dangerous. You're such a fool sometimes. A goddamned fool."

Chase shoves him. Buffalo's back cracks against the wall. He lets out a whimper. His glasses hang crookedly on his nose. He runs a hand through what little hair he has and it stands on end. "I don't understand what's wrong with you. Something is wrong with you."

Chase stalks toward him. He feels as if his heart has experienced an electrical short and the heat of it is still deciding whether to die or catch flame.

"I'm going to go find that boy. I'm going to find this magic bullet. I'm going to go get my hands dirty. That's my decision. Not yours."

"You're not listening to me!"

"I don't have to listen. I'm the goddamn president."

Buffalo slaps him then. The noise like a popped balloon.

Chase's cheek smarts and he puts a hand to it. He staggers away and crouches on the floor as if to contain the anger springing in his chest that will not go away. He can only fight it so long.

Buffalo reaches for him with arms like weak lassos. "Oh my. Oh no. I'm sorry. I'm so sorry, old friend." The same hand that slapped Chase now strokes the bare skin of his back. "I'm sorry."

He pulls his hand away when hair begins to prickle beneath it. He has time to run. He has time to cry out. But he does not. He seems to trust that Chase, his friend, his old friend, will contain himself, will be able to hold back, even when he rises slowly from his crouch and starts toward him with his mouth open as if to kiss.

CHAPTER 65

NIGHT FALLS. Shadows deepen between the trunks of trees, firs and cedars and hemlocks, their branches fingering together overhead in a thick canopy that makes Patrick feel safe from any drones or choppers that might pass overhead. The Mexicans dig a shallow pit and gather wood and arrange it into a flaming pyramid to keep the night at bay. Bats and owls swoop through the sparks. The Mexicans sit upon rocks or the misshapen roots that wrestle the ground. They eat jerky and dried fruit. They sharpen their knives and clean their rifles and pistols. The air grows spicy with smoke.

Claire makes a fire of her own, smaller, separate from them, twenty yards away. She sits next to it in a ball, her arms wrapped around her legs. Patrick watches her for a long time. He wants to be near her. More than that, he wants to embrace her, has wanted to since the moment he first saw her earlier that day, but it has seemed impossible. Because they have been on the run, confined to different vehicles as they drove at a perilous speed from the site of the crash—into the asphalt maze of Portland—and then parked on a service road in the Hoyt Arboretum, with five miles of thick woods between them and the mansion, their plan to attack in the morning. And because, these past few hours, whenever Patrick drew near, she stiffened and offered him clipped answers. "I thought you were dead," he said, and she said, "I might as well have been." He tried to get her talking, but she wouldn't give him anything, always turning the question back on him: what exactly are you doing here?

To which he could only say, "Recon." He was grateful she did not press him further. To tell her anything more would confirm his betrayal.

In his backpack was the inoculation: the vial that made possible her erasure. Only twenty-four hours ago he felt so certain of himself, so positive he had made the right decision. Twenty-four hours seemed now like twenty-four years, his frame of mind so distant, his resolve rotted through with questions.

Above her, through the trees, he can see the moon, a silver sliver brightening the edge of a giant black ball. Sometimes you can see more of what isn't than what is, and this is one of those times.

She must hear him coming, his feet snapping branches, clunking off rocks, but she does not turn to look at him. And she does not say anything when he sits beside her, but she does not move either.

Every time he looks at her, when that old attraction geysers up inside him, he feels as excited as he does anguished. The image of her—skin and hair reddened by the fire—has made him aware of all those sunken feelings, all those things lost and untested.

He says, "Hi," and she says nothing and the space between them seems to widen.

He can only guess how hard the past five months have been for her. That's what he wants to say. That he understands. She must feel she doesn't have a place in this world. She must be sick and tired of living with a knife to her throat every second, of scrounging for food, of running and running and running. She must have reached the breaking point—and that's what tomorrow is about—her either fighting back or lying down and closing her eyes forever.

His thoughts are interrupted by Tío. He appears around a tree, tossing into the air his bone-handled knife, the blade as big as his forearm. End over end, a silver flash. Twice, three times, four. It makes a whistling sound with each arc. Tío stares at Patrick while he plays with the blade. "You're not wearing handcuffs. You're not roped to a tree.

Your mouth isn't duct-taped shut." He catches the knife and then slashes at a nearby cedar. A piece of bark falls away, and then another, and then another. "You might be thinking that means you're free to do as you please." The blade thwacks the trunk and a crude picture begins to emerge—that of a face, the yellow pulp starkly set against red bark—two long eyes, a gash of a nose, and a jack-o'-lantern's smile. "Today we killed some soldiers. Tomorrow we're going to kill some wolves. And I want you to know something. I want you to know that if you do anything that interferes with that, I'll drop you." He notches away the final curve of the smile and then departs, leaving them staring at the face, which bleeds sap. "I'll be watching," he says over his shoulder.

They sit there another few minutes in silence before Patrick says, "Fire is dying," and gets up and brushes off and collects an armload of sticks to set upon the flames. Sparks dance. Pitch pops.

Then he begins to talk. He tells her about the war as if it were a thing alive, with metal jaws and sulfuric breath and a saber rising from its groin. He tells her about the crystal-cold sky of the Republic and the snow that lies over everything like a wrinkled white sheet. He tells her about his father and his fool's mission to find him and what he learned when he discovered the doomed lycan squad. He says he is afraid that she is going to appear and vanish again like his father. He says he is sorry. He says he understands why she might hate him. He says he hopes that another universe might exist in which none of this happened and their only concern would be lying on a beach and rubbing oil all over each other and drinking piña coladas right out of the coconut.

Her expression softens and she smiles when she looks to the sky, and he can tell that she sees there the same thing he sees: a life beyond the walls of this place, where rivers rush with clean water and where gardens flower with spring and where children play soccer and couples walk hand in hand through parks and order large Cokes and buckets of popcorn when they go to the movies and where the two of them, Patrick and Claire, might be together without regard for the past, only the future.

She lifts her arm. He scoots into it. And they are holding each other. "Remember what you said about electricity?" he says.

"I still don't understand it."

"Me either. But I can feel it."

CHAPTER 66

THERE IS A PATTERN in the ceiling. The cracks and water damage melting together into the image of a dark-hooded wraith. Miriam tries to look away, tries to rearrange it into another design—say, a fish breaking the surface of a murky pond—but try as she might, it is always there. It is waiting for her, she feels certain. Waiting for her to give up. And when she does, it will drop like a bat to seize her and flap away to some cave deep beneath the earth where her bones will become jewelry and her teeth dice and her lungs red accordions, her soul sealed away in a locket worn around a demon's neck.

It is morning. She knows this from the pink light leaking through the glass-brick window. Right now, maybe only a few hundred miles away, alarm clocks are blaring, people are rolling out of bed, brewing coffee, burning toast. For her, though, morning may as well be night. She has no routine—day's beginning, day's end. Sometimes they feed her—sometimes they come to clean her or to fuck her—and sometimes they do not. Otherwise everything remains the same.

Her husband once said that he believed some sort of mathematical equation could be applied to life—since the longer you lived, the greater its seeming velocity. She always attributed this to familiarity. If you kept the same habits—and if you lived in the same place, worked in the same place—then you no longer spent a lot of time noticing. Noticing things—and trying to make sense of them—is what makes time remarkable. Otherwise, life blurs by, as it does now, so that she has difficulty keeping track of time at all, one day evaporating into the next.

So she cannot be certain, but she believes it has been a week or more since she last saw Puck. Curiously, she has come to look forward to his visits as much as she dreads them. He speaks to her. He listens to her even when all she has to say is fuck off, go to hell. He is keenly interested in her, even if only to see her suffer. That makes her feel important, adversarial. Like she has some role more essential than furniture discarded to the basement. She hates him. She wants him dead. But she also wants him to bite her, to cut her, because if she bleeds, she lives, and this day then distinguishes itself from the last.

It is not Puck who unbolts the door this morning. It is Caliban. Pale haired and slit eyed and round backed. She can't tell if he is as old as her or old enough to be her father. He carries himself differently than the others do, shuffling about and whispering to himself, more servant than soldier. Sometimes he brings her food and sits on the edge of her bed and reaches the spoon toward her mouth, his own lips always parting just as she bites down. He will not speak to her, no matter what she tells him. And he rarely looks at her, perhaps embarrassed by her nakedness. But maybe he never talks to or looks at anyone. Maybe that is the avoidant way his mind is wired.

He is here to clean her. He carries a metal bowl sloshed full of soapy, steaming water. He sets it down on the floor and draws a washcloth from it and strangles out the water before running it along her face, her belly, her thighs and calves and feet. There is nothing sensual about the act. Nothing rough either. He is simply scrubbing her as he would a floor, spending extra time on her sores, letting the water soak into them, scraping away with a fingernail the dead skin.

He finishes with her groin and plops the washcloth into the basin and goes about stripping the bed. She has just enough slack on her restraints to lean her body sideways, to move her arms and legs enough to position a bedpan beneath her. The sheets on the mattress are rubber—in case she spills—changed every few days. He peels the sheet beneath her and she obliges him. When he leans over her, she notices the keys shining at his waist. He has not shoved them fully into his pocket and they peek out and catch the light and wink at her.

She remembers that when she was a girl, she believed if only she concentrated hard enough, she could move things with her mind. She believed it was like anything else: her mind was a muscle that needed exercise. So she would spend minutes every day staring at a red pebble or a pencil, willing it to move, sometimes staring so hard her head shook and her vision walled. More than once, when trapped in this basement, she has thought the same: that if she imagines hard enough, with the same sort of concentration, she might make something happen. She might escape this place. She thinks about her cabin. The green moss sponging the trees, the white bark of alder shining like bones. She is there. She walks naked through the mist, through a field of dew-soaked sedge, bluegrass, bear grass kissing her bare calves. Her husband is there too. And her daughter.

And now that moment has come.

Her wrists are braceleted with sores that break and bleed when she reaches for the keys, reaches as far as she can. She is an inch short. She wills her fingers into magnets. She wills her joints to come undone, her tendons to snap like rotten rubber bands, and allow her to stretch just a little farther. The handcuffs are cutting her deeply now, the skin peeling away, the blood snaking from her wrist. The blood helps. It lubricates.

Slowly her hand creeps forward and she manages to pinch a finger through the key ring. At that moment, Caliban adjusts his body to reach for the other corner of the mattress. The keys pull away from his pocket with a jangle she masks by coughing hard and shaking her restraints and making them rattle.

She has less than a minute, she knows. He will pour the wash water down the drain. He will ball up the sheets under his arm. He will shuffle to the door and close it and reach for his pocket. And by then it will be too late.

There are only two keys on the ring—one for the door, one for her cuffs—and she pinches the shorter of them between her pinky and thumb. This allows her less of a grip but a better reach to her wrist, to the keyhole. Her eyes dart to Caliban. His gaze is elsewhere, following a spider that scurries along the wall. He leaves the sheets half-undone and pursues it and mutters to himself in a language she cannot decipher.

She drops the key twice before she slides it home and twists hard and shakes free the cuff at the same moment that Caliban slaps a hand against the wall and then examines the black smear on his palm. He wipes it clean on his thigh and returns to the bed.

She lies as stiff as a board until he reaches over her again to tidy the sheet. His face hangs over hers. She can see into his mouth, can feel his breath gusting over her. She shoots her free hand into his neck and he looks at her, looks directly into her eyes, maybe for the first time. "I'm sorry," she says before tearing out his larynx with a sound like an apple bitten.

Patrick is curled up behind Claire, the bigger of two spoons, when he wakes to what he initially mistakes for the snap of a pitch pocket. But the fire has burned down to coals. The woods remain as dark as night, but through the branches he can see a pink dawn spilling across the sky. Then comes the noise again, unmistakably gunfire.

He is only half-awake, and dream logic makes him think, that's right, we were going to attack at dawn. He is staring dumbly at the face carved into the trunk of the tree when a bullet whizzes into it and opens up a pulpy gash between its eyes. Only then does he realize they are the ones under attack.

Claire rips the enormous .357 from her hip holster. He reaches for his own, but finds his belt empty. He bolts over the berm that separates their campsite from the others, his mind still two paces behind what is happening, certain he will find his pistol where he left his pack. The gunfire is constant now—thundering into a fusillade—so that he can barely distinguish the voices calling all around him. Dirt sprays, wood splinters, rocks spark, ferns shake.

Here is Tío yelling out commands in Spanish. Here is a man kneeling behind a stump with a rifle set on top of it. Here is another lying face-first in the fire pit with what looks like a mouth screaming at the back of his head. Patrick steals away the dead man's lever-action and hunkers against a tree to check the chamber for a live round. He looks to the shadow-soaked woods and waits for gunshots to flare and then fires toward them, emptying the brass, chambering a round, until the rifle empties and he tosses it aside. He does not know who is attacking them, only that they are being attacked, and it doesn't occur to him until a chopper darkens the sky overhead that he might be fighting his own.

He finds his backpack then, and another body, another gun, a pistol this time, a .22 Ruger, good for a range of only twenty or thirty yards, which seems to be the distance of the advancing soldiers. He nearly tells them to hold their fire, nearly calls out his rank and squad number, but at that moment a stare seals between him and Tío.

The man is lying behind a log, a shotgun cradled against his chest, and he pats the stock and points to Patrick, as if to say, *for you*.

Their gaze breaks when something clunks off a nearby tree and falls to the ground like a heavy pinecone. Fog fizzes from it—tear gas. Another clatters through some branches and falls among them. A man cries out and brings his hands to his eyes.

A bullet passes between Patrick's fingers with the furious buzz of a hornet. He checks the skin there, a scorched red. It couldn't have gotten any closer. He won't be that lucky again.

His eyes are beginning to water and his throat to blaze. He shrugs on his backpack. He needs to escape this place. He tries to account for Claire but can't see, as if someone has smeared an onion across his eyes and he cannot focus on anything more than a few feet from him. He pops off a few rounds and hunches down and stumbles away.

Miriam has difficulty walking. She trips twice on her way out of the basement cell. She has to will her legs forward, her feet to rise and fall. Her joints feel rusted, her bones brittle, hollow, as if a hard step could shatter them. Her tendons seem to have shrunk. Her calf muscles bunch up like fists and she sits down to massage them, trying not to cry out. She drags herself up, leans against a stack of boxes that rattle. IODINE, the label reads. All throughout the basement, she notices stacks and stacks of the same boxes and wonders whether she has been housed all this time at some sort of medical facility.

The thought doesn't last long, gone once she clambers up the stairs and cracks open the door as slowly and quietly as she can. She spots, hanging from the wall, a tapestry and two oil paintings with gilded frames. She opens the door wider and takes a quick inventory of a marble-topped table bearing a porcelain lamp, a fireplace mantel with a three-faced ornamental clock, a leaf-patterned wooden chair blackened from so many years of polish, an oriental rug that spans the length of what appears to be a sitting room, and assumes she is in some sort of museum.

She leans hard on the doorknob when she steps into the high-ceilinged room. The wainscoting is dark slatted wood. The windows are framed by thick curtains, and through them she can see untamed hedges, knee-high grass in the steadily brightening dawn. She does not have time to wonder at her surroundings. Escape is all that matters.

She tries to imagine the seeming size of a house like this, the rooms stretching on and stacked up all around her, like some vast honeycomb in which barbs and venom lie in wait. The hardwood groans with her every dragging step and threatens to give her away. She is weak, naked, unarmed, but her temper is as hot as blood in the vein when she thinks about anyone stopping her after she has made it this far. She goes to the fireplace—her bare feet cold on its soot-stained tiles—and grabs a poker to serve as a weapon and a cane.

She can see down a short hallway and into what appears to be the foyer. Her way out. She starts toward it and then midway across the room stops short. From this new vantage point she can see a wide spiral staircase reaching upward—and she can hear what sounds like footsteps shuddering down it. Her first impulse is to sneak beside the doorway and raise the poker like a sword—ready to swing its prong into the skull of whoever passes by—but she knows her body is too ungainly to fight, her muscles too weak to even hold the poker wobblingly overhead.

There is a swinging door beside the fireplace. She uses her back to push her way through it, into the kitchen, with its black-and-white rubber-stamp floor and its walls and cabinets painted a blinding white. Something is cooking. Meat. Her body aches at the smell—only for a moment.

In the center of the kitchen is an island. And upon the island lies a naked body. A thin, pale-skinned man with a beard wisping along his cheeks and neck. His mouth and eyes are open and she might think him alive if not for his hollowed-out belly, the skin scissored away beneath his sternum, guts gone. A large metal bowl—the same as the one Caliban used to clean her—sits beside him. Flies orbit the air above. One of them vanishes into his mouth.

She hears a creak. It comes from the sitting room, the hardwood floor depressed by the weight of someone walking. She must hide. She goes first to the pantry, but when she opens the door, she is greeted by another body, a man hanging upside down and bleeding out into a mop bucket. She nearly cries out in surprise. She spins around and sees a square of space beneath the island where someone might stack pots or bowls. It is empty now and she slides into it the moment the kitchen door swings open.

From here, she can see only to his waist but knows him immediately, his trunked legs, his boots big enough for a child to climb inside, the giant Magog. He never visited her in the basement, his one grace, for his weight and size would be an unimaginable torture. He wears black jeans that disappear behind an apron spattered with blood. She hears a *tick-tick-tick-tick* that she at first believes to be the radiator across the room. Then she notices that the poker is tapping the wall of her hiding place, jarred by the slamming of her pulse.

She wants to look away but cannot. She needs to know where he is, needs to know the moment his body stiffens at the sight of her so that she can try to uncurl from her hiding place and stab the poker into his knee or groin. He goes to the counter near the sink. He runs the water, and under the noise of it she shifts her body to better observe him. His red hair spills down his broad back. He picks up a cleaver and sharpens it—fifty times on one side, fifty times on the other—the scraping of the blade, the steel-on-steel sound so tangible that he might have drawn it along her bones. He tests it with a thumbnail and the razor edge peels away a curl.

Then he approaches the island. So close that she can smell him, so close that she can touch him, that she considers attacking him from below. Her hands grip the poker so tightly her knuckles whiten. If only she weren't so weak.

There comes a *thwack* from above. So powerful that the island shakes around her. He has brought down the cleaver. She hears the meaty release of the blade when he lifts it. And then he brings it down again. And again. There is a ripping sound of wet fabric. And then something plops into a bowl. A ten-gallon trash can stands a few feet away. Into it Magog tosses the man's head. The skull has been cleaved, the brain scraped from it.

The butchery continues for the next ten minutes. Him circling the island and slashing and peeling and tearing, the blade occasionally shrieking against bone. Blood oozes to the floor and pools in a puddle, and in it she can see the reflection of Magog raising and dropping the cleaver, like the terrible god of some tiny red planet. When the muscles in her back and legs begin to spasm and knot, she puts her hand in her mouth and bites down on it to get through the pain.

Somewhere in the kitchen an alarm chirps. Magog drops the cleaver with a clatter and walks to the oven and raspingly pulls from it three pans of meat, long thin strips browned to a crisp. From her hiding place she can smell the hellish breath of the oven—and she hates that it smells good, that her stomach gurgles with a hunger she wishes she could correct.

From one of the cupboards he lugs a Cuisinart. He snaps a shredder into place and punches the power and grinds the cooked meat against it until the container fills with flakes. What he is doing makes no sense to her. But none of this makes sense to her—the stacks of iodine, the old mansion, the harvested bodies—so that she wonders whether madness has finally seized her and she remains strapped to her basement bed, lost in some waking nightmare where the alien and ghastly behavior of her fellow lycans makes her question whether they really are men, as they like to claim, or merely beasts hidden in human robes.

The kitchen door swings open and she ducks back into her hole. She spots sneakers, jeans. "She's escaped," a voice says. Then, as quickly as he appeared, he is gone, followed by the booming footsteps of Magog.

They could return any second, she knows, but her muscles are in such a state of distress that she has no choice but to immediately slide out of the island and onto the floor, her body crabbed up. Slowly she straightens each leg and rubs hard at the muscles. She breathes through her teeth. It takes several minutes before she is able to hoist herself upright. She stares at the pile of meat and bones on the table, no longer recognizable as a man, a body unpuzzled. She doesn't know whether to run or remain hidden. They are looking for her now, and if they find her, she doesn't want to imagine what they will do to her.

There is a short hallway adjacent to the counter where Magog was working a moment before. She peers down it and spots a door with a square window that looks out onto an expansive lawn edged by hedges and rhododendrons. She sees—but it can't be—a heifer, a sheep, and several goats grazing there. She thinks again that the alien logic of this place better suits a nightmare. A jacket hangs from a hook and she pulls it down and zips it around her nakedness before scrambling for the doorknob and pushing outside before she can second-guess the decision to run.

She does not look back. Looking back will not help. She keeps her eyes on the wall of rhododendrons ahead, narrows all of her attention on them so that the rest of the world falls away. Glossy green leaves, bright red explosions of flowers. If she can just get to them, if she can just cross these next twenty yards unopposed, she will be out of sight of the house. One step at a time, one decision at a time. First to the rhododendrons. Then to the ironwork fencing. Then to the woods beyond. One step leading to the next, every step crutched by the poker in her hand. She would run if she could, but the best she can do is hobble.

Her muscles scream. Her breath comes out of her throat in a wounded rasp. Her eyes water with tears of pain and fear and relief, making her vision uncertain, so that she at first can't tell if the rhododendrons are shaking.

They are only ten paces away and she wants only to crash through them, the leaves like waxy knives, the blooms as big as fists battering her, a momentary discomfort, like the past few months, that she will grit her teeth through and endure and then emerge out the other side scratched and sticky with pollen, but alive. Then everything will be okay.

At last she is there—she has made it—and her body collapses into the tangle of branches, hidden, safe for now. She can go no farther, even though her legs stubbornly continue to jerk, as if she wants to keep walking.

She hears a rustling and snapping. She raises her head weakly. Twenty yards away, she sees a body push through the rhododendrons, stepping onto the lawn. And another. And another. All of them with shaved heads and American-flag T-shirts. They wear backpacks. They carry shotguns. They do not make sense. Like everything else. She tells herself that they are like the antique furniture and the dissected body and the goats grazing all around her—hallucinations—dreams she can dispel by pinching her skin and saying, *wake up*.

At first she believes they are hunting for her. No, she thinks. No. That wasn't the deal. If she made it this far, she would be safe. She will not allow them to take her. She clutches the poker two-handed, ready to drive it into any who come near.

But they are already jogging away from her, toward the mansion, their backpacks jingling with ammo.

It is then that she smiles. Only for a second. Her face quaking with happiness. The expression does not come easily. And it feels alien to her and the horror of her circumstances. But she cannot stop herself. She is going to make it after all. She is going to live.

☽

When the bullets spray their campsite, Patrick bolts in one direction, Claire another. She has her revolver in one hand and her backpack slung over her shoulder and she isn't sure how long and how far she runs, but by the time she stops, her throat is ablaze, her side is cramped, and she is alone. In the distance she can still hear the crack of gunfire, the *whop-whop-whop* of a helicopter. At first she is in a fury, her body shaking with the dynamite of the moment.

She doesn't understand how they found the campsite, and she doesn't understand why they are here, but it must be because of Patrick. For this she might have shot him if given the chance. He has betrayed her again. She should not have trusted him. She should not trust in anything, not even herself, weak and forgiving as she seems to be.

She keeps going—to where, she doesn't know. Away. For the moment, movement is all that matters. She is used to it. It is what she is best at. Running. She tries to hurry, but the ground steepens into a hillside tangled with vines and spongy with deadfall. With every step, her anger lessens, replaced by worry as she wonders whether Patrick is all right.

She clambers up battlements of basalt and finds herself in a dry riverbed and follows it up and up. She remembers his surprise, his panic. The way, when the gunfire began and they sat upright and blinked away sleep, he put a hand protectively to her chest, the way her father did when he was driving and had to stop suddenly. It was the same hand, as rough as a hunk of pine, that touched her all last night, combing fingers through her hair, tracing the outline of her jaw and neck. He loved her neck, he said. It was the most delicate thing about her. She touches the place he touched, just above her collarbone, and feels there the beating of her pulse.

She tries to make him ugly. Knobby knees. Big ears. Flat butt. His face spooned. Too much white around his eyes. But it doesn't help. His rightness, that electrical feeling, engulfs everything else. She wants him. Right now she wants him more than anything in the world.

All of her running has made her mouth cottony, given her a headachy, dehydrated feeling. She climbs up this dry riverbed, what feels like an immense rainspout, and eventually it peters out and she clambers through a notch and discovers that she is at the top of the hill. She stands on a shelf of rock overlooking a hundred-foot drop. She gets that feeling she sometimes gets. The fall would be long and terrifying—followed by serenity.

For a moment she wobbles there with a sensation not unlike vertigo. Then she climbs down another way, onto a slippery wash of red clay that takes her eventually to an asphalt trail. It is strewn with leaves and half-hidden by mud, but she can still see what appear to be yellow paw prints painted onto it. Though she should have noticed them long ago, she was too caught up in her thoughts and only now observes the buildings rising out of the woods, many of them mossy and vine strangled. The air smells curiously sweet, fecund. Above a glass entryway hangs a sign that reads, in white lettering, EAGLE LANDING.

The zoo. She is at the Portland Zoo of all places. She remembers, yesterday, when studying the map with Tío, seeing it on the other side of the Hoyt Arboretum. She is so far from where she thought she would be, only a day ago.

She tucks the .357 into her hip holster. She wanders the trails and passes by replica ice floes and snow caves, artfully stacked logs, a miniature train rusting on its tracks with seven cars to haul red-faced children and camera-lugging adults. She sees, beyond the fencing and moats, the faded orange coat of a dead tiger, the sunken hummock of a grizzly. A giraffe that died with its body on one side of the fence, its head on the other, trying to reach the leaves of a nearby tree, its long neck rotted through and spiked with white vertebrae. Behind a plate-glass window she spots a stuffed mountain lion unendingly roaring, the only thing here that appears alive. She wanders over to a pond and finds it full of flashing color, orange and red koi that come boiling to the surface when she tosses a handful of pebbles into the water.

"Have you seen this?" someone says. "You should really see this."

For two years she has imagined him always behind or beside her, like a shadow she can't shake. For two years she has not so much as taken a shower without a weapon in arm's reach. For two years she has dreamed of him and what he will do to her when he finally finds her. She will try to run, but her legs will feel entangled in mud. He will strike her. She will stumble. He will strike her again and she will fall. "You've made me angry," he will say. "You've made me so, so angry." She will close her eyes and whimper and there will be a crackling sound and the smell of smoke and when she looks at him again his terrible melted face will have been set aflame by his anger and his volcanic eyes will regard her as dry tinder.

And now here he is, the Tall Man. He wears a black suit despite the heat of the morning. A Glock dangles from one of his hands, gripped as casually as a closed umbrella, but there in case he needs it, there for her to see. His bald, ruined head is spotted with sweat. He withdraws a silk handkerchief from his breast pocket and runs it across his brow. He stands ten yards away, next to a short fence past which the ground slopes to a pond with an island in its center. On the island is a chaotic wooden structure with ropes and tires hanging off it, the grass below it littered with bones.

"He's been eating the others." The Tall Man tucks away the handkerchief and motions to the island with the Glock. "And now he's eating himself." She follows the pistol and sees the ape squatting among the bones. Its thinness is obvious despite its shaggy red coat. It has the wrinkled face of an old man. It is gnawing on its arm and she can see even from this distance the bone peeking out from beneath its fur.

"Anything to stay alive. Amazing resolve." He smiles wretchedly, the burned skin so tight around his skull that it appears it might split at the effort. "But it looks like he doesn't have much time left. It looks like this is the end of the road."

"You followed me?"

"From the woods? Yes. What a surprise to see you there. But of course I've been following you for a long time, Claire." He touches his face. "To thank your father properly for what he did to me. Did you know that my nerves have been damaged in such a way that they feel constantly aflame? All this time I have been burning."

She should shoot him. She should reach for her revolver and shoot him. She feels unsteady on her feet, as she did minutes before at the cliff, drawn to the edge. If she moves, she could die, but so could he, so could they both. But she is unable to move, arrested by his gaze, and so spins on an axis that can't find its course. His eyes are so gray they are almost black. Absent of light. But there is little, she knows, that they do not see. The moment her hand twitches, he raises his gun and studies her down the long line of his arm.

The ape that has been silent up to this point now begins to screech. It has spotted them. It lopes to the shore and swings its good arm into the water, pounding, splashing, trying to get their attention. The Tall Man turns to acknowledge it. It gives a short leap and races in a circle and returns to the water to slap once more.

When he turns away, it is easier. His face is eclipsed by the faces of Miriam, of her father and mother, of Matthew, and the thought of them gives her the gravity she needs.

The ape cries out and the Tall Man brings a finger to his lips to tell it *shh*—and his finger is still there, still at his mouth, when he turns to face Claire as if to silence her drawn revolver before it reports.

She remembers the tree behind the cabin. She remembers the way her bullets bit through it. She remembers its slow collapse. He falls in much the same way.

It takes five slugs to bring down the giant, and even then, he is still alive. His breath whistles and bubbles through the holes in his chest and throat. He lies in the foyer of the mansion, like a fallen grandfather clock, with the Americans standing over him, commenting on what a huge piece of meat he is. He says nothing when they ask him where to find Balor. He only raises a hand to swat away the shotgun Max aims at his face, but it is too late. A second later a thunderclap fills the air and his arm falls heavily at his side.

They make their way methodically through every room on the ground floor, killing two others, before climbing the stairs. Someone fires down on them and they toss a grenade onto the landing and duck down. Plaster clouds the air. The ceiling cracks. In the dusty silence that follows the blast they continue upward. There is a metal gate secured at the top of the landing, and then another at the doorway to a master bedroom at the end of the hall, both of which they blast through with C-4 charges.

He sits on a walnut sofa with green velvet cushions and a floral crest. He wears a white linen shirt unbuttoned at the top to reveal a silvery thatch of hair. His legs are crossed. His hands are folded in his lap. He disappoints Max. He does not race at them. He does not cower. He simply sits there, staring into the empty fireplace, until they surround him. He then looks up with a dispassionate expression, ignoring the shotguns aimed at him, staring into each of their eyes.

"You're him," Max says.

"Who?"

"*Him*."

"Yes. I suppose I am." He sighs through his nose and stares again at the fireplace. "It's too late, you know?"

"Too late for what?" Max says.

"You'll see. Soon enough you'll see. It's already happening." One of his eyes is the blue-silver of sage, the other the purple of an old bruise.

"I used to be like you, you know," Max says. "But then I learned something. I learned that talking is one thing, doing is another." He reaches for his boot and unsheathes the knife there. "You want to do some real damage, use fewer words."

The knife, Max notices, catches the sun and throws a bright blade of light onto the couch. He turns the knife and makes the light slide along the cushions, along Balor's thigh, up his torso, trembling across his face until it settles on his eye, his decayed eye, which glows for a moment like a dying star.

They find stores of gasoline in the carriage house. They splash it along the walls, soak pools of it into the rugs, waterfall it down the stairs. Their eyes tear over. The fumes make them dizzy. They cough and laugh at once.

They make a trail of gasoline through the foyer, down the porch, along the brickwork path, to the driveway, where Max lights a match. "Time to clean house," he says. The match falls sizzling from his fingers and the gas ignites with a huff. A tongue of blue-and-orange flame licks its way speedily into the mansion.

It isn't long before the windows explode and the fire rises through them and the brick around them blackens. Sparks swirl. The roof vanishes in a snapping crown of flame. The heat is tremendous. Everyone staggers back. Smoke shadows the sun. And a smile plays across Max's face as he runs his fingers through the new scalp at his belt, petting it, the hair long, with a light gray sheen, as if woven from silver.

☽

How many have been killed?—what happened to Claire?—is he being followed? Patrick doesn't know; he doesn't know. He can see some way into the woods, but no farther, the air still dim with dawn and everything thickly tangled, draped in moss, ornamented with fungus.

He pops the clip, checks to see how many rounds remain in the Ruger. One. One bee sting of a bullet. He tries not to think about all the different kinds of fucked he is right now. The ground slopes beneath him into a bowl-like depression with a long-dead fire ring at its center, someplace teenagers used to come to drink beer and smoke cigarettes and get lucky. Cigarette butts, faded chip bags, the dried husks of condoms. He steps on an empty can of Busch Light and startles at the metallic complaint.

He sees, carved into the bark of a tree, names and hearts and promises, and among them, in huge block letters, someone has scratched out FUCK YOU AND YOUR LOVE AND HAPPY HANDHOLDING HORSESHIT. Patrick listens to the gunfire still shouting behind him and feels a brief but profound surge of hate, hatred for people in general, their destructive urges.

This is who he wants to hand the vaccine over to, the same sort of creature that sprays down a campsite with an M4, that guns down a pack of lycans and then collects the scalps, that defaces a tree garlanded with declarations of love.

Amid the trash on the forest floor he spots a shattered pink cell phone. It hits him then: this is how they found him. He throws down his backpack and digs around until he finds the satellite phone. He sets it on a log and claws up a sharp-headed rock from the fire pit. He holds it aloft for a long moment. This phone is his tether to the other world. He imagines what awaits him there, the gauntlet of photographers, the cell where he will face interrogation. He cries out when he brings down the rock and shatters the phone into hundreds of glittery pieces.

For a moment he considers doing the same with the vaccine. He unrolls the watch cap and studies the vial in his hand.

It is then that he hears a branch snap. Behind him.

When he spins around, he sees only the graffiti-riddled tree. It has died and rotted from the inside out, its base hollowed like an empty eye socket that seems to follow him when he shoves the vial in his backpack and throws the pack over his shoulders and approaches the tree. He circles the trunk with his Ruger ready, his finger off the guard, on the trigger.

Then a man—helmeted, dressed in a utility uniform—steps from behind a tree.

Patrick falls back and raises his pistol just as the man brings the buttstock of the rifle to his shoulder. They stare at each other through their sights before slowly letting the noses fall and point at the ground. "You know who I am?" the man says. "Hoo-ah?"

It takes Patrick a moment. To see past the beard. To make sense of him in this context. And then it clicks, the voice, the face he has observed so many times on the television, the newspaper. "Yes, sir."

He wonders whether he ought to salute. "Hoo-ah, sir."

Chase Williams. His president.

"We were supposed to have that photo op in the Republic, but you didn't wait for me. You took off. Sort of like yesterday at the recon site. And sort of like ten minutes ago when we were trying to extricate you. You have a habit of not being there when people need you." He is smiling without humor. "You got the vaccine?"

It takes Patrick a long time to nod, but he does.

"And you have the papers. Desai's papers. And his laptop? You said you had them."

Again he nods.

Chase smiles so broadly that he squints. "I'm grateful to you. I am. And you don't need me to tell you this—you wouldn't have come all this way if you didn't know—but your country will soon be grateful to you; the human race will soon be grateful to you."

The gunfire has ceased. The forest is silent and so is Patrick.

"You're worried," Chase says. "You've broken some rules. But know what? I'm a rule breaker myself. And I'm going to make sure nothing bad happens to you. I'm going to make sure only good happens to you. You're going to be rewarded. We're going to get you in front of some cameras.

You and me. That's what people need right now. They need somebody to cheer for, and you're somebody to cheer for."

Sunlight breaks through the canopy and lights up this pocket of forest. Patrick does not cry. Nor does he run. Though he wants to. To forget, if only for a moment, he closes his eyes. The sun backlights the blood vessels in his eyelids so that he sees a wash of red with dark roots creeping through it.

That's it, he thinks. That's how it ends. Quietly. No gunfight. No fistfight. No yelling and pleading. He can see it all so clearly, him handing over the vaccine. He could end it. He could end it all right now. As easy as that.

"How about you let me see the vaccine?" Chase says in a voice with cracks running through it. "How about you give it to me?"

Patrick then notices his skin trembling, his muscles jumping. The president looks like one of those old stop-motion movies, moving too quickly and jerkily. A drop of blood gathers at the corner of his eye and streaks down his cheek, vanishing into his beard.

Patrick is stepping back—he is shaking his head—when he says, "You're one of them?"

Chase seems not to hear him. "You're already a hero." He lifts a palsying hand from the stock of the rifle and reaches for Patrick. "You can remain that way."

"Not interested," he says.

Somehow Patrick finds her. He sees the smoke obscuring the sky, the ash tumbling from the cloud of it, and he walks until the hill rises into a point to find some vista, to get some perspective. He discovers her there. She stands on a lip of basalt overlooking a crevasse. The sky is behind her, and her windblown hair curls in every direction, as if she were floating in a big blue spread of water.

He has pored through the notebook and all those old emails—and his father and Desai have conducted their exhaustive research—each of them longing for interpretation, believing in their own way that they might find some answer to the impenetrable and make right the world. But when Patrick looks at Claire, when he feels that high-pressure need, it all seems suddenly beside the point, every pharmaceutical formula and utilitarian equation irrelevant.

She does not seem to notice him approach. Her eyes are on the crevasse. The tops of trees spike toward her. The wind, a mere breeze moments before, now gusts. If he had been wearing a hat, it would have blown off. She tips toward the open air before catching her balance. He says her name twice before she glances his way.

"Can you get away from there? Please? You're making me nervous."

She squints at him for a long moment before doing as he says, taking one step, then another, away from the long drop.

These past few months his heart has all but disappeared into a dark corner of his chest, a tiny flickering speck, but with her before him, the wind now feels as though it is fanning an ember, blowing it into a spark.

She calls out a question to him, but the wind rises and dashes her words away, and Patrick does not hear her. "What?"

"You should go."

"What if I want to stay with you?"

"We're different. Don't you remember? That's what you wrote to me once." There is a mixture of assault and resignation in her voice, and she looks at him, then looks away, as if she regrets what she said as soon as she said it. "You were right."

"No," he says. "I was wrong."

He holds out a hand to her then. Along the forearm, in the shape and color of a lipsticked kiss, is a bite mark.

Patrick had only one bullet. Killing Chase would

accomplish nothing. His body would fall. Within a minute, drawn by the gunfire, soldiers would appear, knotting around him, knocking him to the ground and flex-cuffing his arms and legs, transporting him to the perimeter, an assassin.

So he lifted his pistol and fired it into Chase's foot. The bullet punched through the leather and blood instantly welled from it. Chase widened his eyes and howled and fell backward and cradled his foot. "I can't believe you did that," he said, heaving a breath between each word. "I can't believe you would do that."

His entire body began to shake. He brought his hands to his face and stared at Patrick through the fingers. When his hands fell away, it was as though he had snatched off a mask, his face different, his mouth bloody and too full of teeth. He seemed not to notice his injured foot when he rolled forward in a crouch—and then launched himself at Patrick.

Their bodies became a mess of limbs, rolling over and over, so that Patrick could not distinguish up from down except when his face crushed into dirt. His backpack jabbed into his spine. Somehow he managed to short-punch Chase in the throat. The president coughed and choked and lost control of his body so that Patrick could knee him in the groin. His body went limp and Patrick shoved him away, separated himself, crabbing backward in time to hear voices and footsteps crashing through the forest.

He spied the rotten tree and scrambled into its dark entry. He barely scraped into the space with his backpack, shimmying upward, not caring what spiders or bats might wait for him, only wanting to be out of sight.

He was not sure what happened next. He heard the soldiers screaming their commands and Chase snarling in response. He heard a single gunshot followed by a cry of pain that trailed into a whine. He heard Chase struggling with them as they secured his wrists and ankles. He heard the helicopter hovering overhead and the trees moaning when they swayed and dropped cones that thudded the ground like grenades.

And then he heard nothing, and when he heard nothing for long enough to feel safe, he crawled out of the tree. Except for a few spots of blood, the ground appeared swept clean. As though nothing had happened.

He swung off his backpack and dug into it. He wanted to make certain that he still had the vaccine, that the vial had not been crushed, the bottom of his pack a mess of glass and powder. His hand closed around it—unbroken—but when he pulled it into the light he did not feel any sort of relief.

He was too distracted by the sight of his forearm.

The gash there. Stamped with teeth. He had been bitten. Chase had bitten him. He stared at it for a long time.

Now his arm is extended toward Claire, and she reaches for it, not to take his hand, but to touch the gash with her fingertips. They come away tacky with blood.

His whole body is leaning toward her. As if he is asking for a blessing. She looks into his eyes. He is waiting for her to say something, but she only brings her mouth to the wound—and kisses it tenderly.

Then he says he has something else to show her—and her face hardens, betrayed from the possibility of a happy ending.

She does not ask any questions—she has no energy to do anything but follow him down the slope and into the zoo, past the dead animals in their cages, past the cool, still body of the Tall Man, to the color-coded, vine-strangled map. Patrick puts his finger on the veterinary offices and says, "There." A few minutes later he kicks down the door and rips through the cabinets until he finds what he is looking for—two syringes and a container of diluent labeled STERILE WATER.

It is then that he unzips his backpack and withdraws the silver vial and sets it on the counter between them like a dare, like a bullet, as if this were some game of Russian roulette. Slowly she reaches out a hand to twist the vial until she can read the label. "That's why you were here? In the Ghostlands?"

"Yes."

"That's what you came for? A vaccine?" Her hand lingers on the vial—and she fights the competing desires to hurl it against the wall and swallow it whole.

"That's what I thought I came for. I found something else." His hand joins hers, and the vial vanishes from sight and she feels some fleeting relief. "You know what it's like, having something inside you you can't control."

"On many levels, yes."

"Here's your chance to put a stop to it."

She thinks for a long time, tugged one way and then the other, and then remembers some long-ago joke her father told her, about how even the best marriages are the result of overlooking the things you hate and focusing on the things you love. He said this just before dragging his wife, her mother, into an embrace and nuzzling her neck. It was and was not a joke. And when Claire looks inside herself now, past the fatigue, past the temptation and convenience of being fully human, she sees the two writhing forms at the heart of her, and she knows who she is and cannot betray that marriage.

She slides the vial toward Patrick. "I want you to take it."

His hand pushes back, but she resists him and he does not battle her further. "There's enough for us both."

"I want *you* to take it."

"Think how much easier things would be. Do you really want to side with these people?"

"I hardly recognize them. But I know who I am."

He takes a long time to nod his agreement, but when he does, she helps him mix the powder with the diluents and reconstitute the vaccine and dose the syringe and find the vein. She swabs the blood that wells at his elbow. Then she kisses him again, this time finding his lips.

EPILOGUE

HE IS A small man. Maybe that is why no one seems to notice him. He wears safety goggles, a white jumpsuit with a General Mills logo along the breast, and a matching ball cap under which his fluorescent hair is nearly hidden. He holds a clipboard and pen and walks along a steel gangway with a chain railing. To either side of him, in this dry milling facility outside Des Moines, conveyors grumble and choppers mash and ovens process corn into flakes, flour, grits, meal, that will then be outsourced.

Yellow dust fills the air. Wide-blade fans, built into the walls, suck it outside. The roar of their blades and the crackle of the corn and the cranking of the machinery make it nearly impossible to hear. The noise doesn't bother him. He feels perfectly at home here, as he should, since this is the twentieth facility—some dry millers, some wet millers—he has visited this month under the false pretense of quality control. Beside him, a seemingly endless stream of shelled corn sizzles down a chute.

His hand is missing two fingers, but he doesn't have any trouble unzipping a custom-sewn compartment at his sleeve. From it falls a white, flaky dust. First one arm, and then the other. As if he is crumbling to ash or performing some funeral rite. He can fit a surprising amount into each sleeve, four liters' worth of seed. That's how he likes to think of it, as seed. The processed remains of the infected. Balor is dead, Magog is dead, but the mission is not: Puck set out weeks before with a pickup stocked full of ziplock containers they prepared for him.

He dusts off his hands once the last of the seed has fallen from him.

Prions, the widely read research of Neal Desai explains, are extremely resistant to standard inactivation methods, including boiling, irradiation, dry heat, and chemical treatment. At best, the prions reduce their infectivity but remain alive, waiting to swarm into a new system and take it over. It takes four and a half hours to kill the infection at 132 degrees Celsius—and even then it must be doused with hydrochloride and hypochlorite. Compared to that, the dry millers are the equivalent of a tanning bed. From here the infection will be processed into everything—toothpaste, yogurt, juice, cereal, chips, crackers, beer, beef, bread—truly everything.

When Puck makes his way out of the facility, the assistant manager, a man with a squat, square body, chases him down in the parking lot. The sky is a dying shade of purple. Puck keys open his pickup and pulls off his hat and tosses it inside the cab. The manager asks if everything looked okay.

"Everything was great," Puck says and checks his hair in the side mirror. "Just lovely."

"Will you be sending me a report?"

Puck climbs into the cab and keys the ignition and says over the engine, "You'll be hearing from me."

And he will. Everyone will. One night or another, likely when the moon is full, they will shut off their televisions or set down their forks or pause in their lovemaking, their heads cocked, before going to the window and staring through their warped reflections and wondering at the sirens that steadily fill the night with their howling.

ACKNOWLEDGMENTS

Thanks to Katherine Fausset, Holly Frederick, and all the rest of the grand old crew at Curtis Brown, Ltd.

To Team Werewolf: Helen Atsma, Kirsten Reach, Oliver Johnson, and all the good and mighty at Hachette for their editorial and marketing muscle.

To Lyric Bartholomay, Cory O'Neel, Jason Ryan Arment, Julie Babbit, Chris Herring, Michael Kimber, Peter Percy, and Elizabeth Whitley for their help with the heavy research that went into this novel.

To Tyler Cabot, Rob Spillman, Kevin Larimer, Donovan Hohn, and Radhika Jones for their support. To Dean Bakopoulos for friendship. To Peter Straub and John Irving for wisdom and encouragement.

To my colleagues and students at St. Olaf College, Pacific University, and Iowa State University.

ACKNOWLEDGMENTS

To the National Endowment for the Arts.

And a special thanks to my family, especially my wife, whose tolerance and enthusiasm and partnership mean everything. I'd lasso the moon for you, Chief.

ABOUT THE AUTHOR

BENJAMIN PERCY was raised in the high desert of Central Oregon. He is the author of the novel *The Wilding* and two short-story collections, *Refresh, Refresh* and *The Language of Elk*. His honors include a Whiting Writers Award, the Pushcart Prize, a grant from the National Endowment for the Arts, and *The Paris Review*'s George Plimpton Prize for Fiction. His fiction and nonfiction have been read on National Public Radio and published by *Esquire*, *GQ*, *Men's Journal*, *Outside*, *Time*, and the *Wall Street Journal*. He is the writer-in-residence at St. Olaf College in Northfield, Minnesota.